Acclaim for Cathy Bramley:

'A fantastic read filled with **laugh-out-loud funny** moments.
A **lovely, heart-warming** story – highly recommended'
Compelling Reads

'Filled with **friendship, humour and genuinely loveable
characters** of all ages, shapes and sizes'
One More Page

'Such a **charming, feel-good** story'
Carole's Books

'**Satisfying, dreamy and delicious** – leaves you
wanting just a little bit more.'
Crooks on Books

'I loved Tilly Parker immediately . . . Cathy is such
a **wonderful writer**'
Girls Love to Read

'This was the one **of the funniest stories
I have ever read** . . . I loved every word'
On My Book Shelf

'I loved every single character! Full of **warmth and belonging**'
Jeras Jamboree

'I adored this **gem of a book** . . . *Ivy Lane* has **everything I love
about a novel** – wonderful characters, a gorgeous setting and
twists ready to be unveiled at any opportunity'
Reviewed the Book

'What a **lovely** little tale this was!'
Fabulous Book Fiend

'There is nothing in this book to disappoint and
everything to **make you smile**'
Sheerie Franks

www.transworldbooks.co.uk

'This is a **perfect book** to take with you to
your garden on a sunny summer day'
Dreaming With Open Eyes Reviews

'I loved it! Cathy Bramley is the most effortless
of storytellers, she has a total knack of drawing you in.
I could read her books every day, forever'
Donna's Room for Reading

'A **sweet, lovely story** that will leave you wanting more'
Laura's Little Book Blog

'**Captivating** . . . A wonderful quick read!'
The Love of a Good Book

Cathy would love to hear from you! Find her on:

 Facebook.com/CathyBramleyAuthor

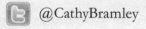 @CathyBramley

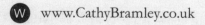 www.CathyBramley.co.uk

Wickham Hall

Cathy Bramley

CORGI BOOKS

TRANSWORLD PUBLISHERS
61–63 Uxbridge Road, London W5 5SA
www.transworldbooks.co.uk

Transworld is part of the Penguin Random House group of companies whose
addresses can be found at global.penguinrandomhouse.com

Penguin
Random House
UK

First published in Great Britain as four separate ebooks
in 2015 by Transworld Digital
an imprint of Transworld Publishers
First published as one edition in 2016 by Corgi Books
an imprint of Transworld Publishers

A CIP catalogue record for this book
is available from the British Library.

ISBN
9780552172103

Typeset in 11½/13pt Garamond by Kestrel Data, Exeter, Devon.
Printed and bound by CPI Group (UK) Ltd, Croydon, CR0 4YY.

Penguin Random House is committed to a sustainable future for our business, our readers
and our planet. This book is made from Forest Stewardship Council® certified paper.

MIX
Paper from
responsible sources
FSC® C018179

1 3 5 7 9 10 8 6 4 2

For Tony, my brightest star
xx

Hidden Treasures

Chapter 1

I puffed out my cheeks as I turned the corner into Mill Lane. My throat was dry, my lungs felt squashed and achy and one of my laces was beginning to come loose, but I was determined not to slow down.

'Come on, Holly,' I muttered under my breath as the finish line came into view. 'You can do this. Nearly there. One last push!'

I broke into a sprint for the last hundred metres. The early June sunshine was warm on my back and I felt hot and sweaty in my T-shirt and shorts, not to mention ready for a drink. There was no stopping me now, though; I was through the pain barrier, I was in the zone . . .

'Good grief!' cried Mrs Fisher, my elderly neighbour, stepping out of her gate, her shopping trolley trailing behind her. 'You nearly gave me a heart attack, charging along like that!'

'Sorry, Mrs Fisher,' I wheezed as I swerved round her. 'Lovely morning!'

'How's your mum?' Mrs Fisher shouted after me.

'Fine thanks,' I yelled over my shoulder. 'Sorry, can't stop!'

I ran on to our gate, arms raised triumphantly above my

head as though I was breaking through some imaginary ribbon. I'd made it all the way back without stopping for the first time ever. Go me! I leapt over the boxes of rubbish that had been left out for recycling and came to a breathless halt at the front door of Weaver's Cottage, the honey-coloured stone terrace I shared with my mum.

I checked my watch: five kilometres in twenty-seven minutes.

Result! A personal best and not bad at all for someone who, until recently, would rather grab a box of French Fancies (lemon ones, preferably) and the TV remote and settle down in front of *The Hotel Inspector* than exercise.

I pulled off my headphones and grinned to myself as the front garden filled with the tinny sound of Shakira singing 'Hips Don't Lie' from my iPod.

You are so right, Shakira, I thought, wiping a line of perspiration from my forehead. *These hips certainly don't lie*. A month spent eating cake whilst applying for jobs had done absolutely zero for my figure. Hopefully, thanks to my new fitness regime, the truth would soon hold no fear for my hips – I was definitely feeling fitter. And as for the job hunt . . . I thought I might have sorted out that little problem, too.

I stood for a moment, hands on hips, while I caught my breath. There were a few weeds poking up between the paving slabs and I bent to tweak them out. I would make an effort to do a few jobs today, I thought, make the most of my last few days of unemployment. Perhaps Mum might even be in the mood to help; we could start with the boxes I'd just jumped over? No harm in asking . . .

Five weeks ago, I'd been made redundant from the Esprit Spa Resort. Since then, despite keeping myself busy with job hunting, I'd found myself with quite a lot of time on my hands and Weaver's Cottage, with its low ceilings and cluttered rooms, had become a bit claustrophobic. And because Mum only worked part time, we'd been spending far too much time in each other's company and I was beginning to feel the strain.

Don't get me wrong, I love Mum to bits. Adore her. I'd do anything for her. In fact, I *have done* anything for her: I'd put up with her 'peculiarities' for as long as I can remember but I'm only human and living with her in such a confined space had tested my patience to the max.

Which was why I found it such a joy to stretch my legs outside. Running was my safety valve; the country lanes around my home village of Wickham gave me the space to let off steam and the time to think.

And I had lots to think about. Because I'd been offered a job. Hallelujah!!

I leaned up against the wall of the cottage and began to stretch out my calf muscles one at a time, taking deep breaths and feeling pretty damn proud of this morning's achievements. Five kilometres, a month of gainful employment and it was only eleven o'clock.

For as long as I could remember, I'd always wanted to work in the events industry, preferably at prestigious international events. *No harm in aiming high,* I'd thought. Sadly, it wasn't to be. By the end of my first year at uni, it had become clear that Mum wasn't coping well without me at home and I'd had to adjust my plans accordingly. After three years living in minimalist heaven in my halls of residence, I came home to Weaver's Cottage. But while that might have hampered my globe-trotting plans, it certainly didn't curtail my ambitions.

The picturesque village of Wickham is in the shadow of Stratford-upon-Avon, a jewel in England's tourist crown and home to numerous jobs in the hospitality industry. After taking on a variety of roles – including a stint as a hotel receptionist and a ticket seller at Anne Hathaway's cottage – I landed 'a proper job' with the Esprit Spa Resort. And I'd stayed there for three years, working my way up to assistant events organizer.

Sadly, the owners had got themselves into a financial mess and Esprit was no more, leaving me and the rest of the team unemployed. I'd been applying for jobs like a demon ever since. I was desperate to stay within the events industry and keen to move up the career ladder, too. But as a 'Plan B' I'd enrolled with a temp agency in Stratford yesterday and lo and behold I'd had a call first thing this morning with the offer of a temporary office job at the conference centre in town.

I'd responded enthusiastically, of course, saying how pleased I was and had promised to let the lady know by close of play today. She'd been a little put out that I didn't snap her hand off there and then, I think, but I had my reasons. At that point the postman still hadn't been and whilst deep down I knew it was unlikely at this late stage, I was still carrying a torch for one of the other jobs I'd applied for.

Cool-down stretch complete, I sat on the front step, picked up the bottle of water I'd left tucked behind the empty milk bottles and took a long drink.

Unbelievably, my absolute, one-in-a-million, what-are-the-chances *dream job* had arisen a mere stone's throw from home: Wickham Hall was looking for a new assistant events manager. I felt my heart thump a bit harder at the thought of the Elizabethan manor house on the far side of Wickham. The stately home was still privately owned by the Fortescue family and was renowned for its calendar of successful events. *This is destiny, written in the stars*, I'd thought when I'd spotted the advertisement in the *Stratford Gazette* two weeks ago. The description read as though it had been written with me in mind: meticulous planner, attention to detail, excellent communications and organization skills and experience running events. The job couldn't have been more 'me' if it had tried!

Plus I knew Wickham Hall inside out; I'd been going there ever since I was a little girl. In fact, when I was small I used to pretend I lived there and dreamed about waking up in a four-poster bed with my own maid, a wardrobe of Disney Princess outfits and acres of space all to myself . . .

I stifled a sigh and shivered a little as my skin began to cool. I rubbed the shin that had been aching and circled my ankles. As usual, my run had allowed my crowded thoughts some room to manoeuvre and I had reached a decision.

The fact was that despite putting heart and soul into my application for the Wickham Hall job, I hadn't been invited for an interview. And I would have heard back by now: the interviews were being held this week and the postman had had nothing for me again today. It was – to put it mildly – a bit of a blow. On the other hand, if I accepted the temp job, I could be out of the house and back at work on Monday. Hall-e-flippin-lujah.

Put like that, what choice did I have?

I jumped to my feet, intent on making my acceptance call immediately. I put two hands on the front door, which usually needed some force to open it, and pushed.

'Ooh, hold on; let me move out of the way!' cried Mum. 'OK, come on in, love.'

I stuck my head round the door and was greeted by the sight of my mum kneeling at the bottom of the stairs amongst stacks of newspapers and bags full of old clothes, wearing one of her favourite Boden summery dresses, a bargain from the charity shop where she worked. Her ample bottom pointed towards me and I caught an eyeful of dimply thigh.

'Sorry about that,' I said, squeezing through the gap. I closed the door and closed my eyes to the mess, focusing on her instead.

Mum and I were the same height, i.e. not high at all. We were both blonde and both prone to gaining weight in the tum and bum department. Her eyes were blue like my grandparents and mine were brown, which I guessed made them the same as 'he who shall never be referred to'. But the greatest difference between us – and incidentally the greatest source of tension – was stuff. Mum had stuff everywhere. I did not.

Right now she was ferreting through said stuff.

'Have you lost something, Mum?' I was still hot and the hallway felt airless. I opened the door again and fanned myself with it.

'Not me, no. But you have,' she said, pushing her hair off her face and dislodging her reading glasses, which nested permanently in her blonde waves.

'Me?' I gave her a wan smile. That was one thing I was careful not to do in this house: put something down and you might never find it again. 'I don't think so, Mum. Anyway, I've come to a decision about that temp job. I'm going to take it.'

'Hmm? It must be here somewhere,' she muttered, ignoring me and sifting through a pile of envelopes.

'What must?'

She shook her head anxiously so I closed the door and lowered myself onto the bottom stair, catching a whiff of my own post-run aroma. Shower-time next, methinks, just as soon as I've made that call.

'Mum,' I said gently, resting a hand on her shoulder, 'let me take all that post. We don't need any of it, it's just junk mail. Please?'

She picked up another handful and flicked through them.

'You should have had a letter from Wickham Hall. A lady called Pippa has just called to see if you'd received it. I was trying to find it before you got back.'

She abandoned her search and sat back on her heels, staring at me guiltily. 'It's my fault, Holly. It must have got lost in amongst my muddle. I'm sorry.'

Mum looked so dejected that it took a moment for her words to sink in. My eyes widened and I swallowed, hardly daring to think what I thought I was thinking.

'Oh my life, Pippa is the events manager! What did she say?' I grabbed Mum's hands and forced her to look at me. 'Exactly?'

Mum blinked her cornflower-blue eyes at me. 'She said you hadn't replied to her letter and she wanted to know if you could still make the interview this afternoon.'

My heart swelled with happiness and hope and pure unadulterated pleasure. The temp agency could wait. The stuff on the front path could wait. I had my dream job to go for.

'Yes,' I squealed, planting a kiss on Mum's cheek. 'Yes, I can!'

At three o'clock that afternoon, I was ushered into a seat at the end of a long oak table by Pippa Hargreaves, events manager at Wickham Hall. There were butterflies in my stomach and I knew my face was a bit flushed, but I was here, where I was supposed to be, and that was the main thing.

'Thank you for coming at such short notice, Holly.' She

smiled, taking a seat opposite me. 'I can't think what happened to your interview letter. I'm normally very organized.'

I watched Pippa as she poured us both some water from a heavy glass jug. She was about five years older than me – mid-thirties at a guess – with carelessly pinned-up hair, a floral summer dress and a welcoming smile. She had talked non-stop since meeting me in the reception area at the bottom of a flight of oak stairs and I already suspected that the two of us would get along brilliantly.

'I'm sure it's not your fault,' I said, accepting a glass from her. 'It probably got lost in the post. I'm just so overjoyed that you rang. I've been keeping everything crossed all week that I'd be successful in getting an interview.'

I felt a flash of guilt for blaming the poor postman. We had, in fact, found Pippa's letter in the end; it had come in a thick cream envelope with the Fortescue family crest on it. It had somehow slipped inside an old Christmas card catalogue along with an unopened electricity bill and a leaflet for Mo's Maids home cleaning service. But I could hardly admit that, could I?

'Right, with any luck, there should be a copy of your details in here.' Pippa gave me a bright smile and pulled a jumbled sheaf of papers towards her.

I itched to take the pile from her and tap its edges on the table to neaten them up. Instead, I crossed my fingers under the table and tried to focus on being the best interview candidate Wickham Hall had ever seen.

'I've brought a spare copy?' I offered, as she flicked though the pile.

'No, it's OK, here we are: *Holly Swift*,' she declared, producing my application letter, which I'd toiled over so painstakingly. She whizzed through my résumé, speed-reading under her breath. 'University . . . degree in hospitality and management . . . work alone or as part of a team . . . excellent organizational skills . . . assistant events organizer at Esprit Hotel and Spa.'

'Esprit? Very posh.' She stopped reading and looked up briefly. 'I was planning on taking my husband there for our seventh anniversary this year. I was surprised when it closed down.'

'So was I,' I said, raising an eyebrow. 'I loved the serenity of Esprit, but unfortunately it turned out to only be skin deep. The financial accounts were in a mess, according to the liquidators.'

Pippa's brow furrowed as she shook her head and I was conscious that I needed to steer the conversation into more positive waters.

'Esprit was very modern and luxurious,' I went on, nodding. 'But I adore the Elizabethan beauty of Wickham Hall. It seems to breathe with history; it's like you can hear the stories from the past whispering in the background. That beats the glass and gloss of Esprit, as far as I'm concerned.'

Pippa smiled and dipped her head again and I glanced around me, committing every detail to memory so I could tell Mum about it later. This part of the hall wasn't open to the public but it was just as charming as the rooms I'd seen on my previous visits. The events department, where the interviews were taking place, was housed on the first floor of the east wing. Somewhere below me was Lord Fortescue's private office. My stomach churned at the thought. A real lord, I could be working with a real lord . . . That would give Mum something to talk about at the charity shop!

The long narrow room was entirely wood-panelled, with

a high ornate ceiling and a beautiful wooden floor covered with a large oriental rug. It smelt of furniture polish and of the blowsy old-fashioned roses arranged in a priceless-looking porcelain vase on the table and, for me at least, it smelt of hope and the possibility of a new career.

My gaze drifted through the windows to the grounds of Wickham Hall beyond. I could see the formal gardens, ablaze with colourful flowers, bordered with wide stone paths and dotted with exquisitely trimmed topiary shapes. A ride-on tractor mower leaving wide green stripes in its wake chugged across the manicured lawns, and in the distance, a plume of spray from the fountains cascaded down towards the deer park. I felt a deep pull of longing in my stomach. It was too perfect for words.

'So, Holly, tell me why I should give you the job as my assistant?'

Pippa sat back, laced her fingers together and smiled. Behind her, bands of sunshine streamed in through the mullioned windows and past the faded elegance of the brocade curtains, illuminating the otherwise dark room and creating a goddess-like halo around her head.

I blinked at her. 'Well, I . . .'

For a moment my mind went totally blank. Usually I'd research and plan and practise all the likely interview questions. But I'd had no time for that today.

Come on, Holly, this is your big chance, the challenge you've been waiting for.

I took a deep breath and leaned forward. 'Because this is my dream job and I guarantee no one wants this job as badly as I do.'

Pippa cocked her head to one side and smiled softly. 'Really?'

I looked directly into her eyes and nodded.

'I've been coming to Wickham Hall with my mum ever since I was a little girl, for the Summer Festival, the fireworks displays, the Christmas decorations . . . every event, actually.' I uncrossed my ankles, which had somehow plaited themselves uncomfortably around the barley twist legs of my chair, and edged forward in my seat, forearms resting on the table.

'I even come here by myself sometimes,' I confided, tucking my blonde bob behind my ears. 'Just to enjoy the peace, the symmetry of the hall and orderliness of the gardens and . . .'

To escape from the chaos of Weaver's Cottage, I added mentally.

'I can honestly say it's my favourite place in the world. And the thought of being part of the team that makes all these wonderful events happen fills me with such joy that I can hardly contain myself . . .'

My chest heaved and a lump appeared in my throat. Pippa's eyes widened and she pressed a hand to her throat. I decided to revert to a more formal answer before we both ended up in tears. I coughed and ticked off my attributes on my fingers: 'I'm efficient, extremely organized, I love a challenge and I'm sure I will learn a lot from working with you.'

And I want this job. So. Much.

I leaned back and exhaled shakily. Maybe I'd overdone it, but it was the truth and telling the truth had to be a good thing, right?

Pippa smiled. 'Thank you. That was very heartfelt, Holly, I must say. Your résumé is very impressive too and it's a bonus that you're already familiar with our events.'

We talked for another fifteen minutes: me telling her discreetly about my personal circumstances and her giving me an outline of the day-to-day role of the vacancy, plus a run-down of her own story (married, four gorgeous children under six including twins, daughter of a vicar, lives in an old stone rectory that reminds her of home). What a superwoman! I was in total awe and it was all I could do not to reach across the table, squeeze her tight and beg her to pick me.

'It's not glamorous you know, this job,' said Pippa, twinkling her eyes. 'It probably sounds it, but running events here at the hall can be physically exhausting. Not only will you have to walk miles getting from one end of the estate to the other and back again, but we often have to set out chairs and tables, carry heavy boxes full of leaflets, climb ladders to fix signage—'

'I'm fit and strong,' I said, possibly sounding a little over-eager.

'Good. And we're rarely acknowledged for our efforts; Lord and Lady Fortescue are the public faces of the hall. Nobody even notices us half the time,' she finished.

'That's absolutely fine by me!' I declared, holding up my hands. 'Honestly. I'm much more of a behind-the-scenes person; give me a clipboard and a to-do list and I'm a happy bunny. I'm really not one to crave the limelight!'

'That's all right then,' Pippa laughed, 'because this job really wouldn't suit a diva who isn't prepared to get her hands dirty.'

'I love dirt,' I said hastily.

She grinned and I smiled and blushed and thought what fun we would have working together.

As Pippa made scratchy notes with her pen in the margin of my CV, I started looking around me again. These four walls would have been privy to hundreds of conversations over the past five centuries, I mused: shared secrets, rowdy debates, idle gossip, and now, Holly Swift's interview for the position of assistant events manager would forever be part of the room's illustrious past. I shivered; I had to get this job, I just had to.

'Do you have any questions for me before you go?' Pippa enquired, pen poised.

'Oh, yes, I do,' I said, thinking on my feet. 'Will I have an induction programme?'

This sort of thing is very important to me. I like to know what I need to know, upfront. No surprises. Be prepared, that's my motto.

'Induction. Right,' said Pippa, tapping her cheek with her pen. 'I'm sure we can sort something out.'

'Good, because I'd like to familiarize myself with the organizational hierarchy, key personnel and working practices first before I leap into the fray.'

Pippa's eyes twinkled with amusement.

'Um. If I'm successful, of course,' I added.

'Of course.' She pressed her lips together and I suspected she was swallowing a smile. 'Any other questions?'

'Ooh, yes, one more,' I said, taking a deep breath. 'What are the opportunities for progression in this role?'

Pippa pulled a face. 'In this department? None, I'm afraid.' She snapped the lid back on her pen and shoved my application to the bottom of the pile. 'Unless I leave. And I'm not planning on going anywhere. We're a small team. Of two, to be precise. Sorry about that. Is that all?'

I swallowed, giving the pile of application forms an anxious glance and worrying that my last question might have been too cheeky. But I was ambitious, I thought, no harm in being honest.

She pushed back her chair and stood up so I did too.

'I'm very pleased to hear that,' I said.

Pippa's mouth lifted into a smile and she gestured towards the door. 'I'll show you out.'

'About you not going anywhere, I mean,' I explained over my shoulder as I walked along the uneven corridor. 'I think we'd make a great team, don't you?'

She was still smiling as she stopped at a door at the top of the stairs. 'There are a number of strong contenders for the job, Holly. I need to have a think about who would be the best fit.'

'OK.' I nodded, sending her positive 'pick me' vibes.

'Right, here's the events office, I'll let you make your own way out.' Pippa shook my hand warmly. 'Lovely to meet you, Holly. I'll be in touch.'

'Will that be soon?' I asked, raising an eyebrow. I'd promised to call the temp agency back this evening and I very much wanted to be able to turn them down.

'You were my last candidate, so yes, very soon.'

'Thank you very much.' I beamed, releasing her hand reluctantly. 'I'll look forward to it.'

Back home at Weaver's Cottage, I called hello to Mum and ran straight up the stairs to my bedroom. My brain was whirring and my heart still pumping like the clappers from my hour at Wickham Hall. My dream job was within touching distance and yet I'd have to give the temp agency an answer before the office closed for the weekend at six o'clock. I needed a few minutes alone in my own sanctuary, my oasis of calm away from the stress of the rest of the cottage, to collect my thoughts.

My room was the same size as Mum's but that was where the similarity ended. All my furniture was white, white walls, white bedlinen and curtains. All the surfaces were clear except for a little dish on my chest of drawers where I kept my keys. I didn't go in for ornaments but photographs, mounted in collages on the wall, added some fun to the room, reminding me of my school and university days and holidays with my best friend Esme. I opened the top drawer, slotted my silver bracelet and earrings into place in my jewellery case and then changed from my interview clothes and into a pair of jeans.

'How did you get on?' shouted Mum.

'Down in a minute,' I yelled back.

I opened the wardrobe, hung my dress and jacket neatly, stacked my heels on the built-in shoe rack, tucked my phone in my pocket and ran back downstairs to find Mum. She was loading empty wine bottles into a plastic crate in the kitchen.

'Oh, Mum,' I breathed, 'I really want that job and I really liked Pippa. And the room was lovely, all wood panelling and sweet little windows . . . even the flowers were stunning.'

'Fingers crossed for you, love,' she said, patting my arm.

The worktop was a jumble of pans and second-hand kitchen equipment – like the breadmaker and coffee grinder that she'd brought home from the charity shop and never used – but I spied the teapot in amongst the clutter. 'Any tea left in that pot?'

'Yes, but it's gone cold,' said Mum, reaching into the fridge for a new bottle of wine. 'How about joining me for a glass of Pinot to celebrate your interview instead?'

'No thanks, I don't want to celebrate yet in case I jinx it,' I said, taking the kettle over to the kitchen sink. 'Let's stick to tea and celebrate when and if I get the job. But . . .' I hesitated, knowing I needed to get the tone right. 'I was thinking, Mum, why don't we have a go at clearing some of the stuff out of the hall before dinner? It would keep my mind off the interview and I might not have so much time soon . . .'

The change in her expression was instant; I'd seen it many times, but it never ceased to amaze me how quickly the shutters came down whenever I tried to make a sensible suggestion. Mum pressed her lips together, shook her head and searched the worktop for a wine glass.

'There's nothing to clear. I need all of that. Anyway, I'm busy tonight,' she muttered. 'I promised I'd knit another baby bonnet for the neo-natal unit. And I can't let the charity down. I won't have tea, thank you.'

My heart sank as she took the bottle and glass and pushed past me into the living room in search of her knitting bag. Classic Lucy Swift; it was always the same. As soon as I tried to make a suggestion to help pull her out of this rut, she would miraculously come up with something else more pressing and disappear.

It was on the tip of my tongue to remind her that charity begins at home but before I had a chance to formulate a suitably diplomatic reply, my mobile rang.

I stared at the screen, which read 'unknown number'. My heart thudded against my ribcage as I answered it.

'Holly Swift?' *Please let it be Pippa, please . . .*

'Holly, hi. Pippa Hargreaves here. Congratulations, you've got the job.'

'Yes!' I yelled, punching the air. 'Thank you. You won't regret it, I promise.'

My new boss laughed softly in my ear. 'Glad to hear it. When can you start?'

'Now?' I offered.

She laughed again. 'It's Friday evening, Holly. Monday morning at nine o'clock will be fine. I'll meet you in reception.'

'Nine o'clock sharp,' I said, beaming. 'Have a lovely weekend, boss.'

Chapter 2

It was a short drive to Wickham Hall – barely even a drive at all, in fact, but as the sky looked a bit threatening I took the car. I was waved into the staff car park by the security man, a dapper old chap in baggy shorts and a cagoule with a name tag revealing him to be Jim Badger.

It was five minutes to nine and my stomach was fluttering with first-day nerves as I stepped through the staff entrance at Wickham Hall. Me – staff – happy, happy days! I took a seat on one of the high-backed velvet armchairs in the reception area at the foot of the wide staircase and waited for Pippa to fetch me.

Almost immediately my phone dinged, alerting me to a text message. I fished it out of my bag and grinned when I saw it was from Esme.

Have a fab first day, Holster. I'm sure you'll wow them with your clipboard skills!

I quickly tapped out a reply.

Thanks Es. And you were right about the dress. I feel unstoppable in it!

Ha, told you! I should be in Hollywood dressing the
stars, I'm wasted here. See you later x

I turned my phone onto silent, tucked it away and smoothed
the skirt of my pale blue and white tea dress. Esme had persuaded me to buy it on Saturday. She and her mum, Bryony,
own a boutique called Joop in Hoxley, which is the next
village along from Wickham. Their clothes are to die for, if
a little above my price range, even with my generous mates'
rates discount. However, Bryony has a knack for spotting
what looks good on people and once she'd persuaded me to
try on this dress, and Esme had offered to turn up the hem,
it was a done deal.

'As Coco Chanel said, "Dress shabbily and they'll remember the dress, dress impeccably and they'll remember
the woman"', Esme had said through a mouthful of pins
as she altered the length to suit my vertically challenged
physique.

And as today was all about first impressions on everyone
at Wickham Hall, I definitely wanted them to remember
the woman.

There was a tall narrow console table opposite me in
the wood-panelled corridor and on top of it was a leaflet
dispenser filled with literature about Wickham Hall. I took
a selection and began reading one about the conversion of
some outbuildings into an art gallery. I'd seen one or two
of the leaflets before because Mum was on the mailing list
and she never threw anything away but there was a new one
about the Summer Festival. She would definitely want to
see that.

Two women came through the door: one in chef's whites,
the other in waitress uniform. 'Are you being looked after?'
one of them asked with a smile.

'Yes, thank you,' I answered. *I think*, I added under my breath, stealing a look at my watch. Ten past nine.

'OK. Lovely dress, by the way,' said the other.

Result.

'Thank you.' I beamed as they walked away.

Actually, maybe I wasn't being looked after, perhaps Pippa had been waylaid. I shoved the leaflets into my bag to show Mum later and was just contemplating making my own way up to the office when I spotted a matronly woman in her late sixties bustling towards me along the corridor. Her short hair was set in perfect silver waves, she had reading glasses on a chain perched on her bosom, and one of those Wedgewood cameo brooches pinned to her cardigan.

'Miss Swift?' she asked briskly.

'Yes?' I leapt up from my seat.

'I'm Mrs Beckwith, Lord Fortescue's private secretary,' she announced, shaking my hand briefly. 'Welcome to Wickham Hall. I've been sent to sort you out. Introduce you and whatnot.'

'Pleased to meet you, and do call me Holly,' I said with a smile. Mrs Beckwith reminded me of my old English teacher: a brisk, no-nonsense woman who forbade us ever to start a sentence with 'but'. 'Is Pippa—'

'Pippa won't be in today. Or possibly all week.' Mrs Beckwith gestured towards the staircase. 'Follow me to the events department please.'

My face fell. That was a shame; I'd been looking forward to spending some time with Pippa this week, learning the ropes. How odd that she hadn't mentioned on Friday that she wouldn't be here this week. Perhaps I could phone her instead, unless . . .

'She's not ill, I hope?' I asked as I followed Mrs Beckwith to the bottom of the stairs.

'No, not exactly, more of a family crisis,' she said, beginning the ascent to the first floor.

'Oh, how awful.' I frowned again.

What did that mean? Poor Pippa. I was dying to ask more questions but Mrs Beckwith was stomping up the stairs so quickly that I had to run to keep up.

At the top, a rich red carpet stretched left and right along the corridor. There was a row of windows on one side and large white-painted doors with brass knobs on the other. The only open door was the one leading to the events office. *My* office.

I was bursting to tell Mrs Beckwith what starting this new job meant to me and how amazing it was to be out of the house and working again but she didn't seem the sort to welcome such confidences, so I followed her into the room, grinning behind her back.

'You'll share this office with Pippa. Make yourself at home. Ladies' loos are along the corridor. And if you need anything, call me. Phone list is inside the top drawer.'

'Thank you.' I stood in the middle of the room, eyeing up the space.

It was a fairly small room with windows overlooking the gardens and just enough space for two desks, a photocopier and a table with a kettle, coffee machine and mugs on it. I glanced at the desks; one was clear except for a laptop and an A4 notepad, the other was barely visible beneath scattered papers, files and catalogues.

'Good grief, she gets worse,' Mrs Beckwith chuckled, walking towards the messy desk. 'I don't know how Pippa works in this turmoil.'

I let out a sigh of relief that that desk wasn't mine and rested my bag on the empty one.

Would Pippa mind if I tidied up in her absence? I

wondered. I really didn't want to have to sit looking at that chaos all week. I had enough of that at home. I'm from the 'tidy desk is a tidy mind' school of thought . . .

'Although I must admit, she always manages to lay her hands on what she's looking for straight away,' she went on, shaking her head as she sifted through the paperwork. 'Ah, here we are: the plan for next year's Wickham Hall calendar.'

Mrs Beckwith picked up a document, flicked through it and sighed. 'Oh dear, Lord Fortescue needs to know what is going on the cover as soon as possible. From the look of this, Pippa hasn't decided.

'Oh well.' She smiled brightly at me. 'That can be your job instead.'

'Of course.' I nodded. 'I can do that.'

How hard could it be? There must be loads of things at Wickham Hall that would make a stunning front cover.

'Right, come along, we must press on.' She marched to the door.

I cast a look back at Pippa's desk and the mounds of paperwork stacked haphazardly all over it and wondered whether I'd manage to lay my hands on what I needed to get me through the next week.

'Um . . . Mrs Beckwith, what would you say are the main events that Wickham Hall is gearing up for at the moment?'

Mrs Beckwith flapped her hand at me to hurry up. 'Walk and talk, dear; walk and talk,' she said as we hurried back down the stairs. 'Well, I'd imagine the priorities, in order, are: wedding, calendar, Summer Festival.'

'I didn't know Wickham Hall did weddings!' I exclaimed. I didn't know *I* did weddings, come to that. I'd dealt with gaggles of hen parties, but never an actual wedding.

Mrs Beckwith shook her head. 'We don't usually but this is Miss Zara's wedding.'

Of course, Lord and Lady Fortescue's daughter! I remembered now; I'd seen it in the society pages of the *Stratford Gazette*. She was marrying some French chappie from a wine dynasty with his own chateau. *Later this month.*

So my first major event in my new job was a society wedding? I felt an anxious knot form in my stomach. No pressure then . . .

'I'm sure Pippa will be back before then,' Mrs Beckwith said reassuringly.

'I'm sure she will,' I agreed confidently.

After all, the wedding was not till the end of the month. What sort of family crisis could take that long to sort out?

Chapter 3

Mrs Beckwith was quite a swift mover for someone of her age and I had to break into a trot to keep up.

'I haven't got long, I'm afraid,' she said. 'And now I've forgotten the blasted thing,' she added under her breath.

I scampered along the corridor wondering where we were going and what the 'blasted thing' might be. 'You mentioned introductions, Mrs Beckwith? Will I still be having an induction?'

'Here we are.' Mrs Beckwith barged through a door marked 'private'. I followed her and found myself in a beautiful office twice the size of the events department.

Although the hall was Elizabethan and the outside of the house remained virtually unchanged, a previous generation of Fortescues had redecorated most of the house in Georgian style in the eighteenth century. Not that I was an expert on history or anything, but I went to the local village school and Wickham Hall and the Fortescue family featured very highly on the syllabus.

This room was light and elegant and very obviously Georgian: the walls were pale primrose-yellow, it was bordered with ornate plasterwork and a handsome chandelier graced the ceiling. All the furniture was of a warm golden wood, from the bookcases that lined one wall to the desks, chests of drawers and filing cabinets. Between two of the windows stood a tall china pedestal topped with the most lavish floral display I'd ever seen outside of a church. The office oozed order and calm and I felt my shoulders relax automatically.

A second, interconnecting door stood open and the sound of voices wafted through.

Mrs Beckwith pressed an urgent finger to her lips and bustled across to close the door.

'Lord and Lady Fortescue are in a meeting with the bank,' she explained in hushed tones. She darted behind a desk, bent down to open a drawer and retrieved a camera.

I waited in the middle of the room, not daring to make a sound. Mrs Beckwith straightened up and spoke into a two-way radio.

'Sheila to Nikki. Where are you? Over.'

My lips twitched into a smile and I set myself a new challenge: I would earn the right to call her Sheila before Pippa came back.

The radio crackled and hissed. 'Nikki to Sheila. Chopping heads off on the terrace. Why? Over.'

'On my way to you. Garden tour for a new starter. Over.'

'Oh, for f—'

She cut off the rest of Nikki's message, clipped the radio to the waistband of her sensible skirt and caught me with my eyebrows raised.

'Nikki Logan, our head gardener,' she said dismissively. 'Don't worry about her. Bark's worse than her bite. Just watch those secateurs. Let's go and find her.'

She handed me the camera for some reason and charged off. 'Come along.'

The two of us marched on again, not back towards the staff entrance, but to the end of the corridor and through a heavy wooden door. We emerged into a room that I recognized as being one of those open to the public.

'Oh, I love this room,' I whispered.

It was large and square with deep red walls and was probably the size of our entire downstairs at Weaver's Cottage. Despite its size it felt cosy and homely, as though it was a room that the family used once the crowds had gone for the day. It was furnished comfortably with occasional tables and squishy red armchairs arranged around a huge fireplace. A myriad of family photographs were dotted around the room, from posed Victorian sepia portraits right up to more recent informal shots of weddings, parties and holidays.

Family photographs are like a giant jigsaw puzzle that defines your own life, I've always thought. Fit them together and the puzzle is solved.

All we had in our sitting room were two framed snaps of Mum and me, buried somewhere in the depths of the alcove next to the fireplace, and a rather starchy shot of my grandparents' wedding on the wall. There were a good few pieces missing from my puzzle, that was for sure . . .

Mrs Beckwith was smiling at me, her eyes crinkled at the corners. 'The Red Sitting Room? Me too. Have you been at Christmas?'

'Yes,' I nodded, 'with my mother.'

Mum and I always visited Wickham Hall at Christmas; it was one of our little traditions. We'd have mince pies and mulled wine in the café and then come into the hall to see the decorations. At Christmas, this room was even more cosy: decked out in garlands of ivy and mistletoe, the mantelpiece lined with candles, logs roaring away

33

in the grate and a real Christmas tree tucked into the corner.

And this year, I could come in here every day if the mood took me. I felt unbelievably fortunate all of a sudden and had to fight the urge to loop my arm through Mrs Beckwith's and skip round the room.

A lady in Wickham Hall tour guide uniform, her wispy white hair swept up into a bun, jumped down from a high stool near the door. 'A new recruit, Sheila?'

'Morning, Marjorie,' Mrs Beckwith waved. 'Yes, this is Holly Swift – Pippa's new assistant.' As I stepped forward to shake the old lady's hand, she went on: 'Marjorie is in charge of our team of tour guides.'

'Hello, dear. Any time you want a special in-depth staff tour, you let me know,' said Marjorie, tapping her nose. 'I'll show you all my favourite bits!'

'I'm on the lookout for things to feature in the new calendar,' I said, waving the camera about, 'so I might take you up on that.'

'Maybe after lunch,' said Mrs Beckwith, steering me towards the French doors. 'Garden tour next. Shame it's such a rotten morning.'

I peered through the glass: it was indeed a rotten morning, the clouds had darkened since I'd arrived and the drizzle had turned into fine rain. I could really do with that security man's cagoule, I thought, pulling my cardigan tighter as Mrs Beckwith opened the door. Stepping out onto moss-covered flagstones on the very edge of a wide terrace, I spotted someone on the far side wearing a wide-brimmed leather hat, khaki knee-length shorts and hiking boots. He or she was snipping away at a riot of pink flowers that were tumbling from an urn on top of the stone balustrade.

'I'll leave you in our head gardener's capable hands, Holly,' Mrs Beckwith said, looping a golf umbrella over my arm and gesturing me to move forward. 'Snap away with the camera this morning. It's always interesting to see what catches the eye of a new member of the team. And we really do need to sort out the images for the calendar.'

'Will do,' I said happily. Aside from the weather, walking round Wickham Hall's beautiful gardens photographing whatever took my fancy was a lovely way to start my morning.

The person in the leather hat waved in response and watched me, hands on hips, as I unfurled the umbrella to protect both me and the camera. I made my way across the flagstones and joined her at the balustrade.

'Oh, I love geraniums!' I said, sniffing the flowers in the pot that she was in the process of dead-heading. I shook Nikki's soily hand awkwardly by tucking the handle of the umbrella under my chin. 'And the colour – almost luminous on a gloomy day. So cheering, aren't they? Pleased to meet you, by the way. I'm Holly Swift, Pippa's new assistant.'

I wasn't much of a gardener myself, but Mum sometimes had a flash of enthusiasm for it. Hence the pots at our front door. Geraniums were one of the few plants I actually recognized.

Wickham Hall's head gardener flashed me a look of exasperation.

'Nikki Logan. And these are pelargoniums,' she said, snipping at a dead stem with gusto.

'Oh.' I stood corrected. I leaned in closer, like I knew what I was looking at. 'Similar, though.'

'Only to the uninitiated.'

Her bark is worse than her bite, I reminded myself.

'That's me to a tee.' I laughed. 'Totally uninitiated. I am, however, a quick learner and if you've got time to show me round, I'd like to take some pictures for next year's calendar.'

Nikki exhaled deeply, flicked a glance at my camera and seemed to relent. 'All right. If it's bold colour you're after, step this way.'

She dropped her secateurs into a trug heaped with faded greenery and dead flower heads and wiped her hands on her shorts.

'Thank you,' I said, falling into step beside her. 'My first major task is to work out what should go on the cover. Any suggestions welcome.'

'And I thought *I* was busy,' she murmured, rolling her eyes. But there was a hint of a humour in her voice and if that was Nikki's form of olive branch, I would take it gladly.

I prepared myself for another rapid stomp through the grounds but in complete contrast to Mrs Beckwith, Nikki led me slowly down the steps into the formal gardens. She examined each plant, reeling off its Latin name, and paused every few paces to pull the heads off dead lavender fronds or pluck out weeds.

'It's like housework but on a grander scale,' said Nikki. 'If you see a weed or a piece of debris you pick it up there and then. Leave it and the problem just gets bigger.'

'True,' I agreed, thinking of the decreasingly small amount of usable space in our living room.

We continued along a wide border edged with some sort of low hedge. It was brimming with plants of every hue: hazy masses of sweet peas clung to twisted willow stakes, delicate roses were woven gracefully over metal arches and clumps of plants from grasses to thistly things (which I didn't have a hope of identifying) filled every gap. Nikki, seemingly oblivious to the rain, continued to pull off leaves, fiddle with plant ties and tuck tendrils of stems around plant supports as we walked.

'So,' I said, determined to eke all the knowledge I could out of her while I had the chance, 'can you tell me about a typical day in the gardens, Nikki?'

'Ha, there is no typical day, that's what I love—'

At that moment my foot slipped on a wet leaf, I let out a squeal and grabbed onto Nikki's cotton shirt as my right leg shot forward leaving my left one behind.

'Ouch, oops, sorry!'

Nikki whooped with laughter and yanked me up.

'And there was me thinking I couldn't do the splits,' I snorted, rubbing the back of my thigh.

'Word to the wise: keep some outdoor shoes at work – trainers, wellies, whatever. Those dainty little things won't last five minutes,' she said, shaking her head at my new white ballet flats.

'Thanks for the advice,' I said, pleased that my mishap seemed to have broken the ice. 'I didn't expect to be outside today; I'm supposed to be having an induction—'

'Take a picture of this, Holly,' said Nikki as we reached the exit to the formal gardens. 'It's a topiary elephant we've been working on for a couple of years. Can you see?'

I snapped away while she explained that Lady Fortescue was a big fan of topiary and how Nikki had been training the new growth to form the trunk and how last year she had got fed up of visitors saying that it looked like a hippo.

'And one last shot with you in it,' I said, looking through the view finder.

Nikki obliged, doffing her hat to reveal short, wiry, honey-coloured hair. She grinned up at the elephant while I took the picture.

'Have you always worked at stately homes?' I asked, following her along a gravel path towards a wooded area.

'No. My last place was a millionaire's mansion near Windsor Castle,' she replied. 'Completely tacky but the gardens were out of this world. Owned by Will Simpson, ex-musician with eighties band Role Play.'

I nodded. 'Haven't they just done a reunion tour?'

'Yep,' she confirmed. 'Twenty dates. Total sell-out. I went to four of them.'

'Wow, you're a big fan, then?'

'Oh, yes.' Her eyes glittered. 'A big fan.'

'So why leave?' I asked, stopping to take a picture of a rose that was growing wild over an old tree stump. 'Sounds like your dream job.'

'Circumstances change. Staying wasn't really an option.' She shrugged, directing me off the path and through the wet grass. My shoes began to collect grass stains to add to the streaks of mud, leaf mulch and watermarks. Wellies were a must as of tomorrow, I vowed.

'Toughest decision I ever had to make. But luckily, the Fortescues' old gardener retired and they remembered seeing my Chelsea show garden and called me up. That was five years ago. And I never regretted leaving Will – I mean, the Simpsons – it was the right thing to do.'

'Well, you couldn't have come to a lovelier place,' I said, detecting a note of sadness in her voice. 'It must be so rewarding being able to show your gardens off to the public.'

'It is. You're right.' Nikki grinned. 'And it's a great bunch of people.'

Phew; happy face.

'That's good to know,' I said. 'Pippa seems lovely, although I only met her briefly, of course.'

'She is lovely. This way.' She pointed towards a clump of tall trees with wide trunks.

We stepped underneath the canopy of branches and out of the rain and I lowered the umbrella.

'I don't mean to pry,' I began tentatively, 'but is Pippa OK?'

'Not really.' Nikki shook her head, jaw clamped tight. 'She woke up on Saturday morning to discover that her husband had run off with the au pair.'

'Poor Pippa; and those poor little children, too.' I felt awful, remembering how warmly she had spoken of her family on Friday.

Nikki nodded glumly.

'Terrible behaviour from the girl. She was in Pippa's home in a professional capacity. Married men should be off limits. No excuses. And as for him . . .' Nikki's lip curled. 'Hopefully Pippa will be snipping the sleeves off all his suits as we speak. Anyway,' she knelt down and beckoned me to do the same, indicating that the subject was closed, 'you're in luck, I wasn't sure if we'd find any left. What do you think of these?'

I followed her pointing finger. In amongst the grass were the most incredible blue poppies I'd ever seen. Their tissue-like petals were such an intense colour that they almost looked unreal.

'These are magical,' I breathed, lifting the camera to my eye. 'A celestial blue.'

'Fab, aren't they?' She chuckled. 'They're Himalayan poppies. I'll never forget the first year I was here when I came to this spot and saw them for the first time. It was

39

like finding hidden treasure. People travel from all over to see them.'

I smiled to myself at the pride in her voice.

In that case, I thought, I'd better take plenty of pictures of them while they were still here. Nikki left me to it while I took a variety of shots from different angles.

I caught up with her fishing leaves out of the huge fountain that formed the start of the cascade leading down towards the deer park.

'Do you look after all of this?' I asked, eyeing up the acres and acres of land that surrounded us.

She nodded. 'I look after the formal gardens; the wild flower meadow; the walled kitchen gardens, which grow stuff for the café; the maze; the polytunnels and the greenhouses, of course. I grow plants for the house and a few for the gift shop . . . In short, I look after anything that doesn't have a cow, a horse or a deer on it.'

'Wow,' I said. 'That's a lot of responsibility for one person.'

'Over the years, this place has become my life.' She dropped a handful of soggy leaves on the ground and plunged her hand back into the water. 'My family, too, I suppose. And I have staff, of course, and a brilliant team of volunteers. I'm planting out this afternoon, but I can spare you another half an hour if you want a whistle-stop tour.'

I glanced at her surreptitiously as she wiped her hands on her shorts. Mrs Beckwith was right: under that prickly exterior was a big loyal heart and I had a feeling that despite me knowing nothing about gardening, she and I could be friends.

'Yes, I'd like that very much,' I replied.

*

As promised, the Coach House Café came back into view thirty minutes later. I was sure we must have walked miles around the estate and I was ready for a cuppa, not to mention a change of shoes. Luckily the rain had stopped for us, a chink of blue had opened up between the clouds and the grass was already beginning to steam in the sunshine.

'I loved your tour,' I said to Nikki as we entered the courtyard. 'I've been round the gardens loads of times on my own, but I've just wandered around, blithely unaware of all the planning and detail that goes in to getting the most out of every plant. That perfumed walkway in the sunken gardens, for example. Really clever.'

'An appreciative audience.' Nikki beamed. 'You can come again.'

And just being outdoors had given me such a sense of well-being. Maybe Mum and I should try to get outside more, lose some of the tension that builds up when we're inside . . .

'You'll find Jenny Plum in the kitchens.' Nikki put her hand on my shoulder and steered me towards the café. 'Through that entrance, look for the swing doors marked "staff only" and she'll be in there somewhere. You can't miss her.'

'OK, and thanks again, Nikki, you've really inspired me.'

'Great! That's why visitors come to Wickham Hall.' Nikki nodded enthusiastically. 'The gardens are by far the most important part of the experience. They want inspiration, to see things they might like to try at home. That's why the Himalayan poppies are so important.'

'Absolutely!' I agreed.

'I think that's a good enough reason to put them on the cover of next year's calendar, don't you? See ya!' She waved her fingers and then strolled off, hands in her pockets.

The vivid blue flowers *would* make a striking front cover, I thought, scrolling through the images on the camera. What a brilliant idea – and it would win me some Brownie points with my new friend. Double whammy! I smiled to myself as I pushed open the doors to the café. Lord Fortescue was going to be very pleased with me.

Chapter 4

The irresistible aroma of fresh baking inside the Coach House Café made my mouth water. I'd always loved it in here: the simple farmhouse-style interior was welcoming and inviting, the staff friendly and the food heavenly. Today it was buzzing with customers enjoying tea and cakes amongst other delicious goodies, and the sounds of clinking cutlery and the buzz of conversation filled the warm and slightly humid air. I left my umbrella in a stand by the door, made my way to the swing doors marked 'staff only' and immediately jumped back as a waitress emerged backwards, carrying a plate in either hand.

'Sorry, love,' she said as she turned round and spotted me, her wide smile almost eclipsing her rosy cheeks. 'I nearly covered you in roasted tomato soup. Oh, it's you from reception this morning. I remember the lovely dress.'

'Thank you. Again!' I said, recognizing her as the waitress I'd met earlier. 'Is Jenny through there?'

The waitress jerked her head towards the kitchen. 'Yes, love, you can't miss her.'

What was so unmissable about Jenny Plum? I wondered, edging my way cautiously through the swing doors. The kitchen was a huge space, although currently only about a quarter of it was in use. The high brick walls were painted white, stainless-steel worktops, huge ovens and hobs crowned with enormous extractor fans divided the room into three aisles and the only reminder of the room's age was the row of leaded windows along one side.

'Hello?' I ventured to the team of three who were chopping, stirring and plating up in the area closest to the door. 'I'm looking for Jenny.'

A girl lifted a tray of mini tartlets from the oven, set them down carefully and smiled. She opened her mouth but before she could speak, someone else beat her to it.

'Are those asparagus tarts ready, Rachel?' A woman's voice boomed from the other side of the room.

'Yes, Chef!' yelled the girl, scooping them from the baking sheet with a spatula.

'That's Jenny,' she added in a softer voice. 'Far corner.'

I thanked her and walked towards the end aisle to locate the source of the voice and saw a woman partially obscured by a haze of white powder, towering over the worktop. She was very tall and had tendrils of purple hair escaping from her hair-net. She was completely impossible to miss.

I began to approach her along the aisle and noticed a man in his mid-twenties, wearing skinny charcoal trousers and pointed shoes, leaning on his elbows over the workbench, where Jenny appeared to be wielding a teeny-tiny rolling pin.

'Apparently the *new girl* has started,' the man grumbled with undisguised animosity.

'Oh, Andy; move on, mate!' Jenny wagged her rolling pin at him. 'Pippa must have had her reasons for choosing her.'

Me. They were talking about me. The hairs on the back of my neck started to prickle and I stopped, rooted to the spot.

'More icing sugar,' Jenny demanded.

Andy lifted a metal pot and doused whatever she was working on with a generous sprinkling of powdered sugar, filling the air with another white cloud.

Now what do I do? I was still edging my way towards them and I didn't know whether to walk away and pretend I hadn't heard their conversation or fess up.

'Sorry, Jenny, but it doesn't make sense.' He straightened up, leaned one hip against the counter, tightened his pony-tail with a flick of his wrist and folded his arms. I couldn't see his face but his body language and tone of voice oozed resentment. 'I'm serious. I've got the experience, the flair, the communication skills . . . that job was rightfully mine.'

'Only it obviously wasn't, was it?' Jenny chuckled, her narrow shoulders shaking with mirth.

Oh, stuff it, I couldn't stand here all day and it would be even more embarrassing if I got caught eavesdropping. I cleared my throat loudly and they both turned round.

'Hi,' I said, stepping in between them. 'I'm Holly Swift.'

Jenny and Andy exchanged glances before Jenny held out a sugar-coated hand.

'Bit sticky, I'm afraid.'

I wasn't sure whether she was referring to her fingers or the awkward situation we found ourselves in but I shook her hand anyway.

'Pleased to meet you,' I said and turned to Andy, hoping he'd shake hands too.

He tucked his hands into armpits and scowled.

'That job was as good as promised to me,' he sniffed.

Jenny snorted with laughter. 'You're breaking my heart, sunshine, you really are. Now back to your shop and fold some posh blankets, why don't you? Here you go,' she said, placing something in his hand. 'Take this marzipan lemon with you as a symbol of the bittersweet reality of life.'

'Whatever,' he muttered, and flounced out of the kitchen without a backwards glance.

I let out a breath. 'I don't think he's my number-one fan.'

'Not at the moment, no.' Jenny pulled an apologetic face. 'Sorry you had to hear that.'

'It's fine,' I said nonchalantly. Although knowing Andy wasn't exactly overjoyed at my presence was a bit of a disappointment; I tried to get on with everyone in life. 'Forewarned is forearmed, and all that. I feel a bit bad for him, actually.'

'Good for you. And don't feel bad, chick, as I said to him: Pippa must have had her reasons.'

I smiled my thanks and watched as Jenny turned her attention back to the edible work of art in front of us. She picked up the tiny rolling pin, rolled out some sort of icing and cut it into the shape of a unicorn's head. Then lifting it carefully with a broad knife she laid it next to two others on top of a large round tart.

'That looks incredible. What is it?'

'This?' She wiped her forearm across her face and smiled. 'It's a marchpane tart: an Elizabethan dessert, their version of marzipan basically. I just need to add the bling.'

I watched as she peeled a glittering sheet of edible gold from a packet and carefully brushed a shield decorated with the three unicorns' heads until it glimmered in the light. I was transfixed; Jenny made it look so easy. Brushing the top of a scone with beaten egg is probably my limit.

'That's the family crest, isn't it?' I whispered as she stroked the fine brush around a unicorn's magical horn.

'Yep. Next stately home I work at, I'm going to choose one with a simpler crest. Like a rainbow.' She grinned.

'How much is a slice of this going to set me back?' I

asked, thinking longingly about my lunch break. 'I bet gold leaf doesn't come cheap.'

'Sorry, it's not for sale in the café.' Jenny pulled a face. 'This is the centrepiece for a demo I'm doing for the Women's Institute later on Elizabethan sugar banquets. I'm taking it over now – come with me if you like.'

'Sure. Oh and can I take some pictures for the calendar while I'm here?'

Her eyes widened. 'For the calendar? Abso-bloomin-lutely! Wait here a mo.'

I waited while she issued orders to her kitchen staff, tasted Rachel's pastry and packed the marchpane tart into a cardboard box.

'Can you manage these?' she said, lifting three heavy cake boxes into my arms without waiting for an answer. 'Let's go.'

The two of us left the kitchen via a door that led directly into the main part of Wickham Hall. We passed a group of foreign tourists taking photographs of the stained-glass panels in the hallway, directed an old lady who had got lost towards the exit and finally made our way up to the second floor.

'Don't you do your demo in the kitchen?' I panted after ascending the final flight of steps whilst maintaining a careful grip on the tower of boxes in my arms.

Jenny shook her head and flung open a door on the landing with a flourish. 'Ta-dah! I use the Long Gallery.'

I followed her in, set my boxes down on a small table and whistled.

'Wow!' I turned in a slow circle, taking in the glorious proportions of the room. 'This is huge and very lovely!'

There were tall windows all down one side to the room, each one furnished with a deep, cushioned window seat.

The views were equally stunning; the Long Gallery was in the centre of the hall and looked out onto the impressive gravelled approach to Wickham Hall and the gatehouse at the far end of the drive. The opposite wall contained carefully sculpted alcoves in which sat shelves of artefacts protected from over-enthusiastic visitors by sheets of glass.

Jenny took off her white hair-net and a tumble of ruler-straight purple hair fell to her shoulders. My eyes widened: I'd seen a few loose strands but en masse, her hair was quite a spectacle.

'Indeed it is,' said Jenny, dropping comically into curtsey. 'Would Miss Holly care to take a turn about the room?'

The two of us, arm-in-arm, must have looked quite a sight as we promenaded around the room: Jenny, a purple-topped bean pole, holding her apron to the side as if she was wearing a period gown, and me, barely reaching up to her shoulder, skipping along in my muddy shoes to keep up with her long stride.

'I get my W.I. girls doing this. They love it, pretending to be Georgian ladies getting their daily exercise. And this,' pronounced Jenny when we reached a long narrow table set with crockery and cutlery, 'is where my sugar banquet will go once we've set out the chairs.'

Pippa was right, I thought, as I helped Jenny set thirty chairs in rows for our lady visitors, this job was physically demanding. I probably wouldn't need to go running so much now. This was a much more enjoyable way to keep fit.

'Do you do the catering for all the events?' I asked, flicking a stray thread from one of the gold brocade chairs.

'Yep. We only have a small staff in for the café most days. But when there's a big event, it's all hands on deck.' Jenny walked to the top of the room to collect the cake boxes. 'Ever done any waitressing?'

I nodded. 'Silver service when I was at uni.'

Jenny began setting up the sugar banquet while I took some shots of her pastries and biscuits.

'We sometimes draft in extras at weekends if you're interested? It's a good laugh and a bit of extra cash. I'd love to have you on my team.'

An unexpected lump appeared in my throat. I'd only been here a few hours and I already felt like I was starting to belong. Jim the security man, Marjorie, Nikki, Jenny . . . even Mrs Beckwith in a starchy way had made me feel at home. Andy . . . well, I might have to work on him, but the rest of them had been so welcoming.

Living with Mum since uni had made me gradually more isolated and I tended to steer away from close friendships through embarrassment. I mean, I could hardly bring people home to Weaver's Cottage, could I? But having a group of friendly colleagues who made my day brighter as soon as I walked into work would make a massive difference to my life.

Jenny was looking at me quizzically and I realized she was waiting for an answer.

'I might be a bit rusty, but yes, I'd love to,' I said happily. 'As long as I know well in advance.'

Jenny settled the marchpane tart onto a cake stand at the centre of the buffet and stood back proudly to admire it while I snapped some more photographs.

'Got family commitments, have you?' She nodded knowingly.

'No, no, but—'

'Boyfriend?' She winked and I felt my cheeks heat up.

'Not that either. I just like to plan ahead, that's all. You know. Put stuff in the diary,' I said with a shrug.

I took my diary with me everywhere, much to Esme's

amusement. It was one of those that showed you a week spread over two pages and I put everything in it. I could lay my hands on a list of all the summer holidays I'd ever been on, a list of what was number one in the charts on my birthday every year since I'd been born. And although she might mock the fact that I've recorded my weight ever since my eighteenth birthday, Esme did rely on me to remember all our friends' birthdays, weddings, important anniversaries and forthcoming gigs and parties.

'I see. Well, I'll do my best and if you're available, you let me know,' said Jenny, chuckling to herself.

'The marchpane looks great,' I said brightly, feeling ridiculous for mentioning my diary. I showed her the image on the digital display and her eyes went all dreamy.

'Food is a great way to learn about the past, and such an important part of what we do here at Wickham Hall.' She sighed, looping her hair behind her ears and bending down to get a better look at the screen. 'Anyone can open a stately home up to the public, but where's the fun in looking at dusty old furniture and paintings of crinkly old men in tights? But I adore the history of food: learning about it. Cooking it, talking about it . . . It's like a secret doorway into the past. And even if you only have a cuppa and a bun in the café, we try to make it memorable. Food is what sets Wickham Hall apart from its rivals.'

'I couldn't agree more,' I said, eyeing up a dainty biscuit that was hanging over the edge of a plate. 'Should I be your official taster, do you think?' I looked at Jenny cheekily and pointed at the object of my desires.

She wrinkled her nose. 'Yeah, why not? That one's called a prince bisket. And you can have it . . .'

She watched as I bit into it and closed my eyes as the delicate flavour of rose filled my mouth. 'Delicious!'

'. . . as long as you put my marchpane tart on the front of your calendar.'

My eyes popped open as a crumb made a quick getaway via my tonsils.

'Well,' I choked, banging my chest furiously, 'I'll certainly suggest it.'

Along with Nikki's blue poppies . . .

'Hell's angels!' cried Jenny, looking at her watch. 'I was supposed to take you to meet Andy at the gift shop half an hour ago.'

'Andy?' I grinned, brushing biscuit crumbs from my chin. 'That should be interesting.'

Chapter 5

As it turned out, by the time I arrived at the gift shop, Andy had disappeared on his lunch break and I had the pleasure of a tour round the shop with the diminutive Edith Nibbs instead. Edith told me she had worked at Wickham Hall for fifty years, firstly as a cleaner, then as a tour guide and now she just did a couple of hours a day at the gift shop over lunchtime.

'This has been my favourite job at the hall, so far,' she said as she wrapped a large filigree hurricane lantern in tissue paper.

So far. I stopped straightening a row of Wickham Hall china mugs so that the handles all faced the same way and smiled at her. How many more jobs was Edith planning to have before she retired?

'Thank you, madam,' she said, handing a lucky customer her bag filled with goodies. 'Come back next week and we should have some more sunflower plants. Goodbye.'

'The gift shop must be a lovely place to work,' I said, leaning on the counter. 'You sell some wonderful things.'

'Yes, dear. It is such a treasure trove. Lady Fortescue does most of the buying; she has quite an eye for beauty. I have to restrict myself to buying one item a month,' she confided, settling herself into a low chair behind the cash desk so that only the top of her white bun was visible.

'I can imagine.' My eyes widened as I fingered the price tag on a luxury wicker picnic hamper. 'What are your best sellers, Edith?'

'Christmas decorations fly off the shelves from November.' She chuckled. 'We can't stock enough. But the rest of the year, I'd say the scented range over here, look.'

Edith got to her feet and I followed her to a table in the centre of the shop. On it was an artfully arranged pyramid of bottles, candles and boxes, interspersed with pots of fragrant herbs.

'This is beautifully displayed, Edith,' I exclaimed.

'All Andy's work,' she said, prodding a terracotta pot of something or other. 'Needs a drop of water.'

I raised an eyebrow. Andy was clearly a talented man under that sulky exterior.

'We have this Wickham Hall range especially made in Stratford,' Edith went on, handing me a tester bottle of rosemary and bergamot room spray. The slim glass bottle had an all-over delicate pattern on it and the label bore the Wickham Hall family crest. I squirted the spray into the shop and both of us inhaled.

'Oh, that's lovely!' I exclaimed, replacing the bottle on the table and picking up a fat white candle from the same range.

'Rosemary and bergamot would have been used in scent in Elizabethan times.' Edith beamed and held up a reed diffuser for my inspection. 'I like to think that this is the original aroma of Wickham Hall. Nothing evokes a treasured memory like smell, I always think.'

'Very true.' I nodded. 'Like the smell of coconut oil on holiday, or cinnamon at Christmas.'

'Exactly.'

I'd buy one of those for Mum's birthday, I thought as I reached for the camera and began taking pictures. Perhaps if our cottage smelt of Wickham Hall, it might inspire her to tidy up a bit.

The rest of the day flew by and after several satisfactory hours at Pippa's desk piling the paperwork into some sort of order, I was amazed to find it was time to go home. Or rather time to go and see Esme, who had demanded a blow-by-blow account of my day.

I reached the door of my office when the phone on Pippa's desk rang.

'Wickham Hall Events Department?' I answered brightly, scouring her desk for something to write on and with.

'Oh, Holly, I am so sorry to have left you in the lurch today,' cried my boss. 'Did someone look after you? Did you find things to do? You haven't resigned already, have you?'

'It was fine, Pippa,' I soothed, casting an eye over her already vastly improved work space. I'd also erected a makeshift noticeboard on the wall with all the forthcoming events written on it and made a short list of some nice images for the Wickham Hall calendar. 'I've had quite a productive day, in fact. Learning on my feet.'

Literally, I mused, looking at my dirty shoes.

'I knew I'd made the right decision choosing you,' she said and sighed.

'And I'm so glad you did,' I said, settling back down on her office chair.

'But your induction?' she groaned, sounding so anguished that I could almost see her furrowed eyebrows. 'I feel so guilty! Did you . . . have you heard about my . . . ?'

'Nikki mentioned that you had a family crisis,' I said gently, helping her out. 'Please. Don't worry about me. Just do what you have to do.'

'Thank you. I'm staying at my parents' in Somerset for a few days with the children until . . . well. Anyway, feel free to call me whenever you like, I'll give you my mobile number and if you have any questions—'

I could hear the sound of children squealing and laughing in the background. Good. At least they sounded happy and not traumatized by their current family saga.

'Oh, there is one thing.' I frowned. 'Zara's wedding! I don't know where to start; I've never organized a wedding before.'

'Piece of cake,' Pippa assured me. 'Lady Fortescue and Zara have everything in hand, even though Zara lives in Bath.'

'Thank heavens for that!' I breathed a sigh of relief; I'd spent an hour researching wedding checklists this afternoon. 'I thought—'

'Arrghh!' she shrieked suddenly, startling me. 'Matilda, come down from that tree! Freddy, go and rescue your sister please. Thank you. No, no, don't pull her by her ankle! Wait a minute, Holly.'

I chuckled to myself and waited while Pippa sorted out her offspring.

'Sorry about that,' she said breathlessly, returning to the phone a few moments later. 'Where were we? Oh, yes, remember, our role is to manage public events. The wedding is private. However, we will both be expected to work on the day of the wedding and ensure that no paparazzi gain unauthorized entrance; they can be tricky so-and-sos, believe me. Now, do you know about tomorrow's meeting?'

We finished the call a couple of minutes later after she'd passed on a few instructions for the following day and I went in search of my diary to add the date of Zara's wedding to Monsieur Philippe Valois and underline it in red pen. A posh wedding! I could hardly wait to tell Esme. What would Zara's dress be like? I wondered. And how on earth was one supposed to handle paparazzi?

Esme was sitting on the floor of Joop, legs crossed, bent down over a heap of taffeta when I tapped on the shop window later that evening.

She and her mum had won several awards for shop design over the years. Clothes were displayed in French armoires with the doors removed, opulent chandeliers made the space sparkle and each spacious fitting room was papered with a different vibrant wallpaper. It looked luxurious; only a select few of us knew that the lights were from a DIY store, the wallpaper was from the remnant bin and the wardrobes were courtesy of a closing-down auction at a local hotel.

'Holster!' Esme yelled, flinging the fabric aside and leaping to her feet as I entered. 'Look at you in your personally selected Joop dress! How did you get on? Did you wow her with your extreme diary-keeping?'

I gave her a hug and laughed.

'My boss wasn't there, but I get the impression that she's not as dogged as I am when it comes to paperwork. Anyway, I loved it. There's such an aura about the place. Oh, and the Long Gallery . . .' I sighed wistfully. 'Close your eyes and you can imagine the Fortescues' ancestors all going about their lives. It must be lovely for the current Fortescues to have such strong ties to their family.'

Esme's eyes held mine. She was the only person who I

shared everything with, the only one who knew I felt adrift sometimes with no one except Mum to anchor me to my place in the world.

'I'm glad for you.' She squeezed my arm. 'I was beginning to worry about you, cooped up in that cottage all the time. I even thought of offering you a job here, but . . .' Her voice tailed off and she bent to gather the fabric, scissors and pin tin from the floor.

'But what?' I prompted, following her to the tiny room at the back of the shop. 'Es, what's up?'

I leaned against the doorframe and watched while she packed up for the day. As well as being Joop's stock room, the tiny space doubled up as the workroom and every iota of surface was filled with pieces of fabric, boxes of buttons, reels of ribbon and Bryony's sewing machine and sewing box.

'Oh, probably nothing,' she said, giving me a lopsided grin. 'But the bank wants to see us about our overdraft and, er . . . Mum's not well. She's getting all sorts of aches and pains. She blames it on her age, but I'm not so sure. What if she's taking after Gran?'

My heart sank. Bryony had mentioned on Saturday that her fingers ached and given that Esme's grandmother was wheelchair-bound with rheumatoid arthritis, it was understandable that Esme was concerned.

I stepped into the stock room and gave her a hug. 'Poor Bryony, I didn't realize. Is that why you shortened my hem on Saturday?'

She nodded. 'Mum finds alterations too painful at the moment. It's not my favourite part of the job but it's money we can't afford to lose.'

'Esme, I am sorry. If there's anything I can do to help, say the word.'

'In that case,' my best friend waggled her eyebrows at me, 'the word is ice cream. Come on, I've got a parcel to pick up from the post office in Henley first and then you can treat me to a double scoop of coconut.'

Half an hour later, Esme had collected a floppy brown-paper parcel and the two of us were sauntering back towards her car clutching our rapidly melting ice creams. I glanced at her; she looked like an exotic flower walking down Henley High Street in her tangerine summer dress, her light brown skin glistening in the afternoon sun and her corkscrew curls lifting gently in the breeze. There was the merest hint of sadness in her eyes, though, and I knew she was more worried about her mum and the shop than she cared to admit.

'So, your birthday,' I said, determined to cheer her up. 'Not long now. Have you had any ideas yet?'

I twirled my raspberry ripple as I licked it to keep it nice and round and looked at her out of the corner of my eye.

'Urgh, can't we just ignore it?' she moaned through a mouthful of coconut ice cream. She was biting huge chunks off hers and was nearly at the cone.

'No,' I insisted. 'It's your thirtieth. I know, why don't I organize tickets to that new Salsa club in Stratford? We might meet some snake-hipped Latinos to sweep us off our feet. Come on, Es, we need to plan something.'

We reached her tiny vintage racing-green sports car and I took the parcel from her while she juggled with her ice cream and handbag to retrieve the keys.

We climbed in, the old cream leather seats creaking underneath us, and I reached across and dropped the parcel in her lap.

'You and your plans,' laughed Esme. She popped the end of her ice cream cone into her mouth and wiped her fingers on a napkin. 'I'm more of a moment-to-moment kind of girl, much more exciting.'

Hmm, I thought to myself, hiding a smile behind my ice cream, that was why she always ran out of money before pay day and had to come to me for a loan.

'Stop trying to wriggle out of it, Esme Wilde. We're celebrating whether you like it or not.'

She rolled her eyes and stuck the key in the ignition. 'I'll think about it, OK? Now wait till you see what's in here.'

She unpicked the sticky tape on the brown paper to reveal a piece of folded ivory lace.

'Look at that,' she breathed, stroking a potentially sticky finger over the scalloped edge. 'Have you ever seen anything so delicate?'

I giggled at the expression of ecstasy on her face. 'More fabric, Es! What's your mum going to say?'

'Fabric!' exclaimed Esme indignantly. 'This is five metres of handmade vintage lace. I don't know what I'm going to do with it, but I couldn't resist it. Now, do you fancy going for a drink?'

'I would,' I said, 'but I'm meeting Lord and Lady Fortescue tomorrow for the first time and I need to present my plan for next year's calendar.'

'And what is your plan?'

I pressed my lips together with a secretive smile. 'I'm still cogitating but I've got a feeling it's going to be brilliant.'

The next morning, I reported to Mrs Beckwith at ten o'clock for the meeting Pippa had briefed me about.

'Go through, Holly,' she said and smiled, eyeing my navy

shift dress with what I hoped was approval. 'Her Ladyship will join you shortly.'

I paused at the door to Lord Fortescue's private office; I hadn't been in this room yet. It was big and square and overlooked the Fortescues' personal garden. French leaded doors stood open, flooding the room with sunshine. Seated together at an oval, polished-wood table were Nikki and Andy. A frowning Lord Fortescue was sitting at a large ornate desk under the window. He was on the phone and seemed to be saying nothing other than 'Yah, yah,' and 'Beg pardon?' His desk, I noticed, was clear except for the phone and his elbows.

Nikki tapped the back of the empty chair next to her and I sat down.

'Thank you,' I whispered. 'I'm so glad to see a friendly face.'

I studiously avoided looking at Andy as I spoke. 'What are you here for?'

'Wedding flowers.' Nikki winked at me. 'I have to give a weekly progress report on every bloom destined for Zara's bouquet.'

She was wearing shorts again today and a multi-pocketed khaki gilet that wouldn't have been out of place in the jungle. She reached into one of the pockets.

'Here, I've saved you a blue poppy.' She grinned, handing over the flimsy collection of petals. 'You can press it and have it as a keepsake of your first day at Wickham.'

'How sweet! That is so kind of you.' I beamed at her, slipping the flower between the pages of my diary. I turned my attention to Andy, who had been inspecting his nails pointedly ever since I entered the room.

Best get this over with.

'Andy?' I leaned across Nikki and extended a hand of

friendship. 'Sorry to miss you yesterday, but Edith did a great job of showing me round your amazing gift shop. I absolutely love the Wickham Hall range of fragrance products.'

Andy raised his eyebrows and returned my handshake limply. 'Glad you appreciate my efforts. I source them myself from a local craftsman.'

Edith had told me that Lady Fortescue did all the buying, but I nodded enthusiastically, ignoring what could have been a snort from Nikki.

'You've definitely got an eye for quality,' I said. 'And what are you here for?'

'Finalizing the Christmas decorations for the hall, *the* most important season at Wickham Hall,' he said in hallowed tones.

'In June?' I exclaimed, wrinkling my nose.

'Of course in *June*; we start *planning* in January.' He tutted. 'What do they want to see you for?'

'The Wickham Hall calendar,' I said, permitting myself a little smile.

I'd spent an hour developing some ideas last night and, though I said so myself, I'd come up with a corker. One that I hoped all my new colleagues would approve of.

Andy leaned forward and fixed me with a pair of piercing pale blue eyes. 'I hope you're going to put the gift shop on the cover,' he said in a low voice.

Nikki raised her eyebrows. 'Excuse *me*.'

'For God's sake, Nikki, we are the most profitable part of the business,' he muttered, holding his hands out. 'It's a no-brainer.'

'Huh!' She elbowed him in the ribs. 'I beg to differ.'

Andy sat back, quite possibly forced back under the weight of Nikki's hard stare. 'Profit on a cup of tea? Fifty pence. Profit on a mohair throw? Um,' his eyes shifted side to side, 'massive.'

'It's not all about profit,' Nikki whispered, turning to me. 'The gardens at Wickham are as much a part of its heritage as the hall itself. You can't put a price on that.'

'I agree,' I said diplomatically. 'All areas of the hall are equally precious, which is why none of them will be on the cover.'

Andy blinked at me in disgust and Nikki made a huffing noise.

I was saved any further examination as Lord Fortescue finished his phone call and strode towards me, hands outstretched.

'And you must be our newest recruit, er . . . ?'

'Holly Swift,' I answered for him, standing up as he pumped my hand enthusiastically.

'Excellent, excellent,' he said, nodding. 'Righty-o, let's get started.' Lord Fortescue clapped his hands together. 'Any sign of Beatrice, Sheila?' he bellowed.

Just then Lady Fortescue glided into the room, a picture of elegance in a silk shirt, fitted trousers and spiky heels. Her dark hair was swept up into a smooth chignon and her brown eyes darted round the room until they stopped at me. I smiled politely as she arranged herself at the head of the table.

'Good grief, Hugo!' She tutted affectionately. 'I'm not sure our future son-in-law's family quite heard you in Bordeaux, would you like to shout a bit louder?'

'What?' He blinked at his wife and sat down next to her.

'Lord Fortescue is a bit hard of hearing,' she explained, her lips twitching with a smile, 'although he denies it most vigorously, of course.'

'I heard that,' he harrumphed.

'Good, then let's get started. You must be Pippa's new assistant,' she said, extending a hand.

She had long slim fingers and the biggest rock on her finger that I'd ever seen.

'That's right, I'm Holly Swift, I'm—'

'You're going to tell us about the calendar,' she finished for me, checking her watch. 'Thoughts?'

Here goes . . .

I cleared my throat and turned to the notes I'd made last night.

'Hidden treasures,' I said mysteriously. 'That's the theme for this year's calendar.'

'Huh?' grunted Andy.

Lady Fortescue regarded me with interest. 'Go on.'

I took a deep breath and told them that yesterday, on my first day, what had stood out to me was that there were so many hidden treasures at Wickham Hall, from the flowers in the garden – I paused to smile at Nikki – to the treasure trove of beautiful things in the gift shop – I nodded at Andy – through to the gold leaf used in the Elizabethan recipes from the kitchen. As a marketing theme, that idea could run and run: treasured memories, treasure hunts, maybe a treasure chest window display for the gift shop . . .

'And who better to be the face of the calendar, on your thirtieth anniversary at the hall, than you, Lord Fortescue, Lady Fortescue. I thought that the cover of the calendar could be a lovely informal photograph of you both, with a collection of your favourite Wickham Hall treasures.'

Lord Fortescue was nodding thoughtfully. Lady Fortescue was smiling. Phew.

I ploughed on. 'And as thirty is traditionally the "pearl"

anniversary, perhaps we could do something with that?' Pearl was also my middle name, for reasons known only to my mother.

'I'm with you there,' said Nikki. 'I was already planning a pearly-white theme for the Summer Festival show garden.'

I flashed her a smile of thanks.

'What about you, Andy?' I asked, smiling innocently at him. 'I know you wanted the gift shop on the front of the calendar, but what do you think?'

He shifted awkwardly in his seat. 'I can work with it, I suppose.'

'Oh, Hugo, it's such a sweet idea. I'm sure we can come up with some lovely treasures.' Lady Fortescue sighed wistfully, laying a hand on her husband's arm.

'My bird hide. That's hidden treasure,' said Lord Fortescue. 'Although I wouldn't want anyone knowing about that.'

I stifled a smile; it was not the most useful suggestion. 'Preferably something you'd be happy to be photographed with, Lord Fortescue.'

'Such a shame about my pearl bracelet,' said Lady Fortescue. 'That would have been perfect. Do you remember that, Hugo, the one I lost?'

'No.' He took a checked handkerchief out of his pocket and blew his nose three times. 'But you've got boxes and boxes of trinkets, haven't you?'

'I used to think I looked like Madonna in that bracelet.' She gazed dreamily out of the window.

'Oh, I adore Madonna's eighties stuff,' Andy gushed. 'All that lace and layers. I wasn't born then, of course—'

Lady Fortescue silenced him with an icy stare, before gracing me with a smile. 'Hidden treasures,' she purred. 'I like it. Well done, Holly, I think you and I are going to get on very well indeed.'

Nikki nudged me under the table.

'Thank you, Lady Fortescue,' I replied, doing my best to keep my elation under control. 'I very much hope so.'

Chapter 6

For the rest of the week, I threw myself into my work, learning on the job as previously organized events took place and getting up to speed with where Pippa had got to on new projects too. I carried on in her absence as best I could: issuing press releases for the Summer Festival, mailing exhibitors their information packs, and dealing with tons of different problems on an almost hourly basis. But by Friday Pippa still hadn't come back. Nor had she returned a week after that and I began to get a bit worried about her. I asked Jenny and Nikki if they'd had any news, but no one had heard a peep from her and they were just as concerned as I was.

On my second Friday afternoon, I was starting to wind down for the weekend when Mrs Beckwith came to see me in my office.

'Have you got a moment?' she said, lowering herself into the spare chair.

'Of course. This is an unexpected pleasure.' I smiled, jumping up to switch on the kettle. 'I don't get many visitors. Tea?'

Mrs Beckwith cast her eye around the room as I made us both a drink. 'You've been tidying, I see?'

'Yes,' I said, adding milk to two mugs. 'I hope Pippa won't be offended, but I function much better in a neat and tidy space. Too much clutter and I get all claustrophobic.'

My mind raced back to the argument Mum and I had had the night before when I'd come home to find her trying to stuff a suitcase full of old clothes under my bed. I wouldn't have minded so much if they'd been winter clothes that she wanted to put aside for the summer or something. But they were my granddad's old suits, for goodness' sake. There was one room in the house that hadn't been stuffed to the rafters with her rubbish – or as she liked to call it her memories – and that was my room. I'd dragged the suitcase out and left it on the landing while she yelled at me for being selfish. The row had left me trembling with frustration and that suitcase would probably stay at the top of the stairs for ever now.

I took a deep breath and hoped Mrs Beckwith didn't notice the tremor in my hands as I set the mugs down on the desk.

'I'll get straight to the point,' she said, pulling a tissue out of her cardigan sleeve and wiping the bottom of the mug.

'Go on,' I said shakily.

'Pippa will be taking the rest of the month off.' She sipped at her tea, wincing slightly and peering at me over the rim.

'The *month*!' I gasped, calculating rapidly how many events that would mean running on my own. 'I see.'

There seemed to be some sort of event at Wickham Hall every day, from coach parties to school trips or garden tours. This morning I'd even had an enquiry about Christmas at Wickham Hall. And of course, there was Zara's wedding in a couple of weeks! Eek! Now it seemed I'd be tackling the paparazzi by myself too.

I took a deep breath. I was fine. I was coping; as Mrs Beckwith had pointed out, I'd finally got the office under control and I was even beginning to feel like I knew what I was doing. And at least I didn't have a philandering husband and four small children to contend with.

'How is Pippa?' I asked.

'Well, apparently the au pair has gone back home to Germany. Alone. And Pippa has asked for some more time off while she and her husband sort out their differences.' She leaned forward conspiratorially and sniffed. 'Lord and Lady Fortescue have agreed. They are very good to their staff, you know. Not many employers would be so generous. But they believe very strongly that family comes first.'

'Well, please reassure them that I'll hold the fort until Pippa returns,' I said firmly, mentally deleting the document I'd just typed entitled 'Things to Check with Pippa'.

'Thank you, dear. I've already told them as much,' she said, sliding her mug back onto the desk. 'And Lady Fortescue is delighted with the way next year's calendar is coming on.'

'Is she?' I felt my face glow with pride.

'Oh yes.' She nodded. 'And I must say I was thrilled to be asked for my input.'

The Wickham Hall calendar was progressing extremely well. Everyone had risen to the challenge and I'd enlisted the help of as many people as I could to pinpoint their favourite hidden treasure at Wickham Hall, including not only Mrs Beckwith but also Marjorie, the tour guide, Pam, the housekeeper and Jim, the security man. Even Andy had put aside his gripe with me to create a wonderful treasure-themed display in the shop for the calendar too.

'You're welcome, Mrs Beckwith,' I said. 'I think the

seventeenth-century Dutch plates you suggested will look lovely on the March page.'

'Oh, do call me Sheila,' she said, beaming.

'Thank you . . . Sheila,' I said, trying to keep the elation out of my voice. *Yes! First-name terms – I must be doing something right.*

'Now, I'd better get on. Miss Zara is coming home this weekend and—'

Before she could finish, Jenny's head appeared round the door.

'Sorry to interrupt, ladies!' she said. 'I won't keep you, but I wondered if you were free on Saturday night to help waitress at Zara's hen party, Holly?'

'As in tomorrow?' I said, pulling a face. Tomorrow was Esme's birthday. I'd tried without success to persuade her to go Salsa dancing with me, but she still seemed a bit down at the moment and I didn't like to push her. In the end we'd agreed on a pizza and movie night at her flat.

'Oh, it will be a lovely evening,' Sheila exclaimed, pressing a hand to her chest. 'Zara's having a twelve-course French tasting menu.'

'The waiting staff will be in and out of the kitchen like yo-yos. I need someone organized. Like you,' Jenny added. 'Please, chick?'

'I would've loved to,' I replied, genuinely flattered. 'But I've got a long-standing engagement and I couldn't possibly back out of it.'

'There'll be VIP guests; sure I can't tempt you?' Jenny's eyebrows virtually disappeared under her hair-net at this.

'Sorry,' I said, shaking my head. 'I've got my own VIP to look after tomorrow.'

Sheila got to her feet, chuckling. 'You're in great demand these days, Holly. I can see you're fitting in beautifully.'

The two of them left and I smiled happily to myself as I finished up for the afternoon. What a perfect note on which to start the weekend.

On Saturday evening I packed two bottles of fizz, my overnight things and Esme's presents (a book on Vintage Couture and two tickets to London's V & A museum for the Chanel exhibition) and popped my head into Mum's bedroom to say goodbye.

'Bye, Mum, see you tomorrow . . . Oh, do you need a hand?'

She was wrestling with the door of the huge oak wardrobe that used to belong to her parents.

'Damn thing won't shut,' she huffed. 'Hinges have given up on me, I think, need a bit of oil.'

'Let me try.'

Her bedroom floor was covered with black bin bags and I felt my skin tingle as I stepped over them to get to the wardrobe. No wonder she'd had to take Granddad's suitcase out of the way; I was surprised there was even room to sleep in here. I certainly wouldn't have been able to. I'd have had nightmares about being suffocated in the night.

She stood aside as I opened the door and half a ton of knitwear sprang out from the top shelf above the hanging rail.

'Mum . . . !' I rolled my eyes at her. 'This wardrobe reached its capacity a long time ago; the hinges have got nothing to do with it. You can't keep stuffing more and more in!'

She picked a glass of wine up from amongst the heap of toiletries on her dressing table.

'Oh, don't start, love. I'm uptight enough as it is,' she said. She sank down on her bed and swallowed a large gulp of wine. 'It's Graham's retirement do tonight and partners are invited. Which means yours truly will be paired up with the only other single person going from work – Keith. He can talk for England about his signed football collection. I mean, why? Just why?'

'Well, you'll have plenty to talk about then, won't you?' I said, shooting her a look. 'You can tell him about *your* unfathomable attachment to old tat.'

I regretted my words instantly as Mum jumped to her feet and started dragging a hairbrush roughly through her wavy hair.

'I won't keep you; you get off to Esme's,' she sniffed, not meeting my eye.

I suppressed a sigh and made my way through the clutter to reach her.

'Mum,' I said gently, placing my hands on her shoulders. 'I'm sorry. It just upsets me to see you like this.'

She drained her glass and settled it back down next to her mother's old jewellery box. I had never known my grandmother – she'd died when Mum was small and Mum had been brought up by my Granddad. Mum opened the box and took out her pearl bracelet. It was her favourite piece of jewellery and she'd had it for years: it had a diamond clasp in the shape of the letter S and three rows of pearls.

Her shoulders sagged. 'I know, love. You're a good girl. Most daughters wouldn't hang around . . .'

I turned Mum's shoulders and forced her to face me.

'Well, I'm hanging around,' I said with a bright smile. 'You'll have to kick me out. Here, let me help you with that.'

She held her wrist out while I fastened the bracelet for her, clipping the diamond sections together firmly. It sparkled in the light and I twisted it round on her arm.

'I love this bracelet, Mum. Was it Grandma's?'

'No, love. It was a present to me just before I had you.' She turned away and picked up her hairbrush. 'By the way, what's going on up at Wickham Hall? Two helicopters flew overhead while you were in the shower.'

'Probably something to do with Zara Fortescue.' I shrugged, glad we'd negotiated our tense conversation. 'She's having a hen party tonight.'

'Arriving by helicopter?' Mum frowned. 'She must have some very special hens.'

I raised my eyebrows. 'Hmm. There was some talk of VIPs.'

Come to think of it, Jim had been with some burly men in dark suits and equally dark shades when I'd left last night. Perhaps extra security had been drafted in for the weekend? I felt a brief pang of regret for not being there to help Jenny out.

'Oh well,' I said, brushing my lips against Mum's cheek, 'must be off, my quiet night on the sofa awaits! Have fun with Keith!'

Ten minutes later I pulled up outside Esme's flat. She waved at me from her second-floor window and was waiting at her front door when I got to the top of the stairs.

'Happy birthday!' I grinned, dropping my bags so I could hug her tightly. 'How does it feel to be thirty?'

'Oh, don't remind me,' she groaned. 'Thirty is so ancient. Honestly, Holster, I swear a massive wrinkle has appeared from one side of my forehead to the other overnight.'

'Rubbish.' I laughed. 'You have the loveliest skin in the world.'

Esme's dad was from Trinidad and she had inherited his colouring and curls and her Mum's complexion and heart-shaped face. I know I was biased but she was gorgeous.

'Thanks.' She grinned. 'Doesn't stop me from feeling old, though. Anyway, how are you, stranger? I've barely seen you since you started mixing with royalty. Too posh for me now, are you?'

'Hardly royalty, Es,' I scoffed. Although Lord Fortescue was something like eighty-fifth in line to the throne. 'Anyway, you're *birthday* royalty today. I've got you some lovely pressies.'

We went through to her kitchen and she oohed and ahhed over her birthday presents while I eased the cork out of our first bottle of Prosecco.

'Here's to you,' I said, handing her a glass. 'Happy birthday.'

'Mmmm,' she said, giggling as the bubbles went up her nose. 'Here's to a night in with Patrick Dempsey, pepperoni pizza and plenty of Prosecco.'

We despatched the first bottle while we watched *Enchanted* and were about to start on *Made of Honour* when our pizza arrived.

'How's everything at Joop?' I asked, clearing a space on the coffee table while Esme fetched the plates and napkins.

She opened the pizza box, flopped a large slice of steaming pizza on a plate and handed it to me.

'We went to see the bank and it was all margins, projections, profit and loss,' she groaned. 'What do I care about all that? I love fashion, not all that financial stuff.'

'No wonder Joop's got an overdraft,' I chastised, biting into the pointy end of the slice. 'Running the business is as important as selling clothes, you know. More so, in fact.'

'Yes. Thank you, Lord Sugar.' She rolled her eyes. 'The main issue is cash flow. Our stuff is quite pricey because we sell lots of occasion wear. We get sixty days' credit from our suppliers. So we have to pay for stock after two months

73

whether we've sold it or not. So it's a massive risk. Anyway, it's my birthday, let's not talk shop.'

She reached for the DVD remote, but before she pressed play I got to my feet.

'More bubbles?'

'Ooh, yes, why not?'

I fetched the second bottle from the fridge and popped the cork. 'And how's your mum? Any better?'

She sighed as she held up her empty glass. 'She hasn't even been to see the doctor yet.'

I gave her a sympathetic smile. 'And does your dad know?'

Esme's dad did something in IT that involved being abroad for long stretches of time. He'd left the UK at the end of May for an eight-month contract in Dubai, which made it very easy for Bryony to keep things from him.

She shook her head. 'No, she doesn't want to worry him. She's so stubborn.'

I slid another slice of pizza onto our plates. 'Tell me about it. My mum is as bad. Sometimes I get so tired of being strong, of being the parent in our relationship, and all I really want to do is shout that no actually I'm not fine. *This* is not fine. And I wonder where it will end and how it will end and sometimes even if it will ever end at all.'

I felt my throat tighten and tears prick at my eyes. 'Oh God, Es, I'm so sorry,' I laughed shakily. 'I don't know where that came from. And on your birthday. Come on, let's watch that film.'

Esme put her plate down and pulled me into a hug.

'You are amazing. Never forget that. You are the best friend and the best daughter anyone could have and if it helps to cry about it, just bloody do it. And it will end. It will. We just have to find a way.'

My mobile rang from my bag in the hallway and I pushed myself up to get it. Mum's mobile number flashed up on the screen.

'Mum?' I answered. 'Is everything all right?'

My stomach churned as I exchanged glances with Esme. It was eleven o'clock – Mum never phoned this late.

'Yes, apart from having to listen to Keith's story about how he nearly won a football signed by David Beckham on eBay but lost out at the last second because his broadband died.'

I exhaled with relief. 'Good, I thought there must be a problem.'

'Problem? Oh no, darling, I just thought you'd like to hear the gossip.'

'Go on.' I sat back down on the sofa, grinning at Esme and put the phone on hands-free so we could both hear. Mum's stories about her work colleagues were legendary.

'Well, you know you said there was a big party on at Wickham Hall?'

Esme nudged me in the ribs. 'You never told me about that, Holster?'

'They asked me to waitress, but I turned them down. It's no big deal,' I said.

'It was a big deal,' Mum squeaked down the phone. 'The Duchess of Cambridge was there. Everyone in Henley is talking about it. Apparently, she's just left by helicopter.'

'Kate?' Esme and I shrieked.

'Kate Middleton, wife of our future king?' I gasped.

'Holly, why didn't you say?' Esme looked completely dazed.

'I didn't know she'd be there.' I shrugged. 'Jenny just said VIPs.'

'Anyway, I thought you'd like to know,' said Mum. 'I must

go, they've persuaded me to go Salsa dancing in Stratford. Bye!'

Esme and I stared at each other in disbelief. Both of us had been glued to the Royal Wedding a few years ago and had followed Kate's meteoric rise to global fashion icon ever since. Esme had even filled an entire sketch book of dresses inspired by her wedding gown.

'Kate Middleton at Wickham Hall.' I sighed, feeling a bit sick that I'd missed all the excitement.

'I wonder what she was wearing,' Esme breathed. 'Such a shame you weren't—'

She stopped and turned to me abruptly. 'You turned down tonight because of my birthday, didn't you? I can read you like a book.'

I nodded and looked down at the phone still in my hands.

'Your birthday was in the diary first, I didn't want to let you down, I'd planned to be with you.'

Esme shook her head. 'Holly Swift. I would have understood. And all I really wanted was a night on the sofa with Patrick Dempsey,' she chided gently. 'And I can do that any night.'

We looked at each other and began to laugh.

'Well, in DVD form anyway,' she added. She reached for the bottle and topped up our glasses.

'Next time you get that sort of opportunity, promise me you'll take it, grab it with both hands. Even if there is something else in the diary.'

'But—' I began to protest but she silenced me with a stern look.

'I know you love to plan, it makes you feel grounded and secure. But once in a while, let it go, live for the moment.' She raised her glass. 'Because sometimes magical things happen when you least expect it.'

'OK. Here's to magical moments.' I smiled, chinking my glass against hers.

Was she right? I wondered. Would something magical happen when I least expected it? If it was going to happen anywhere, I thought, rearranging myself on the cushions as Esme cleared away the empty pizza box, I felt sure it would happen at Wickham Hall; it was just that sort of place.

'Now shall we watch this film and finish that Prosecco?' said Esme, reaching for the remote.

'Whatever you say, birthday girl.'

Chapter 7

The sun was already beating down on Wickham Hall when I parked my car in the staff car park the following Monday morning. I'd had to drop some artwork off at the printers before work and by the time I arrived, there were visitors already in the grounds. I breathed in lungfuls of fragrant summer air as I crossed the courtyard towards the east wing and sighed happily about my good fortune. The situation at home might not be ideal, but having Wickham Hall to escape to suddenly made life a lot more bearable.

After two hectic weeks, I felt as though I was finally getting on top of things in the office; I was more relaxed about the smaller everyday events and could turn my attention to the three-day Summer Festival. This was Wickham Hall's showcase event and their biggest money spinner, and my heart raced at the thought that it was a mere six weeks away.

I was no stranger to the event; I'd been coming all my life. In fact, when I was small, Mum was so in love with it that we used to have tickets for every single day. She had eased up now, thankfully, but I still spent at least one day here with her every year. This year's festival would be very different for me, of course; I'd be one of the ones with a clipboard, two-way radio and furrowed brow, darting from one corner of the five-acre site to the other . . .

Anyway, one day at a time; my diary was bulging with jobs to do and I smiled to myself at the prospect of crossing several of them off this morning.

'Morning, Jim!' I called out as I approached Wickham Hall's elderly security man basking in the early morning sun with a mug of tea in the doorway. 'Lovely day.'

I had a soft spot for Jim; he must have been in his seventies but he seemed to bristle with energy. This morning he was wearing baggy green shorts, a fleece body warmer and an NYC baseball cap.

'Morning, young Holly.' He got to his feet and doffed his cap. 'Got a minute for a quick detour before you head inside?'

I resisted looking at my watch and nodded. 'Sure.'

'You'll like this.' He winked, shook the dregs of his tea into the lavender and set his mug down.

I walked with him down through the gardens towards a cluster of tall trees where the ornate marble fountain sprayed flumes of water into a circular pond.

Jim stopped under the tree canopy, hunched his shoulders and pressed a finger to his lips.

'Now you'll have to be quiet or else you'll frighten 'em,' he said in a low voice.

'OK,' I whispered, amused.

'Come on.' He beckoned me to follow him to the low wall around the pond. 'Look. There on the other side of the fountain. A moorhen and her little 'uns.'

We crouched down to see a black bird with a red head and yellow beak leading a clutch of peeping black chicks to the water's edge.

'Oh, cute!' I whispered. 'It looks like they're all having their first swimming lesson.'

'They come down to the water every morning for a splash. See how fluffy the chicks are?'

I nodded.

'Well, when they get their adult feathers the parents turf them out of their nest. This is a lesson in survival.'

'How did you know they'd be here?'

'I know everything that goes on around here.' He tapped his nose and grinned. 'I've been watching wildlife on the estate for sixty years; you pick things up.'

I watched as Jim reached into his pocket for a camera. I guessed he was about ten years younger than my Granddad Swift would have been now. I felt a sudden wave of nostalgia for what I'd never had; I'd have treasured doing things like this with him.

'Have you got grandchildren, Jim?' I asked.

He shook his head. 'Me and my Betty weren't blessed with children. Would have been lovely bringing kiddies down here.' He smiled, but there was a shadow of sadness behind his eyes.

'Well, now you've brought me,' I said, secretly casting him as my adopted granddad. 'And you've given me an idea.'

'Glad to be of service.' He chuckled.

We both fell quiet then; Jim was taking a few pictures and I was busy thinking about the possibility of him running children's nature trails. There was a big focus on the gardens at Wickham Hall, but the wildlife was largely ignored and Jim would be brilliant at it. It was definitely something to bring up at the next meeting . . .

I stood for a moment, listening to the sound of the fountain, the rustle of the trees and birdsong high up in the branches around us. I watched while the chicks bobbed about on the water and their mother flitted backwards and forwards keeping a careful eye on them and I exhaled happily; I couldn't imagine a more peaceful start to my week.

'Glad you came?' Jim asked, slipping the camera back in his pocket.

'Definitely.' I nodded. 'Thanks, Jim.'

We walked back towards the staff entrance and Jim collected his abandoned mug.

'Word of warning: I'd keep a low profile today,' he said, pulling a face. 'Lady Fortescue's in one of them moods.'

'Really?' My eyes widened. 'Why?'

'His Lordship's in the doghouse.' He chuckled and did a beer-drinking mime with his hand. 'Apparently he had a few jars on Saturday night.'

I cringed. 'Oh dear. Thanks for the tip; I'll stay out of her way.'

'Right, I'm off to inspect the new fencing. We've been having problems with poachers, so we've gone all electric now along where the deer park meets the main road. That'll teach 'em.'

I'll do as Jim suggested and keep my head down, I thought as I ran up the stairs towards the events office. I had plenty to do, so it should be easy enough.

Or maybe not. The door to my office was open and waiting inside it were three agitated figures: Lord and Lady Fortescue sitting on the edge of Pippa's desk and Sheila hovering beside them.

My stomach churned, what on earth had happened?

'She's here. Thank goodness,' exclaimed Lady Fortescue before I had chance to speak. She jumped to her feet and began pacing around the office. Her hair, normally immaculate, hung to her shoulders in shaggy clumps. And no lipstick. That alone spoke volumes.

Lord Fortescue, I noticed, appeared a little worse for wear. He had one hand pressed to his right temple and looked as though he hadn't shaved for a day or two. Surely if he'd been drinking on Saturday night he couldn't still be suffering, could he?

'Holly, I'm afraid we need to arrange a press conference,' said Lady Fortescue. 'This morning. Noon at the latest. You'd better explain, Hugo.'

'Storm in a teacup,' protested Lord Fortescue. 'Least said, soonest mended. It'll all come out in the—'

His wife silenced him with a piercing look. 'Too late for that now, Hugo, and will you please stop talking nonsense.'

'Holly, dear,' Sheila said, fiddling with her cameo brooch, 'we need to call the press and invite them in for a chat. Can you do that?'

I gave my full diary a last lingering look. 'Of course. May I ask what the occasion is?'

Lady Fortescue folded her arms. 'The occasion is crisis management. Hugo inadvertently let slip that we're looking forward to retirement in five years' time.'

'Oh, congratulations; I didn't know that.' I smiled, looking from her to Lord Fortescue and then over to Sheila.

'No, neither did I,' said Lady Fortescue crisply. 'I'm not ready to be pensioned off.'

'*I* am,' retorted her husband.

'I see,' I said simply. I didn't really see but it seemed the only suitable reply.

'Announcing the heir to an estate such as Wickham Hall is usually a formal affair,' Sheila explained quietly. 'A statement with formal photographs and whatnot.'

Lady Fortescue made a horsey sort of harrumphing

sound. 'And it is most certainly *not* announced to a public house, whilst three sheets to the wind and before agreeing it with the heir in question,' she snapped.

Lord Fortescue's head sank lower until his neck was completely invisible. Poor thing, I was almost tempted to give him a hug.

I cleared my throat, not sure if I was missing something. 'And who is succeeding you at Wickham Hall?'

The Fortescues looked at each other and then shiftily at me.

Lord Fortescue smoothed his hair down nervously. 'Ah, well—'

'I'll be in the garden letting off steam,' announced Lady Fortescue. And off she stormed.

The room seemed to breathe a sigh of relief.

'Lord Fortescue, why don't you get back to your office, have a nice strong cup of coffee and carry on trying to ring Benedict, while I explain everything to Holly?' soothed Sheila.

Benedict? So Lord and Lady Fortescue's son was the heir?

'Righty-ho,' he said and shuffled off.

Sheila waited until he was out of earshot and let out a sigh. 'What a palaver.'

Thirty minutes later I'd been fully briefed by Sheila, I'd emailed all the local press and was busy constructing my most important press statement ever.

Lord Fortescue, it seemed, had escaped to the Fox and Hounds in Hoxley while Zara's hen party was in full swing. At some point or other, he had declared that he and Lady Fortescue would be handing over the reins of Wickham Hall in five years. Some opportunist, looking to make a few pounds 'with a scoop', had phoned the *Stratford Gazette*, which in turn had called Sheila.

'This is all such bad timing,' Sheila had said crossly. 'The focus should be on Zara's wedding at the moment. This is a distraction we don't need. But if we don't hold a press conference and issue a formal statement, we'll be besieged with calls.'

'But at noon?' I'd queried. 'I can write the press release, but the journalists don't have much time to get here.'

Sheila had smiled primly. 'Exactly. The fewer the better. Lord Fortescue can say his piece about ensuring the hall remains in safe hands, blah, blah, blah, and you can issue any no-shows with a statement. Most of the press is syndicated anyway, as you probably know. Word will soon get around, believe me.' She made her way to the door and sighed. 'I just hope we get to Benedict before the press does.'

'And does Benedict know anything about Lord Fortescue's plans?'

Sheila leaned her hip against the doorframe and folded her arms, drawing her cardigan tightly across her chest. 'Let's just say it's complicated. You know what families are like.'

I pulled a sympathetic face, whilst musing that no, actually, I didn't. 'Go on.'

She glanced over her shoulder into the corridor, and evidently found it empty. 'Zara can't take on the hall as she's marrying into a wine empire in France, which leaves Benedict and I think he feels a bit trapped.' Her eyes dropped to her wrist watch. 'Heavens, I must away! Let's catch up in an hour or so.'

A noise outside distracted me and I turned to look through the mullioned window. It was a perfect summer's day and the grounds of Wickham Hall had never looked lovelier. A young couple strolled hand in hand through the formal gardens and children ran laughing through the maze. In the distance I could just make out Nikki talking to a group of people, possibly conducting one of her gardening tours. I would never tire of this view, I thought, never.

I turned back to my laptop.

'Trapped, eh? Poor baby,' I murmured to myself.

By the end of the morning, I had printed out a brief statement, organized for Jenny to send refreshments for the three journalists who promised to be here and sorted out a back-up. The plan involved the cooperation of Jim and Pam, the housekeeper, and Lord and Lady Fortescue themselves. And now I was on my way to the library to set up the room for the press conference.

The library was a lovely room, not huge but it somehow made you feel cosseted within its deep emerald-green walls. There was a big stone fireplace in the centre of one wall, hundreds and hundreds of leather-bound books, plus one smaller cabinet stuffed entirely with newer paperbacks. The smell was calming, too: a comforting mix of wood smoke, leather and old books. A small armchair in the corner looked so inviting that I was highly tempted to curl up with a book and disappear into a fictional world for a while.

I'd just set out two armchairs with a coffee table between them when I heard the sound of footsteps along the corridor. Sheila and Lady Fortescue appeared first, followed more sedately by Lord Fortescue. Lady Fortescue, I noted, had recovered her usual poise and looked elegant in a black and white silk kaftan.

'We've had *The Times* on the phone,' said Sheila, taking my arm and leading me to the far corner of the room away from the Fortescues. 'They're running a piece tomorrow and want an interview with Benedict about his succession, but so far none of us have been able to raise him. At least he's only at his studio in London and not in a different time zone for once.'

I raised my eyebrows, wondering how often that happened. 'Should we really be telling the press anything before his parents have spoken to him?'

'Lady Fortescue is going to FaceTime him now. Benedict should be up by noon.'

Sure enough, Lady Fortescue was sitting in one of the armchairs and had set up her iPad on the coffee table.

'Cutting it a bit fine, aren't they?' I whispered, feeling an uncomfortable prickle of sweat under my arms. 'In fact, that must be the press now.' Out in the corridor, I could hear several sets of feet marching towards us.

I positioned myself at the door, armed with a stack of press releases, and plastered on a smile as the feet approached the library.

The next events happened in such a blur that I'm not quite sure what came first. But by the time the three journalists – a redheaded woman, a weaselly boy with a notebook and a portly photographer with a handlebar moustache – had taken their seats, Lady Fortescue's iPad screen had flickered into action.

'Mum, what do you want?' a man's voice grunted, sounding slightly groggy. 'I've been up all night. Only just got to bed.'

As one, we all leaned forward and squinted to see the screen.

'Speak up, son,' tutted Lord Fortescue, cupping a hand to his ear.

'Benedict!' Lady Fortescue gasped.

I clapped a hand over my mouth as Sheila lunged forward

and knocked the iPad onto its front, but not before I – and I guessed everyone else in the room – had seen a naked torso, a tousled head of curly dark hair and one slightly unfocused brown eye amongst a tumble of white sheets.

There was a titter of laughter from all three members of the press, which confirmed it: the Honourable Benedict Fortescue had just attended a press conference wearing nothing but a frown.

Lord Fortescue's face was ashen, which contrasted nicely with his wife's scarlet cheeks.

Holly, time for that back-up plan . . .

I clapped my hands so loudly that the weasely boy flinched. 'Thank you, ladies and gentlemen of the press,' I said loudly, wondering as I did so if that was what you actually said to journalists. Either way, it had the desired effect: every single person in the room was now staring at me.

'Lord and Lady Fortescue have prepared a press statement for you all about their succession plans for Wickham Hall—'

'Hold on a sec,' grunted the boy, 'I didn't come all the way out here for a press release! I could have got that sent to the radio station.'

'Absolutely not, of course,' I agreed. 'I – we – have devised a bespoke press tour for each of you.'

I handed out my press releases swiftly.

'Martha?' I smiled at the lady from the *Stratford Gazette*. 'I've arranged for Pam, Lady Fortescue's private housekeeper, to give you an *exclusive* preview of the Honourable Zara Fortescue's wedding dress.'

'Really?' gasped Martha, bouncing to her feet. 'Goodness, that's . . . well . . . thank you!'

'On the understanding that any pictures will be embargoed until after the wedding service, of course.'

She nodded vigorously. 'Of course!'

I signalled to Sheila to radio for Pam and caught Lady Fortescue's eye. Her eyes twinkled with amusement and she was nodding ever so slightly. Phew.

I turned back to the young reporter.

'David, I thought you could interview our head of security. Bit of a scoop for you. Poachers have been taking pot-shots at our deer. You'll find him in the ticket booth, name's Jim.'

'Oh, wicked! Poachers? With guns?' David nodded, the grin on his face making it plain that this story was a million times more exciting than who would take over Wickham Hall in five years. He bounded to the doorway and then stopped. 'Will there be any antlers going spare?'

'Good heavens!' Lord Fortescue huffed.

'Sorry.' David blushed and then disappeared just as Pam arrived and bore a radiant Martha away to see some bridal wear.

'What can I do?' asked Neil, the freelance press photographer. 'I need a picture of something or I'll have had a wasted journey.'

'I've got something *very* special for you,' I said, gazing at him intently. 'It's Lord and Lady Fortescue's thirtieth year at the hall and I thought you could take a commemorative portrait of them at the bottom of the main staircase.'

Neil seemed to think that this was a marvellous idea and Sheila escorted him off to set up his tripod.

I puffed out my cheeks with relief. I could barely keep my smile in; that had gone unbelievably well. Lady Fortescue pulled her husband out of his chair and linked her arm through his.

'Holly, that was inspired.' She beamed. 'Well done on organizing that so quickly.'

I feigned nonchalance. 'It was nothing. I just thought we should have a back-up plan in case you hadn't managed to speak to your son.'

'It's all in the planning,' said Lord Fortescue heartily. 'Excellent, excellent.'

'You,' said Lady Fortescue, kissing his cheek, 'are never allowed in the Fox and Hounds on your own again. How's that for a plan?'

Peace restored, I thought, breathing a sigh of relief as I made my way back to the office. *Now what was I supposed to be doing . . . ?*

Chapter 8

I gazed out of a window in the Great Hall, where Zara and Philippe's wedding breakfast was to be served in a few hours' time. The sky was that rare sort of azure blue – the colour of Nikki's treasured poppies, in fact – which gave you absolute confidence that it was going to be the perfect day for an English summer wedding. Even the lacy clouds on the horizon looked as though they had been put there specially to decorate the sky.

The setting was perfect, too: outside, the terrace had been filled with tables and chairs and almost invisible wires hung overhead, carrying miles of tiny fairy lights that would twinkle magically once the sky faded into inky darkness. A wrought-iron bandstand had been installed on the lawn to house the jazz band and next to it stood a marquee complete with wooden dance floor, DJ equipment that would make Calvin Harris drool and enough bottles of champagne to ensure the party would sparkle, courtesy of the groom's family's vineyard.

Inside the Great Hall, Nikki's gardeners had performed miracles to provide such an array of blooms: roses in pastel hues interspersed with tufts of gypsophila and fronds of ivy adorned every surface: glass bowls on the window ledges, swags across the tall white fireplace and towering glass vases along the oak table that spanned the length of the room. And arrangements of other flowers, most of which I couldn't name, spilled from every corner.

Wickham Hall was closed to the public for the weekend in honour of the celebrations but even so the hall and grounds were overrun with men and women, dashing about carrying all sorts of things from furniture to food, flowers to photographic equipment, and it was impossible not to get caught up in the sense of urgency that filled the atmosphere.

I hurried out of the Great Hall and along the corridor to the stairs and wondered what to do next. I was armed with press statements and a handful of official portrait photographs of Zara and Philippe, but so far no press had been found lurking in the bushes.

Lady Fortescue had sat me down yesterday morning and given me strict instructions as to what to do in the event of a paparazzi intrusion: firstly, call security. Jim had reinforcements dotted around the perimeter of the grounds especially for the day. Secondly, hand over the official wedding press release and talk about the Anglo–French forging of two great dynasties. Thirdly, on no account mention Wickham Hall's succession or Benedict – whom no one had seen hide nor hair of since the FaceTime fiasco.

Lady Fortescue had closed our meeting by handing me two fifty-pound notes.

'For you, Holly: a little bonus for all your hard work. I thought you could perhaps find a new outfit to wear for the wedding?'

My heart had swollen with pride and I'd nipped off to Joop after work and splashed out on a new dress, which I'd had to leave with Esme to have altered.

I checked my watch: eleven o'clock. Now was probably a good time to go and collect my dress. With any luck I'd be back in time to see Zara in her wedding gown before she left for the church. Perfect plan!

I jumped aside as two men carrying cello-y type instruments in large black cases hurried by and then left the hall by its grand front entrance.

Zara and Philippe were getting married in the little church of St John's. It was right next to the hall and I could see its Norman bell tower peeking over the high brick wall that bordered the grounds. Soon Zara would be walking down this gravel drive on the arm of Lord Fortescue. How lovely to have all this on your doorstep, I thought with a sigh, looking down the drive, past the pristine lawns and topiary hedges to the gatehouse. Imagine being able to call Wickham Hall 'home'. Lucky thing.

'How do I look?' called a voice from above, interrupting my thoughts.

I turned and looked up at the far corner of the hall, where the west wing, which housed the Fortescues' private chambers, met the main hall. Zara was waving to me out of an open window. She was smoking a cigarette, her hair in giant rollers, and her face covered in a chalky-white face mask.

I laughed and waved back. 'A bit pale! Come and join me in the sunshine for a few minutes.'

'Can't, I'm beautifying!' She started to peel off the face mask and squealed in pain. 'Ouch! I think I've just pulled actual skin off. Do you think Philippe will still marry me if half my face is missing? Oh bugger, Mum's coming!' She pulled a face, frantically stubbed her cigarette out on the stone window sill, and flipped the butt into the shrubbery below just as Lady Fortescue appeared next to her.

I laughed at Zara's antics as I continued my quick march down the gravel drive, through the gatehouse and across the path to the staff car park.

Zara had arrived a few days ago and I'd fallen under her charms instantly. She was as beautiful as her mother, but she had her father's fair colouring, temperament and easy smile. She was sweet and nervous and full of excitement at getting married and her happiness was contagious.

Philippe had been here too a couple of nights ago for a grand formal dinner held in honour of the Valois family. I hadn't seen him but Sheila and Jenny had, and they had nothing but good things to say about him. His mum was English, apparently, and he'd gone to university here, so his English was perfect but his black hair and dark eyes were unmistakably French.

Ten minutes later I was congratulating myself on securing a parking spot directly outside the pretty boutique on Hoxley High Street.

Esme's mum Bryony opened the door, planted a kiss on both cheeks and dragged me inside. 'How are the wedding preparations going?' she demanded. 'I want all the gossip.'

'Smoothly so far,' I replied, tapping the white-painted wood counter for luck.

'Not one of them bought their outfits here, you know,' she harrumphed, fluffing up her golden tresses and jamming her hands on her curvy hips.

'I'll take some of your business cards back with me,' I promised. 'Leave them subtly on tables if I can.'

'Ooh lovely, thanks,' she said, scooping up a pile from the counter and handing them to me.

'Your rings,' I blinked at her, looking at her bare fingers. 'All your rings have gone.'

Bryony brought glitz and glamour to the tiny village of Hoxley. She was never one to shy away from loud colours, bright lipstick or bold accessories and her fingers of both hands normally glinted with rings.

She rubbed one hand over the other self-consciously.

'My finger joints have begun to swell,' she sighed, 'so I decided to take them off while I still could. My mum ended up having to have her wedding ring cut off. Broke her heart seeing it sawn through.'

My heart ached for Bryony; it looked as though she was beginning to suffer from arthritis, just as Esme had predicted.

'You know what that means, don't you?' I grinned. 'You'll have to treat yourself to one of those manicures where they set gems into the polish.'

'Ooh, yes! Never thought of that. That would give me my sparkle back!' She beamed. 'Go on through, love, I think she's finished your dress.'

'What do you think?' Esme looked up and swirled a piece of fabric I recognized as my new dress in the air as I joined her in the store room.

I'd chosen a white and navy dress with a boat neck and full striped skirt, cinched at the waist with a grosgrain navy ribbon. Unfortunately, the top half had somewhat dwarfed my petite frame and Esme had offered to rework it.

'Love it!' I said, clapping my hands. 'Can I try it on?'

'Sure!' she said, handing it over. 'But it will fit, I guarantee, Esme's measuring tape is never wrong.'

She was right, of course: it was a perfect fit. I twirled round in the fitting room and examined myself from every angle.

Thank you, Es,' I said, giving her a hug. 'You're a genius.'

'Now don't upstage the bride,' she warned.

I shook my head. 'No chance of that. Zara's wearing the most gorgeous gown I've ever seen. She sneaked it down to the kitchen yesterday for me and Jenny to see.'

Esme folded her arms. 'What I wouldn't give to be at that wedding.'

'Aww, I'll take a few pics of the happy couple for you,' I promised.

She walked me to the door and handed me my old outfit in a Joop bag. 'I'll hold you to that; I want to see the dress in detail.'

Church bells chimed in the distance, reminding me to get a move on.

'Goodness, I'd better dash.' I popped a kiss on Esme's cheek. 'Thanks again.'

'Hey,' she called after me, 'I'm working tomorrow morning on a prom dress. Drop by then with the photos.'

'Sounds like a plan.' I grinned. 'See you then.'

By the time I got back to Wickham Hall guests had started arriving and the Fortescues' private car park was filling up. I spotted Nikki standing next to a side gate in the high wall that surrounded the front grounds. She had a tray of something in her hands and looked the smartest I'd ever seen her in a loose linen suit. She wolf-whistled at me as I walked over to her.

'Wow, you look like a blonde Audrey Hepburn in that dress, Hols. Very glam.'

'And you,' I laughed, tugging on her sleeve, 'I think it's the first time I've seen you in proper clothes!'

'Thought I'd better make an effort as I'm handing out the buttonholes. What do you think? Good, aren't they? Andy did most of it.'

The tray in her hands was full of exquisite roses in the

same colours as I'd seen in the displays in the Great Hall – pink, yellow, white and peach – each one wrapped with sprigs of gypsophila and fern, their stems tied with ivory lace.

'Stunning,' I agreed. 'You've done a brilliant job with the flowers, Nikki, all of them.' I pointed at the gate. 'But why stand here?'

'It's a short cut to the church via the graveyard. The bride won't use it; she'll go through the lych-gate at the front, grand entrance and all that. Ooh, excuse me, more guests. Catch you later, Hols.'

I left her sorting out buttonholes for an immaculately dressed family of four and entered the hall by the main entrance.

'Holly, there you are!' The extravagant feathers on her hat quivered as Lady Fortescue hurried down the main stairs, pulling on her lace gloves. 'Is everything all right? Any problems?'

'Not at all, Lady Fortescue.'

'Take this anyway.' She handed me a two-way radio from a console table. 'Security has got it well covered, I'm sure, but one never knows.'

'Please try not to worry and enjoy your day, Lady Fortescue. You look lovely, by the way,' I said, clipping the radio onto the ribbon on my waistband.

'Thank you, Holly, although being surrounded by Zara and her lovely bridesmaids does make me feel ancient. It doesn't seem five minutes since I was the bride at Wickham Hall. Oh, here they come!'

We both gazed up the wide sweeping staircase as seven girls, giggling nervously and dressed in long satin gowns of varying pastel shades, began to make their way down.

'Oh, don't you look divine!' Lady Fortescue cried. 'Lovely

girls . . .' she muttered as an aside to me. 'I'm hoping one of them might suit my son.'

I pressed my lips together to hide a smile at Lady Fortescue's match-making plans. I still hadn't met Benedict but from what I'd heard about him so far I imagined he'd be unlikely to appreciate his mother's interference.

A photographer in a trendy charcoal suit appeared from between them and jogged down the stairs.

'OK, if we can have you in two lines, please; little ones at the front?'

The bridesmaids hooted with laughter as they battled for the front row, chivvied along by the patient photographer.

'That's great, and now one of you with the bridesmaids, Lady Fortescue?'

Just then a door along the corridor marked 'private' opened and Lord Fortescue emerged. His fine silver hair still looked damp, but he looked very refined in his morning suit and he beamed with pride when he caught sight of his wife.

'Beatrice,' he said, catching hold of her hands and kissing her cheek, 'you look more beautiful now than on our own wedding day.'

My face broke into a soppy smile. Lady Fortescue seemed to be feeling a bit sensitive about her age today and he couldn't have uttered more perfect words to her.

'Oh Hugo.' She giggled, pink with pleasure. 'Now, our daughter is dressed and ready and looking every inch the perfect bride, complaining, of course, that the dress is too tight and she can't walk in it, but I told her she'll be fine as long as she concentrates.'

It suddenly dawned on me that I wasn't doing a very good job checking for errant journalists; I really ought to go and do something. But just then Zara glided into view at the balustrade on the first floor. My heart tweaked and I couldn't drag my eyes away. She looked incredible.

Her long blonde hair had been twisted into a chignon and finished with a headband made of pearls and silk rosebuds stitched onto a lace ribbon. The ivory dress was simple and stunning: the top was made entirely of lace with a V-shaped neckline and cap sleeves. The skirt was one long satin sheath.

I tutted at myself as a lump formed in my throat. This wouldn't do at all, I thought with a sniff, reaching into my handbag. I wasn't even family.

'Here comes the bride,' Zara trilled, holding her arms out. Her bridesmaids turned and clapped. One actually put her fingers to her lips and whistled.

'Darling!' exclaimed Lady Fortescue, dabbing a tissue to her eye. 'Oh, our beautiful girl, Hugo, look!'

'Thanks, Mummy,' Zara grinned, 'and please don't cry. At least not until I say "I do", or you'll have no mascara left for the photos.'

Lord Fortescue opened his mouth to speak but no words came out, his eyes looked suspiciously moist and I thought he was going to expire with pride.

'Right.' Lady Fortescue leapt into action. 'The bridesmaids are ready, so we'll head over to the church and you follow in twenty minutes or so.'

'Right you are. Any sign of . . . ?' He raised his eyebrows.

Lady Fortescue shook her head. 'On his way, apparently. Go and give him another call, will you? Come along, ladies.'

The mother of the bride and bridesmaids departed noisily by the front entrance, Lord Fortescue darted back into the room he'd come from and a moment of calm followed before the photographer started issuing instructions to

Zara. I felt my bottom lip wobble as she made her way gingerly down the stairs.

'You look absolutely beautiful, Zara,' I said. 'How are you feeling?'

'I'm so bloomin' nervous!' she said, fanning her face with her hand. 'Do you think I could risk another fag?' She peered over the banister on the lookout for her father.

'Better not,' I laughed.

'Definitely not,' added the photographer, beckoning her down the last few steps. 'I'm going to take a more formal shot of you with the full staircase in view.'

'Do I look as if I'm waddling like a penguin?'

'You look gorgeous.' He winked, taking a step back. 'Now lower your bouquet so that it looks less like you're holding a microphone.'

'The bridesmaids look good fun, Zara, are they friends or family or both?' I asked, slipping my phone out of my bag to take some pictures of my own.

'They'll all from my university netball team,' she said, pretending to throw her bouquet up in the air like a ball. 'I played centre because I was the smallest and nippiest and I could jump . . . arrgghhh!'

The photographer and I lunged forward to catch Zara as she tripped over mid-netball demo, but we weren't quick enough; her foot missed the bottom step and there was an almighty ripping sound as the side of her dress tore from the hem to the top of her thigh and I caught a glimpse of a pale ankle at an odd angle as she landed in a snowy heap.

Oh God. Why, why, why did I mention the bridesmaids? This was my fault. I thought I might actually throw up.

'Zara, are you all right? I'm so sorry.' I knelt down quickly, removed her shoe and instantly wondered whether that had been the right thing to do. The chances of getting it back on again were slim, which was more than could be said for her rapidly ballooning ankle.

'Not your fault,' she whispered, her face contorted with pain.

The photographer crouched down beside us. 'You've probably just sprained it.'

'Just?' she cried, gripping her ankle with both hands. 'It really, really hurts!'

We both looked at the torn dress and the bare leg complete with lace garter poking through the split then back to each other and she let out a bubble of hysterical laughter.

'At least you'll be able to walk in it now,' I said, casting round for something positive to say.

We looked at each other and did that laugh you do when you know something is really bad and not at all a laughing matter. Seconds later Lord Fortescue flew back out from the drawing room.

'Good Lord,' he whispered hoarsely, dropping to his knees next to his daughter. 'Beatrice is going to kill us.'

That shut us up.

'Holly, the dress is ruined,' wailed Zara, looking very pale all of a sudden. 'What are we going to do?'

I looked back at the ripped fabric and at her swollen foot and I squeezed her hand, my heart beating like humming-bird wings inside my chest.

How on earth was I going to get the bride to the church on time?

Chapter 9

Think, Holly, think. We need a plan and quickly.

'Right,' I swallowed, my mind whirring rapidly, 'don't worry. I know exactly what to do.'

Sort of.

'Ice,' I said rapidly to the photographer. 'Run straight down the corridor, last door on the right. Someone in there will help you. Frozen peas will do.'

A thought struck me that maybe stately homes didn't carry a freezer full of Birds Eye frozen foods like normal homes, but never mind, I was sure he'd find something.

'Ice. Good thinking.' He laid his camera down and stood up. 'Do you want brandy with that?'

'Yes please!' chorused Zara and her father as he jogged away.

I turned to Lord Fortescue. 'And do you have a first-aid box?'

'Of course.' He trotted off, shouting for Sheila.

I asked Zara to wiggle her toes and ankle and between us we established that we didn't think anything was too seriously damaged.

'Except my dress,' said Zara in a small voice. 'I know I laughed, but it isn't funny, is it? People in the church will start getting fidgety soon and I can't walk down the aisle like this, can I? Assuming I can walk at all, that is.'

Her lip started to wobble and my heart went out to her.

'Hey, don't panic,' I assured her, reaching for her hand. 'I've got a friend who is a whizz with a needle and I know she would love to take a look at your dress.'

I picked up my phone and called the number I had on speed dial.

Esme answered straight away.

'You know that piece of vintage lace you bought? Do you think you could cobble . . .' I hesitated. Zara's dress had come from a Mayfair boutique, apparently; cobbling something together at the eleventh hour quite possibly wasn't what she wanted to hear. 'Er, make a last-minute adjustment to a wedding gown with it?'

'Ye-ah?'

I smiled at the fizz of curiosity in her voice.

'Bring it to Wickham Hall, with ribbon and anything else bridal-y that you can lay your hands on. Oh and your sewing box. And drive like the wind!'

By the time I'd confirmed that Esme would be here in a matter of minutes, both Lord Fortescue, accompanied by Sheila, and the photographer, carrying brandy and a tea towel full of crushed ice, had returned. I elevated Zara's leg, resting the tea towel on top of it.

'Right, we'll leave it like that for now. And you go steady with that,' I said, eyeing up the brandy glass in Zara's hand. 'You're wobbly enough as it is.'

Sheila caught hold of my arm. She looked elegant today in a salmon-pink suit and her hair had a newly set crispness to it. She spoke quietly. 'Holly, before you go—'

'Sorry, Sheila,' I whispered back. 'I'd better go and let Lady Fortescue know what's happening. I'll catch you later.'

I hurried across to the side gate where I'd been talking to Nikki earlier. The short cut would save me a much-needed few minutes. I went through the gate and found myself in the far corner of the churchyard on a moss-covered path amid the gravestones.

I ran as quickly as I could, heart racing with the excitement of it all, going over the plan that was unfolding as I travelled: find Lady F, alert her to a short delay, go back to the hall and bandage Zara's ankle while Esme makes some modifications to her dress and then deliver the bride to the groom before he gives up all hope. Simple.

Besides, being a bit on the late side is a bride's prerogative, isn't it? Pleased with my own quick thinking, I allowed myself a little smile as I came to the edge of the graveyard. The sound of organ music, overlaid with the chatter of the assembled guests, increased as I rounded the church and approached the main doors and I took a deep breath, preparing myself to go in.

Suddenly a movement caught my eye: the top of someone's dark curly head was just visible behind the stone cherubs on top of an elaborate headstone and I could hear grunting and muttering.

What on earth . . . ?

I stopped and stared, my pulse thumping in my ears as a white T-shirt was tossed aside, landing on the stone-carved Bible of the grave next door.

I crept closer to take a look. And there, hopping on one leg as he tried to kick his way out of a dirty pair of jeans, was a man wearing nothing but a pair of boxer shorts. What looked suspiciously like a morning suit and top hat were nestled amongst the long grass between the headstones.

With a flash of panic, I realized instantly what was

going on. I couldn't see his camera but he was obviously paparazzi trying to disguise himself as one of the wedding party. And in a graveyard! Security was geared towards preventing unwanted visitors to the hall. It hadn't occurred to me that some unscrupulous lowlife would try this sort of stunt. How . . . how . . . rude!

'Excuse me!' I piped up, fumbling to unclip the two-way radio from my waistband. Security needed to be alerted immediately. Unfortunately, the ribbon of my dress seemed to have got all tangled round the clip and I couldn't free it. 'Do you mind?'

The would-be wedding crasher whirled round, one ankle still trapped in his jeans. Dark brown eyes flashed beneath a head of messy curls.

'Yes, I do mind, actually.' He grinned. 'Can't a man get changed in private?'

'Private?' I retorted, cross with myself because even though this scruffy intruder was clearly in the wrong his body was quite pleasing to the eye. Was that a tiny tattoo about two inches above his right nipple . . . ? Oh God. Now I'd gone bright red. 'Hardly private!' I said, waving my arm around at the gravestones.

'Well, the residents haven't complained so far.' He winked, showing absolutely no remorse whatsoever. He took a pair of trousers off a hanger and stepped into them. 'You, on the other hand, are staring.'

The absolute cheek! Annoyingly I couldn't stop staring at the dark line of hair running down his tanned torso and—

I shook myself briskly.

'For your information, Mr . . . ?'

He bent down to ease his feet into smart shoes and I saw him chuckling to himself.

'I'm doing my job, as I'm sure you are, Mr— oh, damn it.' The ribbon around my waist would not yield the radio so I yanked at it and it came loose from my dress, still attached to the radio clip. I whipped my arm about, trying to get rid of the ribbon but all I succeeded in doing was make the ribbon twirl prettily in the air.

'Grrr!' I muttered through gritted teeth, getting angrier and redder by the second. 'Who are you anyway and where are you from? Not that that means you're welcome, because you're not.'

'From?' he teased. I cast a sideways glance at him. He was openly laughing now, head thrown back, his full mouth exposing a set of perfect white teeth.

'Yes. Which of the local rags . . . ?' I tailed off, remembering belatedly that Lady F had explicitly said I was to give everyone a Wickham Hall welcome, no matter how *un*welcome the person was.

With some relief, I finally freed my navy ribbon from the radio and let it slip to the ground.

'I'm Ben.' He pulled a brand-new shirt out of a packet, shook it out and began to wriggle his arms into it. 'And I work for, er, a new upmarket glossy called *Heirs and Graces*,' that's "heirs" with an "h", not air that we breathe, in case you wanted to make notes.'

I scowled at him; he was definitely teasing me now, he could see I didn't have anything to write with.

He tucked the bottom of the shirt into his trousers and I did my utmost not to watch his hands delving into his waistband. He looked up and caught me staring. 'Don't get any ideas,' he said, raising an eyebrow. 'I've got a wedding to go to.'

What! My jaw opened and closed as words – specifically witty ones – completely deserted me. Did he think . . . ?

'Ideas?' I huffed, finding my tongue at last. 'Here's an idea to get used to. I'm calling security.'

I arranged my face into my best grim expression and without tearing my eyes from him, pressed the button on my radio. 'Security? Holly Swift to security?'

Now if this had been a film, there'd be some gravelly voiced action hero on the other end who'd come to my aid within seconds, shinning over obstacles and throwing himself across the bonnet of fast-moving vehicles, but here, in a sunny churchyard with a hot and stroppy events organizer faced with an unrepentant intruder, all I got from my SOS message was a loud crackly noise that made me jump.

It was all a bit of an anti-climax, actually, especially when Ben perched on the nearest headstone and started whistling nonchalantly. So I picked up my ribbon and retied it, pointedly refusing to meet his eye, as though a delayed response was exactly what I'd been expecting.

All right, so I did sneak a peek at him when I thought he wasn't looking. Wow, he certainly scrubbed up well; the suit emphasized his broad shoulders, the crisp white shirt set off his tan and as much as I didn't want it to, his cheeky smile only added to the attraction.

He looked up and grinned. 'No bodyguard yet, then? And you work here, do you?'

I nodded, red-faced at being caught staring.

'Great. Can you get these laundered for me while I'm here?'

He scooped up his clothes and chucked them at me. A pile of dirty and, now that I looked more closely, paint-spattered clothes.

'I'm going back to London on Monday, so ready by then, please.'

'Do your own dirty laundry!' I fumed, returning his

clothes to him with a swift volley. They landed on the stone cherubs between us and for a moment or two we glared at each other. Correction – I glared, his shoulders started to shake.

Our staring competition came to an abrupt halt when the scraping of high heels alerted us to the fact we had company. I turned to see Lady Fortescue running as fast as her tight dress would allow.

'Holly! What's happened to Z— Benedict! Darling . . .' She ran towards him, holding out her arms.

Benedict. Not Ben. Benedict: heir to Wickham Hall and recipient of my furious outpourings. *Someone please rewind that bit where I lobbed his dirty clothes back at him.* Every drop of blood drained down to my feet and for one blurry second I thought I was going to faint. I leaned heavily on the nearest gravestone instead and wished it would open up and swallow me whole.

Lady Fortescue kissed her son, rubbed the lipstick mark off his cheek and then looked down at the pile of clothes draped on the headstone. 'Oh, please.' Her shoulders sagged. 'Don't tell me you got changed out here?'

'It was to save time,' he protested, eyes twinkling. 'And I thought I'd be alone.'

I'll just examine the toes of my shoes, I thought, *until my face reverts to its normal pale pink.*

'Oh, Benedict.' She sighed. 'And I see you've met Holly Swift, Pippa's new assistant? She's the one I told you about, who came up with the hidden treasures campaign.'

'Did she?' Benedict Fortescue shot me a knowing smile. 'Pleased to meet you, Holly.'

His hand swept down across his groin area so subtly that his mother wouldn't have noticed it. But I did. 'Well, you've certainly seen the crown jewels today.'

'Oh, excuse me,' I said, manufacturing a coughing fit as a cover for my scarlet face. Benedict snorted with unsympathetic laughter as I banged my chest. 'Lady Fortescue, Zara's had an accident. I came to bring you back to the hall.'

When you're the daughter of a lord, it seemed, there was no problem delaying the wedding by a short while. Lady Fortescue had taken her daughter upstairs to undress, Esme arrived with all her sewing equipment and various pieces of ribbon and lace, and Sheila and I organized for the bar staff to wheel drinks trolleys over to the church so that Philippe and the wedding guests could relax in the sunshine with a cold drink.

An hour later, Zara was wearing her newly customized dress and standing barefoot at the bottom of the stairs. Esme was kneeling in front of her, tugging the hem.

'I'm done!' She sat back on her heels. 'How does that feel?'

'I think I love it even more. Mum, look!' Zara twirled round, somewhat clumsily on her swollen ankle.

Zara had insisted that she didn't want the new thigh-length split simply sewn up and so Esme had made a softly gathered lace overskirt that joined the original dress under the bust line. She had sewn up most of the split and made another small slit on the other side seam to match.

'Although I was quite enjoying the extra leg room.'

'Oh no,' Esme argued, shaking her curls. 'Coco Chanel said that a girl should be two things—'

'Classy and fabulous,' Lady Fortescue finished, wrapping an arm around her daughter's waist. 'And you, my darling, are both.'

She turned to Esme, who was packing things back into her sewing box.

'And who do we have to thank for this emergency

repair?' she asked, extending a gloved hand to Esme. 'With all the panic, we didn't get introduced.'

Esme got to her feet and shook Lady Fortescue's hand. 'I'm Esme Wilde, from Joop,' she replied, looking unusually demure for my effervescent chum.

'And also my best friend,' I explained.

'Once again, Holly, your quick thinking got us out of a hole. Thank you both very much,' Lady Fortescue said with a smile.

'The lace is handmade in France,' said Esme proudly. 'So your new husband will approve, Zara.'

'I'll leave some Joop business cards on the terrace,' I added, pulling the handful I'd picked up earlier out of my bag. 'Their summer collection is amazing.'

The church bells pealed out again and Lady Fortescue jumped. 'Goodness! What are we all doing standing about? Quickly, everyone, before poor Philippe thinks he's been jilted.'

She kissed Zara's cheek and sped off out of the door and across the gravelled drive in her high heels. Zara looked down at her feet and then back at me. I knew what she was thinking: she'd never get her wedding shoes on over that swollen ankle.

'Here,' I said, slipping off my own white ballet flats, 'try these.'

'Ooh, bliss.' Zara sighed, closing her eyes. 'We must be the same size; can you wear my heels?'

'Of course.' I nodded and stepped into her vertiginous white satin shoes.

The bride reached out and took one of my hands and one of Esme's. 'Thank you. For everything. You two are life-savers.'

'Zara, darling, we really must go,' murmured Lord

Fortescue as he tucked her arm through his. 'Those French wedding guests will be revolting.'

Esme's shoulders started to shake and I elbowed her in the ribs.

'Daddy!' giggled Zara. 'You can't say that.'

Lord Fortescue rolled his eyes. 'Not that sort of revolting, you silly goose!'

Zara took one step forward and faltered, crying out in pain. 'Ouch! I don't think I can walk at all, let alone all the way down to the church.'

I glanced at Esme, wondering if Coco Chanel had anything useful to say about twisted ankles when Jim turned up, out of breath. He lifted his security cap and patted his forehead with a large white handkerchief. He looked very smart today, if a little warm, in a dark grey uniform.

'Did you want me, Holly?' he asked with gusto, his eyes glinting optimistically. 'Have we had a press invasion?'

Lord Fortescue stiffened and drew a protective arm around Zara.

'Well—' I began.

'Oh, miss,' Jim exclaimed, when he noticed Zara, 'congratulations on your wedding day. I remember you when you was a little girl and now look at you.' He swallowed. 'All grown up and—'

Lord Fortescue cleared his throat. 'Press, did you say?'

'No, no,' I said hurriedly, hoping no one noticed the flush to my cheeks. 'False alarm. Ages ago.'

Just as well, under the circumstances, I thought as I fanned my face. If Benedict had been a bona fide intruder instead of Lord Fortescue's son and heir, I wasn't sure how I'd have been able to detain him by myself for an hour. Sit on him, perhaps? Not an unpleasant idea . . .

For goodness' sake, Holly. Get a grip!

'False alarm? Oh.' Jim's face fell. 'I'm glad to hear that.'

He looked over his shoulder and addressed two of his colleagues on the drive. 'Stand down, chaps, crisis averted. By the way,' he queried, raising his eyebrows at Esme, 'is that your car illegally parked, Miss, only—'

Esme had driven right to the front entrance as instructed to get here as fast as possible. Hardly the Rolls Royce of a girl's dreams, I conceded, as an idea struck me, but better than nothing.

'It's the wedding car,' I blurted quickly. 'Why don't you drive to the church, Lord Fortescue?'

'Well, I . . .' Lord Fortescue stroked his chin.

'Allow me to chauffeur you, Your Lordship,' suggested Jim. He puffed out his chest and pressed his cap on firmly.

'In my old knackered— Ooh, that hurt,' Esme yelped as I pinched her.

'Great idea, Holly. Again.' Lord Fortescue beamed and began to lead Zara towards the door. 'Now take it steady, my dear.'

'Wait a second. Come with me, Es!' I cried, scooping up some remnants of her ivory lace. We ran outside – well, I hobbled in Zara's heels – and tied big bows around the wing mirrors of Esme's battered old MG Midget.

Lord Fortescue helped Zara into the tiny back seat and then lowered himself in to the front and Esme handed Jim the keys.

'Made my day, this has,' whispered Jim in my ear, pressing his handkerchief to his eyes. 'Everybody in?'

'That was surreal.' Esme stared at me. 'And you . . . you were in your element, organizing and delegating and decision-making.'

'I know,' I said with a contented sigh. 'I honestly think I've got the best job in the world.'

Chapter 10

Thankfully the dress disaster was the only mishap of the day and from the moment that Zara entered the church on Lord Fortescue's arm, the wedding proceeded smoothly.

Esme and I had set off to find a glass of champagne but just as I was about to fill her in on my graveyard gaff with the brother of the bride, Jim had arrived back with Esme's car. As soon as he'd handed over the keys, declaring that they didn't make British cars like them any more, Esme had dashed back to Joop and I'd tottered over to the little church of St John's in Zara's heels.

Three completely harmless photographers had turned up and the four of us watched at a respectable distance as the happy couple emerged through the lych-gate thirty minutes later surrounded by friends and family.

The crowd threw handfuls of pastel-coloured confetti and Zara squealed as Philippe swept her off her feet and into his arms. She looked so happy and radiant and I was thrilled that I had played a small part in making her day successful. She caught my eye and waved. I waved back wildly and then set off back to the hall to find out what Sheila had wanted me for.

There was no sign of Sheila; she had had to leave early

for her own family event, apparently, so after checking with Jim that there was nothing pressing for me to do, I spent a contented hour catching up with some filing in my office.

By mid-afternoon, all the guests were seated in the Great Hall for the wedding breakfast, which was my cue to go home. I cast a satisfied eye round the tidy room, wondering what Pippa would make of the changes I'd made when she came back to work on Monday.

I trotted down the stairs, headed along the corridor to take one final peek in the Great Hall now it was full of wedding guests and jumped when my mobile phone rang.

'Pippa,' I said quietly, edging forward to look through the gap in the door, 'I was just thinking about you!'

At the far end of the room a shorter 'top table' had been set up at the end of the long dining table. Zara and Philippe were at the centre of it, heads touching, smiling into each other's eyes. The room hummed with laughter, tinkling silver cutlery and the chink of champagne flutes, and the fragrance from Nikki's exquisite floral displays hung in the air.

'Hello, Holly.' Pippa sounded quiet and subdued.

'The wedding is heavenly; you should see the happy couple. They only have eyes for each other.' I sat down on a dark oak settle under the mullioned windows in the corridor while I chatted. 'Still, I can show you the pictures next week; I can't wait to have you back.'

Pippa groaned. 'I won't be coming back, I'm afraid. Hasn't Sheila told you?'

'What? No, she hasn't.' I frowned. The penny dropped: that must have been what she wanted to talk to me about earlier.

'My husband and I are divorcing, he's keeping the house

and I'm going to move in with my parents for a while, so . . .' her voice trembled. 'Sorry, pathetic, aren't I?'

'Oh, Pippa, not at all! I'm the one who should be sorry,' I soothed. I felt terrible now; blathering on about the happy couple . . . 'It sounds like you're being incredibly generous and brave to me.'

She had spoken so warmly of her children and the old rectory where she lived in our one meeting and it was heartbreaking to think she would lose all of that. And part of me was disappointed, too; whilst I'd coped running the events department singlehandedly, I'd been really looking forward to having some company.

I offered to send her some photographs of the wedding and she made me promise to phone her if I had any problems to do with the forthcoming Summer Festival and we rang off.

I sat for a few more moments on the oak settle and tuned in to Lord Fortescue, who must have been making his father-of-the-bride speech.

'All my most treasured memories are somehow connected to Wickham Hall. Beatrice and I celebrated our own wedding here and I vividly remember returning here thirty years ago when you, Zara, were just a tiny thing, with your brother Benedict. And now I stand here, an extremely proud father, as you embark on a new life with Philippe in France. I know that you have always been proud to call Wickham Hall home, but it's time to build a loving home of your own and I wish you both every happiness in the world. To Zara and Philippe!'

'To Zara and Philippe,' chorused the guests and I joined in silently as I made my way to the front door.

Tears pricked at my eyes as I stepped out into the afternoon sunshine and walked out to the staff car park. Lord

Fortescue had made a lovely, lovely speech but his words struck a chord and I couldn't help but question my own life. Was I proud to call Weaver's Cottage home? Because if not, something had got to change.

When I pulled up in Mill Lane a few minutes later, my heart sank. Mum was in the front garden, knee deep in aluminium cans. She lifted a hand and gave me a cheery wave as I climbed out of the car.

'How was the wedding?' she asked, brushing her hair out of her face with her forearm. 'I bet Wickham Hall makes a lovely venue for a summer wedding. Some of my happiest memories are of days spent in those gardens. And I expect Zara looked beautiful.'

'Perfect,' I said quietly, trying to ignore the thudding of my heart against my ribcage. 'The whole thing was perfect.'

'Lovely.' Her face scanned mine for a second before she picked up an empty can, squashed it flat and dropped it into a refuse sack. 'A penny a can, Holly. Can you believe it! Just for other people's rubbish. I'm going to collect five thousand cans and donate the money to the homeless shelter in Stratford.'

'So it's aluminium cans now?' I swallowed.

There was always a cause, always something demanding her time other than the state of her own house. I loved her for her selflessness but right now I just couldn't bear it.

'I picked up twenty cans this afternoon.' She looked up as I unlatched the gate. 'Littering the path by the canal. Honestly, I don't know how some people live with themselves.'

I cast an eye over our front garden. Black sacks spilling out their contents filled the space under the living-room window and eight large green plant pots, which she'd brought home from the charity shop, lay abandoned on their sides along the path. And now the cans. It was like living in a junkyard.

I thought back to the gravelled entrance to Wickham Hall – the manicured lawns, the perfectly trimmed topiary hedges, the pristine flower beds – and my throat tightened with sadness.

She followed my gaze and turned away quickly, bending down over the pile of metal at her feet.

'Mum?' I said, wanting her to look at me. 'The mess. Mrs Fisher collared me last week and mentioned it again.'

'We have to look after others less fortunate than ourselves, Holly. It's our duty.'

But what about us? *What about me?* Couldn't she see how her behaviour cast a shadow over both of our lives? It affected my friendships, especially with men. Just as I started getting close to someone, I'd pull back, too afraid and embarrassed of them finding out how I lived. The last serious boyfriend I'd has was at uni, eight years ago. When would I get the chance to build a loving home, like Zara?

Something inside me flipped and I felt my legs tremble. I had reached my absolute limit; I couldn't turn a blind eye to this anymore.

'Mum,' I repeated firmly, 'we need to talk about your hoarding.'

'Hoarding?' She looked at me blankly but I noticed a tiny twitch in her eye. 'Oh, love, you're making something out of nothing. I'll get this lot tidied—'

Tears flooded my eyes and I shook my head. 'I can't do this anymore. I just can't. I'm sorry. I know it upsets you every time I broach the subject, but we have to talk about it. If I thought you were happy, I'd leave you to it. But I don't think you are, are you?'

Mum's face crumpled and she dropped her arms to her side, defeated. 'Oh, Holly.'

'Come on, let's talk inside.' I sighed.

I took her by the hand, led her into the house and closed the front door behind us. I knew this conversation was going to be painful for both of us but it had been a long time coming and it was time I got it off my chest.

We stood in the small patch of clear carpet amidst the piles and piles of things and I placed my hands on her shoulders, waiting for her to meet my eye.

'Mum, I think this hoarding is because something makes you very unhappy and as there's only you and me in this family, I can't help thinking that that thing must be me.'

My cheeks burned; I hadn't realized I thought that until now, until the words were out there, hanging between us like a black cloud. But it was true. I could hear my pulse thrumming in my ears. She was a single mother who had never revealed who my father was. Perhaps I was somehow at the root of this?

'Oh darling, you mustn't think that,' she said. 'You're all I've ever had since Granddad died.'

'Then what is it, Mum?' I pleaded, gripping her shoulders.

'I like to keep hold of things. They comfort me.' She sighed, stroking a finger against my cheek. 'Nothing more sinister than that.'

'Look at this,' I said, forcing open the door to the dining room. 'We can't even get in this room. That isn't comforting. When was the last time we were able to sit down together and eat normally?'

'I don't like that room anyway,' she said, peering in. 'It faces north and doesn't get the sun. I'd far rather have a tray on my knees in the living room.'

Give me strength. I felt the frustration rise like a tidal wave inside me and forced myself to stay calm.

'The light is the least of its problems, Mum; it's full of junk,' I said quietly. 'You can barely see the table, let alone the chairs. I mean, do you seriously need to keep Grand-dad's old fishing tackle? Or every newspaper or magazine you ever bought? Or my pram, for goodness' sake?'

'It's not junk. Everything holds a memory, take Grand-dad's—'

'What would Granddad say if he could see you now?' I asked. 'He left you this cottage when he died. What would he think?'

She picked at a bit of loose skin on her fingertip and lifted one shoulder.

'He'd be disappointed, I suppose, but then he'd probably have stopped being proud of me a long time ago anyway, so what does it matter?'

'It matters because . . .' I blew out a long breath, heart pounding. 'It matters because I can't carry on living at Weaver's Cottage. I can't live like this, Mum. Not anymore.'

She stared at me, a mix of horror and fear etched across her forehead. My words seemed to have sucked all the oxygen from the air and my head began to throb.

'I need some air,' I said and stumbled from the hall into the kitchen and beyond into the back garden.

The back garden thankfully was clear of Mum's stuff. It had narrow borders full of self-seeded summer annuals and even though it wouldn't have met Nikki's high standards it was pretty and a million times more relaxing than inside the cottage.

'Holly?' Mum cried, following behind me.

I sank down onto the garden bench tucked under the overhanging branches from next door's apple tree, rested my elbows on my knees and dropped my head into my hands. Mum sat next to me and began to rub my back.

'I'm sorry, love. I couldn't bear it if I chased you away. You're the most precious thing in my life.'

I sat up straight and turned to face her. 'Then help me to understand. Please.'

We stared at each other for a few moments and I watched the dappled shade dance across her features. I knew that face so well and yet I suddenly felt like I didn't know her at all.

Finally she smoothed down the skirt of her dress and took my hand.

'I've never told you this because, I . . .' She paused to take a deep breath. 'Well, I am so ashamed of what happened the summer before you were born.'

'Oh, Mum.' My heart thumped and I squeezed her hand tightly. 'I'm not going to judge you.'

Her eyes sparkled with tears. 'I was seventeen, my life was just beginning and I was so happy. But then I met a man and fell in love.'

'My father?' I whispered.

'We were both at the Wickham Hall Summer Festival and . . . oh God, this is awful.' She lowered her eyes to her lap. 'I thought we'd be together for the rest of our lives. But the night after we made love, we kissed goodbye and . . . I never spoke to him again. You were born nine months later.'

I felt the hairs at the back of my neck stand to attention. I was conceived at Wickham Hall?

'Who is he?' I stared at her in disbelief. 'Is it someone I know?'

She shook her head and pressed a hand to her mouth as tears trickled down her cheeks.

'What must you think of me?'

'Why didn't you speak to him again?' I begged. My body was fizzing with adrenalin; she had never opened up to me like this. I was so close . . .

'Please, I can't tell you anything else. Not now. Except this . . .'

She took my face in her hands and gazed at me. The pain behind her eyes made my heart ache.

'Holly, you were the best thing, the only good thing, to happen to me that year. I thought I had it all that summer and I let everything I loved slip away. And I never want to lose anything important ever again.'

My face was wet with tears and I brushed them away, nodding slowly.

'So you keep it all, you keep everything?' I said, my voice trembling with sadness.

Mum nodded. 'Over the years, it has got harder and harder to let go of anything. I know you don't deserve to live like this, but please don't go. I promise things will change. Without you I—'

She burst into tears and sagged against me. 'I have no one.'

'It's OK, Mum,' I whispered, throwing my arms around her shoulders. 'I'm not going anywhere. I love you.'

We sat, the two of us, surrounded by thirty years of treasured memories, wrapped in our thoughts. I didn't try to make her open up any more; my head was already spinning with all this new information and Mum was clearly too upset to talk. I had learned more today about the reason behind the hoarding than I had ever done and I knew two things for certain: I was determined to help Mum overcome her hoarding and I was going to find out exactly what happened during that Summer Festival at Wickham Hall.

*

The next morning I was up bright and early. The roads were deserted as I drove to the only café open on a Sunday to buy two bacon sandwiches. Mum and I had had an emotional and productive evening: she had agreed to go to see the doctor about some counselling and the two of us had bagged all the aluminium cans and driven them to the recycling centre and cleared the front garden.

It was only a small improvement but it was a start and I was proud of her. And proud of myself, actually, for not pinning her down and forcing her to tell me who my dad was.

What I needed now was a heart-to-heart with Esme accompanied by breakfast and large mugs of tea and as she'd said she'd be working on a prom dress today, I thought she'd be glad of the company.

I pushed open the door to Joop and found Esme standing in front of one of the fitting rooms, hands clasped and pivoting on the spot from side to side.

'Morning, Es. Am I glad to see you.'

'Morning, Hols.' She flashed me a big smile and squeaked as I gave her a quick hug.

'Nice welcome, nice flowers.' I nodded my head towards the vase of roses on the counter.

I did a double-take: they were almost identical to Zara's wedding flowers. Although I supposed roses were pretty much everywhere in June. Nikki had told me it was England's best month for the scented blooms.

'They are, aren't they?' She giggled, pressing her lips together mysteriously. 'You'll—'

'Breakfast,' I said, waving the paper bag under her nose.

She shook her head. 'Er, I'll have mine in a minute, thanks.'

I shrugged and dropped it on the counter. 'Suit yourself.'

I perched on the chaise longue and patted the seat beside me.

'Come and sit down before any customers arrive, I've got so much to tell you.'

'Actually,' she said, widening her eyes oddly, 'I'm a bit busy at the moment.'

I glanced round the shop dubiously, but frankly, I was so desperate to tell her my news that I would probably have spilled the beans even if the shop had been jam-packed full of customers.

'You will not believe the events of the last twenty-four hours of my life. Firstly, well not strictly firstly in chronological terms, but anyway,' I said, taking the bacon sandwich out of its bag. 'Massive discovery in the history of Holly Swift last night. Massive. Turns out, I was *conceived*, yes you heard that right, conceived at Wickham Hall during the Summer Festival. Think about that for a moment, Es.'

'Bloody hell, Hols!' she gasped.

I puffed out my cheeks and shook my head.

'The brilliant thing that came out of it was that Mum has agreed to go for counselling.'

Esme pinched her lips together and shot me an anguished look. 'Holly, you probably shouldn't—'

'I know, I know! What a mystery,' I exclaimed, ripping the corner off my ketchup sachet. 'She wouldn't tell me who he is, though. Could be anyone, could be him out there.' I chuckled, pointing to an old man zipping past on his mobility scooter.

I bit into my sandwich and tugged at a particularly stubborn bit of bacon. Esme jerked her head bizarrely towards the kitchen.

'Don't panic, I won't drop anything,' I tutted. 'Second item on the news agenda . . .'

The saltiness of the bacon was beginning to make my mouth tingle.

'Hold that thought while I make some tea. Want one?'

'Um, no thanks.' Esme's eyebrows furrowed and she was plaiting her legs as though she needed the loo.

'You OK?' I said, frowning at her as I set my bacon sandwich on the counter and made my way into the store room.

'Yep,' she squeaked.

'Secondly,' I shouted, flicking the kettle on, 'Pippa has resigned. So I guess I'll be organizing the Summer Festival by myself, which should be interesting. Although maybe it's in my genes, given my start in life. Ha!'

I clattered around with the tea caddy and spoons and thought I heard Esme speak but couldn't make out what she was saying over the sound of the boiling kettle.

'And lastly, but by no means least,' I said, sitting back down with my tea, 'I met Benedict Fortescue yesterday. And get this . . .' I paused to snort and catch Esme's eye. 'He was stripped down to his boxers in the churchyard. He's quite fit, actually. Made a complete fool of myself by accusing him of being paparazzi and calling security. Hardly my fault, though. I mean, what sort of idiot gets ready for a wedding in a graveyard!'

Esme was now jumping up and down on the spot, waving her arms wildly. 'Holly, um, I don't know how to tell you this but—'

She was saved saying anything at all as the bolt of the fitting room behind her slid back with a thud and the door swung open revealing—

'Benedict!' I gasped, jumping to my feet and spilling hot tea on my flip-flop-clad feet. 'Ouch! Bugger.'

Esme leapt forward, took the mug from my hands and scurried to the store room for a cloth.

Leaving us alone.

My face burned. Possibly even hotter than my feet.

'Holly Swift.' Benedict's brown eyes twinkled with amusement. He was wearing nothing but a T-shirt and a pair of boxer shorts. Again. 'We must stop meeting like this.'

I've just admitted that my mother had sex in your garden.

'Indeed we must.' I swallowed.

'Lady Fortescue sent Benedict down with some flowers from the wedding as a thank-you,' said Esme, bending down to wipe the drips from my feet. 'And he brought a pair of trousers to alter too. Wasn't that kind?'

'Very kind,' I agreed, nodding manically.

My brain scrabbled to try to remember what I'd said about him. *Fit!* Oh God, I'd called him fit. Which, looking at him a second time, was quite accurate, with his soft curls and deep brown eyes. Although not my type, clearly, because everything I knew about him so far pointed to unreliable, scruffy and irresponsible . . . not qualities I normally rated in a boyfriend. Boyfriend? *Boyfriend?* What was I thinking?

I moaned softly under my breath.

Esme did a sniggery sort of laugh from her position on the floor. No help at all.

Benedict picked up a pair of shorts from the floor of the fitting room and pulled them on. 'Thanks, Esme,' he said as he wriggled his feet into a battered pair of Converse. 'I'll pick them up on Wednesday.'

'Wednesday is too late,' I reminded him, finding my voice at last. 'You're going back to London tomorrow.'

'No I'm not.' He grinned, handing Esme a pair of beige linen trousers with pins at the hem. 'Change of plan.'

'But . . .' I began.

He sauntered casually to the door, opened it and turned

back to face me. 'Didn't Ma and Pa mention it? I'm taking over from Pippa for a while. I'm your new boss.'

'You?' I gasped.

'See you in the office. Don't be late.' And with a wink he was gone.

I sank down onto the chaise longue and stared at Esme.

'So,' I said, wetting my dry lips with my tongue, 'to recap. I've just admitted to my new boss that I think he's fit, that my mother got it on with a stranger at his family's Summer Festival and that I think literally *anyone* could be my father.'

'That about sums it up.' Esme hid her mouth behind her hand and I could tell she was dying to laugh.

'Well, Monday morning should be interesting,' I groaned. 'He's never going to take me seriously after those revelations. How on earth am I going to work for him now?'

I watched as Benedict Fortescue drove off in a scruffy hatchback and raised his hand in a wave through the open window. More importantly, had my dream job just turned into a nightmare?

Summer Secrets

Chapter 11

It was the Monday morning after Zara's wedding. I'd got up mega-early and gone for a run before work. I'd been so busy over the last few weeks since starting my new job that I'd scarcely had the time to exercise, but this morning I decided to make the effort. My head was still whirring from the events of the weekend and although I didn't like to admit it, I was a bit apprehensive about being in the office with my new boss, Benedict.

As usual, my run had helped me make sense of my thoughts and I'd come up with a strategy to cope with my first-day nerves: I would be a swan. A graceful swan. All serene and floaty on the surface whilst flapping about like mad underneath.

I practised my calm and unflappable demeanour as I made my way through the grounds and into Wickham Hall. It was only seven o'clock and I revelled in the stillness of the gardens and breathed in the scent of summer: freshly mown grass, fragrant honeysuckle tangled in amongst the borders and old-fashioned roses trailing over archways. The car park had been empty and I didn't meet a single soul as I let myself in through the staff entrance in the east wing.

In theory, the next couple of weeks should be quiet at Wickham Hall: Zara and Philippe would be far away on their honeymoon by now and Lord and Lady Fortescue had jetted off too to the South of France for a few days. And that left only one Fortescue on the premises: Benedict.

There wasn't much chance of him being quiet, I thought with a wry smile.

At least I'd get a couple of hours' work done before he turned up. I had heaps to do and I would have to bring him up to speed on the Summer Festival before this morning's meeting, too. If I could bring myself to look him in the eye, that was, after my rather embarrassing revelations at Joop yesterday.

Swan, Holly, think swan . . .

I ran up the stairs to my office ready to immerse myself in my to-do list, but a noise stopped me in my tracks: someone was in there already. I could hear drawers being slammed, the thudding of what sounded like heavy objects being dropped and above it all the incongruous sound of a man singing a criminally bad version of Taylor Swift's 'Shake It Off'.

I couldn't help but giggle. It had to be Benedict.

Goodness knows what he was up to. But if nothing else, no one could accuse him of being boring; at least Benedict appeared to have a sense of humour and I doubted he took himself too seriously. Imagine if I'd had to work with Andy? Now that would have been awkward . . .

I took a deep and calming breath, opened the door and—

'Oh.' I swallowed.

Pippa's desk, which I had so painstakingly tidied, had been totally ransacked. The drawers were hanging open and empty, there were stacks of paper on top of it, cardboard boxes on the floor next to it and Benedict appeared to be filing all of Pippa's old paperwork under 'B' for bin.

'Morning, Miss Early Bird. Couldn't you sleep? What happened – boyfriend kick you out of bed for snoring?' He grinned and blew out of one side of his mouth to temporarily dislodge the curls hanging over his left eye.

'I came in early to get a head start on the week. Looks like I've missed quite a party,' I said, trying to drag my eyes away from the mess. I blinked at him. 'And for your information I do not snore.'

'Good to know.' He winked.

'Do you have any idea how long it took me to tidy this office when I arrived?' I asked calmly.

The swan thing was working; there was barely a ripple on the water. I was quite proud of myself. Inside, however, my stomach was churning as though I'd swallowed an outboard motor.

'Er,' he screwed up his face, pretending to think, 'I give up. Glad you're here, anyway – grab this box.'

He held a cardboard box out to me. I ignored it.

'Whilst I have every respect for you, Ben – Benedict . . . actually,' I said, sitting at my desk, 'will you please tell me what to call you. Should I call you Mr Fortescue?'

'Officially, I'm the Right Honourable Mr Benedict Fortescue. But my friends call me Ben. *You* can call me Ben.' He set the box down and began piling books and papers into it randomly.

'As I was saying,' I cleared my throat, 'I'm keen to work with, I mean, *for* you, but we need some house rules.'

'Do we? OK, let's hear them,' he said with a barely concealed chuckle.

I cast my eyes around my previous oasis of calm and sighed inwardly. There were only two places on this earth where I felt I had any control over my environment: my bedroom and my office. He wasn't to know that, of course, but seeing my well-ordered piece of the world thrown into chaos really was quite upsetting. Even the shelf above the photocopier had been stripped of most of its contents, only a few books remained. All the phone directories, catalogues and magazines were strewn on the floor.

'Remind me never to let you near my bedroom,' I muttered.

'That's a house rule?' He blinked at me.

'Sorry, no . . .' I felt my face heat up. I hadn't meant to say that out loud. I harnessed the swan again. 'People operate best when their workspace is tidy. It's a well-known fact. The Summer Festival is only four weeks away; there is an almost unconquerable amount of work to do, so let's focus on that first, shall we? And not choose this moment to reorganize the office.'

Ben swiped some of Pippa's files into the box, chuckling to himself.

'I wasn't very good at English,' he said, shooting me a smile over his shoulder. 'But what's that Shakespeare thing, about a short girl being feisty?'

'No idea,' I said airily, recognizing the passage from *A Midsummer's Night's Dream*. 'But it's funny, isn't it, when a man stands up for himself, he's strong but when a woman does it, she's labelled fierce?'

He looked at me all twinkly-eyed. 'Fierce, that's it,' he said and laughed.

Damn it. I couldn't help but laugh too.

'Anyway, enough banter,' he said, face serious all of a sudden. 'Here I was arriving early to get straight before you arrived and here *you* are cluttering up the place. At least make yourself useful.'

'How exactly?' I retorted. 'By putting all this stuff back where it belongs?'

'Look,' he sighed, 'it's a work in progress. Sometimes things have to look worse before they can look better.'

Now that was true; Mum and I had had a go at sorting out some of Granddad's old things yesterday. The dining room was now officially a no-go zone.

'I didn't mean us to get off to a bad start; I just thought I'd have a spring clean, or a midsummer's morning clean. Blank canvas, new broom, and all that.'

I folded my arms, remembering how spotless the office had been when I left it on Saturday afternoon during the wedding.

'Look, if it makes you feel any better, we'll stack the boxes in one corner for a while, to be on the safe side. Just in case there's something we need amongst this lot. OK?'

'OK,' I agreed.

'But anything we don't look at between now and Bonfire Night is going on the fire. Deal?'

'That's in November!' I exclaimed.

'Correct. Give the girl a fish.' He handed me an empty cardboard box and this time I took it from him.

'You're staying for quite a while, then?'

He grinned at me. 'Is that a problem?'

'Not at all.' I smiled.

Swan, Holly, think swan . . .

By eight o'clock, I was thirsty, hot and more than a little dusty, but all the loose paperwork was stacked into a corner and I had to admit, the office did look less cluttered. And I realized, Ben hadn't made as much as one tiny reference to my comments in Joop yesterday and for that I was extremely grateful. I was about to suggest that I made us a pot of coffee when Ben marched to the door.

'Come on,' he said, holding the door open and waving his arm for me to go through it. 'Now the office is sorted, we can go.'

'Go where?' I said, puzzled, automatically collecting my handbag.

'The showground. The Summer Festival is on in four weeks and there's an unconquerable amount of work to do, you know,' he teased.

We left the hall, crossed the grounds diagonally towards the Coach House Café and both turned as a Harley-Davidson motorbike roared into view, ridden by a tall figure dressed head to toe in leathers. The bike disappeared behind the area fenced off for deliveries to the café and the engine stopped.

'Should we be worried, do you think?' I asked, glancing up at Ben as we passed the café's outdoor tables and chairs.

Ben tutted playfully. 'Do you ever *not* worry?'

I was still trying to come up with a suitable reply when the biker reappeared in front of the café entrance, raised a hand in greeting and removed the glossy black helmet to reveal a tumble of long purple hair.

'Jenny! I didn't know you were a biker!' I wondered how many other stately homes had a purple-haired, Harley-Davidson-riding head chef! My head was already whirring with how we could use this to our advantage in some sort of marketing campaign.

'Morning, Benedict; morning, Holly,' she grinned. 'Yes. It was my dad's, actually. I don't always bike to work but I was running a bit late today.'

Ben looked wistfully towards the spot where Jenny had parked the bike. 'Your dad used to ride it to Wickham Hall every day. He took me out on it once; I'll never forget it. I badgered my parents for a bike for ages after that. He was a good man, your dad.'

Jenny nodded and let out a deep sigh. 'He was.'

'Jenny's father was the mechanic and chauffeur here at Wickham Hall for decades until he retired,' Ben explained as Jenny inserted her key into the café's double doors. 'In my grandfather's day, the garage was full of cars, from Rolls Royces to Aston Martins. Now all we've got are sensible cars and quad bikes for riding round the estate.'

'Oh, I've always fancied a go on one of those quad bikes,' I said. 'I've seen the groundsmen out on them. They go quite fast, don't they?'

Benedict nodded. 'My friends and I used to take them out into the parkland. Great fun, especially in the dark. I'll have to take you out on one; I'd quite like to see you letting your hair down.'

I wasn't sure what to say to that so I picked up Jenny's helmet and handed it to her.

'Thanks. Are you both coming to the festival committee meeting today?' Jenny asked, unzipping her leather jacket.

The committee meeting was held in the room where I'd had my interview. It was usually chaired by Sheila, and the committee consisted of Nikki, Jenny and Andy, as well as someone from Radio Henley and the Summer Festival sponsors. And me.

'Just me,' Benedict answered quickly. 'Holly has got an *insurmountable* pile of work to do. In fact, we're on our way to the showground now. I need to familiarize myself with the site again. She's going to fill me in on what has been happening and I should have some new ideas by the time we get to the meeting.'

'*New* ideas?' I said, meeting his gaze. 'I'm not sure we

135

should be introducing new ideas at this late stage. And to answer your question, Jenny, yes I am coming to the meeting.'

Jenny winked at me. 'See you both later, then.'

She disappeared into the café, laughing softly to herself.

Ben and I carried on out of the courtyard and through the formal gardens. I could have quite easily dawdled and stopped to pick daisies in the grass, but Ben was a fast walker. I didn't mind; simply being out in the grounds on a beautiful sunny morning worked its magic and my spirits soared.

'It must have been incredible to have all this as your back garden when you were a child,' I mused as we walked through the trees alongside the cascade that led to the parkland.

'It was brilliant,' Ben said simply. 'I had dens and hollow trees big enough to hide in, rope swings . . . We even made our own BMX track once.'

We emerged from the woods into the parkland and paused to look across at the fallow deer dotted across the grass in the distance.

'I don't think I'll ever get tired of this view,' I said.

'It is nice to come back to,' Ben agreed. 'For a while, at least.'

I frowned, wondering what he meant by that, but before I could ask he began marching again. By the time we came to a halt on the wide path that led down towards the river I had enthusiastically filled Ben in on the highlights of this year's Wickham Hall Summer Festival.

'Hard to imagine, isn't it?' said Benedict as we stood for a moment, surveying the site.

The showground was simply a five-acre area of grassland, which would be fenced off on three sides, the fourth side being bordered by the river. A second adjacent area would be fenced off as a temporary campsite for exhibitors to park caravans and pitch their tents. It was still unadulterated at the moment, but in two weeks' time, the contractors would arrive to set up all the marquees, exhibition stands and toilet blocks, turning the field into a little village complete with temporary roads and an electricity supply.

'It is,' I agreed. 'I've been here loads of times as a visitor but I had no idea how much work it takes to put the event on.'

The festival was a highly complex affair and from what I had seen so far, it seemed to be very well run. And it needed to be; there would be upwards of 23,000 visitors over the three-day show.

'Oh yes,' said Ben, snapping his fingers as though he'd just remembered something. 'I'd forgotten that the Summer Festival has a special place in your heart.'

'Oh definitely.' I nodded. 'I remember one year it was so hot that . . .'

My voice trickled away as I caught him grinning at me, his eyes twinkling. 'Oh you mean *that*. Look, I'm really sorry you overheard me pouring my heart out to Esme yesterday.'

He held up his hands. 'No, I apologize. I shouldn't tease you.' He took a deep breath and gazed into my eyes. 'You mentioned about your mum going for treatment and whatever it is, I hope she's OK.'

I nodded. I was attempting to be swan-like but had a sneaking suspicion that I was erring more towards flamingo, i.e. a delicate shade of pink.

'Thank you.' I cleared my throat. 'Now, about this morning's meeting.'

I raised a hand to shield my eyes from the bright sun so that he couldn't see my face. 'Radio Henley has already started their on-air campaign, the literature is printed and all the people entering show gardens have submitted their themes, including Nikki. Please,' I said, dropping my hand and meeting his eyes, 'please tread carefully with new ideas.'

'I hear you.' Ben nodded, smiling softly.

'Phew. Thank you.' I sighed with relief, recognizing an olive branch when I saw one.

'Come on; let's go back to the office, Holly. Do you realize it's nearly nine o'clock and you haven't made me one cup of tea yet?'

'What!' My jaw dropped but he burst out laughing and draped an arm loosely across my shoulder. 'Only joking, Miss High Horse. Let's go and see if Jenny can sort us out with some tea and toast.'

'That's more like it,' I said primly, not even sure in my own mind whether I was referring to the offer of breakfast or to the tremor of excitement that had just run down the length of my spine.

Chapter 12

By early afternoon Ben and I were back in the events office. Ben's first Summer Festival meeting had been declared a success and I must admit, it had been a lot livelier with him in the room than his father.

However, my jobs list had somehow doubled and I'd yet to cross anything off it, which was making me feel a bit jittery. Particularly as I couldn't find a single document that I needed following our office tidy and now a courier had turned up for Ben. The man had made several trips backwards and forwards to his van and had deposited some large mysterious packages that made Ben even more exuberant than normal.

The courier soon left and Ben began tearing into the parcels, humming tunelessly under his breath. I did my best to block him out and tried to get some work done.

I opened a blank page on my laptop and typed: *Thirty Things to Do at Wickham Hall.* This was first on my list of extra things to do following this morning's meeting.

Ben had blithely ignored my advice to go easy on new ideas. He'd spent the first half an hour of the committee meeting quietly building a tower with drinks mats. But then, as I was outlining my idea for a children's treasure hunt, he'd suddenly rocked back in his chair, linked his fingers behind his head and puffed out his cheeks.

'It all sounds great,' he'd said, flashing a smile around the assembled committee members.

It was the first thing he'd said and everyone had stared. Andy had gazed adoringly and Samantha from Radio Henley had melted quicker than a Solero on a sunbed.

'*But* I can't help feeling that we're missing an opportunity to celebrate all that my parents have achieved in the last thirty years at the hall.'

'With respect, Benedict,' Sheila, who heads up the committee, had said, 'Lord Fortescue has sat in on this committee every week until now and has never once mentioned your parents' thirty-year anniversary.'

'Oh, he's too modest,' Benedict had said, flipping a drinks mat off the edge of the table and attempting to catch it. It dropped onto the floor. 'Neither of them will make a fuss. It's up to us to do it for them.'

Jenny had agreed, citing how many people benefited from the Coach House Café that the Fortescues had built in the early nineties. 'Not just customers, but staff, too. The café works closely with the catering college in Stratford; we've helped train hundreds of young people over the years, me included,' she'd said, twisting a strand of hair around her index finger. 'I don't know what I'd have done without this place.'

'And the gardens owe a lot to your parents, too,' Nikki had added, passing her phone round so we could see her latest pictures. 'See how fantastic the maze looks this year? No offence, Benedict, but your grandfather was more interested in vehicles than visitors and the gardens were too basic to attract the public. The Italian sunken garden used to look like the forest out of *Sleeping Beauty* from what I understand. And the rhododendron was rampant.'

At this point, I'd had a sudden – unwanted, I might add – image of my mum and A. N. Other furtling in the rampant rhododendron. I'd grabbed my glass of water and taken a long drink before anyone noticed my pink cheeks.

'Holly, your hidden treasures campaign is great, very imaginative,' Ben had said, nodding.

I'd coloured a bit more and mumbled my thanks.

'But I think we can go further.'

Sheila had looked at her watch pointedly. 'What did you have in mind?'

'So much of what is special about Wickham Hall is down to old Hugo and Beatrice, and I think we should pay tribute to that in some way.' Ben had looked directly at me as I looked up from my diary having just scribbled out 'make treasure hunt clues'. 'Any thoughts, anyone?'

Andy, who'd been saving a seat for Ben when we arrived, had wriggled to the edge of his seat as close to Ben as he could be without actually sitting on his lap. 'Why don't we have a series of thirty-themed activities? Like, for instance, I could do a "gifts for under thirty pounds" range in the shop?'

'Ooh, yes!' Samantha had waved her hand. 'We could get people to phone in to the radio with their memories of the festival and give away thirty pairs of tickets to the best ones.'

For the next few minutes everyone had shouted over each other with their thirty-themed suggestions: Nikki was going to create a flower bed in the shape of a three and a zero out of white geraniums and position it at the entrance to the show; Jenny would work up a special thirty-pound set menu for the outdoor restaurant that would be set up in the showground and I had come up with a series of press releases entitled 'Thirty things . . .' to send out to the press.

And so here I was. Writing my first press release.

I had to admit Ben had a point. The Fortescues were too modest to make a splash; well, Lord Fortescue was anyway. And so it was up to us to honour them. It was really sweet of Ben to suggest it and his parents would be thrilled that it was he who had come up with the idea. And also, I realized, there was something about the way he talked about Wickham Hall that hinted that he had a real love for the place. Like me.

So there was something we could agree on. Unlike the paint-speckled wooden easel that he was in the process of unpacking and setting up under the window in our office.

I watched him stack pots of paintbrushes onto the newly emptied shelf above the printer. Surely he wasn't planning on painting in here? And when was he actually going to do any work? So far all I'd seen him do was exercise his delegation skills. He was very good at that.

'You're an artist, then?' I said, brushing away the flakes of dried paint that had fallen from the pots of paintbrushes onto my desk.

'Yes, landscapes mainly.'

Ben uncovered a canvas and held it away from him to inspect it. He cocked his head to one side, grunted and set it against the wall. I was dying to see what it was of but the painted side was facing the wall.

'So, if you don't mind me asking, why take Pippa's job?'

'Mum and Dad have got a bee in their bonnets about me learning the business. You probably know they want me to take over in five years.'

I nodded, remembering our thwarted press conference. 'And you don't want to?'

He frowned and I wondered if I'd overstepped the mark. 'I'm not ready to commit to that yet.'

'So why are you here now?'

He grinned sheepishly as he unpacked a blank canvas and set it on the easel. 'I forgot to renew the lease on my London studio. I've been evicted. I've got a new space sorted but it won't be free until January. So this stint back at the old homestead has come just at the right time.'

Ben was leaving at Christmas. I wondered what Lord and Lady Fortescue would think about that. And, more to the point, how did I feel . . . ?

'Oh, good,' I said, in lieu of something more meaningful. 'About you getting a new studio, I mean, not that I want you to leave.'

Oh crumbs, now he was chuckling at me again.

'Right.' He installed himself at Pippa's old desk for the first time that day and pulled the telephone towards him.

I heaved a sigh of relief; finally it looked as though he was going to get on with something.

He flicked a sideways grin at me. 'Now stop chatting please, I've got loads to do.'

'Me chatting? Oh, you are so irri—'

'Irresistible?' he offered, searching through his desk without looking up.

'No,' I stuttered, 'Irri—'

'Oh, Holly,' he looked at me this time, pulling a comical sad face, 'don't say irresponsible, please, look how hard I—'

'Irritating,' I tutted.

He mimed zipping his own mouth and I felt my own mouth lifting in a smile. A bit irritating, perhaps, but in an irresistible way.

*

Half an hour later I'd given up all pretence of trying to work. Ben was simply too distracting to work with. Not because he pursed his full lips when he was concentrating or because the sun was casting shadows across his face in the afternoon light or because there was a lively citrusy scent that got stronger every time he came near me, but because he seemed to be having problems doing . . . whatever it was he was doing and had taken to grumbling to himself, tutting and slamming the phone down.

'Benedict,' I said, using his full name for once. I closed the lid of my laptop to give him my undivided attention. 'What is it you're trying to do, exactly?'

His chin was propped up in his hand and he was drumming his fingers on an empty notepad.

'I thought as all the team were doing something special for my parents' thirtieth year I should contribute too.'

'Good idea,' I said, pushing myself up and heading over to the coffee maker. 'Coffee?'

'Please,' he said, stretching his arms above his head. 'It might perk me up.'

I spooned fresh coffee into the filter and turned the machine on.

'I thought of doing a sort of photographic "retrospective": a look back at thirty years of the festival. I thought we could mount it as a display in one of the marquees.'

'Nice idea,' I said, 'we haven't really got anything arty going on. So what's the problem?'

I left the coffee to gurgle and splutter away, perched on my desk and crossed my ankles.

'We employed a professional photographer from 1990, so I'm OK from then on; I can get the pictures from Sheila, she says she's got them all on CD. It's the first six years I'm struggling with.'

'What about old Summer Festival programmes? There must have been a few on that shelf you cleared out this morning.' My lips twitched. 'In amongst the stuff you decided we didn't need.'

Ben shot me a look with a hint of cheeky grin. 'Sorry to disappoint, but they were all too new. What I really need to do is find some old copies of the *Wickham and Hoxley News*. That was the local newspaper that covered the festival every year until it was bought out by a bigger regional outfit. And when I phoned and asked them about their archives, they said they didn't have any.'

I nodded. 'I remember. They used to cover all our school events, too. But you want actual pictures, don't you, and not press cuttings?'

Ben pushed back his chair and lifted his feet up onto the desk.

'If I can track down the newspaper's photographer, he or she will probably have the original negatives.' He raked a hand through his hair and shrugged. 'But how on earth am I supposed to find copies of an out-of-print newspaper from thirty years ago?

The skin at the back of my neck began to prickle. How indeed?

'Here you are,' I said, putting a cup of coffee in front of him. I took a deep breath. 'Now, I'll do you a deal: if you promise to let me get on with some work, in peace, for the next hour I'll see if I can find you some old copies of that newspaper.'

'Really, Miss Swift?' said Ben, brightening up. 'In that case, I'll leave you to it. I think I've earned my keep for today anyway.'

He picked up his coffee and left the office and I sat down to finish that pesky press release undisturbed. Oh yes, I knew exactly where to find issues of the *Wickham and Hoxley News* dating back to July 1984: our dining room.

I'd agreed to meet Esme after work for a drink at The Bluebell in Henley. She had news, she'd said, and needed to talk. And after bashing out press releases all afternoon, I was only too happy to accept her invitation. She was already at the bar when I arrived, taking delivery of a bottle of Sauvignon Blanc and two glasses.

We kissed our hellos and carried our drinks outside to the back garden. We found a table in the corner and Esme poured the wine while I slipped my shoes off and wriggled my toes.

'Here you go; cheers,' said Esme, nudging a full glass towards me. She giggled. 'Oh Holly, your face yesterday when Benedict Fortescue appeared from the fitting room.'

'Don't, please,' I said with a shudder. 'All those things I said . . .'

'And then he turns out to be your new boss. You were right about him being fit, though. Lucky you.'

I raised my glass to Esme and drank. The wine was ice cold and tangy and hit the spot perfectly.

'I'm not so sure "lucky" is the right word,' I replied, licking my lips.

As much as I admired Ben's energy and creativity, I hadn't been exaggerating when I'd said we had a lot of work to do for the festival and today we hadn't made much of a dent in it.

'However, to his credit, he didn't bring up my indiscretions this morning. In fact, if anything, he was quite sweet about Mum. *And* today was the first time I'd greeted him with his trousers on. So that was a definite improvement.'

She raised one eyebrow over the rim of her glass. 'Oh, I don't know.'

We both giggled.

'I think you'll be good for each other,' said Esme thoughtfully. 'Yin and Yang, opposites attract, and all that.'

'No. Men are off the agenda,' I replied briskly. And even if they weren't, I didn't normally go for the rumpled look. 'All men except my father.'

'I meant as colleagues, actually,' she smirked, 'but go on. Has your mum said something?'

I shook my head. 'Not yet. But I can't shake the feeling that if I can only get to the bottom of the whole hoarding thing, then she'll feel comfortable telling me the rest of the story. So that's my priority at the moment. And she's really making an effort. I'm proud of her.'

Her eyes glittered. 'I'm proud of *you*, Holster. The way you handle life's hurdles . . . you're an inspiration to me. I wish I had half your determination.'

I peered at her, wondering what she was talking about. Esme Wilde was one of the most 'look out world, here I come' people I knew. She dipped her head and stared into her glass and I remembered with a jolt that we were here to talk about her news.

'That is a lovely thing to say, Es,' I said, covering her hand with mine. 'But enough about me. Come on?'

My best friend held my gaze for a heartbeat.

'Mum definitely has the onset of rheumatoid arthritis; she went to see the doctor today, finally.'

I squeezed her hand. 'I'm sorry, Es.'

She gave me a wan smile. 'It could be ages before it really takes hold of her and who knows whether she'll get it as bad as Gran, but in the meantime, we have to think what it means for Joop. We're still sitting on a lot of summer stock, which means money tied up. We need something for Mum to get her teeth into now that she can't sew and I need a fresh challenge too.'

'You need an action plan. Luckily you have a friend who loves a good plan.' I grinned. 'So what is it that you love?'

'Fashion.' she said simply, lifting her curls off her neck and twisting them into a bun. 'Vintage, retro, couture . . . I'd love to get into something a bit more edgy than the occasional wear we sell but it comes back to cash flow.'

I nodded slowly. 'You need to expand what you offer at Joop without lots of upfront investment.'

'Exactly. And preferably something that doesn't involve me turning up posh boys' trousers for the rest of my life.'

We exchanged knowing looks, remembering Ben standing in his boxers in Joop's fitting room.

I drained my glass and pushed it across the table.

'I'll get my thinking cap on, I promise,' I said, reaching across to kiss her cheek. 'But right now, I've got a date with 1984.'

Chapter 13

The next morning I got to Wickham Hall a few minutes before nine. I paused outside our office, holding my breath to listen for sounds of Ben singing while he flung paint around the room. But all I heard was silence and when I pushed open our office door, neither Ben nor his easel were anywhere to be seen.

The room was stuffy so after I'd dropped my pile of newspapers on Ben's desk, I flung open the windows as far as they could go and looked across the grounds.

And there he was.

Beyond the tapestry of the box-edged parterres, at the very edge of the formal gardens, Ben stood at his easel painting, facing away from the hall, looking out towards the deer park.

Without a second glance at my diary, or my to-do list, or the undoubtedly full inbox of emails, I made us both a cup of tea and fled the dim and overheated hall for the beauty of the gardens.

I carried the mugs carefully through the gardens, inhaling the aromas of vanilla, musk, citrus and clove as I brushed past the plants that clung to every gate and archway.

This was definitely my priority, I told myself, spotting Ben at the top of the worn stone steps; he would want to know straightaway that I'd found six years' worth of July newspapers for him. Besides, I was curious to see what he was painting.

He was dressed in flip-flops, T-shirt and shorts, with a paint-smeared rag hanging from his pocket, and appeared to be standing perfectly still, brush in one hand and palette of paints in the other. I cleared my throat softly as I approached, not wanting to make him jump. 'Good morning, boss. I've brought you some tea.'

Ben's eyes turned to mine but it was as if he didn't see me at first. Then he shook his head and smiled. 'Blimey, what time is it?'

'Nineish.' I handed him a mug and he smiled gratefully.

'Thanks,' he said between slurps. 'Ahh. Nectar. I was beginning to wither; I've been out here for hours.'

'You're welcome.' I stole a sideways glance at the canvas he was working on. 'May I look?'

Ben nodded and I stepped closer to the easel.

'Oh my word, Ben.' I stared at the painting. 'You're actually really good!'

He laughed and pretended to stagger backwards. 'Finally, you appreciate my talents. Wonders will never cease, Holly Swift.'

The painting was ninety per cent sky: pink at the bottom, streaked with fiery orange lifting to a pale silvery blue near the top. Smudges of treetops framed the base of the picture, with a sparkling flume of spray rising beyond them and evaporating in the sky. The colours were so vivid that I could almost feel the heat of the sun on my face.

'Consider me very impressed,' I laughed, 'that sky is amazing.'

'Do you know,' he said, sliding a paintbrush in amongst his curls, 'I could paint the sky every day for the rest of my life and never produce the same picture. And the dawn sky, like this one, is my favourite.'

'You were out here at dawn?' I said, raising an eyebrow. 'You *are* full of surprises.'

'Wickham Hall is full of beautiful places to paint.' His lips twitched at my implication. 'I wanted to capture the top of the fountain today but it's not my favourite spot to paint.'

I suppressed a smile. Whatever Ben liked to tell himself about taking over at Wickham Hall, it clearly meant an awful lot to him.

'Where is your favourite spot?' I asked, hiding my face behind my mug.

'See that hill over there?'

He placed his hand on my shoulder and twisted me round so that I was facing to the west of the Wickham Hall parkland. In the far distance was a small hill almost at the boundary of the estate.

I nodded.

'If you haven't sat on that hill and waited for the sun to makes its glorious appearance on a summer's day then you haven't lived.'

'So, sunrises are your thing?' I said, conscious of the touch of his hand on my back.

He shrugged and swallowed a mouthful of tea. 'Milky moonlight across a lake and a sky lit with a thousand stars is just as magical. I wouldn't want to miss either.'

'That does sound magical.' I thought for a moment. 'I'm not sure I've ever seen the dawn.'

'Well, I'm sure that can be arranged.' He smiled, finished the last of his tea and handed me his mug.

'Like the quad bikes?' I said. 'Quad bikes at dawn, perhaps?'

'Oh no,' he shook his head in mock horror, retrieving the brush from behind his ear, 'dawn is about the stillness and silence and being at one with the world.'

And with those words of pure poetry, he reapplied himself to his painting. I wasn't quite ready to leave the sweet summer air and the view of the gardens yet so I took a seat on the top step in front of the easel. The heat of the day was already building and I lifted my hair from my neck. I liked having my hair in a bob; it was nice and easy to look after, but sometimes, like now, I wished that it was long enough to scoop up into a ponytail.

'You're very distracting when you do that, you know,' Ben mumbled.

He had his brush in his mouth while he scraped at his canvas with a finger.

'Sorry.' I got to my feet and picked up our mugs. 'I'll go back to the office out of your way.'

'No, no, stay for a moment and lift your hair up again.' He gestured for me to put the mugs down.

'Why?' I laughed, doing as I was told. 'I promise I've washed behind my ears.'

I raked my hands through my hair, scraping it so that it all fit into one hand. Ben took the brush from between his teeth and laid it on the edge of the easel.

'Turn your head,' he murmured. He cupped my chin and gently twisted my face away from him. 'The curve of your neck, the pale skin under your hair, and such tiny ears . . . Did anyone ever tell you that you have very unusual earlobes?'

The moment felt very intimate all of a sudden and I prayed my face didn't actually look as red as it felt.

'Not that I can remember.' I swallowed.

'It makes me want to paint you.' He smiled softly.

'I'm flattered.' I laughed, releasing my hair. 'Unless you entitled it *Girl with Weird Earlobes.*'

He stared at me with an expression I couldn't read so I looked down at my feet to break the moment.

He touched a finger to my nose. 'I think you're starting to burn.'

'You're right.' I covered my warm cheeks with my hands. 'Which is my cue to get back to the grindstone. See you later.'

I began to walk back to the hall and then stopped and turned round only to find him watching me. My face inched up the colour chart from rosy to crimson.

'By the way, I forgot to say. I managed to get hold of the old newspapers you wanted,' I called.

'Already?' he exclaimed. He dropped his brush instantly and came running after me. 'Swift by name, and all that. Come on, then, let's see if we can track down this photographer between us.'

'Can't you do that by yourself?' I tutted, thinking of my to-do list.

'Yes,' said Ben, nudging me with his elbow. 'But where's the fun in that?'

I grinned at him, shaking my head in despair. 'True.'

Ben dived straight into the pile of back issues of the *Wickham and Hoxley News* that I'd brought in and within seconds there were sheets of newspaper spread out over his desk.

'I can't believe it, you've even got the Festival issue from 1984, the first year Mum and Dad were here,' he said, flicking through them. 'How did you find them?'

I shrugged, as though having copies of thirty-year-old newspapers was the most normal thing in the world. 'They were just lying around at home.'

'They're yours?' Ben frowned.

'Not exactly . . .' I was trying to conjure up a reply that didn't make me look odd when my phone rang. I grabbed it gratefully and mouthed an apology to him.

It was a call from a coach operator confirming details of a coach tour for the next day. I scribbled some notes and rang off. Ben was engrossed in the *Wickham and Hoxley News*, laughing to himself, reading out snatches of headlines and holding up pictures of big eighties perms for me to see.

I whizzed off a quick internal email to Nikki, Jenny and Jim to let them know the details of the coach party. I confirmed their time of arrival, lunch and departure and I booked in Nikki's garden tour, hoping that by the time I'd finished, Ben would have forgotten what he was going to ask me.

I was feeling a bit less stressed about Mum's hoarding now that she had finally admitted that that's what it was, but it didn't stop me being embarrassed about it. Ben had grown up in an Elizabethan manor house; I couldn't even begin to explain to him what it had been like growing up in Weaver's Cottage.

Having an untidy house hadn't bothered me at all when I was small. All families are the same, I'd thought: stacks of mail in the hall, a pile of washing on a chair, an assortment of things at the foot of the stairs waiting to be taken up. There never seemed to be enough room for things but I didn't notice anything different about my home.

I must have been about twelve when I realized Mum's piles of stuff weren't normal. I saw it on the faces of friends when they came round. The way they eyed each other as they inched past a stack of newspapers in the narrow hallway; the way they turned in slow circles in our living room, looking for a place to sit.

'Let's go up to my room!' I'd suggest, knowing that at least there they wouldn't be able to find fault with the clean surfaces, the lack of 'stuff' and the collection of posters, symmetrically Blu-tacked to the walls. But the damage had been done and after a while friends stopped coming round, or I stopped asking them, I can't remember now.

Mum kept everything, although paper was her weakness: newspapers, magazines, all sorts of literature, but anything to do with Wickham Hall was special. Now I knew that she had had an affair with a mystery man there, that part sort of made sense. But I'd already revealed far more than I should have done to Ben thanks to my faux pas in Joop on Sunday; I certainly didn't want to explain why my mother had kept every brochure and newspaper with a mention of the Summer Festival in it since 1984—

'Look at this,' cried Ben triumphantly, breaking into my thoughts.

He was holding up a double-page spread of photographs taken at Wickham. I went round to his side of the desk to read it over his shoulder.

'Wickham Hall Summer Festival 1989. And it's part of a four-page supplement. Look.' He tapped a picture of a dark-haired boy beaming at the camera in front of the coconut shy.

My eyes scanned the caption. 'Benedict Fortescue enjoys the fun and games at— that's you,' I squealed. 'Oh, how cute were you in those little shorts!'

He pulled an injured face. 'Do you mean I'm not cute in shorts any more?'

I opted to ignore that question on the grounds that I could either fan his ego by admitting that he did look cute. Or lie.

'The photographer is Steve Selby,' I read from the copyright notice underneath Ben's picture. 'So all you need to do now is to see if he covered all the earlier years of the show that you want too.'

Ben grinned. 'He did, I've already checked. I just wanted you to see that picture of me and go weak-kneed at my cuteness.'

I rolled my eyes and went back to my laptop. 'Let's see if Mr Selby appears on a Google search. And then I really must send out some press releases and check on the printers to see if the new calendar is ready and then try to source some giant pearls for your new and improved treasure hunt. Ben?'

But he was already sprinting down the corridor.

My 'Steve Selby' search threw up thousands of results but the most likely candidate was a lecturer at Hathaway Arts College in Stratford. Where Esme used to study. I reached for my mobile and tapped out a text message.

You heard of Steve Selby?

Her reply came back immediately.

Yeah, my old photography lecturer. Used to be press photographer, covered all local stuff. Nice bloke, about Mum's age.

Result! I sent her a thank-you message and by the time Ben came back, lugging his easel and paints, I'd put a sticky note with Steve's mobile number on his desk.

'Excellent work, Sherlock,' said Ben, peeling the note off the desk.

He called the number immediately and after a very short conversation ended the call, stood up and rubbed his hands together.

'He can see us in an hour. Are you coming?'

I blinked at him. 'What, now? But . . .' I glanced down at my diary; there was still so much to do for the festival and I had planned to start a Facebook competition this afternoon to win a VIP package including tickets for four, a garden tour and lunch from Jenny's newly devised thirty-pound menu.

'Yes, of course now,' said Ben impatiently. 'If I'm going to mount this photographic retrospective, I need to get a move on or it'll be a disaster.'

It crossed my mind that if he didn't let me get any work done, the whole festival would be a disaster. But . . .

Admit it, Holly, you want to go. Forget your plan. For once.

He punched my arm playfully. 'Come on, Swifty, I'll even let you feed the swans on the river after we've been to the college.'

'I'm not eight, you know,' I said, trying to keep a straight face.

He stopped suddenly and slapped his forehead with his palm. 'You have to be eight years old to feed swans? Why didn't anyone tell me?'

I was giggling so much that he had to put an arm round my waist to propel me through the door, down the stairs and back out into the sunshine.

Chapter 14

Hathaway Arts College was a brightly coloured modern building only a short hop from Stratford-upon-Avon's famous Swan Theatre and was in a stunning location right on the River Avon.

'Lucky students,' Ben commented, striding ahead. 'My school was as isolated as Hogwarts and twice as ancient.'

He pushed his way too fast through the revolving doors, leaving me to play Russian roulette with a spinning plate-glass door.

'But despite such hardships, look how well you turned out,' I retorted sweetly, when I finally joined him on the other side of the doors. 'Such a gentleman.'

Water off a duck's back, I thought, eyeing up the swans pecking at the some unseen titbit at the river's edge while Ben went to reception to get directions.

'Do you think that might be him, by any chance?' Benedict murmured, nodding towards a man who had appeared from a doorway, a large camera hanging from around his neck.

The man extended a hand and darted forward, arms wide. 'Welcome, welcome. This is a pleasure, I must say.'

Steve Selby was a wiry, energetic sort with a trimmed silver beard and grey hair tied back roughly in a ponytail.

Pale blue eyes shone out from a tanned and leathery face. He looked the sort who might spend his free time running up and down muddy hills for the sheer hell of it.

Ben shook his hand. 'It's kind of you to see us at short notice, Steve; and please call me Benedict.'

Ben introduced me and Steve led us into a photographic studio.

It was a large white space with black-out blinds at the windows. An oversized roll of red paper was fixed to one wall and flowed down to the polished concrete floor to form a backdrop and more rolls in every shade from lavender to lime were stacked on their ends on one corner. A tall workbench lined one wall and tripods, lights, silver umbrellas and a wind machine took up much of the floor space. Ben was entranced and I could tell that he was itching to pick up a camera and start playing around.

'Your students are lucky kids, Steve,' he said with a whistle. 'This is better than professional studios in London.'

Steve grinned and folded his arms across his chest. 'You're telling me. And it's a damn sight better than the cubbyhole I used to work in at the *Wickham and Hoxley News*, too. So you mentioned you had some old editions?'

Steve gestured for us to sit at a small white table and we each pulled out an orange chair and sat down while he fetched us all coffee from a machine. Ben explained about this year being his parents' thirtieth at the hall and his idea of doing a photographic exhibition to commemorate their achievements at this year's festival.

'As I mentioned on the phone, I've got CDs of photographic images dating from 1990, which I've brought with me, but it's those earlier years I was having trouble with. According to the newspaper, you were the photographer then.'

'The Summer Festival was one of my favourite jobs.' Steve sat back in his chair and gazed up at the ceiling. 'Always such a good atmosphere. I'd have only been early twenties when your parents first arrived in 1984. I'd photographed the festival the year before, but, I dunno,' he shrugged and smiled at Ben, 'there was a new buzz about it. No disrespect to the previous Lord Fortescue, your grandfather, but it was great having young blood at the hall. And your mother . . .' He whistled. 'What a stunner!'

Ben and I exchanged looks.

'I'll pass that on.' Ben grinned.

'I seem to remember her being a bit nervous that first year,' Steve continued, offering us sachets of sugar for our coffee. 'But then I suppose, it's a lot to get used to, isn't it: moving into Wickham Hall and holding that event for the first time, and you and your little sister would only have been tiddlers.'

'She did have her hands full,' Ben agreed. 'And my father was just as busy trying to get to grips with his father's business affairs. He'd always known he was going to inherit Wickham Hall at some point, of course, but my grandfather was taken ill so suddenly and then passed away that they had no time for a handover.'

I sat up straighter in my chair; I hadn't known any of that. No wonder Lord and Lady Fortescue wanted Ben to work at Wickham Hall now, before they retire. It would be far easier to take over the reins if he already knew how the estate ran. Which was a luxury they hadn't had.

'Getting to know the business now is a good idea then, isn't it?' I murmured, catching Ben's eye over my coffee cup.

A cloud passed across his face and I could have kicked myself; it was Tuesday, I'd only met him on Saturday at his sister's wedding. It was wrong of me to comment on a situation I didn't fully understand. I opened my mouth to make some sort of apology but he winked at me.

'It does have its advantages, I admit.' He grinned and tipped Mum's old newspapers out of a plastic bag. 'Now, Steve, wait till you see what everyone was wearing in the eighties. Talk about crimes against fashion.'

'Oh right,' said Steve, clapping his hands together. 'Better go over here, where there's more room.'

I smiled to myself as he made some space on a cluttered workbench, pushing piles of photographic prints, a box of cables and stacks of old magazines to one side; Steve Selby would get on famously with my mother.

'Blimey, it's good to see these again,' said Steve once Ben and I had spread out the relevant pages across the workbench. He pored over the earliest one, stroking his beard and shaking his head. 'Rolls and rolls of film I used to get through. Then I'd have to wait for them to be developed and only then could I sift through to see if I'd got anything worth using. Amazing to think it all gets stored on a tiny memory card these days and photographers can see straight away whether they've got the shot or not.'

'And do you still have them?' I asked, crossing my fingers under the table.

'I should be able to lay my hands on them; I rarely throw things away, especially negatives. Most things are in my attic at home. Just as well because there was a fire at the paper, you know, in the late nineties. Most of the archive went up in smoke. The days before digital, eh?' He tutted.

I flicked through the old newspapers, half hoping to spot a picture of Mum and me – it wasn't that out of the question: we had attended the show often enough – but I didn't see anything. Ben stretched his arms over his head, circled his shoulder as if limbering up for a cricket game and started jiggling one leg. I suppressed a smile; Steve was enjoying the trip down memory lane but Ben was already getting restless.

'Shortly after that the paper went the way of many smaller presses – swallowed up by a bigger one. So old issues like these are nigh on impossible to get hold of. Where did they come from? Do you have an archive at Wickham Hall?'

Ben shook his head. 'We archive financial records and I believe we hold historical documents about Wickham Hall, but no newspapers, I'm afraid. These all belong to Holly.'

Two pairs of eyes looked at me.

'Yes, I . . . we had them at home, my mum, she . . .' I waved my hands around in the air, going redder and redder, my voice getting faster and faster. 'Well, she's a collector. Of newspapers. Mostly those that covered Wickham Hall events and some other events. Like county shows. That sort of thing.'

Now I've made her sound odd. I eyed their expressions: Ben looked intrigued, Steve looked like he'd found a winning lottery ticket.

'Really!' Steve whistled through his teeth. 'What I wouldn't give to see them. Do you think your mum would mind if I came round to your house for a look?'

'Me too,' Ben added. 'I'd like to thank her for letting us borrow these.'

Oh crumbs, what had I started? Coming round to the house was a big no-no. The last man I'd taken home was someone I'd been sort of seeing, a fitness instructor from Eden Spa called Simon. It was our second date and we'd been for a drink in Henley and had come back to Weaver's Cottage for coffee. It hadn't gone well. He'd been a bit freaked out about the state of the house, even though I'd

162

tried to warn him; Mum had flapped around clearing stuff off the sofa so we could sit down and I had been hideously embarrassed. There hadn't been a third date.

'We-ll, actually, she's a bit precious about them,' I said, pulling an apologetic face. 'Maybe not such a good idea.'

Ben folded his arms and leaned back on the workbench, curiosity etched into every curve of his smile.

Steve nodded. 'Totally understand. But tell your mother that from what you've described a collection like that is a cultural treasure trove, each one a snapshot of village – or even English – life through the last three decades. She would be doing me a great honour if she'd let me see them.'

That was just the right thing to say. I think despite her reluctance to let anything go, deep down Mum was ashamed of her hoarding. Perhaps hearing something like that might give her a boost? It had to be worth a try . . .

'I'll ask her.' I smiled. 'If nothing else, she'll certainly be flattered.'

'Great,' said Ben and Steve together.

I watched as Ben emptied a stack of CDs from the bag and sifted through them. A flash of silver caught my eye as a CD flew off Ben's finger and landed on the floor.

He stooped to pick it up and polished it on his sleeve. 'Whoops. I hope I haven't scratched it or Dad's secretary will never forgive me. 2001, according to the label. Can we have a look at it?'

'Sure.' Steve took the CD from him, blew the dust off it and inserted it into his laptop.

'I recognize this very clearly,' Ben said, squinting at the screen. 'It was the opening of the Coach House Café. Princess Anne came along to cut the ribbon. Look, there she is, all sassy in her navy suit. She got a bit merry later on

Mum's strawberry daiquiris.' He smirked at me. 'Mind you, we all did.'

Like you do.

I blinked at him incredulously. Sometimes Ben seemed perfectly ordinary, just like me, and then whoosh he drops royalty into the conversation and I realize that we are, in fact, worlds apart.

'Oh and there's a picture of me, looking uncomfortable in a suit. I must have been about nineteen.'

I leaned forward, curious to see what he looked like back then. Although I had grown up in the village of Wickham, our paths had never crossed: he went to boarding school and then university and hung out with a different crowd.

He was heartthrob-handsome even then, his hair cropped short at the sides with long curls on top. He had his arm around a pretty girl with a curtain of auburn hair, his lips pressed to her cheek.

'Oh, the pain and pleasure of young love.' Ben sighed dramatically, catching my eye. 'That's Sasha Jones. She broke my heart shortly after that and dumped me for a rugby player.'

I sneaked a look at his profile and couldn't help wondering if he was still single. After all, he hadn't brought anyone to the wedding, as far as I knew.

He caught me staring. 'I'm single now, though, in case you were wondering.'

'I wasn't,' I muttered. I fanned my face. 'Is it me or is it warm in here?'

Not that his status mattered to me, one way or the other; he was *so* not my type. In fact, could anyone be more diametrically opposed to my type? Anyway, I was plain old Holly Swift and he was heir to Wickham Hall.

So that was the end of that.

By the time I had got my pink face under control, Steve had folded and stacked the newspapers in date order and Ben was preparing to leave.

'Well, you must come to the festival this year, as our VIP guest along with your wife,' said Ben. 'And I'll be sure to credit your name in the exhibition.'

'That would be great,' Steve cried, pumping Ben's hand. 'But I'll bring some of my students, if I may. Plenty of opportunity for them to take some interesting shots.'

Ben's face lit up. 'Hey, I've got an idea. Why don't we run a photography competition, Holly? Ask people to send in their snaps and we pick the best one. Do you think the *Stratford Gazette* would run it?'

I suppressed a smile; it had been at least half an hour since he last had a new idea to add to the festival programme . . .

'It would be nice to incentivize Steve's students. Why don't we keep the competition restricted to them?'

'Fine by me.' Ben shrugged. 'Steve?'

He nodded happily. 'They're always up for that sort of thing. Term will have finished by then, so I can't make it compulsory, but if I could give them free tickets in exchange for sending you their pictures?'

'It's a deal,' said Ben, patting Steve on the shoulder. 'We'd better go; I promised Holly she could feed the swans—'

'Good grief!' cried Steve. 'I've just remembered something, hold on a minute.'

He darted over to a series of shelves and crouched down. Ben raised his eyebrows at me and I rolled my eyes.

'I do not want to feed the swans,' I whispered.

His lips twitched. 'Spoil sport.'

The two of us looked at Steve as he pulled out a thick box file marked 1984 with a satisfied, 'Aha!'

The year Mum fell pregnant with me. My ears pricked up and I edged closer to Steve to get a better look.

'I brought this in to show one of my students a few months ago and never got round to taking it home. He opened up the file on the workbench in front of us. 'Now there are loads of jobs in here – not just your festival, but if I remember rightly, I should have some Wickham Hall prints here . . . Yes, here we are.'

Steve extracted a handful of large colour photos and laid them out in front of us. I picked one up for a closer inspection.

'Of course,' exclaimed Ben with a laugh, 'they're in colour! I was expecting them to be in black and white like the newspaper. Imagine these blown up to two or three feet in size, they'll look great, won't they, Holly? Holly?'

'What? Sorry?' I looked at him blankly, not sure what he'd said. In my hand was a photograph of a group of Morris dancers but behind them, to the left of the shot, was a girl with wavy blonde hair wearing a pale pink ra-ra skirt. She had her back to the camera and was holding hands with someone who had been chopped off the edge of the picture. My heart thumped as I gazed at the picture. That girl was my mum, I'd recognize her anywhere, it had to be: her hair, her height and build, even the clothes . . . it all fit. Which meant that the person she was holding hands with was probably my father.

'Steve,' I said shakily, 'can I borrow this?'

'Sure.' He nodded and checked his watch. 'And now I'm going to have to be awfully rude and say goodbye. My next lecture starts in five minutes.'

*

As soon as we got back to Ben's car, I sent Esme a text.

Emergency meeting at yours tonight, OK?

A reply flashed back immediately.

Ooh, sounds exciting. Is it boy-related?

My fingers hovered over the keyboard of my phone as I hesitated over my response.

Let's just say it's a family matter. See you at seven, I'll bring food x

Chapter 15

Jenny and Nikki were waiting for us in the office when we got back to Wickham Hall. Jenny was perched on my desk, hands clasped in her lap, and Nikki was looking out of the window at the gardens.

Nikki turned to face us and folded her arms across her chest. Jenny leapt up straight away and began pacing the floor. Her chef whites were flecked with pink and strands of purple hair had escaped from her hair net.

'Jenny Plum!' Benedict grinned and patted his stomach. 'Wickham Hall's answer to Mary Berry. Did you bring me any food?'

'No I didn't,' said Jenny, shooting him a very un-Mary-like grimace, 'Because I am not at all happy with you.'

'Me?' Benedict sank onto his chair looking wounded and watched her pace.

'Well, someone, anyway,' she said, looking from him to me.

Ben and I exchanged confused looks.

'Jenny, we don't know what you mean,' I said, reaching for the kettle. 'Put us out of our misery.'

'I've just been sent the plans of the festival showground,' she explained. 'My outdoor restaurant is right in the far corner away from all the action. Location, location, location, guys!' she said, stopping at my desk to give it a thump. 'If we aren't in the centre of things we'll fail, we won't take enough bookings, there'll be no atmosphere and people won't come.'

Personally, I thought she might have a point but the lay-out had been done before I arrived at Wickham Hall and it was too late to change it now; there was nowhere else to put it.

Benedict looked at me blankly; he had only seen the plans briefly at yesterday's meeting. I reached for the relevant file and spread the plans out on his desk.

'It is in a corner, Jenny, but there's nowhere else for it,' I said, pointing to where the restaurant was. 'But I will make sure there are plenty of signs and I'll put the reservation number on Facebook and I've done a press release about your thirty-pound menu.'

Ben stood up and put an arm round Jenny's waist. She was taller than him and I noticed her transfer her weight to one leg to reduce the height gap.

'We've put the restaurant there, Jenny, because we wanted to give it plenty of space so that diners feel more comfortable. We thought it would be good to create more of an exclusive ambience, make it upmarket. I know my father is planning on eating lunch there every day with old friends and business associates and word has already got round about your food, you know.'

Jenny's eyebrows disappeared under her white hair net. 'Really?'

He nodded earnestly. 'Oh yeah.'

'That's gratifying to hear, Benedict, thank you.' She sighed. 'I just want it to be a success; we've never done an outdoor restaurant on this scale before.'

'I think you're underestimating the "Jenny Plum" effect.'
He grinned and winked at me.

Jenny studied the plan for a moment, running her finger
along the paths around the showground.

'It does make sense, I suppose, having more space.' She
nodded. 'And we wouldn't want to be next to all the fast
food, would we, with their fried onions and greasy chips?'

'Exactly.' Ben smiled smoothly.

That seemed to appease her and she skipped off, muttering something about silver cloches and linen napkins. Ben
and I turned to Nikki.

She was still at the window, arms folded, mouth twisted
to one side and her sun hat jammed low over her forehead.

'Don't even think about giving me that Benedict
Fortescue patter,' she grumbled.

'Nikki, come on,' Ben said with his most charming smile.
He took a step forward and held his arms wide.

'I mean it, Benedict, you are out of line.' The head
gardener flicked her palms up. 'I've been given the list of
lots for the charity auction. Lot fifteen – an afternoon of
garden design from Nikki Logan. What were you thinking?'

He raised his eyebrows and shrugged. 'What's wrong
with that?'

'So someone – anyone – can bid for an afternoon of my
time?' She shoved her hands in the pockets of her khaki
shorts and glared at him. 'I haven't agreed to that. You can't
just pimp me out to the highest bidder for me to design
somebody's garden. I could end up anywhere. I shouldn't
have to do that sort of thing. I'm a professional and I will
not stand for it.'

Oh dear, I'd never seen Nikki so riled. Not even the time
that Lady Fortescue had suggested that the solution to the
boggy bit of grass at the entrance to the kitchen gardens

could be astro turf. Her bark might be worse than her bite but right now she did look very angry.

'A cup of tea?' I offered, to diffuse the mood.

Nikki shook her head. 'If this is how you are going to treat me then I'm afraid I might have to consider my position at Wickham Hall.'

I glanced at Ben, wondering how he was going to get out of this one. This was his doing; he'd promised me that he would fill in the gaps on the auction list by sourcing a few more prizes. I'd have to check it this afternoon to make sure there were no other surprises on it.

'Crikey, Nikki,' said Ben, running a hand through his curls. 'Please don't get upset, there's just been a misunderstanding. The auction list should read: "An afternoon of Wickham garden design *with* Nikki Logan". Nothing more elaborate than a garden tour here, like you normally do, but with the emphasis on the design changes you've made in your time. That's all.'

Nikki appeared to contemplate Ben's words for a long moment.

'So I'd take the highest bidder on a garden design tour of Wickham Hall?' She eyed Benedict from under the brim of her sun hat.

'Exactly,' he said. He stepped forward gingerly and placed an arm around her shoulders. 'The charity was delighted when they heard; a bespoke tour like that will probably set off a bidding war.'

She bobbed away from him and frowned. 'I don't exactly buy your answer, but I'll let you off the hook. For now.'

'Phew.' Ben pretended to mop his brow.

Nikki ignored him and turned to me. 'I've got tons of salad leaves going spare in the kitchen gardens if you want some?'

I thanked her and agreed to collect some before leaving for the evening, pleased that she didn't appear to be cross with me too.

'What about me?' Ben asked when Nikki walked to our office door. 'Don't I get salad?'

'You can pick your own,' she called over her shoulder as she left.

I snorted as Ben clutched at his heart and pretended to be hurt.

Nikki's boots clumped down the stairs and Ben blew out of the side of mouth, making his curls bounce. 'That was a close call,' he said, accepting a cup of tea from me.

'You handled both ladies very well,' I said with a grin. I sat down at my desk and opened my diary ready to get on with my afternoon.

'All in a day's work,' he said, slurping his tea.

'I was impressed, actually,' I said. 'I think you might be quite a good manager of people.'

'Really?'

I nodded. 'You motivate people, you fire them up. I saw it yesterday at that meeting.'

Plus I'd felt it myself; he had whirled through this office like a typhoon, but I had to admit I hadn't had a single dull moment since he'd arrived on the scene. And, I realized, I was enjoying his company.

I expected Ben to adopt his default setting of confident nonchalance and shrug off the compliment but he looked quite taken aback. And I was pretty sure he coloured a bit under his tan. Ben had a serious side and all of a sudden I liked him a lot more for showing it.

He shot me a sideways glance and rubbed his neck. 'Thanks, Holly. No one has ever said that before.'

'Lord Fortescue is good with people too. Perhaps not as

exuberant as you,' I twinkled my eyes at him, 'but he has a certain aura about him. It must be in the genes.'

'Maybe you're right,' said Ben thoughtfully. 'We all must inherit something from our fathers, mustn't we?'

I thought of the photograph I had in my handbag, which I believed had my father on it, and a shiver ran down my spine.

'I suppose so,' I murmured and wondered what I might have inherited from mine.

At seven o'clock on the dot, I knocked on Esme's door and she opened it dressed in a pale yellow playsuit that set off her golden brown skin beautifully.

'So, what's the emergency?' she said, ushering me inside.

'Food first.' I held up my bags. 'And wine.'

I quite enjoyed cooking; I found it relaxing. Not at Weaver's Cottage. That was anything but relaxing. I like to lay all my ingredients out, do all my preparation before I begin cooking. There simply wasn't room amongst all the kitchen clutter at home to do it properly.

Esme uncorked the wine while I washed the tiny new potatoes that Nikki had given me along with the salad leaves and set a griddle pan out ready to cook a couple of salmon fillets.

'I thought about going for a run to sort out all the mush in my head,' I said, accepting a glass of rosé from her, 'but this is far better.'

'No contest.' Esme pulled a face. 'Cheers.'

We took our glasses out onto her tiny balcony while the potatoes cooked and sat down in the evening sun.

Esme's flat was one of ten in a two-storey building on the edge of Henley. Built in the 1950s it had as much space as a modern two-bedroomed house, a communal garden and this, the pretty balcony that she'd decorated with bunting and fairground-style lights.

I stretched out my legs and exhaled. Esme waited patiently.

'I met that old lecturer of yours today – Steve. He wants to come round to our cottage and look through all Mum's old newspapers. Apparently, they're almost impossible to get hold of. "A treasure trove of culture" he called them.'

'Did he? The old smoothie.' She chuckled.

'Part of me thinks that maybe I should arrange it. He did seem quite excited. And it might give Mum a boost, especially now she's admitted she's got a problem.'

'Do it! Definitely.' She rolled her eyes at my doubtful expression. 'Look, Hols, if the newspapers really are of value to him, he's not going to mind the state of your house, is he?'

'The thing is,' I worried at a piece of loose skin on my lip, 'Ben wants to come too.'

'*Ben* now, is it?' she smirked.

I ignored that remark. 'We've been getting on really well this week and I don't want to spoil anything.'

Esme gave the patio table a triumphant tap. 'You really like him, don't you? I knew it.'

'He's my boss and I want him to think well of me. He's really grown on me. At first he didn't seem to take anything seriously and he was irresponsible, I mean, the way he acted when we were trying to organize a press conference about him taking over from his father . . . ridiculous. And he was hideously late to his own sister's wedding . . .' I shook my head at the memory, although I couldn't help but smile. 'But today I saw a more sensitive side of him, which I liked.'

I set down my glass and gazed at Esme. 'If he comes to

174

Weaver's Cottage and sees the way I live, he'll think differently about me.'

'Well, maybe if he's as sensitive as you say he is, he won't.' She shrugged simply. 'Besides, I hope you realize you fancy the posh pants off him.'

I shook my head. 'He's my boss, and—'

'Are you kidding me? There was enough electricity sparking between you two on Sunday in Joop to light the Eiffel Tower.'

'That was embarrassment, not electricity, Es. Big difference.' I stood up and collected her empty glass. 'Come on, the potatoes will be cooked.'

We tucked into our pan-fried salmon when I dropped the bombshell.

'I think I found a picture of my father today.'

'What?' Esme spluttered, a forkful of salad halfway to her mouth.

I darted back to the kitchen where I'd left my handbag and returned with the photograph from Steve's studio.

'One of these Morris dancers?' Her jaw dropped.

I tutted and pointed at the blonde girl behind them. 'Look at her. It's Mum and she's holding hands with a man.'

Esme squinted and moved the picture backwards and forwards to focus. 'Are you sure it's your dad?'

'Admittedly it is only his hand and a bit of his arm. But that's definitely Mum and this picture was taken in 1984, so yes.' Esme looked dubious but I tapped the picture confidently. 'Don't ask me how I know, I just do. And now I want to know who he is.'

My heart thumped as I stared at the photograph. My head had been full of Mum's story ever since she'd revealed that she'd fallen in love with someone at the Wickham Hall

Summer Festival. In all my twenty-nine years I'd never been particularly curious about my father. I'd just accepted that he wasn't around and that was that. But now I'd had this tiny glimpse of him, I'd never been more curious about anything in my life.

I remember the first time I asked Mum why I didn't have a daddy. She had wrapped her arms around me, pulled me onto her knee and told me how a fairy had knocked at her door and asked her to look after a very special baby. The baby being me, of course. I'd adored the story, boasted to all my slightly less gullible friends about it and it wasn't until I was eleven and along with my classmates watched the excruciating 'Birds and Bees' video at school that I noticed the flaws in her tale.

But I'd never asked her again. Not outright, anyway. It made her too anxious. And if anything remotely related to fathers ever came up, Mum's stock response was that she loved me twice as much to make up for not having two parents.

'Can't you ask her?' Esme asked. She turned back to her dinner, swooping a tiny potato through mayonnaise and popping it in her mouth.

I shook my head. 'Not yet.'

I filled Esme in on the online reading and research I'd been doing. Although Mum hadn't begun seeing a counsellor yet she was making progress in terms of tackling some of the stuff she'd been accumulating. To date she'd managed to part with my cot, my baby toys and a box of old nylon bedspreads that had given us electric shocks every time we'd touched them. But I still felt as though I hadn't got to the heart of it yet.

'All sorts of things can trigger hoarding as a coping mechanism: a traumatic event, bereavement, anxiety, stress . . .' I said, spearing a pile of rocket with my fork. 'Mum says that she felt like she had everything that summer of 1984 and she let it slip away. And she was only seventeen, poor thing.'

Esme pulled a sympathetic face. 'Wasn't your granddad there?'

'I don't know exactly when he died.' I frowned. 'But I know he never met me. So I'm guessing she was completely on her own.'

'Finding herself single and alone and about to have a baby would be traumatic enough to trigger the hoarding behaviour, I guess,' Esme mused, topping up our glasses.

I nodded. 'She said something else, too, about her father not being proud of her. It's as if she is ashamed of something. And that's the key to it.' I gazed at Esme and rested my cutlery against my plate. 'That's when she clammed up on Saturday. But what I don't understand is why she feels to blame. I mean, she's not the first teenage girl to get pregnant, is she? And it was the eighties not the twenties. Besides it takes two . . . Oh God.' I clapped a hand over my mouth as a thought hit me.

'What is it? Holly, you've gone white,' Esme pointed out.

'You don't think he was married, do you?' I whispered. 'That could be it. What if she fell in love with someone she couldn't have? Perhaps he had children of his own. That would explain why Granddad wouldn't have been proud of her. And that might be why she's too ashamed of the affair to talk about it.'

'Possibly.'

We both fell silent then. I was mulling over my theory and Esme appeared to be concentrating on her salmon.

'I've had another thought as well,' I added in a low voice. 'Mum has always said that Granddad left her his savings.

177

That's why she's only ever had to work part-time. But maybe the man is still around and pays her an allowance and Mum can't tell me because she's sworn to secrecy.'

Esme wrinkled her nose and twisted her corkscrew curls around her finger. 'Isn't a savings fund a bit more . . . likely?'

I thought about that. She was right, I was getting carried away. 'OK, but I bet he's local. Mum has never wanted to move away from Wickham. What if she wanted to stay in the village to be near him?'

'You think she had an affair with someone in Wickham?' gasped Esme. 'Blimey, that would be playing a risky game, wouldn't it? She would bump into him all the time; Wickham's only small.'

I swallowed. It would also mean that I would bump into him all the time. Perhaps I had? I let out a groan. Perhaps it was actually someone I knew . . .

Esme frowned. 'I don't buy it. If she says she met him at the Summer Festival, then that means it wasn't someone local, or she would have met him previously. Perhaps it was just a visitor.'

'I'd like to think Mum wouldn't simply fall in love with someone who turned up to Wickham Hall with a day ticket and fifty pence for an ice cream,' I scoffed, pushing my plate away.

'So,' Esme tapped her lip and narrowed her eyes, 'we are looking for someone who perhaps worked there, or at least someone who was there for longer than a day.'

'There are tons of staff at Wickham Hall, especially during the festival,' I suggested. 'And then of course there are all the exhibitors. They arrive three or four days before the start of the event. There would have been plenty of time to get to know one of them.'

'Or – it could be Lord Fortescue!' Esme leaned back in her chair.

I gaped at her. 'Esme! I hardly think—'

'*He's* married.' She raised one eyebrow suggestively.

'Yes, but he's too old for Mum *and* he adores Lady Fortescue, and that was his first year at Wickham Hall.' I shook my head. 'Definitely not.'

'Ha!' She stabbed the air triumphantly. 'There you go. That's why she hadn't met him before; he'd only just moved to Wickham.'

'That's ridiculous. Besides, he's lovely.' I stared at Esme defiantly. 'Far too nice to be unfaithful.'

'Don't you be so sure,' she said knowingly. 'He might be a very nice man but I know what the aristocracy is like. I've seen *Downton Abbey*.'

'This is crazy. Stop right now.' I snatched up the photograph from the table and gave her a warning look.

'Keep your hair on.' Esme chuckled, scraping the last of the salmon off her plate. 'Well, what about the celebrity then? Who did the celebrity appearance in 1984?'

Every year Wickham Hall had somebody famous on the festival programme to pull in the crowds. This year it was a TV gardener. In 1984 it had been the local BBC weather man.

'Someone from the BBC,' I said. 'I can't remember his name.'

'Ah well,' Esme grinned, pushing herself up straight, 'that's it. He'll be the one. I always thought you'd make a good newsreader. It must be in the genes.'

She pretended to tap a pile of invisible papers on the edge of the table. 'News just in,' she said in a plummy accent, 'a rather attractive man was spotted in Joop, wearing nothing but—'

I tried to laugh with her but all of a sudden I found I couldn't. It wasn't funny at all. This was my father we were talking about. I'd always accepted that my family was just Mum and me; the identity of my father hadn't bothered me too much before now. But now it felt very important and I was hurt that my best friend couldn't see that.

I stood up and swigged the rest of my wine, which was quite difficult given the lump in my throat.

'Holster? What are you doing?'

'I'm going home,' I said, ignoring the prickling sensation at the back of my eyes. 'I wish I'd never shown you the picture. You're not taking this seriously. I'm glad you find my life so amusing, but from where I'm sitting, it's anything but.'

'Holly? I didn't mean anything by it!'

I left Esme's jaw flapping and walked out of the flat, my heart racing. She was completely barking up the wrong tree. Mum probably just fell in love with a nice boy her own age and got a little carried away behind the bushes. All this talk and speculation was unhelpful and . . . unsettling. There'd be a very simple explanation, I was sure of it, and I wouldn't stop digging until I'd found it.

Chapter 16

It was mid-July, the sky was as blue as a robin's egg, and the air was so still that not a blade of grass moved nor a willow branch rustled and I was out and about in the gardens. On days like today there was nowhere I would rather be than lost in the grounds of Wickham Hall. I wasn't lost, of course, not physically anyway. I'd just gone a bit starry-eyed with happiness at the sheer fabulousness of my job. I was so lucky to be outside in the sunshine, wandering around, checking up on the events happening that day, all in the name of work. I opened my diary as I rounded the eastern façade of the hall and ticked off my first completed task.

I'd just performed my daily circuit of the festival site and had been thrilled to see that most of the marquees were up, including the big demonstration theatre and the indoor arena. The geography of the festival was beginning to take shape. I'd also been quite distracted by the sight of tanned shirtless men in shorts spreading tarmac for the temporary road that would loop around the showground. Muscles on muscles, some of them. Maybe Mum had had her head turned by one of the construction team all those years ago . . . ?

I snapped myself straight out of that thought. It wouldn't

do to go down that road this morning; I had too much on my plate and needed to keep focused.

The courtyard was busy already and I had to dodge the tourists as I crossed it. The sunshine had brought visitors to Wickham Hall by the coach load, the café was doing a roaring trade in ice cream and Jenny's special raspberryade, and Andy had been boasting that sales of his Victorian-style parasols would take the gift shop profits to new heights.

Andy was on my to-do list today. Negotiating with him was always my least favourite task. I decided to get it over with straight away and made a beeline for the gift shop.

The little shop was still relatively quiet – most visitors tended to save their shopping until the end of the day – and Andy was constructing a teddy-bears'-picnic-themed window display.

'Morning, Andy,' I said breezily. He threw me an icy smile and continued setting up a miniature picnic rug complete with three teddy bears in the window. 'What a lovely display! We've got a large party of small children in today, they'll love it.'

'I can't bear having loads of kids in here fiddling with things,' he muttered.

I was used to his less than welcoming charm where I was concerned and ploughed on regardless.

'We've had some signed books delivered from Suzanna Merryweather's publisher. They've asked if we'll sell them in the shop. Can I get them dropped off here?'

Suzanna Merryweather was the presenter of the TV show *Green Fingers*. She was also our celebrity guest for the festival and would be doing gardening talks in our demo theatre. I wasn't a gardener myself but Mum loved her and even Nikki, who was a bit sniffy about TV gardeners, was keen to meet her.

'No chance,' he said. 'We're up to our eyeballs in summer stock. Books take up too much space and no one will buy them anyway.'

I held my breath and waited for a diplomatic response to occur to me. But before it did, Edith appeared from the stock room. She was wearing a knitted twinset and thick tights despite the July heat but she still looked as cool as a cucumber with her powdered nose and immaculate bun.

'Did I hear you say Suzanna Merryweather?' she chirped. 'I'll have a book. I love that programme.'

I looked at Andy and resisted sticking my tongue out. Seriously, what was his problem? I'd done nothing other than be chosen over him for this job. *And* I went out of my way to compliment his shop at every opportunity.

'All right, well, I'll send over one for Edith and the rest can be arranged on a table in the demo theatre.'

'Rest of what?' asked Jim, poking his head in through the shop door.

When I explained, Jim's eyes nearly popped out of his head. 'I'll definitely buy one, and I'm going to ask for her autograph when I see her.'

'Two down, twenty-eight copies to go,' I said brightly. 'Not too bad. Let's hope we find plenty more fans like you to buy the rest.'

'Send the books over then,' grumbled Andy. 'Or I'll never hear the last of it.'

'Holly, just thought I'd let you know, I'm about to start,' said Jim with a wink.

'Thank you, Andy,' I said, inclining my head graciously, and I followed Jim out of the shop before he changed his mind. Phew, another task ticked off the list.

Jim was looking extra dapper today. He had a Wickham Hall polo shirt on, a clean, non-baggy pair of trousers and,

I reckoned, he had even applied a good splash of aftershave.

'Are you ready for this, then, Jim?' I asked, looping my arm through his as we made our way to the picnic area.

'I'll be all right once I've got going,' he said, 'although I'm not used to addressing a crowd.'

'You'll be brilliant,' I said, squeezing his arm.

Today was Wickham Hall's first ever nature trail, led by the aptly named Jim Badger, naturally. And twelve parents with their preschool children had gathered in readiness.

I stood to one side as Jim introduced himself, gave everyone a sticky badge with their name on and then did that slidy-finger trick that old men do when they pretend they've cut their finger off.

The kids loved him and the mums were giggling too. Jim handed all the children a map and coloured pencils and geed them up ready to go exploring. I took a few pictures on my phone as the little ones crowded round him.

'Right, follow me to the woods; we're going to see how many animals and insects we can find.'

Before they moved off a little girl with brown pigtails and a stripy dress put her hand up.

'Yes, Phoebe?' said Jim, bending down to read her name.

'If you got all the ants in all the world, would they fit under one chicken?' she asked.

Jim and I exchanged glances and I grinned, wondering how he'd answer this and possibly a lot more where this came from.

The mums giggled, especially the one with brown hair standing behind Phoebe.

Jim bent down and pretended to steal the little girl's nose. 'Let's hope not, Phoebe, because I think it would be very uncomfortable for the poor chicken.'

And then he began dancing on the spot and smacking

the back of his shorts as though he was being attacked by invisible ants. The children loved him. Just as I knew they would. Ever since he'd shown me the moorhen and her chicks I'd been trying to give him the chance to be a granddad, even if only for a few hours. He was in his element and I was pleased as punch for him. I ticked 'check up on nature trail' off my list and headed towards the café.

I bought a pot of tea and a strawberry tart and chose a table outside, tucked into a shady corner. In theory my out-of-office jobs were done and I could go back inside, but as Ben had taken over the room with his easel this morning, I decided to work on the festival show guide in the courtyard instead.

I poured a cup of tea, spread out the paperwork and then sliced the strawberry tart into quarters. I blinked at it: I'd bought Esme's favourite cake without realizing, a sure sign that I was missing her already.

It was well over a week since Esme and I had had our falling-out. Technically I supposed we hadn't rowed, I'd been the one to blame, overreacting about the whole 'who's the daddy' thing.

We rarely rowed and it had left both of us shaken but we had smoothed things out by the following weekend.

I'd apologized and she'd admitted that she'd got carried away with her Lord Fortescue theory, forgetting for a moment what the implications were for Mum and me. In the end we'd agreed that it was far more likely that Mum had simply had a fling with someone she'd rather not keep in touch with. I was glad we'd made up when we did because she and Bryony had made a snap decision to close Joop for a couple of weeks, regardless of the profit implications, and had flown off to Dubai to join Esme's dad. I was super pleased for them. Not least because the shop was normally open seven days a week and they were in dire need of a break. But also they could discuss as a family what to do with Joop in the light of Bryony's arthritis.

I was completely used to my friend jetting off to spend time with her little family unit of three, but this year I was particularly aware of the dad-shaped hole in my own life.

I sipped at my tea and mentally brushed away that particular niggle. *No time for daydreaming, Holly Swift*, I told myself firmly: the copy for the festival guide was due at the printers that afternoon and I still had a few pages to check.

I immersed myself in the artwork, sorting any typesetting issues and spelling mistakes with a stroke of my red pen. I'd reached the itinerary page for the last day when a shadow fell across me and a slight breeze made my paperwork lift from the table.

It was Nikki wafting herself with her sun hat. 'What are you doing out here, fallen out with Benedict?' she asked with a grin.

'No, not at all,' I said smoothly, 'the office just gets a bit heated at this time of day with the two of us in it.'

Nikki laughed and pulled out a chair to sit on. 'I bet it does.'

I felt a flush rise to my face. 'The way the sun comes round, I mean, at noon.'

'Sure.' She winked.

I busied myself pouring out a second cup of tea while the colour on my cheeks subsided.

The truth was that I was finding it increasingly difficult to spend time alone with Ben in our office. It wasn't just that he insisted on having a radio on all the time, or that occasionally paint flicked from his brush onto my desk, or even that he was still, even now, with two weeks left

186

until the festival, randomly bursting out with 'hey, what about . . . ?' and then embarking on an enthusiastic explanation as to why we should incorporate his latest idea into the schedule.

No, I could just about cope with all of those things.

My issue was that whenever I looked into his dark eyes, framed by even darker lashes, my heart gave a little flutter and no matter how often I reminded myself that a) he was my boss and b) he didn't treat me any differently to anyone else, the fluttering was getting harder and harder to ignore.

'. . . and on a day like today,' Nikki was saying. 'I'm surprised he's even in the office. Benedict's like me: a free spirit and doesn't like to be hemmed in. Between you and me, I think he finds being at Wickham Hall too suffocating.'

I sometimes felt like that about Weaver's Cottage, but here? I glanced around me at the size of the buildings, the acres of wide-open space.

'Hmm, I've noticed that too, although I can't understand why. I'm sure he loves Wickham Hall but there does seem to be something holding him back from committing to it long term. Do you know what it might be?'

Nikki shrugged. 'No, but I guess it's something to do with his parents. I admire Lady Fortescue, but she does treat him like a child. Family life is rarely straightforward, is it?'

Understatement of the century.

'It certainly isn't,' I said, giving her a wry smile. 'Anyway, how are your preparations for the festival going?'

'The pearl garden is going to look fantastic,' she said. She reached into her pocket and pulled out the head of a white geranium. 'Pretty, isn't it? Problem is that it's scorching

187

out there and the flowers are all blooming like billy-o, I just hope I can extend their flowering until the end of the month. And the watering . . .' She paused to roll her eyes. 'Gallons and gallons of the stuff. We're OK while the plants are in the nursery beds, but once we're down on the showground everything will have to be watered by hand. It's a full-time job just keeping them from drying out! Talking of which, I've earned myself a drink this morning, see you later.'

Nikki wandered inside and I was about to resume my proofreading when I noticed Ben and Lord Fortescue coming across each other at the far side of the courtyard.

Lord and Lady Fortescue had returned from the South of France looking healthily tanned. I was glad to have them back. The place seemed all the brighter for their presence, almost as though Wickham Hall stood to attention for them.

It was the first time I'd seen father and son talk to each other without anyone else around – Ben had arrived during a manic time on Zara's wedding day and the Fortescues had gone away straight after that – and I must admit, I was quite curious to see the two men together.

Even though I couldn't hear what they were saying I could read their body language. Lord Fortescue seemed perplexed: one hand smoothing his hair, the other on his hip. Ben didn't look very happy; he was staring at the ground, shaking his head, waving his arms around until finally folding them defensively. Lord Fortescue laid a hand on his son's shoulder and patted him gently but Ben turned his body away, catching my eye in the process.

I raised a hand and Ben made a beeline for me as Lord Fortescue carried on walking towards the private car park.

'Hello, Mr Happy,' I said as he dropped into the chair Nikki had just vacated.

He leaned forward, resting his elbows on his knees, and rubbed his face roughly.

'Parents,' he said gruffly. 'Dad knows that I'm not really cut out for this role, but asks me loads of questions anyway, which I can't answer, and then he gives me his disappointed face as if I'm not doing a good enough job.'

He looked so dejected that it was all I could do not to pull him in for a hug.

I cleared my throat. 'What sort of questions?'

Ben sighed. 'How many tickets for the festival have we sold, for example? I mean, my grasp of numbers is weak at the best of times. In one ear and out the other. I should know, but I just forget.'

'We've sold eighteen thousand,' I said. 'With thirty per cent of those coming from online bookings. I'll drop him an email. What else?'

'Oh, er . . .' He scrunched up his eyes. 'Have we made sure there are disabled access ramps in the indoor arena?'

'Yes, we have.' I looked back down at my paperwork to hide my smile. That would be the 'Royal' we.

'Oh good.' He nodded. 'And he wanted to know whether the outdoor seating in the VIP area is shaded.'

'It is,' I said. 'Well, it is now. I've just been down this morning and asked them to put a canvas roof over it. It will be a bit like a sail. I didn't want your parents' guests keeling over with sunstroke.'

He stared at me and whistled. 'How do you remember this stuff? I bet I could ask you a thousand questions and you'd be able to answer all of them.'

'Planning. It's all in here. Look.' I held up my diary at

today's page. There was barely any empty space; I'd written reams of notes all over it.

He shook his head and grinned. 'Holly Swift, you're a marvel. What would I do without you?'

I felt ridiculously pleased and too tongue-tied to come up with a witty answer and was relieved when Sheila inadvertently came to my rescue.

'There you are!' she announced, panting slightly as she laid a heavy cardboard box down on the table. 'I've been carting these round looking for you.'

'I'm sorry, Sheila, I thought I'd escape from the perils of sharing an office with an artist.' I smiled, flicking a glance at Ben.

'The new Wickham Hall calendars are in.' She flipped open the top of the box and handed one to each of us. 'I thought you might like to see them before I drop them off at the gift shop.'

'I would, thank you!' I held my breath as I looked at the calendar. This had been my first job on arriving at Wickham Hall, my first chance to prove myself, and I hoped I had succeeded.

The cover photograph of Lord and Lady Fortescue was adorable: instead of a stilted formal pose, Lady Fortescue was sitting on a window seat in the Long Gallery, Lord Fortescue beside her, his arm around her shoulders; the pair were smiling and gazing at a jewellery case containing Lord Fortescue's grandmother's tiara. A lump appeared in my throat as I read the caption: *Lady Fortescue's Hidden Treasure. A surprise on our wedding day from Hugo, this gift, a family heirloom, more than anything truly made me feel like one of the family.*

Even though I'd read her words before when we put the calendar together, it still warmed my heart to read it again.

'Holly, this is great. Really great.' Ben reached across and ruffled my hair as though I was a small boy. 'And different. I don't think the calendar has ever featured people before, has it, Sheila?'

She smiled. 'No, it's usually flowers or views across the estate or various rooms in the hall.'

'The team at Wickham Hall, the people, they're its beating heart. Good on you, Holly.' Ben gazed at me and I stared back, trying to read his expression, my own heart beating furiously at the compliment.

Sheila picked up the box and walked off to the gift shop and gradually the noise and the movements around me came back into focus.

The door to the café opened very slowly and Jenny's head appeared through it, followed by the rest of her.

'Just checking Lord Fortescue wasn't around. I want to keep this a surprise. What do you think?' She held out a small dish of tiny eggs skewered onto cocktail sticks that had been decorated with concertina'd ribbons of Parma ham.

'Very pretty,' I said. 'What is it for?'

'A little *amuse-bouche* for our thirtieth-anniversary menu: the quail eggs represent pearls.'

'Wait a second and I'll give you my verdict,' said Benedict, scooping up two and popping them one after the other in his mouth.

'You're supposed to savour it, you glutton!' Jenny tutted.

I giggled at the look of indignation on her face.

'Very moreish,' declared Ben, reaching for a third. 'If a bit small.'

'Oi.' Jenny twisted away out of reach. 'Let Holly have a taste.'

I bit into one. 'Mmm, delicious. I don't think I've ever had quail eggs before.'

'Too small for me,' said Ben, trying to get past Jenny's hand to pinch another. 'Give me a good old-fashioned hen's egg any day.'

'Actually, quail eggs *are* old-fashioned. Quite popular in Elizabethan times,' I argued. 'I'd have thought you'd have known that, Mr Fortescue.'

'You tell him, Holly.' Jenny held out the last cocktail stick to him and then made her way back to the kitchen.

He unravelled the Parma ham from the cocktail stick and dropped it into his mouth.

'I can see why you like sitting in here.' He grinned.

'I'm trying to finish the festival guide.' I leafed through the loose pages, found the section that mentioned his parents' thirtieth anniversary at the hall and slid it across the table towards him. 'Perhaps you'd read this for me?'

His forehead furrowed in concentration, completely absorbed in the text, his full lips moving as he read silently and I found myself wondering what those lips would taste like . . .

He looked up. 'You're staring.'

'Sorry.' I popped the rest of my strawberry tart in my mouth and prayed my face didn't give me away.

'Yeah, that's good.' He handed back the page and stood to leave. 'Fancy a trip to Stratford? I'm going to the college to collect the photos for my exhibition from Steve.'

'Um . . .' I hesitated. It was tempting to spend a couple of hours with him away from Wickham Hall. But duty called. 'No, too much to do. But would you please let Steve know I'll give him his photograph back when I see him at the festival.'

I'd made a copy of Steve's photograph but I hadn't got round to showing it to Mum yet. The time wasn't right. She had started seeing a therapist. I'd been over the moon at first but she was finding the sessions hard and came back emotionally exhausted. The therapist had given her exercises to do at home, too. But she seemed to have regressed a bit and the dining room, which we'd started to clear, had accumulated another three bags full when I looked at the weekend. It was early days, though, and I was determined to help her crack it.

'OK.' Ben pretended to look wounded and began to stride away.

'Oh and can you ask him for his mobile number?' I added. 'I'll arrange for him to see my mum's newspapers if he's still interested.'

It had to be worth a try.

'Sure.' He grinned. 'Now try not to miss me too much when I'm gone.'

'It will be difficult,' I twinkled my eyes at him, trying to ignore the thumping of my heart, 'but I'll do my best.'

Chapter 17

A week later, very early in the morning, when it was still dark – or at least dark enough not to be able to see my watch – I was woken by an insistent, repetitive noise coming from downstairs. It was the door: someone was knocking on the front door.

What on earth . . . ?

I stumbled out of bed, picked up my phone to turn it on and pulled back the curtain. Adrenalin began to race through me as I spotted movement in the semi-darkness. Beneath the window, a shadowy figure was leaning on the wall of the cottage and then . . . bent to sniff the flowers.

I threw open the window. 'Ben!'

He took a step back, stumbled over one of Mum's plant pots and cursed under his breath. A thin sliver of moonlight illuminated his smile as he peered up at me. I smiled back and wondered for a second whether this was just a dream.

'Hello. I was just contemplating whether to shin up this drainpipe and bounce on your bed.'

'Keep your voice down. And why are you smelling our flowers at,' I paused and squinted at my phone, 'four twenty in the morning?'

'I woke up and thought about you never having seen the dawn and what a travesty that is. So I'm taking you to watch the sunrise at my favourite spot.'

Oh. That was possibly the loveliest thing that anyone had ever done for me. It took me a moment to gather my thoughts.

'That's a relief,' I whispered. 'I thought the festival showground must be on fire or something.'

'No offence, Holly, I know you're amazing and the world's greatest diary keeper and everything, but you wouldn't be my first port of call in a fire. I've been out here for ages.' He grinned. 'Half of Warwickshire would have been razed to the ground by now.'

I laughed softly. 'Sorry, I'm a deep sleeper. It's because I work so hard. You should try it.'

He stared at me and then flapped his arms. 'Well, come on then, get some clothes on, the sunrise waits for no man. Or woman. You look very cute with bedhead hair, by the way.'

I poked my tongue out at him and shut the curtains again, hugging my excitement to myself.

I pulled on a pair of jeans, a hoody and my trainers and ran down the stairs two at a time, trying not to wake Mum, while dragging my fingers through my hair in lieu of a hairbrush.

I hesitated in front of the door and glanced round the hall. Boxes were still stacked behind the front door and a teetering pile of newspapers cluttered up the entrance to the kitchen. I knew there was an improvement, but even so, I didn't want Ben to see it like this.

I opened the door just enough to squeeze myself through and a look of curiosity flicked across Ben's face as he tried to look past me into the hallway.

'Right, I'm ready,' I said briskly, 'let's go.'

I was about to close the door quietly when the cottage was suddenly filled with light and footsteps thumped down the stairs.

'Oh no! We've woken my mother,' I hissed.

Ben pulled an apologetic face. 'Sorry.'

'What's going on?' called a voice. 'Who's there?'

I put my face to the chink in the door. 'Only me, Mum. Bye.'

Mum opened the door wide, yelped in surprise when she saw Ben and darted back behind the door, wrapping her arms across her chest.

My heart sank. Ben must have been able to see the mess in the hall and I felt my face burn with shame.

Mum popped her head round the door and peered into the gloom. 'Excuse me in my nightdress! I didn't know we had visitors. Are you just arriving or leaving, Mr, er . . . ?' Without her glasses on she didn't have much chance of seeing him in any detail.

'It's Benedict, Mum, from Wickham Hall. And we're both leaving.'

'Oh, I see,' said Mum, her blue eyes wide with curiosity. 'Hello, Benedict, I didn't recognize you in the dark.'

'And to be clear, Ben has just arrived.' I caught Ben's eye then and sent up a silent thank-you that there wasn't enough light to see my blushes by.

'Pleased to meet you, Mrs Swift.' Ben extended a hand and then averted his eyes as Mum unfolded her arms from her chest to shake it. 'Are you sure you two aren't sisters?'

'It's Ms Swift, actually, but you can call me Lucy.' Mum gave him a girlish smile and ran her fingers through her hair.

'Oh, Lucy, I just remembered.' He delved into the pocket

of his shorts and held out a scrap of paper. 'Steve Selby asked me to—'

I plucked the paper out of his fingers. 'I'll take that, thanks. Hadn't we better get going? Bye, Mum!'

Mum watched from the door as I darted down the path, closely followed by Ben to where his battered old mini was waiting.

'Sisters?' I said, raising an eyebrow.

Ben turned the key in the ignition and winked. 'What can I say? Flirting comes fitted as standard.'

'Unlike the suspension in this car.' I winced as we bounced over the potholes in my little street.

We drove through the twilight in easy silence and after only a few minutes, Ben pulled over in front of a pair of old metal gates that I'd never noticed before. He unlocked them, we drove through and as he jumped back out to lock them again, I realized that we were inside the grounds of Wickham Hall.

'We'll have to hurry,' he said, glancing up at the sky. Already the darkness had evaporated, leaving a milky blue light in its place. He jammed the car into first gear and we bumped along the track. 'Sunrise can only be minutes away.'

He stopped at the end of the track. We jumped out and Ben pulled a rug from the back seat. We ran over the dewy grass and up to the top of a hill, where he threw the rug down and I dropped down next to him, breathless and exhilarated.

It was the perfect spot. We were in the parkland on the edge of the Wickham estate: directly ahead of us, to the east, lay the hall, its terraces and gardens barely visible in the distance; to our left, the woodland and in front of that, the river meandered silently through the park. The show-ground, deserted at this time of day, was almost complete and I could see the white marquees clustered inside the temporary metal boundaries.

He turned and grinned, panting after our run. 'We made it.'

'With moments to spare, by the look of it,' I said.

The sky was an artist's dream: from inky navy way up high to the softest Tiffany blue on the horizon and every shade in between. Wisps of cloud marbled the sky, tinged candyfloss pink by an as yet invisible sun. And then I held my breath as a golden haze appeared over the turreted roofline of the hall followed by the perfect curve of an enormous golden globe.

'It's too beautiful,' I said, half laughing, 'I think I might cry.'

'Don't you dare, you'll set me off and I'm a very ugly crier.' Ben nudged my arm.

'It feels like the whole world is asleep except you and me,' I said. 'Our secret sunrise.'

'Not quite just you and me, look.' He pointed down the hill to where a fallow deer and her fawn were grazing on the silvery grass.

'Oh, Ben, how gorgeous!'

We watched them for a few minutes, the mother nuzzling her baby tenderly and then they wandered off to join the rest of the herd at the edge of the woods.

'Thank you for this. I . . . I think I'll remember my first dawn for the rest of my life,' I said softly.

'You're welcome.' He gazed at me with such warmth that I felt my heart swell with happiness.

'Some moments are like that,' he added. 'Not many. But when they happen you have to stop what you're doing

– snoring your head off, in your case,' he elbowed me in the ribs and I wriggled away from him, laughing, 'and be in them, really live in that moment. I never feel more alive than when I see the sun wake the earth like that.'

Esme had said something similar last month. What was it? Something about living in the moment because that was when the magic happens. She was right: being here with Ben in the stillness of the morning was magical.

'That's when the magic happens,' I murmured.

'Exactly.'

The sun was rising fast now, almost all of it visible above Wickham Hall. It had changed from orange to white, surrounded by a halo of light, and it was too bright to look at it. I glanced at Ben instead, his face suffused in soft golden shadows, his jawline dark with stubble and his eyes glistening and for a second I wondered if he was OK. He met my eye and smiled wistfully.

'Look at it, at that view. When I see Wickham Hall like this – on the dawn of a brand-new day – it looks so fresh and new I can almost see myself here for ever. I see possibilities and opportunities. And then . . .' He finished with a sigh and I felt his shoulders sag.

Not for the first time, I wondered what was behind this apparent reluctance to take over from his parents at Wickham Hall. Sometimes it almost felt as though he resented his inheritance and the legacy of privilege that went with it.

'And then what?' I asked, confused.

He raked a hand through his hair. 'And then the world wakes up and there are duties and expectations and structure and business as usual. And it's just not . . . me.'

'Welcome to the adult world, Ben,' I said wryly. I stood up and spread my arms out. 'For most people, the chance to call all this home would be a dream come true. It certainly would be for me.'

He stood too and faced me, his jaw tightening. He pressed his lips together and searched my face as though torn whether to confide in me.

'You've seen my home,' I said quietly, 'or at least the hall-way; and it doesn't get any better in the rest of the cottage. Mum can't let anything go, she hoards everything. I don't let people in; I don't even tell people about it. In fact, I'm not sure why I'm telling you any of this.'

'I did notice the stacks of newspapers inside the door.' He smiled softly.

'It has overshadowed my whole life, ever since I was a little girl. She has just begun to accept help and I'm hoping that . . .' I hesitated, wondering whether to tell him about the mystery man in the photograph. I decided against it. For now it was enough that he'd had a glimpse into my home life. Besides, I wanted to know more about him. 'Well, I'm hoping that things are going to get better soon.'

Ben placed his hands gently on my arms. 'It sounds like you've had a lot to deal with. And that's the counsellor that you mentioned?'

I nodded.

I held my breath as he leaned forward and pressed a kiss to my forehead.

'You're an amazing girl, Holly. And that explains why you're so organized at work. And why you almost hyper-ventilated when I made such a mess on my first day in the office.'

'I thought I coped very well, considering.' I grinned. 'Come on, let's go. I'm gasping for a cup of tea and you can tell me what's holding you back from taking over from your father.'

Ben scooped up the blanket, stuffed it under his arm and we ambled down the hill towards the car.

'Don't get me wrong, I'm proud of my heritage, my ancestry and the fact that the Fortescues have managed to hang on to Wickham Hall through the centuries when many other old properties have been sold off to pay death duties. But . . .'

'You don't like being told what to do,' I finished for him.

Ben unlocked the car and opened the passenger door for me.

'Have I ever told you about the school I helped build?'

'No!' I climbed in and waited for him to get in next to me, conscious that he was deflecting the conversation away from himself.

'It's in a tiny village in Cambodia called Mae Chang. I went out there as a volunteer when I was an art student. A group of us built a little secondary school and I've been going back there ever since. I teach art to the kids. These people have nothing. Nothing, Holly. Can you imagine?'

His eyes glinted as they bored into mine and I shook my head, mesmerized, as I tried to envisage him teaching Asian children under a hot red sky.

'It might sound clichéd and don't get me wrong, their life is tough – sometimes if crops fail or if the area floods, they suffer terribly – but they have taught me so much about what is important in life. And what's important to me is my art.'

'More important than Wickham Hall and your family?'

I turned to face him as he sucked in a breath.

'Couldn't you do both?'

He shook his head and blew out through the side of his mouth. 'I've never told anyone this . . .'

'Go on.'

'What it all boils down to is that I'm scared.'

'You? Scared?' I raised a quizzical eyebrow. 'I find that hard to believe.'

He waited until I was buckled in before starting the engine. 'When I'm in London at my studio, or meeting art gallery owners or out with friends, I'm Ben Fortescue the landscape artist. I'm confident in my world. But here I'm Benedict, only son of Lord Fortescue,' he shrugged, 'and those are pretty big shoes to fill. Particularly when it comes to taking over a successful estate. In a way it would be easier if the business was losing money, at least that would be a challenge. '

'But your feet are huge,' I exclaimed. 'Metaphorically speaking.'

Ben grinned at me. 'Thanks, I think. Come on, where to, m'lady?'

'There's a café open early in Henley,' I suggested. 'We could get breakfast there.'

He nodded and we set off more slowly over the bumpy track. I regarded his profile thoughtfully. 'But you will always be an artist, won't you? You've already painted one canvas since you've been back. You wouldn't have to give up your art totally?'

'If I take over from my father, it isn't just the hall I'd be heading up. There are other business interests, too, like property and stuff. I wouldn't have time to be creative; I'd be drained.'

'You're wrong, I'm sure of it,' I argued.

But he turned on the radio and started singing along to Katy Perry and I couldn't help laughing.

I looked out of the car window so that he couldn't read my expression. He was like sunshine, I thought, and I was a sunflower, tilting my face to bask in his light.

He was doing some strange form of dancing in his seat now and drumming his fingers on the steering wheel, in an attempt to attract my attention, and my cheeks ached with the effort of smothering my giggles.

Whether he was ready to admit it or not, he was the perfect choice to take over the running of Wickham Hall. He was charismatic, a natural leader, and he was as happy in the limelight as I was out of it. He didn't have to be stuck in an office if he didn't want to be. All he needed was the right person behind him to keep him organized.

I risked a look at him as he concentrated on the traffic lights ahead and felt a fluttering in the pit of my stomach.

I'd quite like that person to be me.

Chapter 18

The first day of the festival had dawned and miraculously the spell of fine weather continued. We were prepared for record visitor numbers, St John Ambulance was on standby to take care of any medical mishaps, there were drinks kiosks and ice-cream sellers dotted across the showground and we had erected a large shaded picnic area at the eleventh hour to provide some respite from the sun.

I checked the time again – two minutes to nine – and then glanced around me: everything and everyone was in place. Thank goodness. Gathered just inside the festival showground were the Fortescues, myself, Sheila, several marshals in official polo shirts and tabards and our official photographer. And on the other side of the extra-wide pearly white ribbon that Sheila and I had strung across the entrance between the two ticket booths was a pleasingly large throng of the general public.

'Are you ready for the onslaught?' Ben murmured close to my ear.

'As I'll ever be.' I nodded, taking in his smart linen suit. His cotton shirt was open at the neck and my eye was drawn to a tuft of dark hair just visible at his chest. I blinked and looked up. 'You scrub up well, I must say,' I said, tongue in cheek. 'Although I kind of miss the paint splashes in your hair.'

'Thanks.' He pretended to brush fluff off his jacket. 'Don't worry, three days and normal service will be resumed.'

I had bought three new outfits: one for each day of the festival. Today's choice was a sleeveless shift dress, which I hoped would help me to stay cool in the soaring temperatures that this morning's weather report had predicted.

'What about me?' I said, doing a twirl.

He cast his eyes down at my dress and pretended to contemplate my outfit. Served me right for digging for compliments, I thought, going pink.

'You'll do.' He grinned. 'Look, Holly, I've got to do the "heir to the throne" bit today, meeting and greeting Mum and Dad's cronies, a few press and whatever, but I'll keep my radio with me all day. There is usually a fair bit of running around on the first day. Please don't try to sort out every problem yourself. OK?'

'Roger that,' I said, bringing my own radio to my lips and pretending to talk into it. 'Over and out.'

He tutted and jabbed a finger light-heartedly. 'I'm serious, Holly. We're a team.'

'I hear you, boss,' I said, smiling at him.

He shook his head at me and walked over to his father, slapping him on the back. Lord Fortescue cupped a hand to his ear, straining to hear what his son was saying.

At the front of the crowd, a cute little girl with two missing front teeth was tweaking the wide satin ribbon longingly. I smiled at her, remembering the shoebox I used to keep under my bed, full of smoothed-out sheets of used wrapping paper and lengths of ribbon that I couldn't bear to part with.

The little girl caught my eye, dropped her hand from the ribbon instantly and crept behind her mum. I reached into my dress pocket for the spare piece of ribbon that I'd rolled up and handed it to her with a wink, my heart melting as her eyes lit up.

The church bells of St John's rang out, signalling the hour, and the crowd began to inch closer to us.

'The scissors, Sheila?' Lord Fortescue asked, turning to his secretary who handed over a pair of golden ceremonial scissors.

I glanced down at my clipboard, running through the itinerary for the umpteenth time. My stomach clenched just thinking about all the places I had to be and events I had to facilitate today. I thought back to my interview with Pippa just two months ago. How I'd longed to be part of the behind-the-scenes team. And here I was. My shoulders lifted and I let out a happy breath.

Lord Fortescue cleared his throat and a hush fell across the crowd.

'As some of you may know, this is the thirtieth festival since Lady Fortescue and I took over Wickham Hall.' He looked at his wife affectionately and chuckled. 'Although my wife doesn't appear to have aged a day!'

Lady Fortescue's face softened. 'Oh, Hugo.'

The ladies in the front of the crowd pressed hands to their chests and said 'Ahh', although I did hear one whispered suggestion of Botox.

'Thank you all, as ever, for your incredible support. On behalf of my wife and I, we hope you all have a marvellous day and without further ado, I declare this year's Summer Festival open.'

I joined in with the hearty round of applause as Lord Fortescue snipped at the pearly white ribbon with the official scissors and held his position with a smile while the photographer from the *Stratford Gazette* took her shot.

People surged forward, eager to be amongst the first visitors inside the showground and the Fortescues were led away to pose for more pictures in front of Nikki's commemorative geranium flower bed. I ticked off items one and two – ribbon cutting and photo opportunity – on my clipboard and decided to do a lap of the festival, to check all the exhibitors were happy.

I had been here since seven o'clock, making myself available for last-minute queries, of which there had been plenty. In fact, I'd been here early every day this week, as had Ben. But it had paid off, I thought contentedly, as I strolled through the centre of the festival. Visitors were streaming in now, the atmosphere was buzzing and a queue had already formed at the coffee kiosk.

Up ahead, I spotted Nikki sprinting across the path with a watering can in each hand so I headed over to the pearl garden to see if she was OK.

I adored what she and her team had done with this show garden. It was essentially a water feature with plants set around a picturesque pond, the centrepiece of which was a large fibreglass oyster shell, open to reveal an oversized pearl. The plants she had chosen were a serene mix of white flowers, silver grasses and green foliage. I felt cooler simply being in amongst them.

But my heart lurched when I caught sight of Nikki. She looked anything but serene. She was red-faced and her T-shirt was clinging to her in sweaty patches.

'Nikki?' I said in horror, catching hold of her arm. 'What's happened?'

'Bloody disaster!' she groaned, wiping the sweat off her forehead with a hanky. 'One of our volunteers hasn't turned up – food poisoning, apparently. He was supposed to be here early to water this morning. Now everything is drooping. At this rate the pearl garden won't last the morning, let alone the three days of the festival.'

I eyed the plants: now she mentioned it, some of them did look a bit limp.

'I've got no staff based here and I've radioed for assistance but no one's free to help. And that celebrity gardener, Suzanna Merryweather, will be arriving any minute and look at the state of me.'

She made a sobbing noise and turned away towards the water tanks so I couldn't see her face.

'Here, give me the watering can,' I said, dropping my radio and clipboard on the ground. 'I can do this. You go and have a drink, a rest, freshen up and come back in time to meet Suzanna. Her first stint in the indoor arena is, um,' I bent to look at my clipboard, 'one o'clock. Plenty of time to show her round the Wickham Hall gardens before then.'

She eyed me doubtfully. 'Are you sure?'

I smiled reassuringly. 'It's water, Nikki, not even I can get that wrong.'

'Cheers, Hols, you're a mate.' She sighed, passing me a heavy watering can.

She showed me how to operate the taps on the water tanks and then produced a four-leaf clover from her pocket. 'To bring you luck for your first festival,' she said, pressing it into my hand. 'I found it this morning in the wild flower meadow.'

I thanked her and slipped it under the top sheet of my clipboard and Nikki strode away to get cleaned up.

'Leave it to me,' I called confidently, swinging the watering can in my right arm and promptly smearing dirt on the side of my new dress. Damn.

As I bent to examine the mark a familiar voice cried out: 'Don't touch it!'

I whirled round, slopping water over my shoes, to find Mum standing at the side of the garden. She was looking very summery in a brightly coloured maxi dress and flip-flops, her hair pinned up with a variety of combs and clips and held off her face with large sunglasses.

'Let it dry and it'll brush off,' she said, stepping over the rope barricade that surrounded the show garden. 'Rub at it now and the stain will be nigh on impossible to shift.'

'Thanks, Mum,' I said, kissing her cheek. 'When will I stop relying on you for help, do you think?'

'Never, hopefully, darling,' she said, stroking my face with the back of her finger. 'And I'm sure I rely on you more.'

My heart twisted at the note of sadness in her voice.

'In that case, I don't suppose you fancy a job, do you?' I said, handing her a watering can.

I explained the situation and the two of us began watering the pearl garden companionably.

'I'm quite envious of you being at Wickham Hall, you know,' Mum confided as we refilled our watering cans for the second time at the tank. 'I always thought I'd end up here.'

'Did you?' I glanced at her.

She nodded. 'Yes, but it didn't work out.'

She straightened up, pushed a loose strand of hair from her face with the back of her hand and shrugged.

'What happened?' I asked, wondering where this was leading.

'I was offered a job as a tour guide but I had to turn it down.'

I could feel my pulse beginning to race. 'Why, Mum?'

'Because they couldn't offer me enough hours. They close over the winter, don't they? And I needed a regular income. Plus, they wanted someone to work at weekends and I couldn't because I had you to look after. So that was that.' She sighed and marched over to the water tank to top up her watering can.

I exhaled. For a moment there I thought I was about to hear some major piece of news.

'You'd have thought they'd have designed a better irrigation system for this garden, seeing as there's a great big pond in the middle of it,' she grumbled, changing the subject.

'We've nearly finished now,' I said. 'I'm so glad you were here to help, though. I hope I haven't held you up?'

'No, love. I'd just watched Lady Fortescue unveil a gift from her husband before spotting you,' said Mum, stretching towards the bamboo plants at the back of the border.

'Oh knickers, I wanted to see that,' I tutted.

I nipped over to my clipboard and struck through item three on my itinerary. Lord Fortescue had commissioned a local furniture maker to make a love seat for his wife, carved from an oak tree that had been felled on the estate. Eventually it would be placed in her favourite spot in the gardens, but for now, it was mounted on a plinth at the festival for visitors to see.

'Such a romantic gesture,' said Mum dreamily. 'I'm quite envious of Her Ladyship, I must admit; imagine having one man in love with you, forsaking all others, till death do you part . . . Amazing.'

I swallowed. It probably wasn't the right time to bring this up, but when would be the right time . . . ?

'Is that how you felt about my father?'

Mum instantly snapped out of her reverie and dropped

the watering can. 'Gosh, Holly, that question came out of the blue. It was such a long time ago, I . . .' She fanned a hand across her face.

I had the photograph with me in an envelope ready to give back to Steve if I saw him. I pulled it from my clipboard and opened the envelope. My heart pounded as I handed her the print.

'Is this him, Mum? Is this my father?'

Mum's eyes grew round as I pointed to the girl I'd identified as her. Her face crumpled and she pressed a hand to her mouth. 'Where did you get this? Who took the picture?'

'Is it him?' I repeated.

'Yes,' she murmured. 'That's him.'

'Please, Mum,' I said in a shaky voice. 'I want to know the whole story.'

She ran her tongue round her lips and nodded, not dragging her eyes from the picture for a second. 'OK. I'll tell you. But not here.'

'Tonight then, at home?'

She dropped her sunglasses down over her eyes. 'Yes, love, tonight.'

My stomach fizzed as I pulled her into a hug; in a few more hours, I'd know the truth. Finally.

'Oh, Holly,' she whispered, 'I miss having someone special in my life and I worry I've left it too late.'

My gorgeous mum; I could have cried for her.

'I don't think you realize how lovely you are,' I said, pressing a kiss into her hair.

'Ignore me, I'm a silly old fool and I'm spoiling your day.' She sniffed and rooted around in her handbag for a tissue.

'Mum, you're only forty-seven and I'd love you to meet someone.'

'I'm hardly much of a catch, am I, darling?' she said,

dabbing her eyes. She handed me a clean tissue. 'That mud should be dry now.'

I peered at her out of the corner of my eye as I brushed my dress down. We were beginning to get to the root of her hoarding, I was sure of it. Perhaps then she'd feel more confident about herself. Maybe our big talk tonight would help, too.

'Excuse me?'

I looked across to the entrance of the pearl garden to see a boy in baggy jeans with a camera around his neck.

'Hi,' I said.

'Do you mind if I come in to the garden and take some close-ups of the oyster shell?'

'Sure, help yourself.' I smiled.

He beckoned to two others – students by the look of them – and the three of them began taking pictures. Of course . . .

'Are you students at Hathaway College?' I asked.

But before they could respond another deeper voice answered for them. 'They are indeed. Hello again, Holly.'

I turned to find myself face to face with Steve. He was even more tanned than when I'd seen him a few weeks ago and his eyes crinkled merrily as he shook my hand.

'Steve, how lovely to see you!' I said and then lowered my voice, turning my back on Mum. 'I haven't had a chance to ask my mum yet about those back issues of the newspaper we talked about and she's a bit sensitive so . . .'

'That is your Mum?' exclaimed Steve, his eyes out on stalks. 'Wow, she's . . . very . . . young.'

I heard a snigger from the group of students and pretended not to notice Steve's face colour a bit more.

'Mum?' I turned back to her.

'This is my mum, Lucy,' I took a deep breath, 'and this is

Steve. He's the photographer who covered the festival for the *Wickham and Hoxley News* for years. He's interested in seeing your collection of old issues.'

'My newspapers!' Mum raised her eyebrows.

'That's right, Lucy,' said Steve, pumping her hand. 'If your archives are as extensive as Holly intimated, I think you could be sitting on a very valuable resource.'

'Oh goodness, I'd better get going,' I squeaked, suddenly conscious of the time. Suzanna Merryweather would be arriving soon and I wanted to be there to meet her taxi. I left Mum and Steve having an animated discussion about the fire that had destroyed the old newspaper building and they didn't even notice me go.

I looked over my shoulder as I turned the corner: Mum had pushed her sunglasses up into her hair and seemed to be hanging on Steve's every word.

Hurray, I thought, allowing myself a small smile, maybe a bit of encouragement from Steve is just the push she needs.

Chapter 19

When I reached the festival entrance, I found Jim patrolling the area between the ticket booths. He didn't appear to be carrying out any official role but was happily producing lollipops from his pocket for children and pointing visitors in the direction of the toilets.

Edith Nibbs in the gift shop had confided in me recently that Lord Fortescue kept her and Jim on purely because no one could imagine Wickham Hall without them (which incidentally made me admire all three of them a little bit more). So 'head of security' was a nominal title: all the major events such as this one had external contractors looking after the big stuff, but Jim still liked to make himself useful.

'Hello, Jim! Quite a queue now,' I said, taking in the crowd of people waiting to enter. It stretched along the makeshift wooden path and down towards the car park.

'It's the weather, love,' he said, lifting up his baseball cap to wipe his forehead. 'Brings 'em out in droves. We could be in for record visitor numbers, I reckon.'

'I hope so, but I'm guessing you're waiting for one particular visitor.'

He held his hands up and chuckled. 'Guilty as charged.'

I smiled, feeling my body relax in his company as usual. Jim was one of my favourite people at Wickham Hall and I often found myself seeking his advice. He knew so much about the place: where the secret doors were in the hall – the ones that weren't revealed to the public – what time the café was likely to have spare cake going begging, and last week he'd shown me a clearing in the woods where a litter of fox cubs liked to come and play, which was one of the most enchanting things I'd ever witnessed. I'd found out that Jim had bought three signed copies of Suzanna Merryweather's book: one for himself and two as Christmas presents. 'Who wouldn't want to find Suzanna in your Christmas stocking?' he'd chortled.

'You don't mind if I hang around for her autograph, do you?' he asked sheepishly, pulling a notebook out of his pocket. 'I've come prepared.'

'Of course not!' I grinned, looping my arm through his. 'Come on, let's walk down to the road; she'll be here soon.'

We pushed our way through the crowd while he recalled the time he'd seen Dolly Parton at the airport in 1977. He hadn't had any paper for her to sign except for his boarding pass, so she autographed it but he had to surrender it to the cabin crew on the aeroplane and had kicked himself ever since. Suddenly we heard a commotion ahead of us and a little dog appeared through a sea of legs at our feet.

'Oh dear.' Jim tutted. 'A lost dog. We always get one or two who escape their lead.'

The little dog, a white and brown Jack Russell, jumped up at Jim and wagged its tail.

I bent down to stroke it and read the engraved bone in its leather collar. 'He's called Lucky. Any sign of the owners?'

Jim and I scanned the people around us, but no one came forward.

'Jim, can you take him to the festival office for me?' I pleaded. 'Sheila can put an announcement out over the PA system. And get him some water. I daren't go in case I miss—'

We both stared as a black cab pulled up as close to the festival entrance as it could get.

'That's Suzanna Merryweather,' I said.

Jim's face lifted and then fell and he swallowed. 'Of course, I'll take the dog,' he said stoically. 'You go and meet Suzanna; I'll sort this out.'

My heart twanged for him; I couldn't possibly deprive him of his chance to meet his idol. Especially not after that Dolly Parton story.

I scooped up the dog under one arm, still clutching my clipboard under the other.

'Come on, we'll both go and meet Suzanna. Lucky can come too. Then we'll all go to the office together. That way you still get your autograph.'

'Right you are!' Jim punched the air.

We scurried back up the path with Lucky and made it to the taxi just as Suzanna Merryweather alighted from the rear door.

'Hello, Suzanna!' I beamed, juggling my assorted cargo as I attempted to shake her hand. 'Welcome to Wickham Hall.'

She was dressed simply in a white cotton sundress; her face seemed free from make-up and her blonde hair was scooped up in a ponytail. Big inquisitive eyes peered out from under a heavy fringe. She broke into a huge smile when she saw the dog.

'Oh, look at you, mister!' she cooed, instantly taking him off me. 'Is he yours?'

I introduced myself and Jim and Lucky and the curious crowd parted to let us through while Jim recounted the tale of Lucky's escape from his owner.

'Well, I think this might just be our first photo opportunity of the day, Jim. Lucky and I, with Jim the dog rescuer. What do you think, Holly?' Suzanna beamed.

I was thrilled for Jim. He was pink-eared, besotted and overcome with happiness, and I left them in the festival office being looked after by Sheila just as Lucky's owners turned up to collect him.

There was a bandstand ahead, which was currently un-occupied, so I headed for it. Sunlight still filtered through the ivy-covered roof but at least there was partial shade. I perched on the edge for a moment and massaged my temple. I had been exposed to the sun for almost four hours now, my neck felt sore and I had a sneaking suspicion that I was on the verge of a headache.

I checked my itinerary and cringed inwardly; goodness, I was supposed to have spent the last hour with the official festival photographer but I hadn't seen her since the ribbon-cutting ceremony. I was sure she'd be fine; I had sent her a list of the pictures we needed, but even so, I felt bad for abandoning her. Never mind, I decided, getting to my feet, I'd arrange to meet her at the indoor arena later for the start of the charity auction where she could take pictures of Lord Fortescue with the gavel in his hand. If all else failed, I would see her then.

Right now I needed a drink. If I didn't have water soon, my tongue would be hanging out like Lucky's, not to mention the fact that I was feeling a bit light-headed. I set off in search of some water and was almost at the refreshment stall when there was a tap on my shoulder.

'Holly!'

I whirled round to see Jenny dressed in a purple polka-dot dress, her hair flowing loosely.

'I've never seen those before!' I grinned, pointing at her bare legs.

'I'm front of house at the outdoor restaurant,' she explained. 'No need for chef whites today.'

'But no pockets for hidden treats,' I said, pulling a sad face.

'No.' She folded her arms. 'I'm not in the mood for treats, anyway. Do you know we've only got eight bookings for lunch?'

Eek, that was low.

'I didn't know that, no.' I sighed.

'Can you do something about it, do you think?'

'Um . . .' I thought briefly about Ben making me promise not to tackle every problem by myself, but then I remembered what Pippa had said at my interview: the Fortescues were the public faces of Wickham Hall and today Ben was doing his job. It was up to me to do mine.

'I'll go back to the festival office and print out some flyers to hand out at the ticket booths,' I offered. 'That should spread the word.'

'Thanks,' she said flatly.

'Jenny,' I smiled, making an effort to be upbeat, 'it's only eleven thirty; there's plenty of time yet and don't forget that Lord Fortescue is coming with two guests.'

Jenny shrugged, unimpressed. 'All right, eleven. Still not enough.'

'And as soon as passing trade sees those lucky eleven diners, they'll be snapping your hand off for a table.'

She cocked her head. 'But there isn't any passing trade,' she said sarcastically, 'because you made the restaurant

218

secluded and exclusive. Remember?'

I swallowed. To be fair that was Ben's idea but I didn't want to drop him in it. I opened my mouth, hoping that something soothing would emerge but instead my radio crackled into life.

'Sheila to Holly. Over.'

Excuse me, I mouthed to Jenny. 'Go ahead, Sheila.'

I grinned. I couldn't help it. I loved having a radio. So much.

'Please can you locate Jenny and tell her that Lord Fortescue has to cancel lunch. Repeat *cancel* his lunch. She's not answering her radio.'

Jenny threw her hands up. 'Oh, well, that's just fantastic, that's just the icing on the cake. I might as well go home now and turn my quail egg *amuse-bouches* into egg and ham sandwiches.'

I grimaced. 'Will do, Sheila.'

'Tell him I've done his favourite,' Jenny hissed, 'as a surprise. Sea bass and fennel.'

She grabbed the radio from me and brought it to her lips. 'Sheila, tell him sea bass and fennel. Over?'

'He's not here,' came Sheila's crackly reply.

Jenny thrust the radio back at me and scowled. I was fumbling around for words to placate her when Mum appeared in my peripheral vision walking alongside Steve. *Steve!*

'Mum! Mum!' I waved.

The two of them sauntered over.

'You like sea bass and fennel, don't you?' I said, winking desperately.

'Er, yes?' She looked sideways at Steve.

I flicked a glance at Steve. 'Are you two planning on having lunch together?'

Steve raised his eyebrows questioningly at Mum, who smiled coyly and nodded.

'Excellent, book them in, Jenny. My treat. Thanks, Mum.'

I waved them away, possibly a little abruptly, but my nerves were getting frayed. 'There, that's two more. Will that do?'

I swayed and clutched my head, almost falling into the path of one of the quad bikes that were driving round the festival emptying dustbins and collecting litter.

'Steady on, matey.' Jenny grabbed my shoulders. 'Time for you to take a break, Miss Swift, and escape from this heat for a bit. And I'm sorry I'm a bit snarly, it's the anniversary of my dad's death today. Not that that's an excuse; I'm just having a bad day.'

'Oh, I'm sorry, Jenny. No need to apologize.' I gave her a hug and to my horror her eyes started to fill with tears. 'Come on.'

I pulled her by the arm to the nearest bench and we sat down.

'I miss him, Holly. So much.' She shook her head and wiped at the tears. 'We did everything together. Mum used to say that she sometimes felt left out, we were so close. Dad and I never worked here together – he retired before I started in the kitchens – but I like to think it's something we shared. And he loved the festival, never missed a single day of it. He always brought me here when I was little. He'd have loved seeing me in my own outdoor restaurant. He'd have been so proud.'

I took her hand and patted it.

'Of course he would. You're lucky to have such happy memories of him. I didn't know my dad at all. Never met him once.'

Jenny blinked at me. 'That's sad, Holly; I'm sorry.'

'Funnily enough, the one thing I do know about him is

that he was here thirty years ago. At the festival. I guess we have this place in common, so my dad and I share it, too.'

We smiled at each other and Jenny squeezed my hand. 'I'm sure he'd have been proud of you too.'

She stood then and walked back to the restaurant; I slipped the photograph out of its envelope and stared at it for a few seconds. I truly hoped so.

For the next hour I was kept on my toes: running off some simple leaflets advertising Jenny's outdoor restaurant and delivering them to the ticket booths, taking the lovely Suzanna to meet our very own Nikki Logan for a garden tour, dealing with disappointed *Green Fingers* fans who hadn't got tickets to the indoor arena to hear Suzanna's first talk, reuniting three misplaced handbags, two missing children and a teddy bear with their owners and managing to sit down for a grand total of three minutes and two swigs of water.

At fifteen minutes to one I presented myself, a bit nervously, at the VIP tent, where I had been told that Ben was unveiling his photographic exhibition to Lord and Lady Fortescue.

Large screens had been erected along the back of the tent. They were covered collage-style in a timeline of large photographs from 1984 onwards. It had taken Ben hours to do and I knew how happy he was with the result and by the expressions on his parents' faces so were they.

I kept in the background and waited for an opportune moment to interrupt while Ben talked them through how he'd found all the old pictures.

'Bravo, Benedict!' Lord Fortescue beamed.

'Darling, it's wonderful!' Lady Fortescue exclaimed,

resting her fingertips on her lips. 'You couldn't have expressed your commitment to the family in a stronger way.'

'It was *your* commitment that I wanted to celebrate, Mum,' Ben insisted. 'You two had a vision for Wickham Hall and made it the success it is.'

'But it took us years, Benedict, thirty years,' Lord Fortescue pointed out. 'It didn't happen overnight and you'll bring your own personality to the hall, just as every other Fortescue has.'

'No, Dad,' Ben shook his head vehemently, 'I couldn't compete with what you've achieved.'

'Nonsense,' Lord Fortescue retorted. 'The estate is ready for new blood.'

'I think that might be going a bit far, Hugo,' Lady Fortescue chided gently. 'I adore being lady of the manor at these things.'

'No, no,' Lord Fortescue shook his head, 'we're ready for a quiet life away from the public eye. All Benedict needs to do is—'

'Dad, let's not get into this today,' Ben interrupted, ruffling a hand through his hair.

I decided that this was probably a good time to intervene and cleared my throat.

'Hello, Holly.' Lady Fortescue smiled. 'You look as though you're enjoying the festival, you're rather flushed.'

'Oh, yes, Lady Fortescue, very much.' I pressed a hand to my hot face – actually, my clammy face. 'I wondered if I might borrow Lord Fortescue? It's time for the charity auction.'

Sheila had advised me to collect him personally rather than just let him know what time he needed to be there. 'It's not that he deliberately misses things. I don't think, anyway,' she'd added. 'He's just easily distracted and of course he's hard of hearing.'

She had also said that I shouldn't accept any excuses from him not to come with me, that it was a time-honoured tradition that he introduced the first few lots at the auction and the charity depended on the exuberant bidding that his presence produced.

'Yes, Hugo, you must go,' Lady Fortescue said, brushing the lapels of her husband's blazer.

'Good lord!' stuttered Lord Fortescue, running a hand over his hair. He was staring at the mobile phone in his hand.

I suppressed a smile; whenever he said that it always seemed to me as if he was patting himself on the back for a good deed.

'What is it, Hugo?' Lady Fortescue enquired affectionately.

'A hoopoe!' He gazed around, a look of joy on his face. 'I don't believe it! A hoopoe, Beatrice! This is indeed a special day.'

He grabbed her face and kissed her cheeks.

He was such a sweetie, I thought.

'A who what?' Ben laughed and rolled his eyes at me. I grinned back.

'Just had a text from a birding chum. There's a Madagascan hoopoe heading this way, apparently.' He whipped his head up from his phone and dropped it in his pocket. 'Must have been aiming for southern Europe and overshot. Right. I'm off.'

He began to stride to the exit of the marquee, muttering under his breath about this being such a rare treat. 'Oh,' he whirled round and tapped his nose, 'mum's the word, though. Don't mention it to a soul. We don't want all and sundry turning up with their binoculars.'

My shoulders sagged and a sudden wave of tiredness flooded me. 'But the auction . . .'

'Come on.' Ben grabbed me and steered me towards the edge of the marquee away from the Fortescues' gathered guests. 'This isn't like you. What's up?'

'Your father is supposed to start the bidding in the auction. It's a time-honoured tradition, apparently. What am I going to tell the charity?' I pressed a hand to my hot face. Lady Fortescue was right: I was flushed.

Ben grinned at me and shrugged. 'I'll do it instead. How hard can it be?'

I could have kissed him. 'Thank you,' I breathed. 'Gosh, I'm so hot, can we get out of this tent?'

'Sure,' he frowned, leading me outside.

'You're a lifesaver,' I said weakly, as we made our way to the indoor arena.

He nudged me with his elbow. 'I knew it. I knew I would crack that steely exterior one day.'

'Me?' I said, feeling peculiar all of a sudden. The people around me were zooming in and out of focus and they sounded like they were underwater. 'I'm as soft as . . . as . . .'

And then everything went black.

Chapter 20

I don't know. One minute she was talking and the next . . . blurrgh. Sunstroke . . . On her feet all day . . . St John Ambulance . . . Can someone fetch some water . . . ?

Muffled voices floated above me from miles away, across the sea maybe or down the telephone. Someone shook me gently and I groaned, not wanting to wake up, and then one voice pierced through the general noise.

'Holly? Holly, can you hear me?'

When I opened my eyes I was lying on the ground. A crowd had formed around me but there was Ben, hovering over me, his nose almost touching mine. The sun was directly behind him, glinting through his curls. The brightness hurt my eyes and I had to squint to look up at him.

'Hello again.' He was grinning and I made an attempt to smile back. 'You had me going for a second there.'

He was kneeling beside me, holding one of my hands.

'What happened?' I croaked.

'You took one look at my chiselled jaw and fainted.'

I made a noise somewhere between a laugh and a sob and tried to remember what knickers I was wearing in case my dress had ridden up.

Ben addressed the sea of faces that was still looming

above me. 'I think she's OK, folks. Let's just give her some air.'

The crowd melted away and he searched around on the ground for my dropped radio and turned away while he spoke to someone. I took the opportunity to check out the dress situation; it was fine. I may have lost my dignity by collapsing in public, but at least my choice of lingerie was still a private concern. I patted my dress pocket; my phone was still there.

'Holly, do you think you need medical attention?' Ben asked.

I shook my head, which really hurt. 'Ouch. I don't think so. Just take me somewhere cool. And quiet,' I whispered, clutching my forehead. More than anything I wanted to be out of the heat and out of public view. I'd chosen a particularly busy place to faint – in the aisle between the indoor arena and the children's face-painting stand – and people were rubbernecking as they passed by.

He grinned. 'There's a pub I know off the Portobello Road . . .'

I pushed myself up to sitting and chuckled, making myself feel woozy again. 'Oh, head rush.'

Ben winced. 'Sorry. Just hold on, I'll get you out of here.'

He radioed for one of the refuse collectors to come to our location, which was slightly worrying, and then helped me to my feet, keeping one of his arms around my waist. He led me to the edge of the aisle, out of the path of onlookers.

I remembered the charity auction with a jolt.

'You need to go. Auction starting,' I mumbled, my dry mouth fumbling to form a sentence.

A lady arrived with a bottle of water and I took it gratefully. The cold liquid ran straight down my throat and into my empty stomach and made me shiver.

'Do you think I'd leave you on your own when you've got a green face?' he chided softly and nodded towards the face-painting stand. 'You look like you've asked for a "Kermit".'

'Green?'

He nodded. 'I'd ask for a refund if I were you, it appears to be fading already.'

'Good.' I took another sip of water and exhaled. 'That's better. I've got my power of speech back.'

'Excellent.' Ben winced. 'Anyway, I can't go anywhere; you're gripping me too tight.'

'Am I?' I looked down to where my fingers were leaving white marks on his wrist and eased off slightly. 'Sorry.'

'And forget the auction; the chap from the charity is sorting it out. Oh look, your chariot awaits.'

A quad bike pulled up beside us and one of the refuse collectors jumped down and handed Ben the keys.

'Cheers, mate. I'll leave it up at the hall.'

The driver scooped up the bin liners full of rubbish from the back of the quad bike and Ben helped me up to the rear part of the seat, climbing on in front of me. We set off slowly through the crowd towards the exit, Ben tooting the horn at people in our path, me clasping my arms loosely around him. I inhaled his familiar citrusy scent and allowed myself to relax against him for a moment before remembering something . . .

I tapped his back. 'Ben! The itinerary, my clipboard!'

I must have left it on the path where I fell.

He shook his head. 'Forget the clipboard. For once, OK? Just—'

'If you dare say "live for the moment", I might have to thump you,' I grumbled.

'And normal service is resumed.' Ben laughed and I felt

the vibrations through his ribs and into my arms.

We drove on, taking the long route as Ben tried to avoid the bumps across the parkland and away from the noise of the festival and the bustling crowds and on towards the hall. The plume of the fountain sparkled ahead of us and I sat quietly, enjoying the ride, as my body gradually returned to normal. This was better, I thought, leaning my cheek against his back, definitely much better.

Ben would probably have to drop me at the hall and then go straight back to his duties at the festival and I realized that I didn't want him to leave me. Not just yet.

'Do you mind if we don't go back to the hall?' I said over his shoulder. 'Can we go to the sunken garden instead?'

'Sure.'

Ben changed direction and we headed left past the maze and the wild flower meadow and he stopped the quad bike at the edge of the sunken garden. This was my favourite part of the grounds; it was the furthest away from the hall and very restful. Even today when there were thousands of extra visitors at Wickham Hall, it was very quiet: just one or two groups of people strolled amongst the paths and under flower-covered arches.

'You look much better, I'm glad to report,' Ben said, helping me down from the leather seat. 'Your freckles are back. They disappeared for a few minutes under the green.'

'Thank you, Dr Benedict.' I grinned.

'You had me really worried.' He frowned.

What a sweetie. He looked genuinely concerned and I leaned forward to give him a hug when I remembered: Ben was my boss, he felt duty-bound to look after me. That was all. My heart drooped a little.

'Sorry,' I said, giving him a bright smile. 'I'm fine now. I'd been rushing around in the heat and I hadn't had anything to drink; all my own silly fault.'

I turned and walked down the wide stone steps that led to the cool shade of the sunken garden and onto the gravel path and Ben followed behind. My legs still felt a bit wobbly and when we reached an oak bench I sank down immediately.

Ben sat beside me, sighing contentedly. 'Well, this is nice,' he said, stretching out his legs.

I looked sideways at him and grinned. 'I give you thirty seconds before you start jiggling your leg or pulling leaves off that ivy.'

'No, no,' he said, sliding up the bench towards me. He took hold of my wrist and pretended to take my pulse. 'I'm quite happy to do my doctor bit for a while longer. Let's just sit here quietly. I want to be completely sure you've recovered before either of us goes anywhere. If that's all right with you?'

His habitual grin had been replaced with a solemn gaze and I nodded slowly at him. It was just as well he wasn't a real doctor: my pulse was galloping and my legs were even more wobbly now that his firm thigh was pressed up against mine.

I hadn't been this close to a man for ages. My last boyfriend had been Simon the fitness instructor from Eden Spa and that had finished over a year ago. There was my dentist, of course. He was a man. And he made my pulse race, but only in a scary, what-are-you-doing-with-that-drill sort of way. This was a more delicious type of racing. It was nice. Better than nice. My insides felt quivery in a good way and I had fizzing sensations in my stomach that I hadn't felt for a long, long time.

'Well, that all seems to be in order,' Ben said, releasing my wrist. 'My mouth's gone a bit dry, do you mind . . . ?'

He gestured towards my water bottle and I handed it over. He began to unscrew the lid and I stared at it, wondering if he would wipe it before putting it to his lips.

He didn't.

My lips had touched that bottle. Oh my God, what was I thinking? I felt my face flush.

'So that's two of your wishes I've made come true: watching the sunrise and riding a quad bike.' He raised a smug eyebrow and took another sip of water.

'Quite the genie, aren't you? If I rub your lamp will you grant me my third wish?'

Was it just me or did that sound rude?

Ben choked on his water. Maybe not just me.

I took the bottle from him and swigged at it to cover my embarrassment and managed to slosh water on my chin. He leaned across and wiped the drips away with his thumb. One of his curls, like an uncoiled spring, fell over his eye and without thinking, I brushed it away.

We were inches apart. Touching each other's faces.

'You want a *third* wish?' he murmured. 'And what would that be?'

We both lowered our hands and stared at each other and my breath caught in my throat.

I had only known Ben for a month. One month since he burst into my life, trouserless, outside his sister's wedding. Not long at all. And yet so much had changed. I didn't mean all the stuff I now knew about Mum and my father. I meant me. I felt a brighter, more alive version of myself when he was around. It was almost impossible to remember what I used to smile about before he arrived.

And suddenly I knew what my third wish would be: I

wished I had the courage to lean forward and kiss him. Or even better for him to kiss me. Or both, in which case that would be wishes three and four . . .

But that wasn't going to happen, was it? He was just being kind because I'd fainted. I might have to resort to fainting more often. Maybe that should be my wish . . . a daily faint into Ben's arms.

'Earth to Holly?' Ben grinned.

I stood up and pulled him to his feet, breaking the moment before my thoughts strayed into more dangerous territory. 'We should be getting back to the festival.'

'Come on, what's your third wish? I want to know your deepest desires,' he persisted, taking my arm and linking it through his. 'And no, we shouldn't. Doctor Benedict's orders.'

I looked down at our joined arms.

'In case you still feel weak.' One side of his mouth lifted in a sheepish smile and a little bubble of joy burst inside me.

'Um, my deepest desires?' I mused aloud. *Your lips on mine. Right now.* Better not tell him that. Might make Monday morning in the office a tad awkward, I'd have to think of something else. 'I'll tell you mine if you tell me yours.'

'Deal.' He shot me a cheeky grin. 'You first.'

We headed towards a trellised walkway laced with thousands of delicate wisteria fronds, a froth of lilac on every side. It was breathtakingly beautiful but it was a bit lost on me because Ben's arm was touching mine and my stomach was all fluttery and—

I pulled myself back sharply from my reverie. What was I doing, getting all tingly about Ben? This was Benedict Fortescue, the next lord of Wickham Hall, and I was Holly Swift from Weaver's Cottage; he was so far out of my league it was laughable. Only I didn't feel like laughing . . . I let out a tiny moan.

'Holly?' Ben's voice was soft with concern. 'You're not feeling faint again, are you?'

'Sleeping in a four-poster bed,' I blurted. 'Waking up at Wickham Hall in a four-poster bed. That was always my dream when I was a little girl. There. That's my third wish.'

We had reached the end of the wisteria walkway and Ben stopped and turned to me.

'You ask a lot of your genie.' His deep brown eyes twinkled at me. 'But it can be arranged.'

Something in his tone made the heat rise to my face and it dawned on me that I'd effectively just asked for a sleepover at his house.

He must think I'm a lunatic.

'Thank you for looking after me, for rescuing me, but I really must get back to the festival,' I stuttered, untangling myself from his arm.

He caught hold of my hand and raised an eyebrow. 'Not so fast, Miss Swift. You haven't heard my wish yet.'

I exhaled, trying to calm my breathing, and smiled. 'Of course. How rude.'

He stepped closer and tucked a strand of my hair behind my ear. 'I wish you'd have dinner with me. On Saturday night.'

'Dinner?' I swallowed. *Dinner to celebrate the end of the festival or dinner as in a date?* 'Why?'

He chuckled and scuffed his toe on the ground and then gave me the sweetest, shyest smile I'd ever seen. My insides melted and I was very tempted to cover his lips with wishes three, four, five and possibly six.

'I like you. Very much. And everything I know about you so far has only made me more intrigued and I want to get to know you better. Plus,' he paused and held my gaze, 'you're so single-minded and determined about everything and I find that very . . . appealing.'

You know when you roast a marshmallow over an open fire and your face goes pink from the heat and then you bite into the middle and it's all gooey? Well, all of that.

'It's very kind of you to invite your employee out for dinner but there's really no need—'

He blew out a sharp breath and frowned. 'I'm not— this has nothing to do with you being an employee and everything to do with you being a very lovely girl.'

My heart skipped a beat. *Dinner as in date, then. Because I am a lovely girl. Yippee!*

'Ben,' I said kindly, trying to ignore the bubbles of excitement in my tummy, 'I'm flattered. But you're aristocracy, I'm staff. Would Lord and Lady Fortescue be happy if they knew you'd asked me out on a date?'

He opened his mouth and there it was: a tiny hesitation, so tiny that I almost missed it. But it was there and my heart sank. 'It's nothing to do with them.'

I gave him a sad smile and turned to walk towards the lily pond. Ben leapt forward and twisted me round to face him, his eyes boring into mine.

'Holly, listen. You are a breath of fresh air. Most girls I meet are more interested in the fact that I'm expected to inherit Wickham Hall than in me. Which is a bit of a blow to the ego.'

I smiled up at him. 'I can imagine. But you must have met some girls who aren't like that.'

He gave this some thought. 'True. My last girlfriend, Sam, wasn't interested in Wickham Hall, but then she wasn't interested in art either and as I wasn't into horses, we ran out of things to talk about after six months.'

I held out my arms. 'I don't know much about art either. Except that I like yours.'

'There you go; you have an eye for talent.' He grinned. He caught hold of my fingers.

I shook my head sadly. 'We're worlds apart, Ben.'

He brought my hands up to his mouth and kissed my fingers lightly. 'Holly. Can we . . . ? Let's forget that for a moment. And just be Ben and Holly.'

I paused and blinked at him. Being attracted to my boss wasn't in the plan. But it seemed to have happened anyway and maybe this was another of those unplanned magical moments that I needed to just go along with. And maybe I was being a bit harsh on Lord and Lady Fortescue: they were nice people, kind to their staff. Perhaps they would see what Ben had seen and be happy for him.

'Holly?' he prompted.

'I'm always just Holly,' I replied simply, lifting one shoulder.

'You are far more than just Holly,' he murmured. 'I thought I'd hate working in the events department, stuck in an office doing boring organizy-type things. But you've made it bearable, enjoyable even, and I think . . . Well, you bring out the best in me and I think my parents will be forever grateful for that. So don't say "just Holly".'

I swallowed. Hard. No one had ever made me feel as special as he had just done in those few words.

His eyes locked onto mine and he traced a line with his fingertip along the side of my face.

A thousand thoughts whirled through my head then but the most vivid one was that I might forget what he'd actually just said or exactly what he did but I would never, ever forget the way he made me feel.

He dipped his head lower and I felt my breathing begin to race.

We were going to kiss, we were actually going to kiss. How had this even happened? One minute I was arguing about the obstacles that stood between us and the next . . . Frankly, I couldn't care less about any awkwardness on Monday morning in the office. It was days away whereas now was . . . very, very real. Ben took my face gently in his hands and I closed my eyes as the gap between us disappeared. And for a blissful, heart-stopping fraction of a second my lips touched his and we shared the sweetest and briefest of kisses.

A crash in the bushes behind us frightened me half to death and I leapt out of Ben's embrace as though I'd been prodded with a sharp stick, pressing a hand against my thundering heart.

And not a moment too soon. Lady Fortescue appeared from amongst a thicket of rhododendron bushes dotted with fuchsia-pink flowers. Her eyes darted from her son to me and she arched her eyebrows and sucked in her cheeks.

'What are you two doing here?'

'Ben was just—'

Lady Fortescue blinked at me. 'Ben*edict*, Holly, his name is *Benedict*.'

'Sorry,' I corrected. 'Benedict was just—'

'I brought Holly to the gardens for some peace and quiet, Mum, because she was ill,' said Ben, taking a step towards me. 'And she calls me Ben because I asked her to.'

He took my hand and squeezed my fingers. My face was now pinker than the rhododendron flowers.

Lady Fortescue raised herself up tall and I almost expected her to yell, 'Off with her head.'

She pursed her lips at him for a moment instead before turning to me. 'And how are you feeling, Holly? I hear you fainted.'

Actually, I was feeling a bit light-headed from what had looked set to be one of my all-time favourite kisses before she'd gate-crashed the party, but I didn't think she'd appreciate that observation.

'Much better, thank you, Lady Fortescue.' I smiled. 'I'll be getting back to work in a moment.'

'What about you, Mum,' Ben said curtly. 'What are you doing frolicking in the bushes?'

'Hardly frolicking, darling,' she chided. 'I'm looking for my bracelet.'

'Oh dear,' I said, anxious to help. 'Would you like us to look? Where did you lose it?'

'No, no, thank you for the offer,' she sighed, 'but it's a futile search. I'll leave it, I think. I'm ready for a cup of tea and a sit-down in the gazebo. Anyway, I'll let you get back to work, Holly.'

She gave me a pointed look, air-kissed Ben's cheek and strode away along the gravel path.

'Do you think we should have a look for her bracelet?' I said as soon as she was out of earshot.

Ben rolled his eyes. 'No. Like she said, it's a waste of time. She's talking about a pearl bracelet she lost in the gardens thirty years ago.'

He took a step closer and placed his hands on my waist.

'Oh, shame. She must have really cared for it if she's still searching after all this time. Was it a family heirloom?' I said, inching my toes towards his.

Even as I was asking the question, I'd already lost interest in the answer. Which sounds a bit mean. But it looked as though Ben was intent on revisiting that kiss and even though it had come from nowhere, and pretty much stopped as soon as it had started, I had a feeling that I would very much enjoy seeing where it would go next.

'No. Don't think so,' he murmured, lowering his head towards mine again. I felt my knees weaken and I boldly slid my hands up to his shoulders. 'My dad gave it to her. He gave one similar to his mum and his aunt, apparently.' He chuckled. 'Trust Dad to buy the same thing for all the women in his life. Perhaps he bought in bulk for a discount.'

I focused on Ben's lips and tilted my head to his to give him some encouragement. 'Perhaps he just really liked that style. What was it like?'

Why was I still talking about Lady Fortescue's bracelet, when I could be kissing that mouth . . . ?

He shrugged. 'Um, three strands of pearls, with an S-shaped diamond clasp. Not that I've ever seen it, but she's been harping on about it for so long that I feel an intimate connection with the damn thing.'

A lump of ice lodged itself somewhere in my stomach and froze my entire body.

Ben pulled me closer. 'Anyway, where were we?' he murmured, flashing his dark eyes at me.

A pearl bracelet with an S-shaped diamond clasp? Just like the one Mum was given around that time too.

A chill ran along the length of my spine and my body gave a shudder.

Oh, no. Oh God, no . . .

I swallowed desperately as a wave of sickness rose up from my stomach and I struggled free from Ben's arms. I think I knew where Mum's bracelet had come from.

'Holly?' He frowned, trying to catch my hand.

'I'm sorry, Ben, I have to go, I . . . I'm not well.' I stumbled backwards away from him.

'Holly, wait! I'll take you.'

I turned and began to run. 'No need. I'll be fine. Early to bed and I'll be OK tomorrow. '

'But what about my wish, what about our date on Saturday?' he called after me.

His words struck my heart like tiny arrows, piercing me over and over again.

'I can't,' I shouted. 'Please, just let me go.'

'This is crazy, come back,' I heard him shout.

He was right about that: it was crazy. But I didn't stop, I didn't turn round, I ignored him and ran and ran.

All the women in his life.

Mum must have been one of the women in Lord Fortescue's life.

I felt sick and confused and, above all, desperately sad. But I didn't slow down until I reached the end of Wickham Hall's long drive. All I wanted to do was to get home and confront Mum, to force her to tell me the whole story. Because I couldn't wait another minute to hear the truth.

Was I Lord Fortescue's daughter? And more importantly, had I just kissed my brother?

Sparks Fly

Chapter 21

The tiny cottage I shared with my mum was a mere fifteen-minute walk from Wickham Hall, along a narrow side street at the far end of the village. But this afternoon it felt like the longest journey I'd ever made, every step taking me nearer to the truth about my father but further from Wickham Hall and further still from Ben and his mischievous brown eyes and cheeky smile.

I still felt wobbly from my fainting spell earlier at the summer festival and wondered briefly whether the sun was making me a bit delirious but as I walked through Wickham village I forced myself to concentrate on the facts.

I'd asked Mum about that bracelet recently and she'd said it had been given to her as a present just before she'd had me. I was born in April 1985. Who would have given my mother, a seventeen-year-old girl, a diamond and pearl bracelet if not a wealthy lord?

I walked along Wickham High Street playing genetic snap with His Lordship. Brown eyes: snap; fair hair: snap, OK his was silver, but it *had* been blond: I'd seen photographs . . . And now that I thought about it, I even bore a slight resemblance to his daughter Zara.

And Benedict. I rubbed the palm of my hand over my

forehead. For a moment back there in the sunken gardens, I thought we might have been right at the start of something special. Especially when he'd said that thing about me bringing out the best in him. My imagination had run riot, fantasizing that his family might welcome me into their home like a daughter . . . but not that I would actually *be* another daughter.

Oh God. I paused momentarily and leaned against a red postbox as a wave of nausea took hold.

Whatever happened next, I resolved, turning into Mill Lane, I had no intention of causing trouble for the Fortescue family. If my worst fears were realized, I'd resign from my job at Wickham Hall and disappear – simply start again, setting all dangerous feelings for Ben aside. Eventually, I suppose, I'd forget how he had exploded unexpectedly into my life, bringing fun, chaos, noise and his irresistible charm with him.

And perhaps I'd forget how adorable he'd looked when he'd asked me to have dinner with him.

Perhaps.

I sighed, a long shuddering sigh.

I sped up as much as I could as Weaver's Cottage came into view. I'd gone past the tearful stage but my legs had turned to jelly, my head was spinning and my stomach was leaden with sorrow.

I had abandoned my handbag up at the Wickham Hall festival office. I had my phone, but no purse, and no door key. But I was beyond caring about my possessions and I knew I could let myself into the cottage: we always kept a spare key hidden in the garden. I lifted a geranium-filled terracotta pot to reveal it, unlocked the door and almost collapsed with relief as I stepped into the cool, cramped hallway.

Stopping briefly in the kitchen to pour myself a glass of water, I stumbled up the stairs to my mum's room and sat at her dressing table, my stomach quivering as I stared at her jewellery box.

I lifted the lid, removed the satin-lined inner tray and let out the breath I hadn't realized I was holding.

There it was, right at the bottom: the pearl bracelet with its S-shaped diamond clasp.

I picked it up, coiled it into the palm of my hand and closed my fingers around it.

Lord Fortescue had bought at least three bracelets like this: one for Lady Fortescue, one for his mother and another for his aunt. Was it possible he'd bought a fourth for the seventeen-year-old Lucy Swift? Only Mum could tell me the truth and she wouldn't be home until the festival closed at the end of the day.

A wave of tiredness washed over me, every inch of my skin felt raw and despite the heat of the afternoon I shuddered feverishly. I picked up my glass and dragged myself into my own bedroom.

Sometimes, I thought, as sleep began to steal my consciousness, life deals us a blow so cruel that we are convinced the bruises will never fade . . .

I squeezed my eyes shut and tried to banish the puzzled look on Ben's face as I'd run from the sunken gardens and out of his sight.

The sound of a key rattling in the wooden front door jolted me from sleep. My bedroom was bathed in a golden evening light and the edge of my curtains fluttered in a gentle breeze through the open window. I was still clutching the bracelet and when I looked at my palm it was pitted with the shape of each pearl.

I didn't have the energy to call out, so I listened instead, waiting for Mum to find me. She pottered around downstairs for a few minutes, opening the doors into the back garden, and then I heard her coming up the stairs humming merrily to herself.

My heart thumped with tension as she reached the landing.

'Mum?' I called.

'Holly! You frightened me to death!' she said, poking her head around my bedroom door. 'I thought you'd be . . . Good gracious, love, what happened to you?'

She crossed the room, sat on my bed and pressed a hand to my forehead. 'You're very hot. How long have you been lying here like this?'

I shrugged weakly.

Mum held out my glass of water and I raised myself up enough to drink. She bustled out of the room and returned with some headache tablets.

'I've been expecting something like this to happen ever since you started working at the hall.' She sighed, popping two tablets out of the foil wrapper and putting them in my hand.

'You did?' I rasped, blinking at her. My heart ached, wishing we'd had this conversation twenty-four hours ago, before Ben and I had . . .

'You work too hard,' she scolded, shaking her head. She sat back down on my bed and stroked the hair back off my forehead. 'Darling, I know you're a perfectionist, but working so hard isn't good for the soul. What . . . ?'

Her voice faded as I unfurled my fingers and dropped the pearl bracelet into her lap.

'Where did you get this, Mum? Tell me the story. And please, I need the truth.'

Mum held the pearls up to her cheek and her shoulders slumped as she looked at me.

'I should never have kept it.'

I held my breath and stared at her as she squirmed beside me. 'Then why did you?'

'It was the only thing I had left of him, I—'

'Who?' My mouth dried and I took another sip of water. 'Mum, I know this is hard for you, but you don't understand. I need to know. Tonight, before . . .' I shook my head and swallowed. *Before I make any more mistakes with a man who may be my half-brother.*

She pressed her hands to her cheeks and groaned. 'I've been dreading this coming out.'

'Who gave this to you?' I repeated, peeling her hands from her face.

Her blue eyes looked haunted and my heart went out to her. I held her hands gently in mine and waited.

'The truth is that I found it in the bushes at the edge of the sunken garden at Wickham Hall. The diamond fastening glinted through the undergrowth and caught my eye.'

'You *found* it?' My eyes locked onto hers. 'So it wasn't a gift?'

She shook her head. 'Holly, I was seventeen and I had never seen such a beautiful bracelet. Pearls were really in fashion at the time. But even then I knew that this was the real thing, not like the cheap stuff we were all wearing at school. I knew I should hand it in but Antonio said—'

'Antonio?' I sat up quickly and then instantly regretted it as a wave of dizziness blurred my vision.

'Yes.' She nodded, cheeks pink. She smoothed the skirt of her dress and cleared her throat. 'Antonio was my first love. Your father.'

I gazed at her. In twenty-nine years I had never heard

the name Antonio. Was this a rapidly concocted story to disguise the truth? I so hoped not.

'Mum,' I took a deep breath, willing my voice to stay steady, 'Lord Fortescue bought bracelets like this for his wife, his mother and his aunt. Are you sure he didn't buy one for you, too?'

She frowned. 'Darling, I think you might have had a little too much sun. Why on earth would he do that?'

'Because . . .' I shook my head, my thoughts spinning and colliding as I tried to get the facts straight. My mind whooshed backwards to the conversation I'd had with Esme. What if this is why Mum had never wanted to move away from the shadows of Wickham Hall?

I looked at my mum's pretty face, creased with confusion.

What reason would she have to lie after all these years?

'Why have you never mentioned Antonio before?'

An insistent pulse was beating in my temple and my head ached. I forced myself to stay focused on Mum's face. She closed her eyes for a few seconds and I held my breath. I wasn't going to rush her any more; I'd waited long enough for her story. A few more minutes wouldn't hurt. After a long moment, Mum took my hand in hers and stroked it gently.

'Holly, you are the most precious thing in my world and I don't regret a thing. Even though you weren't planned, I have loved you with every fibre of my body, every beat of my heart, since you lit up my life.'

I squeezed her fingers and she smiled, her eyes glittering with tears.

'When you were little it was easy to keep you safe, but then almost overnight it felt like I was a young mum with a beautiful teenage daughter and I desperately didn't want

246

you to follow my example. I have always been afraid to tell you the whole story in case you thought less of me or, worse, made the same mistakes that I made.'

'Mistakes?'

She gazed at me and it was impossible to miss the pain behind her eyes.

'Falling in love so instantly, giving myself to someone I barely knew, which meant an accidental pregnancy and years of solitary motherhood.'

Poor Mum. My heart ached with sadness for her.

'But how can falling in love ever be a mistake?' I argued. As soon as I uttered the words, Ben's face appeared in my mind. I squeezed my eyes shut tight and heard Mum mumble my name sadly under her breath.

I touched her arm. 'But if Antonio is my father, if you were so in love, where is he now? Why have I never met him?'

Mum sighed and dropped her eyes to her lap, allowing the pearl bracelet to fall from one hand to the other.

'Good question. It's so stuffy in here; shall we go and sit in the garden? And I promise I'll tell you everything.'

I wasn't sure I could trust my legs to carry me downstairs, but I nodded and five minutes later we were sitting outside on the garden bench with glasses of iced water. I positioned myself at the shady end and Mum sat down beside me.

'Whatever happened,' I said softly, 'I'm not here to judge you. I love you and I hope you know that. But I do need the truth.'

'OK,' she said, taking a shaky breath. 'Thirty years ago, a week before the festival started . . .'

I looped my arm through hers and laid my head on her shoulder and as the sun sank slowly over the rooftops turning the sky crimson, Mum began her story.

School had finished for the summer and she had spent the days in the run-up to the Wickham Hall Summer Festival hanging out with friends, sunbathing and having fun on the village green. Her world changed for ever when Antonio appeared one morning and asked the girls for change for the telephone box to call his mother in Italy. His mama missed him when he was away, he'd said, in faltering English, and when he turned his soft brown eyes towards Mum, her heart had melted and she'd thought that if he was hers she would never let him out of her sight.

Mum didn't see him again until the first morning of the Wickham Hall Festival; he spotted her working at the ice-cream kiosk and asked her to meet him at lunchtime. His family had a leather business in Italy, he explained, and he and his father spent the summer months travelling around county shows and festivals like this one selling their purses, belts and bags. Antonio had kissed her hand, telling her that she was the most beautiful girl he'd ever seen, and declared that she had stolen his heart. Mum, of course, was besotted.

For the next two days, they spent every spare minute together: walking in Wickham Hall gardens, sitting outside his father's caravan, or sharing a bottle of wine by the river and always, always, wrapped in each other's arms.

Mum had never known such happiness and on their last night together under a sky sprinkled with stars amongst the rhododendron bushes, Antonio laid down a blanket and they made love, whispering their promises to somehow stay together for ever.

As the sky began to lighten with the promise of dawn, they stood to leave. Mum had to go back to the cottage to get ready to return to the festival for work at nine. And it was as they kissed their goodbyes that she noticed the bracelet glinting on the ground.

Antonio had kissed her one last time, telling her to keep it, saying that it would always remind her of their first night together. Mum had nodded, dropping it into her pocket, but secretly thinking as she did so that it had been a night that she would never forget for the rest of her life.

It was the third and last day of the festival, he and his father would be packing up to leave at the end of the day, but Mum and Antonio would have one last afternoon together to say their goodbyes, exchange addresses and arrange to meet up in the autumn.

Mum slipped into the cottage hoping that her father hadn't noticed that she'd been gone all night. But as she climbed the narrow staircase she heard him gasping for breath. She rushed into his room and found him, eyes wide with terror, clutching his heart in agony.

The ambulance ride, the interminable wait in the hospital corridor, gripping onto the pearl bracelet like a talisman, guilt threatening to overcome her entirely . . .

And then it was all over. Her father didn't recover from the massive heart attack, and Mum was left alone in the world at the age of seventeen. By the time she made it to the Wickham Hall campsite late, hollow with grief and shaking with exhaustion, the place was deserted. No caravans, no tents, not even a scrap of rubbish; the area had been completely cleared and no evidence remained of Antonio or of their stolen night together. He had left without trace; she had no contact details, no photograph of him, nothing . . . She didn't even know his last name.

Despite being numb with loss, she spent the weeks after her father's funeral trying to track Antonio down, buying every newspaper and magazine she could lay her hands on with festival coverage, scouring them for a picture, a name . . . anything that could lead her back to him. Throughout August, she even journeyed around the country, visiting other shows and festivals, searching for leather goods makers, asking everywhere she went if anyone had seen an Italian boy with golden hair and brown eyes. But he had vanished.

'And then September came around and I went back to school to finish my A levels . . .' Mum sighed.

There was such pain in her eyes that I thought my heart would burst with sadness for her. 'I was nearly eighteen and I had the cottage, so I was allowed to live on my own but by October I realized I was pregnant.'

I reached across and wiped the tears from her cheeks with my thumb.

'Mum,' I whispered softly, 'I had no idea that Granddad died that summer. You poor thing, having to go through all that alone and so young.'

'I was torn apart with guilt: for leaving my dad on his own the night he had his heart attack, for not turning up to say goodbye to Antonio and then when you were born I felt guilty for not being a proper family.'

'Hey, there's no need for that.' I put an arm around her and pulled her close. Her shoulders were shaking with silent tears. 'You got Granddad to the hospital, that was the main thing. And you were with him. It wasn't your fault he had a heart attack. And don't worry about me; I turned out all right, didn't I? And as for my father . . .'

Words failed me then, it was such a tragic tale and a lump formed in my throat, blocking my voice.

'Antonio would have been so hurt that I didn't show up, Holly. I didn't even let anyone know where I was that day as I waited in the hospital, not even my employer at the ice-cream stall. What if he thought I'd stayed away to avoid him?'

Her eyes searched mine and I shook my head, not knowing what to say.

'He never came back to Wickham Hall. Not once. I didn't stop looking for years. He would have got over it eventually, of course, moved on, probably married and had a family of his own. But I have never been able to move on; my biggest sorrow is that he has missed out on having you in his life.'

I exhaled as the missing pieces of our jigsaw puzzle began to slot together. I had an Italian father. Antonio. Who sounded charming. And just as I'd hoped, Mum had fallen in love with a boy her own age. Relief filtered through me like sunshine on a rainy day. Something else dawned on me too . . .

'I think you've just located the source of the hoarding, Mum.'

She nodded. 'I had lost so much in such a short space of time that I couldn't bear to part with anything. I know it sounds crazy, but those newspapers, the things I kept and collected, those are my memories. It started with the issues of the *Wickham and Hoxley News* in the summer of 1984. Although I didn't have pictures of Antonio, there were pictures of the festival in there, images that kept my memories alive in my head. And Granddad's things, too. I couldn't throw anything away that reminded me of him. I couldn't lose anything else.'

I pulled her towards me and hugged her tight, feeling guilty for all the times I'd been angry and frustrated by her inability to let go. Now, at last, I felt I'd got to the heart of her hoarding and I understood the deep sadness behind it.

'Holly,' she murmured, 'I'm sorry you've had to deal

with this all your life. Have I been a total nightmare to live with?'

I thought back to the humiliation of opening the door to people over the years and witnessing the shock on their faces when they saw the piles of clutter in our hall and swallowed. 'No, Mum. But I do think it's time to move on, don't you?'

She nodded and the two of us sat in silence for a few moments. The sun had sunk from the sky and a cool breeze ran over my skin giving me goosebumps.

'I'm so glad we've had this chat, Mum,' I laughed sheepishly. 'I'd worked myself up into a panic thinking that Lord Fortescue was my father.'

'Oh, Holly.' She giggled. 'You always did have a vivid imagination.'

We looked at each other and laughed.

'Esme even thought you might have had an affair with the BBC weather man that appeared at the festival that year.'

'Urgghh, I remember him.' She recoiled. 'Mustard-coloured tank top and a comb-over!'

I snorted at the look of disgust on Mum's face.

'Lady Fortescue still looks for that bracelet, you know,' I said, chastising her gently.

'Does she?' Mum chewed her lip. 'I had every intention of returning it, but there was so much going on that it went out of my mind. And it reminded me of my and Antonio's last day together.'

'Is that why my middle name is Pearl?'
She nodded.

'In that case,' I said, resting my head on her shoulder, 'you've got me as a reminder and I'm not going anywhere.'

'You're right. I should return it.' She nodded decisively. 'But how do I do that?'

I hugged her tightly and shivered in the breeze. 'I love you, Mum. And leave the bracelet with me; I'll get it back to Lady Fortescue somehow.'

A few hours later I paused from closing my bedroom curtains and leaned on my window sill, mesmerized by the huge pale moon that dominated a clear night sky dusted with stars.

I listened to my own breathing for a moment, revelling in the silence and the peace. A smile spread slowly across my face as realization dawned; all night I had been so wrapped up in Mum's heartbreaking story that I had forgotten what her revelation meant for me.

There were hundreds of reasons why Benedict Fortescue shouldn't make my heart flutter whenever he came near. But he did. And now there was nothing to stand in the way of my feelings for him. Or, I hoped, his for me.

I climbed into bed, my body relaxing as soon as my head touched the pillow, and set the pearl bracelet down on my nightstand.

There was also no reason not to accept Ben's invitation to have dinner with him on Saturday night. There was the small matter of apologizing for turning him down flat and then fleeing the scene. But I could do that in the morning.

And if, as my eyelids succumbed to sleep, it occurred to me that Lady Fortescue's disapproval might stand in our way, I dismissed it. Anyway, after all that I'd been through today, Lady Fortescue would be the least of my problems, wouldn't she?

Chapter 22

The second day of the Wickham Hall Summer Festival dawned and it was another impossibly bright and sunny summer's day. Spur-of-the-moment visitors would no doubt turn up and boost our numbers, Andy's Victorian parasols would probably sell out and hopefully diners would be queuing to reserve a table in Jenny's shaded outdoor restaurant.

I, on the other hand, woke up with a splitting headache and managed one sip of water before I had to make a dash for the bathroom to be sick.

'You, young lady, are going nowhere,' Mum pronounced, frowning at the thermometer after removing its tip from under my tongue.

So that was that.

Returning to work was unthinkable. I spent the next forty-eight hours bathed in sweat, drifting in and out of consciousness and clutching my mum's hand.

I missed the rest of the festival and by the time I returned to work the following Monday, at the beginning of August, it appeared I'd missed Ben too. The events office was empty and Ben's half of the room was abnormally tidy. His easel, paint box and canvases had gone as had the little radio he normally played as loud as I'd let him.

I swallowed my disappointment and sat down at my desk. Five seconds later my heart swooped. Tucked inside the lid of my laptop was a note, written in such scrawly writing that it could only be from one person.

I read it, pausing every other word to exclaim in surprise and laugh out loud, my cheeks aching with happiness.

Dear Miss Clipboard,

I've had some rejections in my time, but of all the excuses not to date me, yours gets the prize for the most extreme! Anyway, I'm slinking away to lick my wounds for some time while I gather the courage to ask you out again (see date marked in diary) and also to do some serious thinking. My easel and I will be braving the elements in the Orkney Islands in search of some windswept landscapes. Think of me often, won't you? A tortured soul, hopes and dreams in tatters, sobbing into my pillow at night . . .

I'm sure the fact that you're reading my thoughtfully placed note means that you are back up to full strength, wielding your trusty clipboard and pen at your in-tray like St George in pursuit of dragons, pink cheeks a-glow and tongue poking out when you write. (Did you know the tip of your tongue goes left for emails and right for your diary?) So you've got time to think up ways to drum up ticket sales for Bonfire Night and also to conjure up a more plausible excuse than exhaustion and sunstroke (yes, I have spoken to Lucy while you were on your deathbed, she chewed my ear off for nearly an hour on the phone) for the amazing date I've got lined up for you (see marked page in diary – again).

See you in September,

yours

Ben

PS I used your clipboard while you were away so it didn't get too lonely.

I sat back in my chair, a wide grin splitting my face in two. The note was so 'Ben' that I could almost hear his voice reading it to me. And he'd planned ahead for another date. Ben – *planning?* Unheard of. Despite leaving him in the lurch to run the festival without me and not having dinner with him on Saturday night, it looked as though he hadn't completely given up on me.

Phew!

My smile drooped slightly when I reread the bit about being in the Orkneys for a few weeks, but at least I had a date to look forward to. I grabbed my diary and flicked through the next few pages and laughed to myself when I found the entry for the last Saturday in September. Ben had written a message inside a large heart in pink chalk which had smudged across the opposite page: *Keep entire day free for date with irresistible chick magnet.*

I read it several times before realizing that my tongue was sticking out.

'Come back soon,' I murmured, touching my finger to the page.

I glanced at my desk, which seemed to have morphed into one huge in-tray in my absence. I'd really wanted to go and find Nikki in the gardens for a confidential chat, but there was no way I could leave the office until I'd got that lot under control.

I began to hum quietly to distract myself from the silence that Ben had left behind and turned my attention to my workload, trying very hard not to mull over what sort of serious thinking Ben had disappeared to do.

Three hours later, I'd planned my schedule for the next two weeks, written a post-festival press release and emailed it to the local media, approved the leaflet for our Halloween pumpkin-carving activities and selected some pictures taken by the festival photographer to use in next year's marketing campaign. And after such an intense session, I was ready for some company and a bit of fresh air.

I closed down my laptop and headed off to find Nikki in the gardens.

The weather had turned cooler over the weekend and the sky was heavy with ominous grey clouds. It didn't seem to deter the public, though; the courtyard tables outside the café were busy, there was a large party of silver-haired visitors wandering amongst the outdoor display at the gift shop and when I paused at the top of the stone steps leading away from the formal gardens, the scene in the parkland that spread out before me was dotted with clusters of distant figures.

I turned then to gaze at Wickham Hall behind me. Its reddy-brown walls edged with large pale cornerstones, the rows of mullioned windows and the three copper-domed turrets across the roofline were so familiar to me now and my heart swelled with warmth. To me it represented grace and beauty and an unbroken link to an almost fairy-tale past. But what did it mean to Ben? I wondered.

This would all be his if his parents had anything to do with it. And if he genuinely didn't want it, I supposed it would have to be sold. I felt a sharp pang of loss, as though it were my own, and hurried down the steps and along the roped-off pathway marked 'staff only' towards Nikki's shed in the Victorian walled kitchen garden.

'Shed' was perhaps doing Nikki's domain a disservice. Wickham Hall had several sheds as well as numerous greenhouses and polytunnels, but the one in the kitchen gardens where she had a desk, a phone and a million pots of cuttings was a very pretty, single-storey brick building. It had proper Georgian windows and a pair of soft green wooden doors, framed with a red climbing rose that scrambled over the doorway. A long bench ran alongside the building for gardeners to perch on while they pulled on their boots and a row of upended wheelbarrows leaned against the wall ready for action.

Nikki was outside with a lorry driver, signing for a delivery of huge sacks full of bulbs, and I took a seat on the bench to wait for her. She handed the driver his paperwork, waved him off and then pointed at the sacks with a grin.

'Are you feeling strong?'

My three days of illness had left me feeling a bit wobbly, actually, but as Nikki didn't wait for an answer, I helped her drag the sacks into the dry shed.

'Are these all for spring?' I panted as we stacked the last couple inside.

'Yep.' She grinned and wiped a hand across her face, leaving a streak of dried mud. 'Bulbs are the first signs of new life at Wickham Hall; just when the landscape needs a boost in February — ping — little pops of bright colours start appearing. And when I see that first bulb in spring, it does my system more good than vitamin C.'

'New life.' I nodded thoughtfully. 'I reckon I might get some bulbs for our garden.'

I hoped that by next spring much of the clutter in Weaver's Cottage would have disappeared and Mum would be in a happier place. Perhaps getting her involved in a garden project would make her focus on a new life outside the cottage and help her to let go of the past? It was worth a try . . .

'Here, look at this. Lovely, isn't it?' she said, handing me a battered photograph from her back pocket. 'A wild flower meadow in spring.'

258

The picture was of a swathe of grass smothered with a mass of tiny flowers in white, yellows and pinks.

'Very lovely,' I agreed. 'I might even have a go myself.'

'That was my inspiration,' she said, stowing the picture back in her pocket. 'But I've got massive ambitions for these gardens. Wickham is going to be *the* destination for spring colour next year. I've bought twenty thousand bulbs to plant between now and November.'

'By hand?' I said, impressed.

'Yep.' She nodded, a determined glint in her eye. 'I might need a few more volunteers, come to think of it; it's back-breaking work. I've got eight thousand polyanthuses for the wild flower meadow, four thousand tulips for the parterres in the formal gardens and crocuses and snowdrops for the woodland.'

'And I wrongfully assumed you'd be heading for a quiet period.' I grinned as a thought struck me. 'Hey, perhaps we could have a bulb-planting party: invite the public to come along with their trowels and—'

I spotted Nikki's raised eyebrow and stopped immediately.

'And have people not burying them deep enough and trampling all over the flower beds?' She shuddered. 'No thanks. Why don't you just work on getting us visitors here next spring to see the flowers and leave the bulb-planting to the professionals?' She chuckled. 'Working with Benedict must be rubbing off on you, that sounds like the sort of hare-brained idea he'd come up with.'

'He's not hare-brained,' I said defensively, 'he's just creative and imaginative and if that's rubbing off on me . . .'

Nikki's eyebrow was up again and a smirk hovered at her lips. I snapped my mouth shut.

'You look hot,' she said, walking over to the far end of

259

the room to her desk. 'Here, have a drink. I don't want you keeling over on me.'

She picked up two bottles of water and handed one to me. I smiled my thanks and unscrewed the lid. Nikki took a long drink from hers and wiped the back of her hand across her mouth.

'I had Ben down here on Saturday, wittering on about how it was his fault you were ill. He left you to do too much . . . blah, blah, blah.'

I hid my smile by sipping at my water.

'He flatters himself,' I said, secretly pleased that he'd been worried about me. 'I'm quite capable of managing a heavy workload, even if he did keep adding to it. I just had too much sun, that was all.'

Nikki stared at me for a long moment until I began to feel uncomfortable and then she sat down on a sack of bulbs. 'Did I ever tell you where I worked before I came here?' she said, with a sideways glance.

'Wasn't it for Will Simpson from Role Play?' I said with a frown, confused at the change in topic.

I didn't fancy perching on a lumpy sack, so pulled her desk chair closer instead and sat down.

She swigged from her water bottle and nodded. 'Did I say why I left?'

I thought for a moment, sifting through all my memories from the last two months. I was sure she'd mentioned something about it on my first day at Wickham Hall.

'Not really,' I said, wrinkling my nose. 'You said something about circumstances changing and staying not really being an option. I assumed he'd fallen on hard times and had had to let staff go.'

She shook her head. 'I was the one who'd fallen . . . in love. Completely and utterly. But Will was married and I had no intention of coming between him and his wife. It was me who had to do the letting go. Before either of us did something we'd regret.'

I nodded, and memories of Nikki's angry response to Pippa's husband's affair with the au pair came trickling back to me.

Nikki had never even hinted at her own romantic past before now. In fact, I realized, I didn't know much about her private life at all. She pulled her wallet out of her pocket and passed me a creased photograph from inside it. It was unmistakably Nikki leaning on a spade – short wiry hair, easy smile and her usual uniform of shorts and a wide-brimmed hat. Standing beside her with his arm casually draped around her shoulders was a tall thin man with bleached-blond hair and a crumpled shirt open to the waist.

'You look very happy, Nikki. And did he feel the same about you?'

I gave the photo back to her and she stroked it tenderly with her thumb.

'I'll never really know. Nothing ever happened between us; he was too lovely to cheat on his wife. But he'd started to spend a lot of time with me in the garden and our friendship deepened into something very precious. Keeping my feelings hidden got too hard in the end; I simply loved him too much to stay.'

My heart twanged with sorrow at such a sad story of a love that could never be. My stomach clenched. Was that the moral of the story she wanted me to hear: a forbidden relationship?

'I think you're amazing, Nikki. You acted so honourably,' I said, reaching over to pat her knee.

'Thanks, Hols,' she said with a wistful smile. She tucked the picture back into her wallet. 'I think he's the only man

I've ever properly loved. Which is why I left. I'm married to this place now. And there are worse relationships, believe me.' She lifted a shoulder and sighed.

I took a deep breath, not sure if I wanted the answer to my next question.

'Why tell me all this now?'

She looked at me for a long moment, as though she was reading my innermost thoughts.

'Because I've seen the friendship between you and Benedict grow and it reminded me a lot of Will and me. The difference is neither of you is committed to anyone else. So my advice is this: if you get a chance at happiness with someone, grab it, hold on to it for all you're worth. I couldn't have my man, but there's nothing stopping you going after yours. Well, nothing except . . .' She waggled her eyebrows and gave me a wry smile.

'Lady Fortescue?' I finished for her.

She nodded.

'I hadn't realized it was so obvious. Ben and me, I mean.' I smiled awkwardly.

Nikki sniggered. 'It's obvious to me.'

I felt my face flame. 'Nothing has happened between us,' I said. Except the briefest of clinches in the gardens, which had been rudely interrupted by Lady Fortescue herself . . . 'Do you think she'd kick up a fuss if anything did?'

'Honestly?' Nikki exhaled. 'She's got a good heart, but she's a snob. I think she's hoping for a daughter-in-law with a trust fund and a family who owns at least half a county.'

I sighed wistfully. Put like that the daughter of a charity shop assistant and an Italian market stall holder might not go down too well with Her Ladyship.

Nikki nudged me sharply with her elbow. 'But you're not going to let that stop you, are you?'

I recalled the look on Lady Fortescue's face when she'd found us up to something in the sunken garden. It was anything but pleased. But then I remembered Ben standing up to her on my behalf . . .

I lifted my chin defiantly and grinned. 'Absolutely not. If it doesn't bother Ben that I'm not well-to-do then it shouldn't bother me either.'

'That's the spirit.' Nikki clapped me on the back.

Picking up a pair of scissors from her desk she inclined her head towards the door and I followed her outside and into the walled garden. 'Now, I'm sure you didn't come down here to hear all that stuff about my love life, so what can I do for you?'

We stopped at a raised herb bed and she began snipping at soft basil stems.

'Well . . .' I hesitated and automatically snaked a hand into my pocket, curling my fingers around Lady Fortescue's pearl bracelet. It was probably a crazy idea but in the absence of anything else . . .

'You know that bracelet that Lady Fortescue lost years ago in the sunken garden?'

Nikki flicked an amused glance at me and folded a basil sprig into her mouth. 'Mmm. Not personally, but I know the one you mean.'

'Do you think it would be worth digging up the soil in that area, perhaps when you're planting some of those spring bulbs, to see if you can find it?' I gazed at her innocently. My half-formed plan was to plant the bracelet back in the garden where it would almost certainly be found.

She laughed softly and shook her head. 'Has she got you on the trail of it now? That area has been dug up before. Rhododendron is rampant, we have to dig it up and cut it back every five years or it takes over and suffocates all the other plants. I remember Her Ladyship watching the ground like a hawk in case we found anything at the time.'

My heart sank. That was the end of that idea, then. I'd have to think of something else, and now, I realized, Nikki might be a bit suspicious when the bracelet did resurface.

'Well, just a thought, forget I mentioned it,' I said nonchalantly. 'I'm going to the café for lunch to fortify myself before tackling my bonfire plan, fancy joining me?'

She shook her head. 'Can't. But deliver this to Jenny for me, would you?'

'Sure.' I took the bunch of basil from her and inhaled its fresh aroma.

'Oh, and let her know I've got tomatoes coming out of my ears.'

'OK.' I laughed, turning to leave. 'And thanks, Nikki, you know, for sharing your story about Will and for the advice.'

I left her snipping through some woody rosemary stems and made my way to the café. Nikki's story reminded me of Mum's experience in a small way: both women had lost the love of their lives through no fault of their own. It was very early days with Ben and me: a sum total of one brief kiss and the promise of a date were hardly enough to base a relationship on, but there was a tiny flame deep within me that was cheerfully flickering away and I was going to prevent anyone from snuffing it out.

I found Jenny enjoying a rare break at a table in the far corner of the café. She buried her face in the basil, face beaming with pleasure, and when I told her about the glut of tomatoes heading her way she began listing the things she would make with them.

'And gazpacho. On a hot day. Oh and homemade smoky ketchup. We can bottle it and save it until Bonfire Night. I love a bit of sauce.' She giggled, tucking a purple strand of hair back into her ponytail.

'You're in a good mood.' I chuckled. I fetched a cup and saucer and poured myself some tea from her teapot.

'I know!' she squeaked, leaning forward and squeezing my arm, making me spill the milk. 'You'll never guess what's happened!'

'Um . . .' I frowned, blotting up the spillage with a napkin.

'Daniel Denton has followed me on Twitter,' she proclaimed, shoving her phone under my nose so that I could read her Twitter notifications. 'Me – Jenny Plum!'

'Daniel Denton the celebrity chef?' I grinned at her excitement.

She clapped her hands together. 'And even better than that, I've invited him to come to Wickham Hall at Christmas and he said if he can fit it in, he will.'

My eyes widened at that. I had already started a folder for 'Christmas at Wickham Hall activities' and this would be a massive draw.

'That would be amazing!'

'Do not breathe a word,' Jenny hissed, tapping her nose. 'Let's keep it a secret for now.'

I stared at her for a moment. I really liked Jenny: she was pragmatic, reliable and, apart from getting a little starstruck at the prospect of a visit from Daniel Denton, very levelheaded. More than that, she was a good friend and I trusted her.

I reached across the table, laid a hand on hers and took a deep breath.

'Jenny, I've got a secret too. But mine is a terrible secret. I can't ignore it, but if I try to sort the problem out myself I'm worried it might cost me my job.'

Her forehead furrowed and she leaned forward but before she had a chance to reply a shadow fell over the table. My head jerked up instantly. Andy was right behind me carrying his lunch on a tray, a wide smirk across his face.

'Room for a little one?' he said, plonking the tray next to Jenny's tea things and settling himself at the table.

Jenny shot me a look of apology and my stomach lurched. Andy had never warmed to me and if he had heard my last comment I was in no doubt that he would try to make things awkward for me.

I whipped my hand away from Jenny's.

'I'd better get back to the office,' I said, jumping to my feet, sending the chair scraping across the floor noisily.

'Something I said?' Andy murmured to Jenny, cocking an eyebrow.

'Holly?' Jenny frowned at me. 'Is everything OK?'

'Never mind, it can wait,' I mumbled.

I strode away, feeling a bit sick. Could it wait? Now that Andy had wind of a possible reason for me to lose my job, the sooner I got this bracelet off my hands the better.

Chapter 23

It was bank holiday Monday in August and although Wickham Hall was open to the public, there were no official events in the calendar and I had a welcome day off. I was already wearing a bikini underneath my shorts and a vest top but I packed a bag with the other essential requirements for spending the day sunbathing with Esme – cans of Coke, a bottle of wine for later, sunglasses, sun cream and a selection of magazines – and headed outside to say goodbye to Mum and Steve.

Steve seemed to be around all the time these days. I wasn't complaining; Mum had blossomed in his company and it made me realize just how lonely she had been before his arrival on the scene. And what was even more heart-warming to watch was how unfazed he was by all her clutter. He was divorced and his ex-wife had taken almost all of their possessions and he liked our 'homely' cottage. I loved that he was kind and sensitive towards Mum and had already gently offered to help her dispose of several boxes of junk from the dining room. At this rate, there was more than a slight chance of actually being able to eat Christmas dinner in there this year.

So, so far so good in their budding romance, I'd decided.

They were having coffee in the early morning sun on the patio. Steve had his arm around the back of Mum's chair and discreetly withdrew it when he noticed me.

'Have a lovely day, you two,' I called with a wave. 'And don't do anything I wouldn't do.'

Although the chance would be a fine thing in my case, I mused wryly. Ben had been away for a month already and I hadn't heard a word from him. I tucked a big bag of crisps in my bag as a last-minute addition; Esme and I were planning on sunbathing on the communal grass slope outside her flat that served as a garden and I could never rely on her to have anything edible in the cupboards.

The back door opened and Mum materialized by my side in the kitchen, her smile overly wide. I knew that smile; it meant 'I'm about to say something that both of us could find uncomfortable'. Usually me more than her. The last time this smile had an airing was a few months ago when she'd thrust a leaflet in my hands about egg freezing. She thought I might want to 'put a few young ones by' in case the right man didn't come along to fertilize them before my embryos were past their best. Talk about mortified!

'Sorry for teasing,' I said instantly. 'I hope I didn't embarrass Steve. Or you.'

'No, no.' She shook her head and ran a finger slowly over the kitchen work surface, which looked remarkably tidier these days. I waited. Uncomfortably.

'Holly,' she began and then paused. She looked back to the garden and pulled the door to behind her so that Steve was no longer visible.

'What do you think of him, of Steve?' she hissed, nestling her sunglasses on her thick blonde hair.

'Oh, Mum, he's lovely.' I pulled her into a hug. 'Not that it matters what *I* think. How do *you* feel about him?'

'He makes me feel special.' She eased back to look at me. 'He makes me feel as if I could move on. But it's moving too fast, I—'

She paused and pulled her top lip between her teeth.

My mind flipped back to the way she had described her life to me recently: the years of solitary motherhood, her loneliness. I couldn't let her return to that, but at the same time I understood how hard it would be to share her life with someone new after all this time.

'Hey,' I said, taking a step back and forcing her to look me in the eye. 'You know how you hum when you're happy?'

She nodded.

'Well, you hum a lot now and also . . .' I hesitated, not wanting to ruin the moment. I kissed her cheek and decided to go for it. 'The kitchen looks loads better and I noticed the dustbin is full. Have you been having a clear-out?'

She nodded again. 'Steve tripped at the top of the stairs so I thought I'd better do something in case one of us had a more serious accident.'

I smiled brightly. 'Well, there you go! You never throw stuff away when you're feeling low. So that has to be a good sign. Right?'

She twisted her hands together. 'It's just that he's started dropping hints lately. Making, you know, suggestions . . . and I don't think I'm ready.'

She blinked at me and two pink spots appeared on her cheeks.

Fighting the urge to ram my fingers in my ears and sing 'lalalala', I took her hand instead. I was only twenty-nine, I wasn't sure if I was ready to dispense this sort of advice to my mother.

'Go on.' I swallowed.

She took a deep breath and gave me a tight smile. 'Steve

269

thinks that Henley library might be interested in my collection of old newspapers. He thinks they'd be grateful if I donated them for their archives, as a contribution to local history.'

'Mum!' I exclaimed, not a little relieved. 'That's fantastic.'

I could hardly keep the smile off my face. This was excellent news and ultimately it was Ben's doing. It had been his idea to do the photographic retrospective for his parents' thirtieth anniversary at Wickham Hall that had started all this. I sent up a silent thank-you to Ben for introducing us to Steve.

'But they're my memories, my collection,' Mum went on softly. 'If I let them go . . .' Her voice faded and a heartfelt sigh escaped. 'He's right, I suppose.'

We gazed at each other for a few seconds.

I laughed softly. 'For one awful moment, I thought you were going to say he wanted to . . . you know . . .' I winked at her playfully.

'Oh, darling!' She gave a tinkling laugh and pressed a kiss onto my cheek. 'We're well beyond that stage. Why do you think Steve was at the *top* of the stairs? In fact, when you've gone—'

'I'm going, I'm going!' I cried, darting for the door.

I was still chuckling about having heard more information than any child should, no matter what her age, when I arrived at Esme's flat ten minutes later. I'd spent the short drive with the radio cranked up loud to blot out all thoughts of what the two of them might be up to.

Esme was leaning over the open stairwell of the block of flats, waiting for me. She waved and ran down to greet me.

'Holster!' she yelled, thundering towards me with her

arms outstretched. I gasped as she subjected me to one of her rib-crushing hugs. It was fantastic to see her and I was so glad there was no atmosphere between us since that silly fight.

'I've missed you so much! We are such idiots for letting work get in the way of our social life.' I grinned when she finally released me. 'And I've got loads to tell you.'

She was dressed in a strapless pink sundress and white flip-flops and her skin looked dark and exotic after her trip to Dubai to visit her dad. I had no chance of catching up, but I was prepared to do my best. Even if it did mean returning to work tomorrow looking like one of Nikki's tomatoes.

'Agreed and ditto. Let's go straight outside,' she suggested. 'I've already set up some beach towels and the cool box.'

'Good plan.' I beamed. 'And I've brought the wine.'

She tucked her arm through mine and we made our way along the communal hallway and through the glass door that led to the patch of grass at the back of the flats.

'I'm sorry I've been incommunicado since Dubai, Hols. But the work had piled up while we were away and I was snowed under.'

'It's fine,' I replied, squeezing her arm. 'I've been almost bursting with news though and I wanted to save it until we could talk properly.'

I was looking forward to spending some time with her; I'd barely seen her over the past few weeks. I had been too preoccupied with the festival in July and then she went on holiday and since then she'd been busy in Joop supplying all the ladies in the vicinity with their posh dresses for summer weddings and parties.

'So what's the latest on Benedict the bootylicious boss?'

asked Esme once we'd stripped off to our bikinis and stretched out on towels.

I tore open the crisps and offered her the bag. She took a handful, popped one in her mouth and raised her eyebrows waiting for a response.

'Still AWOL,' I said glumly, all at once conscious of exactly how much I needed to fill my best friend in on. 'I think he needed to escape from the pressure his parents are putting on him to take over at Wickham Hall. I don't think they're too impressed at his disappearance.'

I missed his cheery presence more than I cared to admit. I still had his note and I still had our date written in chalk in my diary and I couldn't help peering at it every day. But I really wanted his help with Lady Fortescue's pearl bracelet; maybe he would dream up a way to return it. There just hadn't been the right opportunity to give it back and the longer I held on to it, the more bothered about it I became. It didn't help that every time I caught Andy with a smile on his face, I was convinced that he was about to drop me in it.

'My heart bleeds, the poor love,' said Esme, getting herself comfortable. 'Tell him that I'll inherit the hall if he doesn't want it.'

I thought back to the magical morning when the two of us had watched the sun coming up over the turreted roof of his Elizabethan home and the fear on his face at the prospect of filling his father's shoes. I imagined it was as far away from his independent artist life in London as it could possibly be.

'Hmm, I used to think like that, but now I'm not so sure.'

'That's only because you fancy him,' she said smugly. She looked left and right and seeing no one around, unhooked the back of her bikini top and slid it from underneath her.

'Oh, I forgot: men are off the agenda until you find your dad.'

'The agenda has changed a bit since I last saw you.' I grinned. 'My father now has a name and a nationality and Mum has a new boyfriend.'

'What?' Esme's mouth gaped. 'Blimey, what else have I missed? You're not married too, are you?'

'No,' I replied with my best enigmatic smile. 'No need to buy a hat just yet.'

The sun was already beginning to sting my shoulders and I reached into my bag for the sun cream while I told her the whole story, beginning with when Mum met Antonio and ending with the pearl bracelet and how I might have inadvertently let my secret slip in front of Andy.

'So there you go,' I said, smiling at Esme's stunned silence. 'I'm half Italian. How amazing is that!'

She whistled under her breath. 'And what a story your mum has been keeping to herself all these years!'

I nodded. 'I feel so sad for her, losing her dad, missing Antonio before he left for Italy and then having to bring me up on her own. All that trauma could easily have brought on her hoarding.'

'Hey, we should go to Italy, Holster!' She sat up suddenly and then yelped when she remembered she was topless. She grabbed her sundress and pulled it over her head. 'On a mission to find the mysterious Antonio. A bit of Google detective work and I'm sure we can come up with some clues.'

'I don't think it will be that easy to locate an Italian called Antonio who came to England thirty years ago, Es.' I grinned at her. 'Now that is as crazy as me being Lord Fortescue's daughter.'

'I'm serious,' she said, pushing her sunglasses up to

show me her serious face. 'You must be due some time off soon. And you'd be doing it for your mum – you know: closure.'

'I can't just disappear, not while Ben's away,' I retorted. That was Esme Wilde all over: spontaneous and fancy free . . . It had crossed my mind to try to find Antonio but I wasn't sure about it yet; Mum was doing so well getting over her hoarding, especially with Steve's help, and I didn't want to jeopardize anything by announcing a hunt for my father.

'I might think about it again in the spring,' I suggested tactfully. 'There's no rush.'

Besides, it would be something to look forward to if Ben left Wickham Hall at Christmas and returned to his art studio in London, I mused, aware suddenly of a sinking sensation in my stomach.

Esme's face had dropped too. 'As it happens, I might be at a loose end in the spring. Unfortunately.'

'Oh?' I frowned.

She sat up, hugged her legs and dropped her chin to her knees. 'Dad has convinced Mum to put Joop up for sale. He wants her to stop work and look after her own health and as the shop isn't doing that well anyway, she has reluctantly come to the conclusion that it's the right thing to do.'

'Oh, Es, I'm so sorry to hear that.'

My heart twisted for her. *And* Bryony. They had both put everything into Joop and it would be such a shame to see them walk away from it.

'Dad thinks Mum should accompany him on his next contract abroad for the sake of her arthritis.' She sighed. 'But she's always worked; I can't imagine her sitting at home playing house while Dad's at work.'

'And what about you?' I asked softly. 'How do you feel about it all?'

She stared down at her feet and shook her head. 'Gutted,' she said quietly. 'I've been there all my working life. I don't know anything else and I love that shop to pieces.'

I got up off my towel and plonked myself next to her, wrapping an arm round her shoulders.

'Maybe this is your chance to do your own thing, Es. You said you wanted to break away from occasional wear. Perhaps you could move into something a bit edgier, like you said? Let's make a list of options and help you build a plan.'

I pulled my bag towards me, automatically reaching for a pen and some paper. This was my forte: planning. I was sure I could help Esme pin down her next move.

Esme groaned and flapped a hand. 'Urgh, planning schmanning. Not now, Holster. Not while the sun is shining. I'm just taking it one day at a time. Anyway, you know me: I'm rubbish at all the businessy stuff. I'm never going to be organized like you and write everything in my diary, like when I next need a haircut and how much I weigh on every birthday.'

I threw a flip-flop at her, pleased that she'd cheered up. 'I don't do that.'

She cocked an eyebrow.

'Well not any more, anyway,' I conceded. 'Working with Ben has made me much more relaxed about things.'

She picked up the flip-flop and pointed it at me, regarding me slyly. 'Holly Swift, you really like this guy, don't you?'

I hesitated for a moment and then sighed dreamily. 'He is rather gorgeous.'

'Well, now that you've overcome all your obstacles,

what's stopping you from giving him a test drive?' She grinned cheekily.

'Esme!' I laughed, shaking my head at her.

She looked at her watch, pulled a face and took the wine out of the cool box. 'Oh well, I'm sure it's wine o'clock somewhere.'

She poured us both a glass of chilled wine and we chinked glasses.

'So how should I play it, do you think, with me and Ben? I need your advice.'

Esme sat back cross-legged and thought for a moment. 'OK, now listen to Auntie Esme. Don't plan every move, don't second guess every moment, just relax and go with it. Enjoy the chase.' Her eyes twinkled with mischief. 'That's the best part.'

'He's taking me on a date,' I breathed. 'End of September. I don't know where to yet, but it's a Saturday and he's told me to keep the whole day free.'

'Oh Lordy, Holly, I don't believe you've been sitting on that information for the past hour,' she squealed. 'Right, come on!'

She leapt to her feet and began stuffing our belongings into bags.

'Where to?' I laughed. 'The date isn't for weeks yet!'

'I take it back about not planning. There's no time to lose. We're going to plan this date in infinite detail. You, Holly Swift, are going to blow his socks off. Starting with your underwear. I've got just the thing.'

I followed her inside obediently, a big silly grin on my face. Even talking about Ben made me feel all warm inside. If anyone could make me sparkle on my date with Benedict Fortescue it was . . . Well, it was Ben himself, actually, but Esme would send me off looking a million dollars.

And if that was what it was going to take to convince Lady Fortescue that I was worthy of a date with her son, then it would be worth every penny.

Chapter 24

Towards the end of September, Ben still hadn't returned to Wickham Hall and I had been running the events department single-handedly. Whilst I suspected that Ben had chosen the Orkney Islands for its remoteness and seclusion, he hadn't been in touch with me at all. Not once. And it was beginning to bother me. Not only that, I was still in possession of Lady Fortescue's bracelet and I'd been hoping he could help me out with returning it to her somehow.

Unable to stand the suspense any longer, I waited until I knew Lord and Lady Fortescue were lunching in the Great Hall with the Mayor of Stratford and our local member of parliament and went to see Sheila in her office.

I found her on her knees rummaging in the bottom drawer of a filing cabinet in Lord Fortescue's private office.

'I knew it.' She tutted under her breath as she clambered to her feet clasping two British passports. 'Swore blind he hadn't got them. His Lordship has had me up hill and down dale looking for these.'

'Are the Fortescues planning another trip?' I asked, watching as Sheila retrieved her reading glasses from the chain around her neck and checked the expiry dates in the burgundy passports.

'Thank goodness, fine for another year,' she exhaled. 'No, not until Christmas. Lady Fortescue is off to Paris by herself and then they're spending part of the holiday with Zara and Philippe in France at their chateau. Not travelling until Boxing Day, of course – they wouldn't leave Benedict on his own at Christmas.'

I pressed my lips to hide a smile. That would be thirty-two-year-old Benedict. But good news anyway . . .

'So he is coming back to Wickham Hall?' I said, aware that there was possibly a hint of desperation in my voice.

Sheila glanced at the door to check we weren't being overheard and drew her cardigan across her bosom. 'He has promised to be back soon. Well, at the very latest, Bonfire Night.'

November? That was ages away. And what about our date next week, was he still planning on coming back for that? Or perhaps that had simply been one of his spontaneous ideas, forgotten as soon as it was uttered . . .

'But he has been gone so long,' I said.

Sheila regarded me for a second. 'Perhaps it feels that way to you.'

I felt the heat rise to my face and looked down at my shoes. Whoops, I hadn't meant to wear my heart on my sleeve quite so blatantly.

'This is Benedict all over,' she continued, settling herself back at her desk. 'He disappears on a whim, claims to be in the middle of a creative surge and then,' she snapped her fingers in the air, 'he returns with a car full of daubs on canvases. You'll get used to it.'

I nodded, privately thinking that I doubted I would.

'Confidentially,' said Sheila, lowering her voice, 'there have been some heated discussions between father and son about Benedict deserting the events department and not pulling his weight in the family. The whole idea of coming back to Wickham Hall was to learn the ropes. He can hardly do that from the Orkneys.'

My heart sank. I'd been secretly hoping that this painting trip would have given him time to realize that his future was at Wickham Hall and maybe even to have missed me. I mean, missed *the hall*.

And taking my own feelings out of the equation for a moment, I genuinely believed that his energy and enthusiasm could do so much for the Wickham estate and bring a whole new generation of visitors through the gates. I just hoped he hadn't clashed terribly with Lord Fortescue and made any rash statements about leaving. Sheila was still talking, I realized, and I tuned back in to catch her beaming at me.

'Anyway, according to Benedict, the events calendar is under control and is perfectly safe in your capable hands.'

At which point I'd left her to it, feeling suitably cheered by Ben's apparent faith in me and keeping my fingers tightly crossed that our upcoming date was fixed as firmly in his heart as it was in mine.

The following day I was at my desk putting the finishing touches to my hand-outs for the Bonfire Night progress meeting. It was late in the afternoon and I'd be heading home straight after the meeting. I stapled the last copy, shuffled the papers into a neat pile, scooped up my handbag and set off for Lord Fortescue's office.

I was feeling pretty pleased with myself about our winter events and was sure that Ben would be impressed too when he finally returned. The first big date on the calendar was Bonfire Night. I had secured us an award-winning pyrotechnics expert to put on our fireworks display; Jenny had agreed to run the catering in the courtyard, which included a hog to be roasted for pulled pork rolls, local beers, bonfire toffee apples and the usual teas and coffees; I had persuaded Jim to build the biggest bonfire Wickham Hall had ever seen and he had already started amassing firewood on the bonfire site; and Andy had found a supplier of the most beautiful faux-fur scarves, mittens and muffs to sell at the event. It promised to be a night to remember.

My Christmas Activity Plan was coming along nicely too: we would have all sorts going on from carol-singing to homemade Christmas crafts and – drumroll please – Jenny's celebrity chef had confirmed he would be at Wickham Hall to kick off the celebrations with an Elizabethan Christmas demonstration.

Jenny was waiting for me at the bottom of the staircase, waving a sheet of paper.

'I've had another email from Daniel Denton today, agreeing to my recipe suggestions.' She shivered fan-girl style as we walked along the plushly carpeted corridor. 'We might even make the local news. This could be my big break into TV.'

I shuddered. 'That would be my worst nightmare.'

Jenny laughed. 'I was born to cook, but to cook on TV, now that is the stuff of dreams.'

'Then I hope your dream comes true, Jenny,' I said, squeezing her arm. 'But on a more practical level, we need his PR agent's details for photos and stuff. It will make a great press story. Has he got a book out? We could do a book signing too.'

'Good idea. His PR lady is actually his wife; I'll give you her number. It'll be a sell-out.' Her eyes sparkled. 'As soon as word gets out – whoosh – tickets will sell like Jenny Plum's hot cakes!'

Sheila ushered us into Lord Fortescue's office and I headed for an empty chair between Nikki and Lady Fortescue, opposite Andy. I handed round my Bonfire Night documents while Jenny headed for the teapot and began pouring everyone cups of tea.

Lord Fortescue cleared his throat and pulled a sheet of paper towards him. 'Before we begin on the Bonfire Night preparations, I'd just like to report on the final financial figures for the Summer Festival. Visitor numbers were up five per cent on last year.'

There was a mumble of general approval from around the table.

He paused, making eye contact with each of his team and smiled. 'Might not sound like a lot, but there's a lot of competition out there. And anyway, we don't want to give ourselves too much of a challenge next year, to beat this year's figures, do we? But all in all, it was a cracking do, so well done, everyone.'

I smiled at Lord Fortescue; he had such a gentle way about him and it was a lovely positive way to kick off the meeting.

Unfortunately, it didn't last long.

'That's all very well, Hugo,' said Lady Fortescue as she flicked through my hand-out, 'but Bonfire Night ticket sales are looking distinctly lacklustre.'

She took a cup of tea from Jenny and shook her head at the plate of ginger biscuits that Sheila passed along.

'But there are over six weeks to go, Beatrice,' Lord Fortescue reminded her gently.

'Even so!' she retorted. 'We need big parties, large bookings, coach-loads if we're going to cover our costs. I mean, look at this – three thousand pounds to pay the firework display company. Three thousand! That's hundreds of tickets to sell just to cover the cost of that alone!'

I gulped as suddenly all eyes turned to me.

'They are the best,' I said boldly. 'We can choose our own soundtrack and they'll even finish by creating the Wickham Hall logo in the display for that.'

'I'd expect them to project the logo on the moon, for that price,' Andy sniggered.

'Wow, sounds amazing,' Nikki pulled an impressed face.

'And didn't you say they're award-winning, Holly?' said Jenny, nudging the plate of biscuits my way.

I shot them both a grateful smile but before I could reply, Andy slid his eyes slyly towards mine.

'Perhaps Holly has something secret up her sleeve, something she hasn't told us yet.' He smirked, pushing my hand-out across the table pointedly and folding his arms. 'Something *terribly* good.'

Andy hesitated on the word 'terribly' so long that I thought I might pass out. My heart began to race nervously. He wouldn't, would he? I'd been dreading this moment. Please say he wasn't going to mention the conversation he'd overheard between Jenny and me last month, when I'd admitted having a terrible secret . . .

And still all eyes were on me.

My mouth had totally dried up. 'Um . . .' I croaked.

'Holly?' Lord Fortescue nodded at me encouragingly. 'Have you got something to share with us?'

Lady Fortescue chose that moment to swivel her gold bangle round and round impatiently and I could barely drag my eyes away from it. Her pearl bracelet was at this moment in my bag hanging on the back of my chair. My face must have been puce.

'Well? Ideas as to how to make the evening *go with a bang*?' Lady Fortescue tittered at her own joke.

'Um,' I repeated, feeling frustrated with myself. *Think, Holly, think*. Ben would have come up with something in a flash, something creative and fun . . .

'Actually, I have got a good idea,' I said, thinking on my feet.

'Bravo!' cried Lord Fortescue. He leaned his elbows on the table and cupped a hand around one ear. 'Fire away.'

'Well, we could, er, have a Guy Fawkes competition.'

It dawned on me just a fraction of a second too late that maybe encouraging something that had its roots in treason was a bit 'un-PC' when you were eighty-fifth in line to the throne but Lord Fortescue clapped his hands with pleasure.

'Guy Fawkes! I haven't made a guy since I was a boy. Excellent.'

I heaved a sigh of relief and quickly fleshed out my proposal. Actually, it wasn't a bad idea at all, now that I thought about it.

'We could launch it via the five local primary schools. Each school can enter their very best Guy, we judge them and the winning school gets a prize. Something educational, perhaps—'

'A couple of Kindles for the school library, maybe, or an iPad?' Lord Fortescue stroked his chin thoughtfully.

'Sorry,' Andy frowned, folding his arms, 'but I don't see how this is going to cover the outrageous fees for the fireworks. Especially as we've got to fork out for prizes too. Ha – *fork out*, Guy Fawkes, get it?'

'And your idea is . . . ?' Jenny glared at him.

'Me?' Andy sat bolt upright and blinked rapidly. 'OK, well, we could run a Facebook competition to win thirty tickets, using the thirtieth anniversary theme . . .' His voice faded as he noticed the unimpressed look on Lady Fortescue's face.

'We've already done the thirtieth thing.' She dismissed his idea with a wave of her hand. 'And I don't see how giving away tickets will help.'

'Er, thank you, Andy,' Lord Fortescue said diplomatically, 'but perhaps we could let Holly finish.'

I cleared my throat and carried on. 'If the schools have a vested interest in winning, they will promote the event to their pupils for us. And if the children want to come, the whole family will come too. As a rough estimate, I'd say that this idea could generate over a thousand guests.'

'Well, I must say, Holly, that is inspired.' Lady Fortescue's face was wreathed in smiles.

Andy made a derogatory noise that was somewhere between a hiss and a huff, Sheila made a note in the minutes about the Guy Fawkes competition and the discussion moved to the safety arrangements in the parkland.

I picked up my teacup and caught Andy's narrowed eyes over the rim. I might have won that round, but I had a feeling that the fight wasn't over yet.

Thirty minutes later the meeting drew to a close and everyone began to gather their belongings. I wanted to jot down a few notes about contacting the fire service before I left so I stayed in my seat and waved the others off. Only Andy remained.

I looked up from my notes to find him staring at me.

'I don't appreciate being embarrassed in public, Holly.'

It crossed my mind that he didn't need any help from me in that department. His attitude this afternoon had been pedantic and his one idea ill thought out. But I kept my opinions to myself.

'That was never my intention, Andy, I can assure you. Lord Fortescue asked for my idea and I gave it.'

He shook his head slowly. 'You think you're so smart, don't you? Well, just you remember that I heard what you said to Jenny. About having a secret that might cost you your job. And if I ever find out what that secret is, you can rest assured I will be only too happy to share it with the Fortescues.'

My breath caught in my throat. He stretched out a hand in front of him and examined his nails. 'In fact, I might just tell them anyway and let them wheedle it out of you.'

My stomach churned with fear but I refused to let it show on my face. Ignoring the thud of my heart, I got to my feet and leaned both hands on the table.

'I wouldn't if I were you,' I said in my best sinister voice. 'You have no idea what you're dealing with.'

He lifted a finger and pointed it directly at me. 'And neither do you.'

There was a noise at the door and Andy and I turned in unison.

'Ben!' I gasped.

Chapter 25

Ben was back!

His hair was all mussed up and longer than when I'd last seen him, his jaw was dark with stubble and his cheeks had a healthy weather-beaten glow. He stood in the doorway, waterproof coat rustling as he lifted his hands to his hips and gave Andy a suspicious look before turning to me.

'Sorry, Holly, didn't mean to make you jump,' he said, breaking into a smile.

'You didn't, it was just that . . .' I looked quickly at Andy and then back to Ben. 'I'm fine.'

I attempted a casual smile instead of the big soppy one that was threatening to escape. Warmth spread through me like molten chocolate and I felt a pull in the pit of my stomach.

I hadn't seen him since I'd fled from him in the gardens on the first day of the festival eight weeks and three days ago. Not that I was counting. Obviously.

This was ridiculous, I mused, aware of my quickening breath; I'd only known him for a few months. And he'd been away for a lot of that time. And I was grinning like a model in a toothpaste commercial.

Oh, who cares? Ben was back again. Back at Wickham Hall.

I smiled at him. 'Welcome home, stranger.'

It was probably just as well that Andy was in the room; left to my own devices I'd have probably launched myself at him, hugged him tight and proclaimed how much I'd missed him.

From nowhere Esme's words came floating through to me: *just relax, enjoy the chase . . .*

Best not say a word then. And I should preferably wait for some sort of indication that there was even going to *be* a chase before jumping on the poor man.

'Benedict!' Andy's hand flew to his hair as he began preening. 'What a surprise! You've just missed the Bonfire Night meeting. We've got some very exciting ideas.'

He was babbling, which was fine with me; it gave me a chance to recover from Andy's threat and get over the shock of Ben's sudden appearance.

Ben slid his gaze from Andy and his face softened as our eyes met. 'You look pale, Holly. Everything OK?'

I nodded vigorously. 'Absolutely.'

He nodded, looking unconvinced and turned back to Andy. 'I've just unloaded some of my paintings into the gift shop store room for temporary safe keeping.'

'Oh lovely, I can't wait to see them,' Andy simpered. 'I've always said that we should be selling your paintings in the gift shop; you are sooo talented.'

Ben exhaled. 'The place was a tip, Andy. Empty packaging strewn all over the place, boxes piled in front of the doorway. If nothing else it's a fire hazard. I want it cleared up first thing tomorrow.'

Andy grimaced. 'Yes, but we had a big delivery and there's been a problem with the bin collection—'

Ben held up his hand. 'Just deal with it, Andy.'

Andy pulled a face like he was chewing a particularly nasty wasp and began to put his jacket on. 'Fine,' he muttered.

'Holly, I'm sorry to drag you away, but can I borrow you for a second?'

My heart flipped: borrow, keep . . . whichever.

'Of course,' I said, focusing on not sounding too joyful.

Ben strode from the room and I jumped to my feet, scooped up my papers and shoved them into my handbag. Andy caught my eye and I just about restrained myself from sticking my tongue out at him triumphantly.

I pushed Andy from my mind as I scurried after Ben. He was already at the end of the corridor, pushing open the door that led to the Red Sitting Room. The hall was closed now for the day and we had the room to ourselves. He held the door open for me and grinned as I brushed past him. He smelled of the outdoors, the faint tang of the sea and his own special scent – all citrusy and male – and my heart performed a perfect somersault.

'Are you absolutely furious with me for deserting you for so long?' He watched me carefully as he stooped to switch on a table lamp.

'Are you kidding me?' I arched an eyebrow. I walked to the French doors and looked up at the evening sky. 'The peace and quiet was divine. My clipboard has been permanently on duty and my diary is almost full from now until Christmas.'

But I've missed you. A lot.

'Well, that's a relief,' Ben said, pretending to mop his brow. 'I would hate to think of you pining for me while I was gone.'

He came to lean on the doorframe by my side, close but not quite touching me.

'And me,' I asked, keeping my voice light. 'Did you cry into your pillow at night from missing me?'

He scratched his chin thoughtfully. 'Only once. Although I will admit to wondering what you were up to.'

'Working hard to keep the events department running as smooth as silk. Single-handedly,' I said, nudging him with my elbow. 'Without a word from my boss. For two months.'

'God, I'm sorry. My painting was going so well that I couldn't drag myself away.' His eyes sought mine and his face looked serious for a moment. 'I probably shouldn't do this in case you sue me or something . . .'

I looked up at him, holding my breath.

'But I'm going to do it anyway.'

I was in his arms before he'd even got the words out and then he was laughing and swinging me round and I was laughing too and thinking that I hadn't been this happy since the last time I'd been in his arms.

'This is a definite improvement on the last time I saw you.' His lips tweaked into a smile. 'I'll have to go away again. Remind me to check my diary.'

'You haven't got a diary,' I retorted, pulling myself out of his arms reluctantly. 'And besides I need you here.'

'Oh? That's the nicest thing you've ever said, Miss Swift.' He pressed a hand to his chest and pretended to swoon.

'I've talked myself into running a Guy Fawkes competition with the local schools. But you'd be much better at that sort of thing than me.'

'Guy Fawkes!' He grinned. 'I love it. I haven't made a guy since I was about twelve.'

I shook my head affectionately. 'You sound just like your dad.'

A shadow passed over his face and he exhaled sharply. 'Hmm. I haven't seen him yet, or my mum.'

I winced. 'Ah. Well, I'm sure they'll be glad you're back.'

He sighed, and dropped down into an armchair and I did the same.

'They're piling the pressure on for me to officially agree to take over at the hall. I've asked for more time and some space. And it didn't go down well. Especially with my mother.'

'I guess they just need to know where they stand so they can plan for their retirement,' I said diplomatically.

Ben nodded and gave a heartfelt sigh. 'I'm proud of my heritage and of this place, even if my mother does try to smother me on a regular basis.'

We shared a wry smile at that.

'But equally I'm proud of the career I'm making for myself. As an artist. I just can't see myself sitting in some boring boardroom having meetings with the trustees, day in, day out.'

He sat back in his chair and rubbed a hand through his dark hair.

'Everyone has to submit to responsibility at some point,' I pointed out gently. 'And you have dodged it pretty well till now.'

'Nothing wrong with that.' He grinned and shrugged his shoulders.

'Ben . . .' I paused, waiting for him to be serious. 'You will do a brilliant job when you take over from your father. Believe me.'

'Yes, well, that's a long way off.' He frowned and slapped his hands down onto the arms of the chairs, signalling the end of the conversation, and I sighed under my breath, hiding my frustration.

'Anyway, what was I interrupting there in Dad's office? Between you and Andy?'

I wrinkled my nose and shook my head, hoping that my cheeks didn't betray me. 'Oh nothing,' I said breezily.

He leaned closer and tapped my nose. 'Come on, Miss Tiny-but-Fierce, out with it.'

I chuckled and lifted my eyes to his, wondering if I should confide in him. It was a risk, but quite honestly, I was more than ready to get the whole bracelet thing off my chest and if anyone could think of a way to get it back unobtrusively into his mother's possession, it was Ben.

I took a deep breath. 'Would you like to hear a love story?'

'Am I in it?' He lifted an eyebrow mischievously.

I couldn't help but laugh as I shook my head. 'Sorry, this one is before your time, Romeo.'

'Holly . . .' He hesitated and my heart missed a beat. 'I've driven for what feels like a week. Can we go up to my apartment so that I can grab a beer and shed all these layers?'

His private apartment? Eek!

I lifted a shoulder nonchalantly. 'Sure.'

Two minutes later we were in the west wing of the hall on the top floor. Benedict stood back to let me into his suite of rooms ahead of him.

'Wow, Ben! This is amazing!' I walked into the room and span round slowly. This room alone could fit our tiny cottage in it and I imagined it was as far removed from Ben's life in London as it could possibly be.

'Welcome to my humble home,' he said, extending an arm towards a gold brocade sofa.

'It's very . . . gold,' I said, taking a seat on the rather stiff sofa.

Everything was gold: the sofa, the two armchairs and the large rug. There were various drawers and cabinets in the room in a Chinese lacquered style — gold, of course — and, rather incongruously, a beer fridge in the corner. Through an open door I caught a glimpse of a sumptuous four-poster bed hung with gold drapes. There was a further door, which I guessed led to a bathroom or dressing room.

'It is, in fact, the imaginatively named "Gold Room",' Ben said, opening the beer fridge.

He popped the lids off two bottles of Budweiser and handed one to me. I sipped the froth from the top while he peeled off his coat and jumper.

'Zara and I had children's rooms until we went to boarding school.' He grinned as he lowered himself onto the other end of the sofa. 'But now I get this when I'm back. It's a bit full-on, isn't it?'

'But beautiful,' I said, examining the exotic birds on the pale blue printed wallpaper.

'Right,' said Ben, setting his beer down on the low table in front of us. He rubbed his hands together. 'I'm all ears for the love story.'

'OK.' I took another sip for fortification purposes. 'Remember me saying that I was conceived at the Summer Festival?'

'Hardly the sort of thing I'd forget,' he said, his lips twitching playfully. 'That thought kept me occupied on many a draughty night in my hermit's cottage in Orkney. Lucky Lucy, the naughty minx.'

'Ben, please,' I said, wiping my palms on my skirt. 'This is serious.'

'Sorry,' he whispered. And to give him credit he sat completely silently, as I told him how Mum had met Antonio and the story of that traumatic day when my grandfather died and she lost touch with Antonio for ever. Finally,

I reached for my handbag and saw his eyes widen as I withdrew the pearl bracelet.

'Mum had no idea that it belonged to Lady Fortescue, Ben.'

I held my breath as I handed him the bracelet. He stared at it, shaking his head slowly. My pulse was sky high; I had no idea how he would handle this new information about Mum and me.

'Antonio had gone, her father had died and she'd lost everyone in the world who she'd cared about. She just couldn't bear to part with the bracelet.'

Ben still hadn't said a word. I looked down at my leg and realized it was trembling. I swallowed.

'Of course, I'll understand completely if you think I should leave Wickham Hall,' I murmured.

Setting the bracelet down on the table, Ben turned to face me and took hold of my hand, encircling my fingers in his. 'I'm so sorry, Holly.'

My heart sank. I nodded and lowered my gaze to our intertwined hands, loving the contrast of his rough skin against my pale soft fingers. Of course he'd have to tell Lady Fortescue the whole story, I didn't blame him. Which made this potentially my first and last visit to his apartment. I swallowed a lump in my throat and looked up at him.

He peered at me from under his curls. 'Poor Lucy having to face all that alone. And she never managed to trace him?'

I shook my head, thinking of all the newspapers she'd collected over the years, hoping to find a mention of his leather business at some other county show. 'She tried, but it was pre-Google and she only had his first name to go on.'

'Look,' he tugged gently on my hand, 'don't give the

bracelet another thought. I'll get it back to Mum somehow. Leave it with me. OK?'

'Really?' My shoulders sagged with relief. 'Thank you.'

I grabbed him round his neck and pressed a kiss to his cheek.

'Oh my goodness,' I sighed, 'you have no idea how pleased I am to hand that over.'

Ben smirked as he tucked the bracelet into his pocket. 'The kiss is a bit of a clue.'

Just then the door opened without warning and Lady Fortescue barged in.

'Benedict, I've just heard you're home!'

She glided towards him, arms outstretched, and then froze.

'Holly!' she gasped, flaring her nostrils. 'What on earth are you doing in Benedict's room?'

Chapter 26

Lady Fortescue looked at her son and then at me and then back at him. The shock on her face couldn't have been any more exaggerated if she'd caught us both stark naked. I took a sip of my beer to hide my discomfort.

Ben stood and walked towards her. 'She's drinking a beer, Mum. Not giving me a Thai massage.'

Was that the one with no clothes on? The beer slipped down the wrong hole and I began to splutter.

'Benedict, really,' she fretted. 'As much as we all appreciate Holly's role at Wickham Hall, this really is too much. And I must say I'm surprised at you, Holly. Staff are not permitted here, as well you know.'

'I . . . I'll go.' I jumped to my feet, face blazing. But Ben touched my arm.

'Mum,' he said firmly, 'Holly is here as my guest.'

She straightened her spine and shook her head, completely ignoring him. 'Well, I'm afraid I'm very strict about privacy. These are Benedict's private rooms. Whatever it is you need to see him about, I really don't think—'

'I invited Holly in, Mum,' he warned her. 'She's staying.'

Lady Fortescue looked about to object but apparently

thought better of it. 'Well, it's lovely to have you back, darling.'

Ben pulled her in close for a hug. 'Thanks, Mum,' he said, kissing her on her cheek. 'Now close your eyes, I've got a surprise for you.'

She frowned at him for a moment but he grinned in response. 'Go on,' he urged.

'Oh all right,' she said with an exasperated tut.

As soon as her eyes were shut, he winked at me and pulled the bracelet from his pocket.

I stared at him, my face getting hotter and hotter. Surely he wasn't just going to . . . ? Not with me in the room?

He took her hand, uncurled her fingers and dropped her long-lost bracelet into the palm of her hand. Her eyes sprang open immediately.

'Heavens above, Benedict! Where on earth has this appeared from?'

Oh, hell. I pressed myself into the hard sofa wishing I could just disappear between the cushions like a dropped coin.

He pulled a face and shrugged. 'No idea. It was left in an unmarked envelope at the gatehouse. I saw it when I picked up the spare key for the gift shop. Is it the one you lost?'

He flicked his eyes towards me and I detected the faint twinkle of humour, but I wasn't ready to reciprocate yet. Adrenalin was coursing round my bloodstream like a tidal wave.

'Yes!' she exclaimed, eyes glittering. 'Yes, it is! How lovely! Help me put it on, Benedict.'

She held out her wrist and Ben fiddled with the diamond clasp.

'Such a shame I don't know who to thank.' She sighed, admiring the pearls.

'Now you can go and relive the eighties.' Ben grinned. 'Put your Madonna album on and strut your stuff. Your secret's safe with me. And Holly.'

He winked at me and I tried to laugh but made a noise like a goat in pain instead. This was so awkward.

'I'm not the only one who should be going,' Lady Fortescue murmured at Ben and inclined her head in my direction. She was so unsubtle that if I hadn't been worried about emitting a second goat noise, I'd have laughed.

Ben shepherded his mother towards the door and kissed her cheek again. 'We're just leaving, actually. I'll catch up with you and Dad at dinner, OK?'

I gazed around the room and through to the bedroom and my stomach clenched; would Ben remember my third wish, I wondered, about how I'd always dreamed of waking up in a four-poster bed?

'Holly? Earth to Holly?' Ben bent down, resting his hands on his thighs to look into my eyes.

I shook myself. 'Sorry, miles away. Thanks for sorting the bracelet out. I've been carrying it around for weeks.'

'No bother,' he shrugged. 'Come on, I've just had an idea.'

'Oh, really?' My lips twitched; I'd missed his spontaneous ideas.

He pulled me up to my feet and cocked an eyebrow. 'One of my best, actually. But first I want to make a deal with you. If I can find out some more information about this Antonio, will you come on a date with me? This Saturday? I wrote it in your diary.'

'Oh yes.' I wrinkled my forehead, pretending to search my memory. 'I remember. But do you really think you can track down my father?'

'I do.' He grinned. 'Do we have a deal?'

He stuck out a hand and held my gaze.

I pretended to consider his offer carefully and then shook his hand to seal the deal. 'Done.'

He sighed with satisfaction and shrugged his coat back on. 'Wrap up then, it's cool out there this evening.'

I frowned, intrigued as to where he was taking me. 'I haven't brought a coat today. I'll be fine.'

'Here, borrow this.' He opened a tall Chinese lacquered wardrobe and pulled out a battered leather jacket.

He helped me into it. It was huge but the leather was soft and when I buried my nose in the collar it smelled of Ben and I immediately wondered how long I could hold on to it before he asked for it back.

I followed Ben out of his private rooms, along to the end of the west wing and down a narrow flight of stairs. He unhooked a torch from a peg by the door and turned a large old-fashioned key to let us out.

'It's not dark yet, but the place we're going will be,' he said, handing me the torch.

I couldn't imagine how this could possibly lead to information about Antonio, but I was having fun anyway.

'A magical mystery tour.' I smiled. 'How exciting.'

It was nearly seven o'clock, most of the staff had left and we had the grounds to ourselves. We walked along a path lined with topiary shapes that led to the long row of brick buildings at the far side of the Fortescues' private car park.

'All of these used to house my grandfather's vintage car collection,' said Ben as he struggled to push open the heavy wooden door of the end unit.

'And what's in here now?' I squinted.

'Archives. Financial stuff mostly. It's all computerized now, of course, but there's something precious about these old handwritten records, I think. Back in the early days when Mum and Dad first took over at the hall, they had an old chap working in the office who had been here for decades. He kept a big book and listed all the names and addresses of the exhibitors who came to the Summer Festival. Then he used to write them a letter every autumn, inviting them back for the following year.'

'How do you know all this?' I marvelled.

'Zara and I used to have a job stuffing envelopes and licking postage stamps to earn pocket money. We did all manner of jobs around the estate, actually. Looking back, we had a great childhood,' he said wistfully.

I gave him a sideways look. He adored Wickham Hall; it was obvious to me, even if he couldn't see it himself. When would he see the light? I wondered.

'Brilliant, I've found another torch.' He switched it on and I turned my beam to a shelving unit, stacked from top to bottom with ledgers, files and cardboard boxes.

'OK. In theory, the shelves should run chronologically,' said Ben, stepping up to the first shelf. 'Which year are we looking for?'

'1984.' I ran my torch up and down the rows of books and files. 'Over here, look.'

'Ha. Success,' said Ben after a few minutes. He stuck the torch between his teeth and used both hands to pull out a heavy blue book. A label with 'Summer Festival 1984' written in thick black pen was peeling from its spine.

Between us we cleared some room on the top of an old bookcase and began flicking through the alphabetical list of exhibitors.

'This is so weird,' I murmured. 'All those years Mum spent searching for Antonio and the answer was right here all along.'

'We hope,' countered Ben.

I shivered. The old storage building was damp and cold, but it wasn't just the temperature that was making my skin tingle. I knew the story of how my parents met now, and it was lovely and sweet and had wrapped itself around my imagination like a fairy tale, but this was hard facts. This made Antonio real.

I was possibly on the cusp of learning more about my father than even Mum knew.

'Do you . . .? Should I leave you alone?' Ben asked gently.

I touched his arm. 'No, please stay.' I gave an embarrassed laugh. 'I know it sounds silly, but this feels like such a major moment. I mean, I've always been just Holly Swift. I've never had a clue about my own father's surname.' I lowered my voice. 'Your mum would have a field day with that.'

'Don't let her starchy demeanour fool you for a second.' He grinned. 'She's an old romantic at heart. She's always reading lovey-dovey books, when she's not trying to run my life, that is.'

'That sounds like my mum. Oh wait, what's this?' I lowered my head to decipher the loopy writing in the ledger. 'Biancardi leather goods.'

'Sounds Italian,' Ben agreed. 'Address in Bergamo, Italy. There you go, that must be it.'

'Let's double-check there aren't any other Italian names,' I said in a shaky voice.

We checked right through the list of exhibitors, but the only other Italian name was an artisan ice-cream maker based in London. I flipped back to the leather goods listing.

'Biancardi,' I murmured, tracing my finger over the letters. 'Biancardi. What a lovely name.'

The hairs at the nape of my neck prickled. Holly

Biancardi . . . What should I do now, find his number and ring him up with a cheery 'Hi, Dad'? Could it really be that simple?

I reached into my handbag for my phone and took a picture of the Biancardi company's details.

I looked at Ben and his eyes glittered back happily. 'So. What next, Miss Swift? Will you be leaping on the next plane to,' he pulled the ledger closer, 'Bergamo?'

I dropped the phone back in my bag and shook my head. 'This has to be planned carefully. There's Mum to consider and Antonio, too. If he's as lovely as my mum says, no doubt he'll have a family of his own by now. As well, I mean.'

'So you're going to make a plan?' He smiled. 'How very Holly Swift.'

I shrugged self-consciously. He might be the sort to jump on a plane on a whim, but I preferred a more organized approach.

'Hey.' He put an arm round my shoulders. 'I shouldn't tease; I do understand what a big thing this is. Do you want to borrow the book?'

I shook my head. 'I've got all I need. Thank you, Ben. So much.'

I smiled up at him and we were so close that I could feel the warmth of his breath on my face.

'I'd better go; I've got plans for this evening,' I murmured.

I took a step back and a look of disappointment flickered across his face.

It was a white lie; my plans entailed nothing more riveting than hand-washing my angora cardigans ready for the approaching autumn, but something Esme said was ringing in my ears.

I handed him the torch back and said goodnight but as I reached the door he called my name and I turned to see him leaning against the shelf, a cheeky smile playing at his lips.

'I'd still have helped you find that information even if you'd said no to our date.'

'Saying no to our date never crossed my mind.' I winked. 'Not for a second.'

The sound of his laughter echoing around the old garage made my heart skip as I headed towards the staff car park. Esme was right about the thrill of the chase: it was completely intoxicating.

Chapter 27

It was noon on Saturday and I was in Joop. I had one hour until Ben was due to pick me up. Sixty minutes! At this rate I'd be going out *au naturel*. I glanced at my watch for the umpteenth time.

'All I know is it's a smart occasion,' I said, feeling slightly panicky as I rejected outfit after outfit.

'Men,' huffed Bryony. 'A surprise is all well and good and very romantic.' She glanced at me slyly. 'But it's not very helpful when it comes to choosing an outfit, is it?'

I blushed and pointed to a beige linen dress with a full skirt. 'How about that?'

Bryony looked at me as if I was bonkers. 'That colour will wash you out.'

I pulled a face, suitably chastised. 'Maybe not, then.'

She took a silk dress in baby blue with a row of beads around the neck from the rail. 'Put this on.'

'Pale blue?' I looked at it doubtfully.

Esme grinned. 'You've done it again, Mum. Perfect.'

'Silk is smart, I suppose,' I conceded. 'OK.'

'But smart can mean anything.' Bryony sighed, slipping the silk dress off its hanger and handing it to me. 'It could mean ball gown or cocktail dress, or even formal work wear.'

I shuddered and disappeared behind the curtain of the fitting room. 'Or hopefully none of the above.'

'Hey!' Esme piped up. 'Maybe it's a private jet to the opera, like in *Pretty Woman*! Maybe Italy.'

Italy? My stomach took a nosedive at the sudden thought that Ben had somehow contacted my father, Antonio Biancardi (I still enjoyed rolling his name around in my head), and we were heading off to meet him. But that was silly; the date had been in the diary long before Ben had even heard the story. Besides, he wouldn't go behind my back like that and if he did I'd be furious.

Despite checking repeatedly that I was still free on Saturday, Ben had given me no details about our date at all until last night when he'd suggested that I 'might want to wear something smart'.

So here I was, in Joop, frantically combing the rails for the perfect 'smart' thing. The outfit Esme and I had originally planned all those weeks ago – jeans, heels and a nice-but-not-too-sexy top – had instantly been dismissed as unsuitable and if there was one thing I hated, it was not being prepared.

I zipped myself into the blue dress and took a deep breath as I looked in the mirror: slightly too long but otherwise, lovely.

I slid back the bolt on the fitting-room door. Bryony gave me the thumbs-up and Esme instantly dropped to her knees and began to pin the hem.

'He did say we'd be gone all day, but he didn't mention needing a passport so—'

'A day at the races,' Bryony exclaimed, clapping a hand over her mouth. 'A hat, you need a hat. Esme, what have we got?'

I laughed. 'Thank you, Bryony, but I don't want a hat. I'd

feel uncomfortable and I'm nervous enough as it is. I just want to be me. That is who he asked on a date, just ordinary me.'

Esme stood up, spat the pins out of her mouth and plonked a kiss on my cheek. 'You are far more than ordinary, Holly Swift.'

I smiled my thanks and then yelped as she accidentally stabbed me with a pin.

'Don't you dare bleed on it,' she warned.

I stood as still as a statue in the centre of the shop while she pinned up my hem and my eye suddenly noticed a 'For Sale' sign in the uppermost part of the window.

'You're definitely selling up, then?' I asked Bryony, who was leaning on the counter inspecting her sparkly nails.

She let out a heart-felt sigh. 'Well, I can't do the alterations any more, my fingers get too sore, and we aren't bringing in enough money to make a profit so . . .' She shrugged.

I nodded sympathetically. Esme kept silent, I noticed.

I smoothed my hands down the dress and caught a glimpse of myself in the mirror. I'd never in a million years have picked this colour by myself. Bryony just seemed to have an eye for colour and style and could easily pick out outfits to suit her customers. And then the idea came to me . . .

'Bryony,' I exclaimed, 'you should offer a personal shopping service. You could do one-to-ones or even group bookings for hen parties. People would pay good money for personal fashion advice to sort their wardrobes out.'

Esme stopped pinning and Bryony raised her eyebrows with interest.

'She's right, Mum, you'd be brilliant at that,' said Esme. 'Do you know what, Holster? I think you might be onto something.'

'You're welcome.' I smiled serenely.

*

Miraculously, an hour later when I saw Ben pull up at the kerb, I was ready; my hair had been swept up into a pretty chignon, the dress had been shortened to a suitably youthful length and my arm jingled with a selection of Bryony's silver bangles.

Ben walked through the door and I swear I heard Esme's sharp intake of breath. At least I hope it was hers. It might have been mine: in a tight-fitting navy suit and white shirt open at the neck, Ben looked insanely hot.

'He is rocking that suit,' Esme murmured and I had to cough to cover up my giggle. Even Bryony took a staggering step back to lean on the counter.

Ben whistled and took his time looking me up and down. I think my entire body was alight with blushes. And the fact that Esme and Bryony were whispering behind me didn't help.

'Is this OK?' I asked in a shaky voice, giving him a twirl. I felt a breath escape when he nodded.

'Much better than OK.' He beamed. I waited for the joke about me scrubbing up well or something, but he simply smiled proudly, holding my gaze until I looked away.

'Which jacket, do you think?' I held up a silvery silk bolero jacket and a pale blue cashmere cardigan.

He pointed to the cardigan and I gave Esme a secret smile as I folded it over my arm. We hadn't been sure which would suit the occasion best and it had been her idea to be led by Ben.

'Your carriage awaits.' He made a flamboyant arm gesture towards where Lord Fortescue's Range Rover was parked outside. 'Excuse us, ladies.'

I followed him out of the shop, pausing to wink at Esme and Bryony over my shoulder as I left.

'Don't look,' said Ben, shielding the SatNav from me while he tapped in the destination address from a small card.

'It can't still be a surprise, surely?' I laughed, trying to see what he was reading.

'You're peeking.'

'OK, OK.' I grinned. I smoothed the skirt of my pale blue dress instead, wondering why I'd never worn this colour before; it was very pretty and suited my English rose skin tone perfectly. And Bryony, I thought, noticing her at Joop's window, should definitely consider offering a personal shopper service.

And then we were off.

The roads were quiet on Saturday afternoon and soon we'd left the villages behind and were zooming down the motorway but I was still none the wiser about the location for our date. After thirty minutes I could no longer stand the suspense, particularly as Ben kept shooting me gleeful smiles.

'OK, I give up,' I said, caving in. 'I need to know where I'm going so that I can enjoy the ride.'

He laughed and I peered at him, taking in his handsome profile and wondering for the millionth time why, out of all the girls he could be with, he had chosen me. But extremely glad he had.

'We are going to Oxford.' He clamped his lips together infuriatingly, sliding a sideways glance my way.

'And?' I demanded, folding my arms. 'If you don't tell me exactly where we're going, I'll start singing. You don't want that, believe me.'

He snorted with laughter but his lips remained closed.

I filled my lungs and belted out the chorus of 'Let It Go'.

'I surrender!' cried Ben after the second chorus. 'Open the glove box and you'll find all you need to know.'

I smiled triumphantly and followed his instructions. Inside the glove box was a square envelope with my name on it. I shot him a curious look.

He nodded. 'Open it.'

I lifted the flap carefully and removed a thick piece of embossed card. It was an invitation to the opening of an art exhibition this evening at Leith's Gallery in Oxford. The artist's name was Ben Fortescue and the collection was entitled 'New Dawn'. That had to be the loveliest idea for a date ever and my heart gave a little skip of joy.

I pressed a hand to my chest. 'Oh Ben, this is amazing! I'm . . . I'm honoured and thrilled.'

'And I'm honoured to have you as my guest,' he said simply, giving me a modest smile. 'I wanted you to see the other "me": Ben the artist, away from Wickham Hall.'

'I can't wait to see your paintings.' I sighed happily, until a thought struck me. 'I don't know much about art, though; perhaps I should look up some of your other work, will they be on Google?'

I reached for my bag to get my phone out, but Ben grabbed hold of my arm.

'I didn't tell you precisely for that reason,' Ben argued. 'I didn't want you planning ahead. I just want you to relax and enjoy it.'

I blinked at him. 'But what do I say if people ask me what I think of your work?'

'Tell them the truth, say what you see; tell them how it makes you feel.'

I chewed my lip doubtfully, worried that I might let the side down with my inferior art knowledge.

'Holly, you have never had a problem telling people

what you think,' he said, noticing the look on my face. He reached across and squeezed my hand. 'Just be yourself. Just be you and you'll do great.'

My mouth lifted into a smile at the compliment and I settled back into the Range Rover's leather seats and relaxed. Just be me. I was sure I could manage that.

We arrived in Oxford in plenty of time to wander around some of the university buildings, admiring the architecture. We dropped into a brasserie called Browns and arrived at Leith's Gallery at around five o'clock.

The gallery was still closed and the exhibition didn't begin for another hour but Ben needed to be there early to sign off the hanging of his new collection and discuss 'interest' from prospective buyers with the gallery owner. He knocked on the door firmly and we stood on the narrow pavement outside the gallery waiting for someone to answer. Ben had just taken my hand when the door flew open.

'Ben! Come in, come in!' A man in his late forties dressed head to toe in black flung his arms wide and beckoned us in. He had wispy sandy hair and small round glasses.

Ben placed a hand in the small of my back and nudged me forward. 'Miles, this is Holly Swift, my friend. Holly, this is Miles Leith, the gallery owner.'

'Delighted, delighted,' said Miles, pursing his lips in a flirty sort of way as he took my hand and hung onto it.

'Pleased to meet you too,' I said, endeavouring to retrieve my fingers from his meaty paw.

'I'm his friend too, of course,' he added with a hearty laugh.

Miles turned to Ben and clapped him on his back and extended his arm to take in the room. 'So, what do you think?'

'The place looks great, Miles. Thank you.'

'I genuinely think this is your best work, Ben. And you've been away, I believe. Scotland?'

Ben blinked at him. 'The Orkneys, yes.'

'So there are more landscapes in the offing, then?' Miles rubbed his hands together.

'Hey, slow down, Miles,' Ben said with a grin. 'Let's get this show out of the way before we plan the next.'

Miles guffawed as though Ben had told the world's funniest joke. 'Of course, of course!'

Ben touched my arm. 'I just need a few minutes with Miles to go over the arrangements for this evening. Why don't you have a look round? I'm dying to know what you think.'

'Sure.' I nodded.

Miles bore Ben away to a small side office and I wandered further into the room.

The gallery was narrow and on two levels. The walls were white and Ben's canvases – some framed, some not – were displayed all around the room, artfully highlighted with spotlights. With one exception: there was an easel set up in the centre of the room that looked to have a canvas on it but it was covered with a black cloth. At the far end on the upper level, two waiters were unloading champagne flutes from plastic crates onto a long table.

I approached the first painting. It was a huge canvas in tones of red and gold, a fiery sky reflected in a yellow cornfield. A small plaque underneath the picture informed me that it was entitled *Morning Glory*. It was absolutely glorious and I felt my throat tighten with emotion. I'd seen Ben's paintings before, I knew he was talented, but seeing his finished work displayed like this was overwhelming. His art was beautiful and he had chosen me to share this evening with. I thought my heart might burst with pride.

'Miss?'

I turned to see a waiter holding a tray of champagne.

I smiled my thanks and took a glass from him and then I turned back to the picture, raising my glass in a silent toast. *To the other 'you': Ben the artist.*

An hour later and the opening party was in full swing. Ben was thrilled with the turn-out and I'd been introduced to everyone from old art tutors and fellow artists to collectors and the gallery's regular customers. Miles had whisked Ben off on several occasions to talk to clients and sold stickers were beginning to appear on the corners of the paintings.

As far as I could see there were three groups of guests. There were the arty types with brightly coloured dyed hair, wearing trousers baggy at the knee. They seemed to be drinking the most champagne. A second social group consisted of smartly dressed women in their thirties who seemed more interested in the gossip than the art. A third group – older, more sedate, mostly in couples – took their time admiring each painting as they made their way round the gallery. So far this third group was responsible for most of the sold stickers.

'How does it feel, knowing that all these people have come to see your work?' I asked, raising my voice above the background music and the chatter.

'Fantastic.' His eyes sparkled with satisfaction. 'All the months of getting up early to paint the dawn, the self-doubt when I thought the paintings weren't up to scratch and of course the fact that Mum and Dad wish I'd hurry up and grow out of painting.' He made air apostrophes around 'grow out' and my heart went out to him.

'I'm sure they're proud of your work, though,' I soothed, wondering, if that was the case, why they weren't here today to support him.

He laughed softly and shook his head. 'As far as they're concerned it isn't work, it's just a hobby.'

I'd had a couple of glasses of champagne by now, which had knocked the edge off my inhibitions nicely, so I didn't think twice about putting my arm round his waist and kissing his cheek.

'What was that for?' Ben grinned. 'Not that I'm complaining.'

'It's for bringing so much sunshine to Wickham Hall.' I laughed. 'Especially to me.'

He didn't respond other than to smile and hold my gaze for a long moment.

'Come on,' he said, breaking the spell and grabbing two fresh glasses from a passing waiter, orange juice for him and more champagne for me, 'let's go and mingle. And then I've got my big reveal.'

We headed towards the upper end of the gallery, chatting and smiling to guests as we moved through the crowd.

I was more relaxed now, no doubt helped by the champagne; so far no one had asked me anything more challenging than how I'd met Ben and several people had been interested to hear about my job at Wickham Hall.

'I'm curious where this one was painted, Mr Fortescue,' one lady asked, tugging his arm. '*Shoreline Silence.*'

I turned to see the painting in question.

It was a large canvas featuring a stretch of deserted beach, a blue-grey sea with frothy waves and the pale yellow glow of the first glimpse of dawn in the middle of a sleepy sky.

'Ah.' Ben grinned and tapped the edge of the canvas. 'This is Holkham in Norfolk, painted in quite possibly the coldest April on record, fuelled by flasks of beef tea and charcoal hand warmers.'

'Goodness, that's quite an evocative image,' the lady said, clearly charmed by Ben's story.

I could totally see why; I was fascinated by Ben's paintings, too. Each picture was like a window into his soul; from the electric energy of a stormy sky to the exhilaration of clouds scudding across a wintry sea. It was as though Ben's emotions were visible in every brushstroke.

'All of the seascapes here are Norfolk. It's one of my favourite places to paint.'

'If you don't mind me saying,' she smiled shyly, 'your work reminds me a little of Lawrence Coulson.'

'Not at all.' Ben puffed his chest out. 'Coulson is a big inspiration to me.'

'Well, I adore *Shoreline Silence*,' said the lady. 'Yes, I think I'll buy this one.'

Ben signalled for Miles to attach a sold sign to it and I wandered off, leaving them to talk details with the customer.

I found myself in front of one of the smaller framed paintings. It was another coastal scene: lilac-grey clouds hovered over a tranquil sea pierced by the pink globe of the rising sun. I bent to read the nameplate and as I straightened I almost bumped into the waiter and his tray of canapés.

'Miniature Yorkshire pudding, miss?'

I looked at the silver tray. Each Yorkshire pudding had a wafer-thin curl of roast beef in the centre and was probably no more than a mouthful in size. My stomach growled with joy. I'd missed lunch due to my outfit dilemma and suddenly realized how hungry I was.

I popped one in whole and then, grinning at the waiter, took a second. It only took a moment before the taste exploded in my mouth: first the crispy shell of the batter, then the tender beef, followed by . . . Oh my word, something was hot, very hot, in a mustardy-singeing-my-nasal-passage way.

Horseradish sauce. Lots of it.

Tears sprang to my eyes as I forced the mouthful down and then swigged at my champagne. It felt as though my sinuses were on fire. I pinched my nose and dabbed the tears from my eyes and looked around for somewhere to dispose of the second canapé.

'How's that for you?' A dark-haired man sidled up to me with a grin.

'Well,' I sniffed, smiling self-consciously, 'fiery, unexpectedly so. I can still feel the heat burning the back of my throat.'

The man flicked a glance away from me and then nodded. 'Gosh. It does get you like that sometimes when the image is so real it becomes almost tangible. Go on.'

'Um . . .' I floundered. That was all I had to say about it really, I mean how much can you say about a mini Yorkshire pudding? 'Quite took my breath away.'

'Yes,' he nodded rapidly, 'I had that too, anything else?'

I blinked at him. Seriously? It was a flippin' savoury snack.

I shrugged. 'Beefy?'

'Beefy?' he repeated, shaking his head. He stepped up closer to the painting behind me. 'Extraordinary.'

Oh God. I cringed. He'd meant the painting. I moved in the opposite direction, taking my empty glass, unwanted food and burning face with me.

I spotted a bin, dumped the canapé and had recovered enough to face more food by the time the same waiter returned. This time with tiny crab cakes.

'Are they spicy?' I asked, helping myself.

They weren't, apparently, so I risked taking two again.

Ben was deep in conversation with a group of the arty types and caught my eye and waved just as I bit into my first crab cake. I grinned back and walked to the next painting where I was immediately joined by the same dark-haired man.

'That looks good,' he said. He pressed his lips together and nodded.

The painting was another seascape. Which meant it was somewhere in Norfolk. I bet he didn't know that. He wasn't going to catch me blathering about food this time.

'This one is from Norfolk,' I said, nibbling the edge of my crab cake. 'You can almost smell the sea, can't you?'

'Oh yes.' The man dipped his head forward into my personal space and swooped, bending his neck and inhaling sharply. 'Probably Cromer. They're famous for it.'

I cocked an eyebrow at him. Famous for what, smelling of sea?

'You can taste the saltiness of the breeze, the tang in the air,' I continued airily.

'Indeed,' exclaimed the man. 'Well, you've sold it to me.'

The waiter went by again and the man pounced on him. 'I'll have one of those Norfolk crab cakes please, they sound delicious.'

Oh heavens, I'd done it again. I sucked in my cheeks to stop myself from giggling, excused myself from the man and went off in search of Ben.

I found him coming out of the men's loos.

He snaked an arm round my waist and gave me a squeeze. 'I was just coming to find you. Sorry to have abandoned you for so long.'

'Don't worry about it,' I laughed, 'I've had fun. I've even discussed art with someone. Sort of.'

'But I should have known you'd spend half the time on your own. I'm sorry, Holly.' His eyes were soft and I felt my insides melt. 'We'll go for dinner afterwards and then I promise, I'm all yours.'

I opened my mouth to respond but Miles tapped Ben on the shoulder.

'I think you should do your thing now, Ben; if you don't mind excusing us, Holly?'

Ben smiled an apology as Miles led him away and the two men made their way to the painting in the centre of the gallery that so far had been hidden by a cloth. Miles tapped the side of his glass to call the room to order and said a few words of introduction. Then it was Ben's turn. I moved further forward to get a better view.

'Thank you all for coming to see my New Dawn collection, and thank you to Miles Leith for putting on this exhibition in your stunning gallery. This particular collection means a lot to me. I began it last year on the coast of Norfolk, then moved to the Yorkshire Dales in the autumn and finished up with my favourite piece of all, which I've only just finished.' His eyes flicked briefly to the easel beside him. 'The beauty of being a land-scape painter is that I will never see the same landscape twice. The sun, the sky, even the air changes moment to moment.'

Ben paused to take a sip of water and I glanced round the room. Everyone was hanging on his every word. They all seemed as mesmerized as me and I felt my heart swell with pride.

'The best I can do is to try to capture the moment, suspend it in time to evoke the atmosphere and the aura of the place, so that we can continue to enjoy that moment forever on canvas.'

He handed his glass to Miles and placed his hands on the cloth that obscured the painting.

'There is one particular landscape that is very close to my heart and that's the view across the Wickham Hall estate where I grew up. Recently I had the intense pleasure of witnessing a very special sunrise with a very special person. I captured the moment on canvas and I hope she will think that I've the done the memory justice.'

Ben tugged at the cloth and let it fall to the ground.

My breath caught in my throat when I realized what the canvas depicted: it was our sunrise. That perfect morning when he'd showed me the dawn back in July. The rising sun gave Wickham Hall a rose-gold glow and the clouds were candyfloss pink. Long golden shadows fell across the dewy grass where a deer and her fawn grazed fearlessly at the edge of the frame.

His eyes sought mine in the crowd and my body glowed warmly under his gaze. 'This one is called *Secret Sunrise*.'

And then people were clapping and chatting and moving again. The crowd faded into a blur until it was just Ben and me, staring at each other across the room. He raised his eyebrows and then we were jostling through groups of people to get to each other.

'I love it,' I murmured, throwing my arms round his neck. 'Did you do it all from memory?'

He nodded. 'And I went back to that spot for the next three days to make sure I got the magic right.'

I released him and shook my head slowly. 'You are ridiculously talented, Ben Fortescue.'

He smiled. 'I painted it as a gift for you. As soon as the exhibition is over, it's yours to do with as you want.'

'My first piece of art.' I beamed, pressing a kiss to his cheek. 'I love it, thank you.'

Ben grinned. 'Thank God for that, you have no idea how nervous I've been about that all evening.' He eased himself out of my arms. 'Now I have one last high-spending customer to talk to and then we are going to find a restaurant nearby before driving home. These tiny canapés don't even touch the sides for me.'

I watched him walk away and shake hands with a stooped man with sparse white hair and my stomach twisted with nerves.

Home.

Home is where the heart is and for me that had always been the little village of Wickham. Until tonight I'd thought that that was where Ben's home should be too. But maybe I wanted him to stay at Wickham Hall for the wrong reasons – selfish reasons? This was Ben's world, a world of art and artists and passion and talent. Now I'd seen the other Ben, Ben the brilliantly talented artist, I wasn't sure that he could ever be completely happy at Wickham Hall. For him it would mean sacrifice, compromise and possibly even unhappiness.

And if I did persuade him to stay, would I want that on my conscience?

Chapter 28

I sneezed for the umpteenth time and then stooped to pick up a stray leaflet from the living-room carpet. Mum and I were having a mammoth clear-out and it was the happiest time we had spent together for years. I was so pleased for her that she'd finally decided to declutter the living room, even if we had created clouds of dust as we scooped up years' worth of old magazines and brochures. It was a bright autumn day in October, three weeks since my date with Ben and a low sun shone through the living-room window making the dancing dust motes sparkle in its rays. Both of us were doing a lot of sneezing.

'Now are you sure you can bear to part with the Wickham Hall Christmas brochure 1999?'

I held it up to show Mum, tongue firmly in my cheek.

'Oh, let's see,' she said, grabbing it out of my hand and ignoring my despairing sighs. 'They had a big firework display that year, to celebrate the new Millennium. There was a marquee, a three-course dinner, a band and then fireworks to finish.'

I frowned. 'Did you go?'

She shook her head. 'You were fourteen: too old for a babysitter and too young to be left on your own. We watched the fireworks out of the window.'

I put my arm round her waist and gave her a hug. It had always been just the two of us on special occasions; sometimes it felt like we were the only people in the entire world without any family.

'Look at that tree.' She sighed, pointing to a festive picture of the main staircase at Wickham Hall decorated to the hilt. There was a towering Christmas tree at the bottom of the stairs and garlands of fir and ivy were looped around the banisters and tied with red ribbon.

I obliged, scanning the leaflet and joining in with her oohs and ahhs, secretly disappointed that there weren't any pictures of Ben as a little boy in it.

'And it will be just as magical this year,' I said, retrieving the leaflet from her fingers and dropping it into a large refuse sack. 'Although right at the moment all my efforts are being poured into the Bonfire Night display.'

And trying to play it cool with Ben.

I sat on the sofa for a moment, rubbing my nose and waiting for the next sneeze.

My heart twisted as I remembered his confused face when I'd turned him down for a drink last night.

Life in the events department at Wickham Hall had returned to normal – on the surface, at least. Ben spent his days in the office creating havoc: making last-minute changes to the Bonfire Night posters, ringing up the fireworks company to quiz them about some detail or other every five minutes and generally setting me on edge until I sent him off on a spurious errand in an attempt to get some work done in his absence. But something between us had changed. There was an electrical charge to the atmosphere whenever we were together and I could feel it building with every passing day.

The problem was, I hadn't quite worked out how to behave around him.

Our date at the art gallery had been one of the most memorable nights of my life. We had left Oxford and stopped for dinner at a French bistro, sharing a platter of seafood so delicious that it even made Esme's mouth water when I described it to her afterwards. But the date had been eye-opening in all sorts of ways. It had deepened my feelings and confirmed my attraction to Ben. But it had also sent me into a spiral of doubt about the wisdom of Lord and Lady Fortescue's wishes that Ben take over at Wickham Hall. How could he live out his dreams of being an artist without crushing those of his parents?

And on a personal level, how would I feel if, or when, Ben chose his art over Wickham Hall? I already knew the answer to that and the only way to avoid heartache, I'd decided, was to keep our relationship on nothing more than a friendly basis until I knew exactly where things stood.

So I'd said no to a drink last night, even though my heart was urging me to say yes. Mum took a seat beside me and I leaned my head briefly on her shoulder.

'Ben asked me about Antonio again, Mum. He's obsessed with the story.'

'Is he? Ahh.' Mum's face softened. She'd had a soft spot for Ben ever since he'd 'mistaken' us for sisters.

I nodded, trying to hide a smile. In fact, Ben, in true man-style, was more taken with what Mum and Antonio had managed to get up to in the bushes undisturbed, but she'd be mortified if I told her that.

'It was over almost before it began, Holly.'

I blinked at her, wondering for a moment whether she'd been reading my mind. I so hoped not.

'We were from different worlds, different backgrounds.

I was naïve to think it would have worked out between us.'

Different worlds. I flinched as her words touched a nerve. That was exactly how I felt about the obstacles between Ben and me.

'I thought love was supposed to conquer all,' I said wistfully. 'People overcome all sorts of barriers when they feel strongly enough about someone, don't they?'

Mum sighed and closed her hand over mine. 'It was thirty years ago, Holly. I'm a different person and I'm sure Antonio will be too. I have no wish to go down this road for myself. Especially when things are still new for Steve and me.'

Steve had taken to spending the night here quite regularly, which had meant Mum having to have a drastic sortout of her bedroom, which he'd helped her with. And now that she was cooking dinner for them both, she'd made an effort to clear the kitchen worktops too. So not only was the house looking better for his presence, he'd put a smile on her face and a new spring in her step and it was heartwarming to witness.

'When you first told me about losing Granddad and losing touch with Antonio, I thought if I could track down my father, it would give you closure, and maybe help you overcome your . . . attachment to stuff,' I said, avoiding the word 'hoarding' as Mum didn't like to refer to it as that.

'But it's actually a new love which has done that. I'm proud of you, Mum. And pleased.'

I gazed at the three boxes of newspapers ready to go to Henley library. Mum and Steve had selected these after he'd persuaded her to donate all her copies of the *Wickham and Hoxley News* to the local archives. The library staff were really excited and planned to put on a big display sometime in December.

'It wasn't just Steve, love.' She smiled, squeezing my hand. 'You've helped too.'

'Good.'

I felt my foot slide on a piece of paper and bent to retrieve it. It was one of the leaflets I'd picked up on my very first day at Wickham Hall, one about the restoration of the art gallery. I frowned, wondering why that project had never been mentioned in all the months I'd been working at the hall.

I folded it up and stuffed it into the pocket of my jeans to read later. I'd find out more about that, I decided. Perhaps Sheila would know something?

Mum's chest lifted as she inhaled a deep breath before speaking. 'Holly, Antonio is your father and I want you to know that if you do decide to trace him, I support you one hundred per cent. It's completely your choice.'

I kissed her cheek. 'Thanks, Mum. I'm not going to do anything in the foreseeable future, I'm still thinking it through. And if I do anything, I promise I'll tell you first.'

I'd sat down and drawn up a plan of how I should get in touch with Antonio countless times. But I wasn't sure what I'd achieve other than to throw the poor man's life into disarray, not to mention possibly throwing the cat amongst the pigeons for Mum and Steve, despite her assurances. Maybe one day when I wanted children I might feel differently; maybe I'd want to check his family history for medical problems or something. For now, I concluded, it would be kinder all round if things remained as they were.

Bonfire Night had finally arrived and in an hour the sky above Wickham Hall would be heavy with smoke from the bonfire that Jim was currently prodding to check for sleepy hedgehogs. But for now the air was clear, the moon was full and the sky was purpley-black and glittered with pin-pricks of tiny stars.

We had opened the gate to the car park for the firework display at five thirty ready for a six o'clock start and already the lamp-lit courtyard had taken on the appearance of a street scene straight out of a Dickins novel – there were crowds around all the stalls selling snacks and drinks, Andy was doing a roaring trade with his faux-fur winter warmers and the queue for Jenny's pulled pork rolls was beginning to build. The scene made me glow with happiness; the event was turning out even better than I'd hoped.

Jenny held out a piece of pork for me and I opened my mouth like a baby bird as she popped it in.

'That Guy Fawkes idea of yours was spot on, chick.' She grinned. 'I can't remember seeing crowds like this for a bonfire before.'

I closed my eyes as the delicious smoky flavour of the pork filled my mouth. 'I'm not so sure I can take all the credit, Jenny. The smell of that pork has probably had all the mouths in a ten-mile radius watering!'

'By the way, I'm liking the neon yellow look.' She winked.

'Thanks,' I said, giving her a twirl.

Along with a group of other officials I wore a high-visibility tabard over my clothes. Essential at an event like this, of course, but it didn't do much for my sartorial elegance.

She served the next customer, handing the man a juicy pork-filled baguette and pointing him in the direction of the napkins. 'If you see Nikki on your travels, tell her I'll save her a roll. At this rate they'll have all disappeared before the firework display starts at seven.'

'Will do. Last time I saw her she was down at the bonfire site fretting about the state of her grass.'

I pilfered another piece of pork, narrowly dodging a smack from Jenny's spatula and then set off to find Ben. He was due to judge the entries to the children's Guy Fawkes competition at six fifteen and I wanted to make sure he knew where he needed to be and what the prize for the winning guy was.

I found him at the toffee-apple stand struggling to peel the cellophane off his toffee apple.

'These flippin' things should come with an instruction manual,' he groaned, holding up his fingers. They were covered with shreds of cellophane.

I laughed and took the apple from him.

'Here.' I handed him a tissue and he wiped his fingers while I carefully removed the rest of the cellophane and gave it back to him.

'Thanks, Mum.' He grinned. 'Want a bite?'

'No thanks,' I giggled, 'now don't get it all over your face, will you? You've got an audience of impressionable children to address.'

Down on the field, Jim had lit the bonfire and despite the several hundred people surrounding it, I could already feel the heat from it as we approached the area set aside for the Guy Fawkes competition.

'That's some fire,' Ben marvelled as we both watched the flames dancing several metres high. 'I hope Jim can cope.'

I tapped my nose with a grin. 'All carefully planned, Mr Fortescue, never fear.'

We had tanks of water nearby and the fire service were primed and ready should something untoward happen. Not that it would. The fire had been built from garden rubbish and branches pruned back for the winter by Nikki's volunteers. Jim was more than capable of keeping it under control.

Ben put an arm round my shoulders and squeezed me to him so swiftly that it was all over before I could return the hug.

'I'd expect nothing less where you're concerned, Hols. I'm perfectly aware that you run the events department single-handedly. In fact, if anything, I'm probably more hindrance than help.' He laughed. 'You wouldn't miss me at all if I left, would you?'

Was he leaving? Was that his decision? I tried to smile at him but I felt a lump rise to my throat.

'I wouldn't miss your singing, that's for sure.' I laughed shakily. 'Come on, your public awaits.'

Far enough away from the bonfire to appease safety-conscious parents, Ben and I had erected five plinths – one for each of the schools to display their entries to the Guy Fawkes competition – and quite a crowd of children and their families had gathered.

Ben handed me his apple core on a stick with a cheeky smile and plunged to the front of the throng.

'Hello, everyone!' he yelled, waving his hand in the air.

I watched, entranced, for a couple of minutes as Ben chatted to some of the children and shook hands with the teachers. He was in his element, I thought, hugging my arms round myself. All of a sudden the crackle of my two-way radio from my pocket made me jump and I answered the call from Jim.

'Holly, they've run out of room in the car park. There's a queue of stationary cars all the way up to the road leading into the village and it's causing an obstruction. Can you deal with it? You need to go to the gatehouse and get the key for the overspill car park. This fire's getting very smoky and I daren't leave it. Over.'

'No problem, Jim; leave it with me.'

I strode away from the school group, leaving Ben entertaining the children by making up ventriloquist's routines with all the guys. One of the car park attendants came back on the radio: customers were beginning to get angry about the parking situation and demanding ticket refunds if they missed the fireworks.

My stomach twisted and I broke into a run. Having record visitor numbers was all well and good, but if we had to start giving refunds, my name would be mud. It crossed my mind to ask the fireworks people to delay the start of the display, but then I remembered that everything had been timed to the split second; there was nothing they could do about it now. I'd just have to get the car park opened as quickly as I could.

I let myself into the gatehouse, conscious of the prickle of sweat under my arms, and grabbed the key from the key cabinet. I pulled my woolly hat off and tucked it into my pocket. Wrapping up warmly in four layers topped off with Ben's leather jacket had seemed a good idea earlier in the day but now I was practically steaming. I darted back out of the gatehouse and ran as fast as I could to the overspill car park.

Five minutes later the parking issue was abating and frayed tempers were cooling. I breathed a sigh of relief and began a fast walk back to Ben.

I made it as far as the courtyard when I heard my name being called.

I turned round with a smile, expecting to see either Esme or Mum and Steve. They were supposed to be here somewhere and I hadn't bumped into them yet. But it was Lady Fortescue, looking impossibly elegant in a full-length fur coat and matching hat. She had her hands on her hips and was tapping the toe of her boots and scanning the crowds.

'Hello, Lady Fortescue. I like your hat, is it from the Wickham Hall range?' I asked, walking towards her.

'Absolutely not,' she said, adjusting the brim over her fringe. 'I bought it in Harrods last week. Naughty really, I've got a dressing-room full of coats and hats, I really should have a clear-out before Hugo tells me off.'

I made a mental note to ask Pam the housekeeper about Lady Fortescue's cast-offs. I could give them to Mum for her charity shop. They'd have a bumper year selling her second-hand furs, that's for sure.

'You called me, Lady Fortescue?'

'Have you seen Benedict?' She frowned, still looking around her.

'Yes,' I replied. 'He's down near the bonfire, judging the Guy Fawkes competition.'

She pressed her lips together and gave a disapproving sniff. 'That Guy Fawkes thing was supposed to have been your idea, Holly.'

'I did offer,' I said, which wasn't strictly true. 'But Ben*edict* thought it would be a good way of introducing himself to the wider community.' Also not strictly true.

Lady Fortescue brightened instantly.

'Good idea. Such a clever boy,' she said, looking at her watch. 'Would you mind fetching him as soon as he's finished, please? Hugo and I have guests and we're supposed to be watching the fireworks from the private gardens.'

'Of course.' My heart sank; I'd been hoping Ben and I could watch the fireworks together.

'And do tell him to hurry up.'

'OK.' I smiled and prepared to move away when she grabbed hold of my sleeve.

'Is that Benedict's jacket?'

My cheeks burned as I juggled my words to come up with

a suitably valid excuse for being dressed in her son's leather jacket other than that it smells of him and when I wear it, I imagine being wrapped in his arms.

'Yes, he kindly lent it to me a few weeks ago,' I mumbled. 'I was planning on returning it. Tonight, in fact.'

She shot such daggers at me that I wouldn't have been surprised to find myself pinned to the floor.

'Now I know Benedict is a grown man and entitled to do as he chooses, but as a member of staff, you are expected to keep a professional distance. It is inappropriate for you to be wearing my son's clothes.'

My heart was hammering against my ribcage but I looked her squarely in the eye. 'I understand, Lady Fortescue.'

I almost added that we were only friends, but that wouldn't have been completely true. Ben was becoming much more than that. Far more.

She stared at me coldly. 'I hope so, Holly.'

'I . . . I'd better go and find Benedict, Your Ladyship,' I said, turning to go, keen for this conversation to come to an end.

'Yes, do. There's someone I think he'd like to meet. A lovely girl; very biddable. She's the daughter of one of my friends, Baroness Allthorp,' she said. 'Benedict is going to be *so* pleased she could come.'

'Of course, Lady Fortescue,' I muttered.

I left then and pushed through the packed courtyard in search of Ben, feeling cross with myself for letting her get the upper hand.

There was only one woman I wanted Ben to be spending the evening with and that was me.

Chapter 29

Down on the field, the sky was heavy with bonfire smoke and millions of ash flakes fluttered in the air, settling in people's hair and on coats like tiny snowflakes. I began to walk towards the Guy Fawkes area when someone grabbed my arm.

'Holly, love, what do you think?'

I whirled round to see Mum wearing one of the Wickham Hall fur hats. Steve stood beside her, his hands full with two bottles of beer and a pork baguette.

'Suits you, Mum. Hi, Steve,' I banished all thoughts of Lady Fortescue and beamed at the pair of them.

'It was a present from Steve.' She looped her arm through his and relieved him of one of the beers. 'The fireworks are about to start, I think. Can you stay and watch with us or do you need to dash off?'

'Um,' I hesitated, searching the Guy Fawkes area for Ben, but it was deserted. I should really find him and deliver Lady Fortescue's message. After all, we didn't want to keep Baroness What's-her-face waiting, did we?

'Sure, why not.' I grinned.

The three of us walked towards the roped-off area set aside for the fireworks, not that we could get very close;

there must have been hundreds of families already lined up ready for the display to start.

'I'm surprised you haven't brought your camera,' I said to Steve.

'No way.' He chuckled. 'You wouldn't believe the number of events I've been at over the years when I've been so busy making sure I got the perfect shot that I end up not really seeing anything. I want to enjoy tonight as it happens, with my best girl,' he smiled at Mum and my heart melted at the look they shared, 'not wait to see it tomorrow through the lens.'

At that moment classical music boomed out of the speakers and a split second later the fireworks display began. The sky lit up time and time again with burst after burst of bright colours, shooting stars soaring across the night, huge spheres of multicoloured lights, bluey-white flares that were almost too bright to look at, all exploding and fading in time with the music.

'This is great,' shouted Steve above the noise. 'I've never seen fireworks like it.'

'Holly organized it all,' Mum yelled proudly, 'didn't you, love?'

I nodded. 'Glad you like it. It's Handel's "Music for the Royal Fireworks". Quite apt, I thought.'

We stood and watched the whole of the display, joining in with the oohs and ahhs with the rest of the spectators. Though I said so myself, it was the best fireworks display I'd ever seen and when the Wickham Hall logo lit up the sky at the end, I found myself clapping and cheering along with everyone else.

I lowered my gaze from the sky and noticed how smoky the air around our heads had become in the last few minutes. No wonder my eyes were smarting; I could barely see a few feet in front of us. Ben's jacket was going to reek of smoke when I gave it back to him.

'Brilliant, absolutely brilliant,' said Mum, lowering her beer bottle to the ground so that she could join in with the applause.

'I'd better go, Mum,' I said, kissing her warm cheek. 'I was supposed to—'

Before I could finish, Mum and I stumbled backwards as the crowd seemed to surge at us. Steve grabbed Mum's arm and the bottle got kicked over.

I held onto her other arm and stood on my tiptoes, trying to see over heads towards the fire, but the view was obscured by thick smoke. This didn't look right to me and my heart began to race.

'What's going on?' gasped Mum.

'Sorry, love. Everyone just started pushing us,' said a man, with a little boy on his shoulders.

'I wanna get down,' yelled the little boy.

'Smoke! Smoke! Get back!'

I could hear shouting and screaming from down at the front nearest the fire and the air was getting more and more foggy. The crowd was surging backwards as people in the audience yelled and pushed. Some were already coughing as smoke hit the back of their throats.

'Make your way up to the courtyard, you two,' I urged. 'I need to go and check on Jim, see what's happening.'

'Holly, be careful!' Steve warned. 'You don't know what's causing this smoke.'

I nodded and pulled my scarf up across my mouth, dipped my head low and attempted to push against the tide of people. It was no use; the force of the crowd was too strong. I was beginning to get seriously worried and grabbed my two-way radio.

'Jim? Come in? Jim? Over.'

I tried him twice but got no reply. I radioed for Benedict instead. 'Benedict, this is Holly. Where are you? Over.'

'I'm in the courtyard and it's madness, people pushing and shoving through the gates from the field. What's going on down there? Are you OK?'

More and more people were knocking against me and that, coupled with the acrid smoke, was beginning to make me panicky and short of breath.

'I'm not happy with this, Ben. The bonfire is really smoky,' I yelled. 'And Jim's not answering his radio. I'm trying to get to him now.'

'I'll meet you down there,' he replied.

It was ridiculous trying to fight the crowd, so I headed towards the 'no access' roped-off area instead, jumped over it and ran along the area cordoned off for the fireworks. I was nearly at the bonfire site when the radio crackled into life.

'This is Nikki. I think we're going to need the fire service; the bonfire is pumping thick black smoke into the air. Over.'

I yelled into the radio. 'Nikki, I'll call them now. Can you see Jim? Over.'

'No, but I'll keep looking.'

My skin prickled with fear as I dialled the fire service. Where was he?

'Wickham Hall,' I shouted into my phone when the operator asked for my location.

I gave them the details and as soon as I'd ended the call I ran towards the bonfire as fast as I could. The smoke stung my eyes and my thick scarf did nothing to protect me. My lungs began to ache with the lack of oxygen in the air. Then my heart missed a beat as I caught sight of Nikki ahead, kneeling over my dear old friend.

'Jim!' I screamed and I dived to the floor beside his limp body.

The next hour whizzed by in a blur of adrenalin and fear as the emergency services took over. An ambulance arrived in record time and paramedics fitted an oxygen mask to Jim's face before bearing him off into the night towards the hospital in Stratford. A fire engine had eventually got the bonfire under control although the smoke still hung poisonously in the air. Apparently Jim and one of the other marshals had been throwing buckets of water at the fire in an attempt to subdue the smoke. But Jim must have got too close and had collapsed from smoke inhalation.

All of the visitors had gone, including Mum and Steve, and I could finally breathe a sigh of relief that no more disasters could possibly occur tonight. At least everyone had been able to evacuate the grounds quickly enough; the marshals had speedily opened extra exits to the estate and cars had been able to drive away without delay. Lord Fortescue, having satisfied himself that everything was under control, had gone back to the hall. Only Ben remained, thanking everyone for their hard work and helping to clear up where he could.

The St John Ambulance team were packing away, too. They had had their hands full dealing with the public, from panic attacks to asthma to mild smoke inhalation. But thankfully no one had needed hospital treatment – only Jim.

My colleagues were all still here except Andy and Sheila. Andy had been really upset by Jim's accident and Sheila had had to take him home.

Ben and I sat side by side at a table in the courtyard,

sipping at the sweet tea that Jenny had brought round on trays for all the helpers.

'I feel awful about poor Jim.' I sighed.

'The paramedics say that there's no serious harm done, Holly.' He bumped against me gently. 'Try not to worry, OK? It's not your fault.'

He smiled at me and it crossed my mind that I probably looked a terrible sight; I ran a finger under each eye to wipe away any traces of mascara and shook my head. 'But I think it is my fault. Even you wondered if Jim could cope, I should have—'

'Hey.' He reached an arm around me and I held myself stiffly, wondering if anyone would spot us. 'Jim should have alerted us to the problem sooner instead of trying to deal with it himself. Believe it or not, Holly, some things are out of your control.'

He cocked an eyebrow teasingly.

Nikki walked past carrying a fold-up table, caught my eye and winked. I sprang away from Ben and jumped to my feet.

'I'd better, er, do something useful,' I said, jamming my hands in my pockets.

Ben set his plastic cup on the table and got to his feet. 'Me too. And then when we're all finished I've got something to talk to you about, unless you've got to dash off?'

'*I* haven't.' I gave him a mock stern look. 'But aren't you supposed to be entertaining your guests?'

'Mum's guests,' Ben corrected. 'Anyway, this can't wait.'

Happiness bubbled up inside me and I beamed at him. 'In that case, I look forward to it.'

Half an hour later everyone had gone home except for me. And Ben. Ben, who had something to tell me. Although he didn't count because technically he was at home. Unless you counted London where he *felt* more at home, which was a sad thought and not one to dwell on right now . . . Perhaps that was what he wanted to tell me, perhaps he was going to make Wickham Hall his home – permanently . . .

I exhaled and shivered, watching my breath form a cloud in the cold night air.

Ben's eyes glittered as he held a hand out to me. 'Come on, let's walk quickly to warm ourselves up.'

I took his hand, and wove my gloved fingers through his, aware of the fizz of excitement flooding through me. He was full of surprises. It was one of the things I liked most about him.

'Where are we going?' I giggled breathlessly as my legs tried to keep pace with his longer ones. We left the court-yard and began walking away from the smouldering remains of the bonfire and out into the dark parkland.

He looked sideways at me. 'Secret.'

'Ben!' I tugged his hand. 'I thought you said you had something to tell me. Can't you just spit it out?'

He threw back his head and laughed. 'Some things can't just be *spat* out, Miss Swift. Where's your sense of occasion?'

I had no suitable response to that, so I just pressed my lips together instead and tried not to let my smile get completely out of control.

I was glad I'd worn thick boots; the further we got from the hall, the longer and wetter the grass became. But on the plus side, the clearer the skies became too and although the smell of smoke and fireworks still hung in the air, a magical canopy of stars twinkled above us.

Ben opened a wooden gate and we tiptoed gingerly over a cattle grid.

'I've got torches if you like, or we can just be guided by the moon?' he asked.

I snorted and he grimaced.

'Sorry, that was a bit cheesy, wasn't it? I blame you; you bring out the cheese in me.'

'Don't blame me!' I protested. 'Anyway, it's fine; I'm partial to cheese. But to answer your question, let's enjoy the moonlight.'

We walked along for a few more minutes and I stopped trying to second-guess what it was he wanted to tell me and instead immersed myself in the moment. I absorbed every little thing from the feel of his hand wrapped around mine, to the sound of our feet swishing through the grass and the beauty of the silvery moon as it lit our way.

'I know where we're going!' I exclaimed, squeezing his hand as I began to recognize the landscape ahead.

He lifted his eyebrows in amusement and dropped my hand. 'Race you then.'

He shot off and I failed to catch him up until he held out his hand again and then we ran hand in hand up to the top of the hill – our hill – where we had watched the sunrise back in the summer – and collapsed laughing and breathless on the grass.

'Wait, Holly, get up,' he laughed, shucking his coat off for us both to lie on. 'Stay dry on this.'

We lay side by side on the warmth of his thick winter coat, our chests rising and falling as we tried to catch our breath. Nothing and no one could have made me any happier than I was in that moment, lying next to Ben, listening to him breathing and gazing up at the velvety, star-studded night sky.

Ben peeled the glove from my hand and laced his fingers through mine.

'It's just as beautiful as the sunrise,' I said and sighed. 'Thank you for bringing me here again.'

'It was either this or sipping sherry with my mother's cronies.' He twinkled his eyes at me. 'No contest.'

'She is so going to kill you,' I murmured.

He smiled back, his warm brown eyes peering through those irresistible curls. The moon cast a milky light across his jaw and I really wanted to touch him, to stroke his face. But first I wanted to hear what he'd brought me here to say.

'My crimes pale into insignificance beside my dad's.' He laughed, rolling over onto his side and propping himself up on his elbow. 'Last time I saw my parents, Mum had just caught Dad trying to escape into the grounds with his new night-vision binoculars.'

I chuckled at the image of Lord Fortescue tiptoeing out of Wickham Hall without permission.

'Bird-watching again?'

'Yep.' His body shook with laughter. 'He'll be out there now somewhere, probably crouching behind the bushes fiddling with his focus and straining to hear the sound of screech owls.'

'Oh dear, your poor mum.' I pulled my lip between my teeth, trying to dredge up some sympathy after the dressing-down she had given me earlier.

'She'll cope,' Ben huffed. 'Neither of us wanted guests tonight anyway; serves her right if she has to entertain them by herself.'

I rolled onto my back, gazing up at the pale yellow moon and the acres and acres of stars. 'It's massive, isn't it, the sky?'

'Huge.' He chuckled.

'It's funny to think . . .' My voice petered out when I realized how daft I'd sound. 'Nothing.'

Ben poked me in the ribs. 'Go on.'

'Well, I was just thinking that it's odd that somewhere out there my father could right this minute be looking up at the same moon as me. And I'll never know.'

Ben pushed himself up until he was sitting cross-legged in front of me. I blinked at him and sat up too. 'That's a serious face,' I murmured.

He took a deep breath and suddenly he was back to normal, a smile playing at his lips. He took my hands.

'Holly?'

I don't think my heart dared to beat in case I missed his next words. I swallowed. 'Yes?'

'I've got a surprise for you.'

And then my heart did beat, fast and furiously against my chest. He leaned in towards me until the warmth of his breath caressed my lips and I felt something unfurl inside me; this is it, our moment, on our hill. I tilted my chin and gazed into his eyes, every nerve alive, and I could hear the steady insistent beat of my heart as I waited for the surprise.

'I know that finding out about your father means a lot to you.'

I frowned and edged back, feeling confused; I'd thought he was about to kiss me.

'And I know that contacting him out of the blue would have been difficult for you. So . . .'

A wave of nausea hit me as I realized what he was about to say.

'So I've written to him for you.'

He sat back and exhaled, as though he was glad to get

that off his chest. He looked at me expectantly.

Blood whooshed around my body so fast that my head span.

'You've done what?' I whispered, stumbling to my feet.

'I sent him a letter explaining who I was and who you are and—'

'You arrogant arse,' I hissed.

'Huh?' He gawped at me.

'How dare you?' I gasped, pressing my hands to my hips. 'How dare you presume to take control of my life? You may be the heir to Wickham Hall and you may be my boss, but that doesn't give you the right to make those sorts of decisions for me. My relationship with Antonio Biancardi – or not, as the case may be – is my affair. Mine.' I tapped my chest. 'Do you understand?'

Ben staggered to his feet, his face an eerie pale colour as the blood drained from it. 'But, Holly, I—'

'Get off!' I sprang back as he reached to touch me.

'I thought I was doing you a favour.' He let his arms fall to his side helplessly.

I stared at him incredulously, trying to find the right words to express my horror and hurt.

'If I'd wanted to contact him, I would have done. By myself. And for the record, I don't need any favours. No, Ben,' I clenched my jaw, 'you were being selfish, doing what you wanted to do, just like you always do.'

And then I ran, down the hill, through the grass as fast as my pounding heart would allow.

'That's not true, Holly, it's not true,' I heard him yell.

But I didn't look back and to my immense relief he didn't come after me.

My car stood alone in the staff car park and my hands shook as I unlocked the door. Mum would be back at

Weaver's Cottage with Steve by now but I couldn't face them yet. I suddenly realized that I hadn't seen Esme all evening despite her having bought a ticket to the bonfire event. I brushed the tears from my cheeks, reached for my phone and called her.

'Esme? Where are you? I need a hug.'

Chapter 30

Ten minutes later I was knocking on the door of Esme's flat.

'I meant to come to the bonfire thing but I lost track of time,' she said, rubbing a hand over her face. She was covered in shreds of purple fabric and she looked exhausted. 'I've got dresses for identical twins to alter for a masked ball and— Blimey, Hols, what's wrong with you?'

My shoulders sagged. 'I've had fireworks of my own. Ben and I have just had a big row.'

Esme cocked her head to one side and folded her arms. 'Oh dear. I think this calls for Grandma's hot chocolate.'

I followed her into the kitchen, picking my way over a sea of purple satin, and watched in silence as she mixed cubes of dark chocolate with hot milk, whipped cream and a dash of Jamaican rum. By the time I sank onto her sofa and took my first sip, I could already feel it working its magic.

'By the way,' Esme blew on the top of her mug, 'that personal shopper idea of yours has been a big hit. Mum's got four sessions booked in for this weekend and one of those is a group of friends. I haven't seen Mum so fired up about Joop for ages.'

I nodded. 'I'm so pleased.'

At least it seemed I was able to get something right.

'So.' She slurped her hot chocolate, wiped a creamy moustache from her upper lip and looked at me expectantly. 'Tell me about these fireworks.'

I took a deep breath and wrapped my fingers around my mug. 'Well, after we got rid of the fire engine and ambulance and finished clearing up . . .'

I nodded at Esme, whose jaw had dropped open wide. 'Oh yeah, it has seriously been a night to remember on all counts. Anyway, Ben asked me to stay behind because he said he had a surprise for me.'

'Oh yeah?' Esme snorted into her mug until she spotted my eyes bulging with tears. 'Sorry. Go on.'

'I've been trying to keep Ben at arm's length, Es, because I don't want to fall for him in case he ends up leaving Wickham Hall. But when he said that,' I sighed, 'he was just so irresistible I couldn't help myself.'

'And then what?' she asked, staring at me intensely.

'It started off perfectly,' I whispered, and I told her the whole tale about our walk across the moonlit fields, hand in hand, and about how when I lay on his coat snuggled up against his side under a canopy of tiny stars I thought I might explode with happiness.

'Bloody hell, Hols,' she blinked, 'this is like something from a film. At the moment I'm totally in love with him myself. Carry on.'

'It was going well,' I agreed, setting my hot chocolate mug on the table, 'until he leaned towards me and took my hand. And then instead of kissing me, like I was sort of hoping, he announced that he'd written to Antonio, my dad, telling him all about me and Mum. Just like that.'

I folded my arms and sat back, staring grimly at my best

friend, who shook her head slowly.

'That is the sweetest thing I've ever heard, Hols,' she said gravely.

'What are you talking about?' I squealed.

'Apart from painting a picture especially for someone – that was quite sweet too.'

I paused for a second; painting *Secret Sunrise* for me had been a lovely gesture. But pushing that aside for the moment . . .

'This has nothing to do with being sweet,' I fumed, 'and everything to do with bulldozing over my life.'

Esme sighed. 'I take it this is when the fireworks started?'

'Too right,' I said, prickling with indignation. 'How dare he presume to make contact with *my* father, on *my* behalf without *my* permission?'

She raised an eyebrow. 'Maybe because he really, really likes you and he thought this was a way into your heart? After all, his attempts at getting you on a second date have failed.'

A way into my heart. I swallowed a lump in my throat.

'Do you think?' I murmured.

'Why else would he do it?' She shrugged. 'It was quite a brave thing to do really. I would imagine he's regretting it bitterly now.'

'But I would rather have had a snog under the stars.' I pouted.

'Obviously.' Esme let out a tiny snort. I glared at her but she let a second snort escape. And then we both collapsed in a fit of laughs.

'I called him an arrogant arse,' I said, pressing my hands to my face.

'It might have been misguided, but he was probably trying to do you a favour and protect you at the same time.

Assuming Antonio even gets the letter, getting the news of a daughter you never knew you had from a third party might be easier than hearing it directly from you.'

I thought about this for a moment. 'True.' I sighed. 'But I wanted to do it in my own time.'

'Yeah, I get that and Ben should have understood that too. But what if Antonio is delighted to hear about you? Wouldn't that be amazing?'

I nodded. The thought made my head spin.

She pulled me into a hug. 'All I'm saying is that it was very thoughtful and selfless of Ben and I genuinely think that he has taken it upon himself to find Antonio with your best interests at heart.'

'Well, now you put it like that . . .' I chewed my lip between my teeth. And perhaps if I'd let him explain properly before charging off like a demented fire-breathing dragon, this evening might have ended up with Ben's arm round my shoulders instead of Esme's. 'I'm just not sure how it will work out and you know me, Es, I like to deal in certainties.'

'Oh, Holster.' Esme rolled her eyes. 'Life would be boring if we knew how every story ended. This is a new story, it may be the start of a family saga, it may be over in a few chapters, but it's yours so don't be scared to turn the pages.'

I nodded, feeling soothed by her words and tired all of a sudden, which was hardly surprising after the long day I'd had.

'So what do I do now, wise woman?' I asked with a smile.

Esme leaned her forehead against mine. 'Tell your mum so she knows the score. Then first thing Monday, breeze into work and make up with Ben.'

I planted a kiss on her cheek. 'That sounds like a plan.'

*

346

I arrived at work on Monday, a bright smile at the ready and full of good intentions and humble apologies, but the lights were off and the events office was empty.

No problem, I told myself, shrugging off the disappointment. It was still early; there was plenty of time to make amends with Ben. While I waited for him to turn up, I decided to visit Sheila to see if she had any news about Jim.

I trotted back downstairs, along the corridor towards Lord Fortescue's private office and knocked on the door.

Sheila beckoned me in. 'Good news from Jim's wife.' She beamed. 'He's back home and other than a bit of wounded pride for letting himself get in such a state, he'll be as right as ninepence.'

'Phew!' I said, raising my eyes heavenwards. 'I'm so glad. Should we send him some flowers, do you think?'

'Lovely idea, Holly,' she replied, nodding thoughtfully. 'And maybe a gift hamper from the shop. I'll get Andy to sort it out.'

She reached for her phone but before she picked it up, it began to ring. Sheila smiled, her eyes crinkling at the corners.

'And so another busy week begins,' she trilled.

She answered the call and my eyes roamed her perfectly ordered office with its beautiful golden furniture and handsome display of books. As usual there was a lavish arrangement of flowers from the garden on top of the china pedestal and I walked across and bent down to inhale the scent of the lilies.

'Good gracious!' Sheila's hand flew to her mouth. 'Really? How awful! . . . Of course, of course. I will. Goodbye.'

She replaced the phone and tutted. 'That was the

fire service with their initial report from Friday's fire. Apparently the bonfire gave off such thick poisonous smoke because right at the centre of it was a large amount of polystyrene, like packaging materials. It gives off carbon monoxide when it burns, according to the fire officer.'

I frowned. 'But how . . . ? The fire was made from garden rubbish, branches from the fruit trees, just green stuff. Nikki wouldn't have put polystyrene in the fire.'

Sheila pressed her lips together. 'Hmm, it is odd. I'm sure you're right but I will ask her, just in case.'

'Carbon monoxide poisoning. Poor Jim,' I said with a shudder. 'He could have been far more seriously hurt. I think I'll go and see him this evening.'

'He'd like that, I'm sure,' said Sheila, handing me a cup of tea. 'Drink this, you look pale.'

I murmured my thanks and sank into a chair to sip my tea as the grandfather clock in the corner struck half past nine. And still no sign of Ben . . .

'Where's Ben today, Sheila?'

At that moment, the door flew open and Lady Fortescue swept in.

'I assume you're referring to Benedict?' She scowled at me and I nodded.

My heart sank; I seemed to be slipping further and further down in Lady Fortescue's good books.

'He's in Cambodia,' she said with a sniff, answering on Sheila's behalf. 'He upped and left yesterday morning. Just like that.' She snapped her fingers in the air.

'But he can't have . . .' I yelped, earning myself another frown from Her Ladyship.

'Good grief, Your Ladyship!' Sheila cried, scurrying to the teapot. 'Was this planned?'

I stood up and offered my chair to Lady Fortescue, who

348

sank down into it delicately. Sheila dispensed more tea and I hovered anxiously, not quite knowing whether I should stay or go. My throat was throbbing with sadness.

Ben had gone. Without telling me. If I hadn't lost my temper with him on Friday, he would at least have phoned me to let me know, I was sure of it. Did that mean our friendship was irreparable?

'No.' Lady Fortescue sighed dramatically. 'He had a call on Saturday morning to say that Mae Chang village had been flooded and some of the houses had been washed away. All the villagers have been evacuated and the school is in danger too, apparently. So off he shot: he caught the first plane from Gatwick yesterday.'

My heart tugged with affection for him; what a brave and selfless thing to do. Like writing to Antonio Biancardi. He had done that for me and now he was in South East Asia helping those poor people and the last thing I'd said to him was that he was selfish . . .

I felt a sob rise up in my throat and I turned to the window to hide my face from Lady Fortescue.

'I don't know, Sheila, I despair, I really do. All we asked was for him to stay here until Christmas, for him to get a feel for the role of running the estate. But every chance he gets, he escapes.'

For the right reasons, Lady Fortescue, I argued silently. His beautiful heart was in the right place.

I blinked away my tears and turned back into the room. 'When will he be back, Lady Fortescue?' I gulped.

'Huh!' she scoffed. 'As if he'd tell his mother a minor detail like that. This is Benedict we're talking about.' She waved a hand in the air. 'He'll be gone for at least a month, knowing him.'

My breath caught in my throat and I had to stop myself

from gasping aloud. A month? I couldn't wait that long to put right the mess I'd made of Friday night.

'I'll say something for him, though.' Lady Fortescue sighed. 'He's a good boy. He does far more for charity than I do. I think I might start some good works in the New Year.'

'In that case, Lady Fortescue, can I give you Benedict's private mail?' said Sheila, flicking through a stack of post on her desk. 'An envelope came for him this morning. From overseas! Ah here it is.'

My ears pricked up instantly and I strained my neck to see what was on the envelope in Sheila's outstretched hand.

'Overseas?' I leapt forward. 'Where exactly? May I see? Benedict was expecting a letter—'

'Excuse me!' exclaimed Lady Fortescue, jutting out her chin. 'Do I have to remind you again, Holly, that you are a member of staff? Under no circumstances do you inspect my son's private mail!'

She whipped the letter out of poor Sheila's hand. But not before I'd had a good look at it. I could hardly believe what I saw. It had the distinctive striped edge of an airmail letter and the postage stamp bore the word ITALIA in bold capital letters.

My stomach quivered.

It had to be from my father, it had to be.

What was in it? What did he say? Would he want to acknowledge his daughter after all these years, I wondered, or would he deny ever having met a seventeen-year-old Lucy Swift at Wickham Hall? I was desperate to read that letter. Almost as desperate as I was to have Benedict back.

'Holly, dear, are you sure you're all right?' Sheila asked, resting a kindly hand on my back.

A wave of nausea passed over me but I attempted a business-like nod.

'Thank you, Sheila. Forgive my rudeness, Lady Fortescue, I do apologize. I'll do my best to carry on without Benedict in the run-up to Christmas. I'll miss him, of course,' I added, sliding my eyes to meet hers.

'Of course, Holly.' Lady Fortescue smiled and got to her feet. 'We'd expect nothing less. Your *work* has always been exemplary.'

She glided into Lord Fortescue's adjoining office with the pile of post and emerged a few seconds later. 'Sheila, the time has come to have a sort out in Zara's room. She has prom dresses that I know she'll never wear again. And do let me know if you hear anything more from Jim.'

'Right you are, Lady Fortescue.'

We both watched her leave and Sheila pulled her jacket on. 'I think I'll go over and see Andy myself about that gift hamper.'

'And I need to be getting on too,' I said, walking out of the office in front of her.

I strode to the staircase and ran up the first few steps. As soon as Sheila was out of sight I ran back down the stairs and crept along the corridor to her office, checking over my shoulder every other second.

My heart was thudding against my ribcage as I scurried across the floor and peered into Lord Fortescue's office. It was empty.

I entered and pulled the door to behind me, leaving it slightly ajar.

Adrenalin coursed through me. This was possibly one of

the most stupid things I had ever done but I had to get a proper look at that letter. My eyes scanned Lord Fortescue's desk until I spotted a pile of envelopes jutting out of his in-tray.

Oh God. I swallowed nervously. This was crazy.

I flicked a glance at the door and strained my ears for any signs of footsteps. But there was nothing. I tweaked the envelopes out and flicked through the pile until I found the one with the red and blue striped airmail edge.

My hands were shaking so much I could hardly read the writing. But it was definitely to Benedict, definitely hand-written and . . . I squinted at the smudged postmark . . . I was pretty sure it said 'Bergamo, Italia'.

I blew out a breath and picked up Lord Fortescue's letter opener. This was so dodgy. Wasn't opening someone else's post actually a criminal offence?

A line of perspiration broke out on my forehead.

I lowered the envelope to the desk.

But no one would ever know, I reasoned and besides, if Ben were here he'd want me to open the letter.

Sod it.

I slid the letter opener under the flap of the envelope and—

'Morning, Holly. Any tea going?' Lord Fortescue greeted me perkily, appearing at the door.

I flung the letter opener and the envelope down on the desk as though they were burning hot. Like my face.

He looked at the desk and then back to me.

'Everything all right?' he said, looking a bit startled as he approached his desk.

'No. Yes. Everything's fine,' I said, picking up the envelope and stuffing it back into the in-tray. 'Silly me, I've misplaced an envelope from an Italian . . . um . . . ice-cream man and I thought it had got mixed up with your mail, but it hasn't so—'

'Ice cream in November?' He frowned.

'Planning ahead for summer, they get very booked up . . .' I shrugged.

Oh God, what was I babbling on about?

'I'll see about that tea,' I stuttered. 'Won't be a moment.'

I fled from the office and ran back out into the corridor. I pressed myself against the wall and gulped in air as my lungs struggled to breathe.

A month. That was how long I might have to wait until Benedict came back and showed me that letter. Was it from Antonio? Was my father even alive? And if so would he want to meet me? And what about Ben? We'd parted on such bad terms on Friday night that I didn't even know whether we were still friends.

I had so many questions. And Ben held all the answers.

How was I going to get through the next day, let alone the next month, without him?

White Christmas

Chapter 31

Weak winter sun filtered through the mullioned windows and out on the lawn at the front of Wickham Hall I could see Lady Fortescue's new oak love seat under a winter-rose-covered arbour and the gatehouse beyond. It was a stunning view and I was filled with warmth as I cast a glance over to the Fortescues, who sat side by side at the head of the table.

It was early December and Lord Fortescue had called us all to a meeting in the Great Hall to update him on our 'White Christmas at Wickham Hall' festivities. This room was the hall's show-stopper as far as the public were concerned. It still had the raised dais at one end where dignitaries would have eaten in Elizabethan times, but the décor was elegantly Georgian with white ornate plaster-work panels on the pale blue walls, three huge candelabra spaced along high ceilings and a long oak table with twenty chairs filling the centre of the floor.

I had taken a seat at the end of the table with the other assembled staff members – all except Nikki, who appeared to be running late.

Jenny removed the lid from a red and white cake tin and the smell of Christmas instantly filled the air.

'Not mince pies already,' Andy said mulishly, peering into the tin.

'It's December,' said Jenny, pressing a fragrant miniature mince pie into my hand as she moved around the table, dishing out moreish morsels to all of us except Andy, whom she glared at until he took one for himself. 'So it's officially Christmas in my kitchen. Tell me what you think, everyone; we've gone for filo pastry this year and added a frangipane topping.'

'Absolutely delicious, Jenny, and they smell heavenly. What is it that I can smell?' asked Lady Fortescue, breaking off a piece of crispy pastry and popping it into her mouth.

'Orange zest.' Jenny beamed proudly and offered Lady Fortescue a second one. 'And booze.'

'We'll have two hundred of them, please, for our "Christmas at Home" evening,' said Lady Fortescue.

'Excellent idea!' declared Sheila, making a note on her pad. 'And much lighter than traditional pastry.'

'Quicker to make, too,' added Jenny.

Lady Fortescue began issuing further orders for Sheila to scribble down about her Christmas at Home event and Jenny handed round the tin for a second time.

The Christmas at Home party was the social event of the year for a lot of local people, according to Sheila. The Fortescues invited everyone they'd worked with during the year to join them for festive drinks just before Christmas. Sheila had told me that people all over the county would be keeping their fingers crossed this week, hoping that they'd made the guest list.

'Will you be there?' I whispered to Jenny.

She laughed softly. 'No, we have a staff do in the café on Christmas Eve. Christmas at Home is a much posher affair held in the Red Sitting Room. The guests knock back vats of mulled wine and several tonnes of my mince pies. And then once the majority have gone, the Fortescues have a select group of people to a four-course dinner in here, which is even posher.'

'Sounds gorgeous.' I grinned. 'The Red Sitting Room is my favourite room at Christmas.'

I was so excited about Christmas, partly because Wickham Hall looked wonderful when it was decked out in decorations but also because Benedict would be back and I was dying to get my mitts on him *and* that letter from Italy . . .

'Jenny, you have a lightness of touch worthy of a Parisian patisserie,' exclaimed Lord Fortescue, brushing a cluster of crumbs from his chin.

'Indeed,' agreed Lady Fortescue as she handed her husband a napkin. 'Talking of Paris, Jenny, you must let me know if you need any gourmet treats for the kitchen bringing back from my Paris trip.'

Jenny's eyes widened. 'Oh, I will; thank you. Perhaps some marrons glacés from Fauchon or some French mustard from La Grande Épicerie or caramels from—'

'Goodness!' trilled Lady Fortescue. 'I won't be able to carry all that. Just make me a list and I'll see what I can do.'

'A buying trip? Perhaps I could come? I've got some great ideas,' Andy suggested, edging forward on his seat hopefully. He was looking very festive today in a red tartan shirt buttoned tightly to his neck.

'No, it's a personal trip, I'm afraid, Andy,' Her Ladyship replied. 'Besides, we need you here making sure the hall looks its best for Christmas.' She took out a small mirror from her handbag and dabbed at her mouth delicately. 'I shall be shopping for outfits in Paris for our Christmas break with the Valois family.'

'She's exhausted all the London shops, haven't you, Beatrice?' Lord Fortescue chuckled.

'I don't want my wardrobe to be judged by Madame Valois Senior and be found wanting, that's all, Hugo.' She frowned. 'Anyway, Zara will be joining me in Paris and then we'll return to Wickham Hall together.'

'While we're all sitting here,' said Sheila, flipping open a small cardboard box, 'please can you all add your signature to the official Wickham Hall Christmas cards. Sign and pass them clockwise please, Holly.'

She held a pile out to me and I stared at the picture on the front of the card.

It was a modern watercolour painting of a robin perched on the edge of a terracotta pot. The pot was filled with red cyclamens and topped with a thick layer of snow and there was an unmistakable snow-covered Wickham Hall in soft focus in the background. My pulse raced as I flipped the card over to read the back, even though I could already guess who the artist was.

'*White Christmas at Wickham Hall* by Ben Fortescue.'

I pressed my lips together to hide my smile; how much persuasion had he had to use on his mother to have his preferred name printed in black and white?

Once again, Ben's passion for both his art and his home shone through. I stroked the card with my fingertip. I missed his presence in my life and couldn't wait to see him again. He'd be labouring in the sun under the Cambodian sky now, repairing the school that meant so much to him while we discussed the frippery of Christmas with its decorations and parties and cards . . .

He had been gone for almost a month already; would he be back in time for Christmas? I wondered.

I bit back a sigh and began to sign my name in card after

card, passing them on to Jenny. An industrious silence fell across the room for a few minutes as we all concentrated on producing our best handwriting.

Lord Fortescue circled his wrist in the air before checking his watch. 'I really think we should start our Christmas planning meeting, we've waited for Nikki long enough.'

'Oh!' Andy's hand shot up. 'Can I kick off? I've just put the finishing touches to the décor plan for the Great Hall and I'd really love to share it with you.'

Lady Fortescue sighed. 'I'm not convinced about this year's theme.'

'Oh, I think it will be beautiful,' I said, earning myself a faint smile from Andy.

The idea of 'White Christmas' that Andy had come up with – both in the hall and outside in the part of the gardens that Nikki would be converting into a winter wonderland – would use natural materials, mostly sourced from the estate, such as seed heads, fruit and vegetables, a wide variety of leaves, sticks and twigs all given a snowy finish with white and silver spray paints. He had grand plans to suspend a series of angels all the way down the main staircase and fill the Long Gallery entirely with snow-sprayed Christmas trees. I had my doubts about Andy, but there was no escaping the fact that he was incredibly talented.

Lady Fortescue turned away from me slightly. A snub that wasn't lost on me; she'd been giving me the cold shoulder ever since she found me drinking beer in Ben's private rooms back in September.

'The decorations at Chatsworth this year have been supplied by Liberty of London and must have cost a fortune. Wickham Hall's decorations are going to look a little . . . well . . . "low budget" by comparison.'

Andy shook his head confidently. 'Have faith, Lady Fortescue.' He stood up and laid a large sheet of card in front of her. 'As you can see from this mood board, we'll be making a bold statement with our white and silver sprayed—'

At that moment, the door flew back on its hinges, knocking into the wall, and Nikki appeared carrying a large handful of long twigs sprayed white and silver.

'So sorry I'm late, but I've been experimenting with a few bits and bobs for Christmas and I thought you'd like to see the finished article.'

'Bits and bobs?' sniffed Lady Fortescue. 'The mind boggles.'

'Bear with,' Nikki said, flashing us a grin as she produced glass baubles from her pockets and hung them randomly on the end of the twigs. 'Ta-dah!'

'Now, imagine that on a grander scale,' said Andy, waving his hands around. 'Armfuls of them along the length of the Great Hall, all snowy and covered with silver-sprayed pine cones.'

'It'll be like Narnia,' I said, glancing round the room. I could picture it perfectly. And I thought the simplicity of using natural materials, bringing the outside in, would look magical.

'Bravo,' said Lord Fortescue. 'It does have a simple charm to it. What do you think, Beatrice?'

'Oh, very simple,' she agreed, which judging by her folded arms and furrowed brow was evidently not a compliment.

'Harvey Nichols did something similar a couple of years ago, Your Ladyship, and the *Sunday Times* said it was the classiest display they'd ever seen,' Andy countered.

She raised an eyebrow at that. 'Well, all right, let's run with it.'

Nikki and Andy exchanged looks of relief and took their seats at the table.

While Jenny and Sheila sorted us all out with more hot drinks, Nikki gave us a rundown of the White Christmas decorations for the garden.

'I'm delighted to say that Jim will be playing Santa again this year.' She beamed.

She had sourced a Nordic-style wooden hut that would be accessed via a temporary covered walkway directly from the formal gardens. Tens of thousands of tiny white lights would lead the way – wound around trees, gateways and hedges – and dozens of decorated Christmas trees, cut from the estate, would create impact. And finally, once inside the hut, the children would be greeted by elves before getting to meet Santa himself.

My heart lifted at the thought of Jim in a Santa suit. He would love entertaining the children and it would be his last job at Wickham Hall before he retired on Christmas Eve.

'How is Jim, Sheila?' I asked. The Fortescues had insisted on him having a whole month off on full pay to recover fully after collapsing on Bonfire Night and I hadn't seen him for a while.

'Desperate to come back to work.' She chuckled. 'Goodness knows how they are going to cope when he begins his retirement proper in January.'

'He'll never retire,' laughed Jenny. 'Same as Marjorie the tour guide and Edith in the shop.'

'But he couldn't speak highly enough of you, Andy,' Sheila added. 'I didn't realize that you'd been going round to their house to help out.'

'Bravo, Andy, bravo,' bellowed Lord Fortescue, reaching across to pat Andy's shoulder.

Andy squirmed in his chair, blushed the colour of his shirt and picked up his teacup to hide his face. 'It was the least I could do,' he mumbled.

Hmm, I had my suspicions as to why that should be.

I looked at him sharply and for a split second he caught my eye and a look of panic flashed across his face. Nikki had been adamant that her team hadn't put any polystyrene in the bonfire. The gift shop, on the other hand, had piles of the stuff . . .

Today was the day, I thought, I'd collar him on the way out of this meeting and confront him.

'Holly?' Jenny prodded me with her teaspoon. 'Sheila asked for a progress update?'

'Oh, yes, sorry!' I gave an embarrassed laugh. 'Nearly all the Christmas events are sorted. A lady from Henley library will read stories around the Christmas tree in the Red Sitting Room every day at four. All tickets are sold out for the celebrity chef demo with Daniel Denton.'

'Told you.' Jenny nodded smugly.

'The only thing still to be arranged is someone to run our Christmas crafts workshop. The man who had originally agreed has broken his wrist, so I'm searching for a new person.'

Andy cleared his throat and shifted in his seat. 'I'll do it.'

'Really?' I blinked at him.

He nodded. 'The hall will be decorated by then, so I'll have time. Edith can cover for me in the shop.'

I could hardly believe it: Andy, offering to help me out? Wonders would never cease.

'Andy's wonderful with stuff like that,' said Nikki. 'Remember the button holes he did for Zara's wedding?'

'Well, OK.' I shrugged. 'Thank you.'

'Right, everyone.' Lady Fortescue clapped her hands

together to signal the end of our meeting. 'I think we'll leave it there. If you could just stay for a minute, Jenny, to talk me through Daniel Denton's recipe choices.'

Andy was first to leave the room and I hurried after him.

'Andy?' I called as soon as I was in the corridor. 'A word please.'

He looked shiftily back towards the Great Hall.

'Make it quick then,' he said, folding his arms. 'I've got a delivery of hampers due any second.'

'Sure,' I said, gazing at him intently. 'It's about the bonfire.'

Andy shifted his weight from one foot to the other. 'I don't know what you mean.'

I gave an exasperated sigh and mirrored his body language by folding my arms. 'Admit it, Andy. You hid a load of toxic packaging in the middle of the bonfire, didn't you?'

His face drained of all colour. 'I . . . um . . . I . . .'

'Well?' I demanded. 'It's time you and I cleared the air.'

'Oh hell,' groaned Andy, lowering himself to the bottom step.

Chapter 32

'So it was you!' I gasped. 'You do realize that someone could have died – Jim, for starters. We were very lucky that none of the spectators were seriously injured.'

'I'm so sorry.' Andy pressed the heels of his hands into his eyeballs. 'What an idiot. It was all me, all my fault. Are you going to tell the Fortescues? I wouldn't blame you if you did. But, please don't, Holly, please don't.'

To my horror his shoulders began to shake.

Along the corridor, the door to Lord Fortescue's office opened and I heard Jenny saying her goodbyes to Sheila. She would be appearing at any moment and even though there was no love lost between Andy and me, I didn't want our discussion to become public knowledge.

I grabbed Andy's arm and pulled him up the stairs to my office, closing the door behind us.

'Sit down,' I muttered, handing him a tissue. 'Now, tell me everything.'

I busied myself making us both a coffee that probably neither of us wanted while he sat at Ben's desk and sniffed.

'It was that bonfire meeting.' He sighed. 'I'm ashamed of it now, but I felt so humiliated. Everything I said was dismissed and everything you suggested everyone was like:

"Oh, yes, Holly, a Guy Fawkes competition, fabulous idea."
And then when Benedict turned up after being away in the
Orkneys for weeks, I was so pleased to see him and he only
had eyes for you.'

'Me! Really?' My voice went a bit wobbly and I turned
away before Andy noticed my secret smile. That was
lovely to hear, especially as I'd really missed Ben since he'd
left in November and I was tempted to press Andy for
more.

'Yes. And when I tried to compliment him on his art, all
he did was order me to clear up the rubbish. It was the final
straw.'

'So you hid the packaging rubbish on the bonfire?'

'I cleared it away from the store room, as Ben asked,
but there was no bin collection for weeks and rather than
dispose of it properly, I hid it in one of the old sheds. That
was back in September. By the time I came across it again,
Jim had started to build the bonfire.' He shrugged weakly.
'It seemed like a good idea at the time.'

I frowned. 'That explains the smoke, but why have you
been so against me ever since I arrived?'

'I've always wanted to work in a creative environment.'
He sighed. 'And when the job came up in the events department as Pippa's assistant, I thought it was meant for me.
And Pippa was going to give it to me, I was sure. Until she
interviewed you and then my dreams went up in smoke.'

'But isn't your job in the gift shop creative?' I frowned,
setting a mug in front of him.

'Huh,' he grunted. 'Lady F is so controlling; other than a
free rein with the window displays, my hands are tied. And
I never get to choose stock.'

'Well, my job is ninety-nine per cent organization,' I
argued. 'Only the initial ideas for events and marketing

campaigns are creative. I spend a lot of my time writing copy for press releases and leaflets.'

Andy blinked at me. 'Oh, I didn't realize that. I'd be rubbish at that, I'm a bit dyslexic. I have to get Edith to check anything I've written.'

'There you go, then!' I attempted a smile and sat at my desk. Inside I was gritting my teeth. All this childish behaviour for a job he'd probably have hated anyway.

'You still get to work with Benedict, though,' he muttered. 'I'd love to be in your shoes.'

'But you do know that Benedict is unlikely to . . . you know,' I waved my hands awkwardly, 'reciprocate?'

'I know,' admitted Andy, twirling his diamond earring distractedly. 'As soon as you came on the scene, that was it.' He mimed a knife across his own throat.

I blinked at him. 'But . . . Oh, never mind.'

'Anyway, Holly, other than stealing my thunder, my job and my prince, you've really done nothing wrong,' Andy said with a rueful smile. 'So I apologize wholeheartedly and I promise not to be such a bitch in future, starting with running the Christmas craft workshops for you.'

He stood up and walked over to me, holding his arms out. 'Hug it out?'

I suppressed a snort and submitted to his dainty hug. 'Yes, sure.'

'Now I really must dash,' gasped Andy, 'or poor Edith will have disappeared under a sea of wicker hampers. Laters.'

He blew me a kiss and dashed out, leaving me bemused by the whole experience.

I didn't have long to dwell on it, though, as my desk phone rang its special internal ring and I swooped to answer it. 'Events department, Holly speaking.'

'Holly, sorry to bother you, but could you join me in the library?'

I jumped to my feet.

'Of course, Lord Fortescue. I'm on my way.'

I skipped down the stairs as quickly as I could, curious to know what he could want me for. I decided to take the quickest route, which was to walk along the east-wing corridor past his office.

Wickham Hall closed for the season at the end of October and didn't reopen until Easter, with the exception of the last two weeks of December when we opened the doors to the public for the Christmas season, and I still hadn't got used to the lack of people around the place. The hall felt lonely without Marjorie waiting at the door to impart some unusual facts about Lord Wickham's ancestors, or members of the public asking me questions.

But as I drew level with Lord Fortescue's office, Sheila called out to me.

'Holly, do you happen to have an address for Esme Wilde?'

I nipped into her office and she held up an envelope.

'Invitation to Lord and Lady Fortescue's Christmas at Home evening,' said Sheila, answering my questioning expression.

'Wow. Of course.' I beamed at Sheila. 'She'll be flattered. In fact, I doubt I'll hear of anything else from now until Christmas.'

'How lovely.' She chuckled, her blue eyes crinkling with delight. 'Your presence is required too, Holly, although on a strictly professional footing, of course.'

'Sure,' I said and wrote down Esme's address for her.

I turned to go and then remembered something that had

been niggling me for ages. 'Sheila, what do you know about the renovation of the art gallery?'

She removed her reading glasses and peered at me. 'Goodness, Holly, that's an old one. What made you ask?'

I shrugged. 'It was a leaflet I found months ago. Nothing really, I just wondered about it because nobody has ever mentioned it in all the time I've been here.'

'That project got mothballed several years ago, unfortunately.' She frowned thoughtfully and pushed her chair back from the desk. 'Take a pew; I think I might have a folder about it somewhere.'

'Actually,' I smiled mysteriously, 'I have an assignation with Lord Fortescue in the library. Can we do it another time, Sheila? Sorry.'

'No problem, dear,' she chirped. 'Run along now.'

Which I did. All the way to the library.

I knocked lightly on the door and Lord Fortescue called me in. I hadn't been in the library since that press conference when I'd caught my first glimpse of Ben, courtesy of Lady Fortescue's iPad, looking tantalizingly naked in full view of our local press. The room was every bit as inviting as I remembered it: several reading lamps were lit against the fading wintry light, and the smell of leather and old books was mixed with woodsmoke from the roaring fire in the grate. There was no iPad in sight, although Lord Fortescue had a laptop balanced on his knee.

'Sorry to keep you waiting, Your Lordship,' I panted.

He waved me into a seat and I chose a leather armchair facing him, cosily close to the fire. We sat in silence, watching the flames for a moment or two, until I couldn't bear the suspense any longer.

I cleared my throat. 'So. How can I help?'

Lord Fortescue templed his fingers together and peered at me.

'There has never been anywhere else for me but Wickham Hall; I knew from an early age that my future lay here. So I finished my law degree, got married and started working as a solicitor, biding my time until I found myself as the new owner of the hall.'

'And I understand your father passed away quite suddenly?' I asked, wondering where this conversation could possibly be heading.

'Indeed.' He nodded. 'Benedict, on the other hand, forged another life for himself as an artist as soon as he left home for university, a world away from anything his mother and I have ever known. He seems to have found something that makes his heart sing and if running Wickham Hall doesn't have the same hold on him then who am I to force him down a road he doesn't wish to travel?'

'That's exactly how I feel,' I blurted out.

Lord Fortescue blinked at me, looking startled.

'I think he'd do a brilliant job here,' I continued boldly, 'but I also know how much it means to him to stand in front of a blank canvas and create something beautiful, to do his own thing.'

'Well put,' he said, smiling softly. 'And I agree with you. I am proud of what he's achieved with his art.'

My heart lifted; Ben would be over the moon to know that his father was proud of him. I cast my mind back to the launch of his art collection at the gallery when Ben said that neither of his parents valued his work. It would completely change their relationship if only they would talk to each other.

'You should tell him, I don't think he knows how you feel at all,' I urged.

'You're right. I'd rather come to that conclusion myself.' He clasped his hands across his chest. 'That's where I need your help.'

'Well . . . of course, I'll help if I can,' I said, intrigued.

'Thank you, Holly.' He swivelled the laptop around so that I could see the screen. 'I haven't a clue with all this techno stuff. Zara has given me Benedict's Facebook address. Apparently he has been posting to his page, whatever that means. But I must be doing something wrong . . . I can't seem to find him.'

I stared at the picture on the screen.

'Facebook?' My face broke into a wide smile of relief. 'You want to join Facebook?'

If anyone had told me a year ago that I'd be spending a winter's afternoon teaching a man in his sixties, who also happened to be eighty-fifth in line to the throne, how to work Facebook, I'd have laughed my head off. And yet here I was: doing just that. One of the many reasons why I loved my job. *Loved* it.

Within thirty minutes Lord Fortescue had a profile, although we decided to keep it private for the time being until he got the hang of it. He'd sent friend requests out to some of his chums who included several high-profile politicians and quite surprisingly a few celebrities too. My eyes were out on stalks by the time we'd finished, and when the friend request to Daniel Craig was accepted I nearly fell off my chair.

'How do you know him?' I squeaked.

'Um?' Lord Fortescue smoothed a hand over his fine silver hair and pondered their connection. 'Ah, yes! Sat next to him at the rugby once, hit if off straight away.'

Wait until Esme hears this . . .

But not even the fluttering I got reading Daniel Craig's

posts could compare with the tug at my heartstrings when we clicked on Ben's private profile.

There hadn't been many posts since he'd been in Cambodia. It seemed that the village he was staying in, unsurprisingly, had no internet access but occasional visits to a nearby town meant that he could log on to Facebook every so often. I could have kicked myself; why hadn't I thought of this earlier? Ben had been gone nearly a month and in that time, the pain of missing him had been almost physical at times. The breath caught in my throat as we scrolled through the images he'd uploaded of the village, of the damaged school that they were repairing and the people he was working alongside. The most recent post showed him surrounded by children, all wreathed in smiles and holding up their paintings to the camera.

'He looks happy, doesn't he? Totally at home,' Lord Fortescue marvelled.

I nodded, the lump in my throat stealing my speech. Ben was in his element, sharing his love of art with an appreciative audience.

'I don't know.' He sighed, smoothing his hand over his silver hair. 'This is clearly where his vocation lies, how can I ever hope to compete with that? What chance does Wickham Hall have? What can we possibly offer to make him stay more than five minutes?'

He looked so despondent that I had to fight the urge to fling my arms round him and hug him tight.

'Ben loves a challenge, that's why he gets such a kick out of being in Cambodia; he can see the difference his work makes. You and Lady Fortescue have done so much here and he can't see how to take Wickham Hall forward. It's not a blank canvas.'

'No, I can see that.' Lord Fortescue chest heaved with a sad sigh.

And then suddenly my heart twanged as my brain kicked into action. Perhaps there was a part of Wickham Hall that *was* a blank canvas. A project that he could really get his teeth into . . .

I jumped up from my chair. 'If you have any more problems on Facebook, just give me a call, Lord Fortescue. I'll be in my office.'

He nodded but was so engrossed in his son's photographs that he barely noticed me leave. I strode back to my office purposefully.

I loved Wickham Hall and deep down I knew that Benedict, the next lord of Wickham Hall, did too. It *could* compete for Ben's attention, I was sure of it, and I had the beginnings of an idea that just might work.

Chapter 33

With just over two weeks to go until Christmas, Wickham Hall would be opening to visitors on Monday and we were almost ready.

My week could be summed up in three words: holly (no pun intended), ivy and glitter. In fact, I had been sparkling for five days straight. I hadn't expected to be involved with decorating the hall but of course it was a mammoth undertaking and it had been all hands on deck all week. Andy had directed us all admirably in our tasks of wiring seed heads, weaving ivy and untangling fairy lights, and so by Friday afternoon our White Christmas theme was almost complete.

It was slightly chaotic at times, which rather goes against the grain with me. But despite the hard work, frayed nerves and occasional disasters (yes, eucalyptus leaves and poppy seed heads, I'm talking about you) it had been a magical few days and every so often I'd caught myself sighing happily at my good fortune. Wickham Hall was one of my most favourite places on earth and I was making it sparkle for Christmas *and* being paid for it – how lucky was I!

My last job of the day before finishing for the weekend was to decorate the huge Christmas tree in the Red Sitting

Room with head tour guide Marjorie. The fireplace had already been hung with garlands of fir interspersed with fragrant tufts of rosemary, bay leaves and lavender, which filled the room with a wonderfully pungent aroma. The huge fir tree, cut from the Wickham estate, was at least twice my height and decorating it would require three sets of stepladders, a thousand white lights, several hundred baubles and a steely head for heights.

'How is it looking, Marjorie?' I called from the top of the medium ladders. 'Can you spot any bare bits?'

I grinned at her as she took a step back and inadvertently managed to get her ankle trapped in a pool of silver tinsel. Marjorie was a gem; despite being in her late sixties she had worked ceaselessly all day and I'd had to persuade her to come down from the ladder after she insisted on being the one to run the fairy lights right to the top of the tree.

She circled the tree, moving backwards and forwards, and I had to bite back a giggle at how seriously she was taking her duties.

'Just there, Holly, by your knee looks a bit sparse,' she said finally. 'Here you are, I'll pass you a couple of silver pine cones.'

Bare patches dealt with, I joined her at the base of the tree to inspect the near empty crate of Christmas decorations. We both stared at the final item left at the bottom and shared a nervous look.

'I'll do it,' I said, taking a deep breath.

'Right you are, love. I'll make sure to hold the ladder tightly.'

Marjorie reached into the crate and picked up a rather battered angel, chuckling as she straightened the angel's glittery halo.

'I remember the year young Benedict insisted on being

the one to put the angel on the top of the tree.'

My heart flipped at the sound of his name. 'And chaos ensued, I imagine?' I grinned.

After leaving the library the other day, I'd logged on to my own Facebook page and sent Ben a friend request. So far he hadn't accepted. I kept telling myself that this meant nothing; I was well aware that his internet access was limited. Even so, days had gone by, and I was sure he must have seen it by now. How long should I keep hoping that it was simply a lack of opportunity that explained his silence, rather than our row on Bonfire Night?

'Oh, yes.' Marjorie laughed. 'He was a teenager but quite small for his age, I seem to remember, and certainly too small to reach but that didn't stop him trying, of course. He climbed to the top of the ladder but was still miles away from his target.'

'Did he admit defeat?' I asked, already guessing the answer. I selected the tallest of the three ladders and began my ascent gingerly, grateful for Marjorie's steadying presence at the bottom.

'Not likely!' she continued. 'He launched himself at the tree like a basketball player, shouting something like, "Slam dunk the funk". He just managed to hook the angel over the top before getting himself stuck in the branches. We were picking pine needles out of his curls for hours.'

We both burst out laughing and I nearly fell off the ladder myself.

'Poor thing, did he cry?'

'Oh no!' she exclaimed. 'He was as proud as punch. Benedict adored seeing the hall all dressed up for Christmas; it brought out his creative side.'

'I can imagine,' I panted, reaching up as far as I could to the very tip of the tree. 'There.'

Angel deposited, I clambered back down the ladder and shook out my aching hands.

'I bet he enjoyed joining in with all the Christmas activities at the hall too, didn't he?'

'He did.' She laughed softly at the memory. 'There was never a dull moment when he was around.'

I nodded. I knew just what she meant; things had been much more subdued at Wickham without him charging through the place like a whirlwind, disrupting my day and disarming me with his cheeky smile. And I never thought I'd say it, but I quite missed the interruptions to my schedule.

'I think we're good to go, shall we do the grand switch-on?'

I stood back from the tree while Marjorie disappeared underneath the branches to find the electric socket. The lights came on and the tree lit up the room.

'Ta-dah!' I laughed.

Marjorie wrapped an arm around my waist. 'A job well done, I think. Benedict would approve of your angel-arranging skills. Will he be back for Christmas, do you know?'

'Fingers crossed, Marjorie.' I sighed. 'I really hope so.'

After work, I drove straight home, keen to catch up with Mum. Hathaway College had already broken up for the Christmas holidays and Mum and Steve had spent the afternoon together. Today was the big unveiling of the display that Henley library had made from a selection of her newspapers and I was looking forward to hearing all about it. I parked in Mill Lane behind Mum's car, but aside from the twinkling lights around the porch and on the Christmas tree in the living room, which came on automatically, the cottage was in darkness.

I let myself in and set to work lighting the fire. It was at times like these – increasingly often these days – when I came in to an empty house that I longed for a cat. Or a dog. Or anyone really who made a fuss of me when I arrived home. I knelt down in front of the grate and began shaping sheets of paper into tight twists. Ironically, since Mum had stopped hoarding, we never had enough old newspaper to light the fire with and I'd resorted to bringing home scrap paper from work.

A few minutes later, with the help of several matches and a screwed-up copy of last month's events round-up, the fireplace was alive with flames and the wood began to crackle and hiss. I sat back on my heels, prodding and poking it until I was sure it was properly alight and glanced round the room. Our living room was quite cosy now that all the surfaces were clear. Mum's counsellor had set her the task of having one room clear enough to invite guests into and Mum had succeeded with bells on. She had even arranged some new framed photographs over the fireplace of the two of us, one of her parents that she'd found in an old suitcase and a new one of her and Steve.

I smiled to myself, thinking how much happier she seemed these days, and went to make myself a cup of tea. I was just scooping out the teabag when the front door opened.

'Cooee, Holly, we're home!' chirped Mum.

I stuck my head into the tiny hallway where she and Steve were divesting themselves of thick coats, scarves and gloves.

I gave them both a hug and Mum pressed her cold cheeks against mine.

'Hello, you two . . . Oh, you're cold!'

'We've been for a walk round, haven't we, love?' said Steve.

'A walk?' I laughed. 'In the dark?'

Mum nodded and I looked at her properly; she was so brimming with happiness that she could hardly contain herself. 'Yes, Steve and I have lots to talk about and we thought a walk might help.'

'But first,' said Steve, rubbing his hands together, 'let's have a cuppa and tell Holly all about the library exhibition.'

We settled ourselves cosily in front of the fire and sipped our hot drinks, soaking up the atmosphere created by the sparkle of the Christmas tree and the glow from the roaring fire. And for a moment I had a sudden image of what it would have been like growing up as part of a family with two parents.

'Well, what a day I've had.' Mum sighed.

She was sitting beside Steve on the sofa and he reached across and patted her knee.

'So how did it feel to see your collection of newspapers mounted in an exhibition, Mum?' I asked, tucking my feet underneath me in the armchair.

Mum took a deep breath before replying.

'Do you know, Holly, I felt really proud,' she said, with a wistful smile. She set her mug down and clasped her hands tightly in her lap. 'The library staff had done a great job and they seemed genuinely grateful to have the archive; they had one wall completely filled with local news dating right back to 1984 with a banner saying: "Remember when . . ." And then they had a pile of sticky notes on a shelf for people to write their own memories and add it to the wall. It was lovely.'

I smiled proudly at her. 'Sounds fab, I might go and see it myself tomorrow, perhaps drag Esme along if she's got

time. It'll be weird to see newspapers that we've been trip-
ping over for years pinned up neatly!'

'I knew they'd jump at the chance of getting their hands
on your collection, Lucy.' Steve put an arm round Mum's
shoulders and pulled her close. 'What did I say?'

'A cultural treasure trove, you called it!' I laughed,
remembering that summer's day when Ben and I first met
Steve and we pored over the issues of the *Wickham and
Hoxley News* that I'd managed to purloin from Mum. 'I
know it meant a lot to you, Mum, but I can't say I miss all
that clutter.'

'No, well,' said Mum primly, '*all that clutter* may have gone,
but at least I know I can always go and have a look at it
in the library if I get withdrawal symptoms. But it's funny:
now that I've cleared out all of that stuff, my life seems
fuller than ever.'

A loaded silence fell over us then as Steve wriggled closer
to her and the two of them shared a smile. I felt myself
tearing up. After Mum admitted to me in the summer how
lonely she had been, it was heartwarming to see her so
happy.

I suddenly remembered their wintry walk, which seemed
like an odd thing to be doing on a dark evening, and I
opened my mouth to ask about it. But as I did so Mum
picked up her mug again and lifted it to her mouth. The
reflection of the flames caused something to glint on her
hitherto unadorned finger.

'Mum,' I gasped, 'what's that on your . . . ? Is that a ring?
Are you two . . . ?'

I looked from Mum to Steve and back again and their
joyful faces said it all.

'Steve asked me to marry him,' Mum gushed. 'And I
said yes!'

We both jumped up and I grabbed her hand to see the most beautiful diamond and topaz engagement ring on her finger.

'Congratulations!' I squealed. 'This calls for champagne, not tea!'

A second later Steve got to his feet bashfully. 'Does this mean that you don't mind, then, Holly? I know it's all happened very fast. I was a bit worried about what you'd think, although Lucy seemed confident that you wouldn't mind.'

'Mind?' I yelled, wiping away the tears that sprang to my eyes. 'I'm thrilled!'

I flung one arm around his neck and the other round Mum's and hugged them warmly until eventually I pulled away and grinned at Steve.

'Does this mean I get to call you Dad?'

Which I meant as a joke but instantly regretted because it reminded me of Antonio and the letter that I'd seen arrive, which may or may not have been from him. So while the two of them whooped with laughter, my stomach churned and I escaped to the kitchen to find alcohol.

We didn't have any champagne in the fridge, so we made do with a nice bottle of red wine that Lord Fortescue had given me as a thank-you for helping him join Facebook.

'To the happy couple,' I said, raising my glass in a toast. 'Lovely ring, by the way.'

'Thank you, darling.' Mum sighed and stretched out her hand to inspect her new ring for the umpteenth time. 'Steve took me into that little antique jeweller that I love in Stratford.'

'The one she drops hints about every time we go into town,' said Steve, rolling his eyes.

'So will this be a long engagement?' I raised my eyebrows over the rim of my glass.

'We're not in any rush,' they both answered in unison and then giggled.

Mum cleared her throat. 'Holly, ever since you were born it has just been you and me and that means that we've always shared a special bond.'

I nodded. 'You've been the best mum I could have wished for but I'll be thirty next year, it's time you put yourself first.'

Mum tucked a wayward strand of hair behind her ear and shot Steve a nervous look. 'I'm so glad you said that, love, because we've decided to move in together over Christmas.'

I choked on my wine. 'In here?'

OK, so the cottage was a lot less cluttered these days, but even so, it was still *bijou* and that was putting it mildly.

'Well, yes, we thought it was the best solution,' said Mum, chewing on her lip. 'Granddad left me this cottage and it has a lot of happy memories, Holly. Whereas Steve's only been in his flat since his divorce.'

'My place isn't suitable for two of us,' Steve added.

'And this place isn't suitable for three!' I retorted. And then I noticed their discomfort.

Oh. This was my cue . . .

'Hey! I'll move out,' I cried, as though the suggestion had just occurred to me. Let's face it, it *had* just occurred to me, but it was better than them having to actually ask me.

'Really, Holly?' Mum's forehead furrowed.

'Because I wouldn't want you to leave on my account,' said Steve, leaning forward and placing a hand tenderly on my knee. 'And we don't want you to feel pushed out.'

'No, it's fine, honestly. It's time I cut the apron strings.' I laughed.

'Well, if you're sure . . . and there really is no rush,' said

Mum, reaching for her fiancé's hand. 'What do you think you'll do?'

I had to swallow a giggle; they *so* hoped that I would rush . . . I thought about it for a long moment and a smile spread across my face.

'Do you know, I actually don't have a plan. How exciting is that!'

I planned everything in my life. In fact, I planned things in other people's lives, too. And for once I didn't have a clue what I was going to do, where I was going to live and who I was going to do it with. And it was actually incredibly liberating.

I might not have had a plan for my future living arrangements but I did have a plan for Wickham Hall. Or at least, I was working on one. And as soon as Mum and Steve disappeared into Henley for a celebratory engagement dinner, I retrieved the slim manila folder from my bag that Sheila had slipped to me earlier in the week, poured myself another glass of wine and settled back in front of the fire to read it.

It seemed that the Fortescues had begun a project some years ago to convert the row of stone garages that Lord Fortescue's father had used for his car collection into an art gallery. Plans had been drawn up, contacts made with various art institutions and cost estimates had been gathered. The Fortescues had been initially advised that there was a possibility of attracting funding from the Heritage Lottery Fund to finance the building works but when this had failed, the project had been abandoned. Instead, they had ploughed their money into the café and gift shop on the basis that it would provide a more consistent revenue stream and offer employment opportunities to local people. Besides, neither Lord nor Lady Fortescue had a particular passion for art.

But Ben did.

I reached for my notepad, heart pounding, as the ideas began to flow. This could be just the sort of project that would entice Benedict Fortescue to take up the mantle and allow his parents to retire. Could I turn these half-formed ideas into a workable plan before Ben came back? And even if I did, would he listen to me? He still hadn't responded to my Facebook friend request and I really didn't know how he felt about me.

Just then my phone flashed up with a Facebook message and my heart swooped with joy.

It was Ben.

Chapter 34

I paused in front of Joop's front door the next morning to admire the blissfully romantic Christmas wreath that hung from the brass door knocker. It was made from dried rose heads frosted with a shimmery coating and dotted with pearlescent baubles.

Once inside, the elegant, understated Christmas theme continued with matching miniature white trees either side of the entrance covered in strings of pearls and a colour palette of pale pink, cream and rose-gold decorations. Twinkling lights covered every edge of the little boutique from the mirrors, the fitting rooms and even all along the counter. The effect was breathtaking.

'Morning, with you in a moment!' chimed a voice as a figure emerged from the back of the boutique, hidden beneath an armful of clothing still in their plastic garment bags. Esme's eyes suddenly appeared over the top of it and several of the bags slipped out of her arms and onto the floor.

'Holster! You're up early for a Saturday.'

I dashed forward to scoop the dropped items and kissed her cheek. 'I was hoping to tempt you out for breakfast and a trip to the library, but I see you're on your own.'

'Library?' Esme pulled a face. 'Not your most irresistible offer. Anyway, you're right: Mum's not feeling too great today so, regretfully, I'll have to give the library a miss.'

She looked about as regretful as Mum had last night when I'd offered to move out.

'Poor Bryony; give her my love.' I glanced round the shop. 'Love the Christmas decs, by the way, especially that antiquey-looking wreath.'

'Mum made it from the bouquet of flowers that Wickham Hall sent me after Zara's wedding.' She lowered the rest of the clothes onto the floor gently and began removing the plastic covers.

'You two are so talented.' I sank onto the chaise longue. 'If I'd known how good your mum was, I would have asked her to help me out at the hall with our Christmas craft workshops.'

Esme wrinkled her nose. 'It took her ages, to be honest, Hols. Her joints are getting worse; her shoulder has been sore this week too. Anyway,' she shook herself and smiled brightly, 'thanks for wangling me an invite to their Christmas at Home gig. I can't wait! Me, Esme Wilde, rubbing shoulders with the aristocracy; who'd have thought!'

I slipped off my boots and stretched out my legs. 'Nothing to do with me. I think the Fortescues genuinely go through their diary and pick out everyone who has done them a favour of some sort. You came to the rescue at the wedding; they don't forget things like that.'

'And you, you'll be there, won't you? We can party together.' Her eyes sparkled mischievously.

'I will, but only in an official capacity,' I explained. 'Clipboard in hand, whispering everyone's names to Lord Fortescue as they make their way along the receiving line to shake hands with him and Lady F.'

Esme's eyes popped out on stalks. 'Flippin' 'eck, I didn't realize it would be *that* fancy. Now I'll have to re-think my outfit. Never mind, as luck would have it we've just had a delivery of new stock, as you can see. I'll have a look through this lot while I hang. Are you staying for a bit?'

I grinned and waggled my eyebrows at her. 'I have so much news, Es, I could be here a while.'

'In that case, make yourself useful.' She deposited a selection of slidy plastic-covered garments on top of me. 'I'll stick the kettle on.'

She made it as far as the back room and turned. 'Oh, and I'll say yes to breakfast, you can fetch us both a bacon roll from the café over the road.'

I did as I was told and when I returned from the café bearing bacon, two customers, intent on trying on every-thing in the entire shop, were in the fitting rooms. Esme was tied up for the next half an hour helping them choose an outfit each for their work's Christmas party and so I wrapped the bacon rolls up to keep warm and busied myself hanging up the new stock on the rail on wheels that Esme kept for moving stuff around.

As soon as the two ladies departed, clutching their Joop bags triumphantly, we dived into the back and demolished our breakfast.

'OK, ready for part one of the news?' I said, tearing a hole in my ketchup sachet and zigzagging it across the bacon. Esme squirted both brown sauce and ketchup inside her bun and nodded. 'I am burning with curiosity; I never thought those two women would leave.'

I peered at her over my bun for a few seconds to build the tension. 'Mum and Steve are engaged and I'm moving out of the cottage.'

Her jaw dropped open. 'Wow. Fantastic for them. How do you feel?'

I lifted a shoulder. 'Happy. I keep waiting for a wave of nerves to hit me about leaving Weaver's Cottage but so far, I just feel . . . exhilarated. Like next year is going to be different. And I can't wait.'

She nodded encouragingly. 'Go on, then, hit me with your plans.'

'That's what is different,' I said, beaming. 'I don't have any plans. You know, all my life I've freaked out if things aren't in order or tidy or "in the plan". Maybe it's time to, as you would say, "live in the moment". So as far as plans go, I'm going to be taking a leaf out of your book. Trying it your way. What's so funny?' I said suddenly, noticing that Esme's shoulders were shaking.

She dropped her bacon roll onto her napkin. 'Just that I was going to say the same to you. From now on I'm doing it *your* way.'

I blinked at her and slurped my tea. 'What do you mean?' She took a deep breath.

'I need a plan. And quick. I think we might have a buyer for the shop.'

'Oh, that's good, isn't it?'

Esme's shoulders sagged. 'Well, Dad's delighted. Mum's having second thoughts. She's had a new lease of life since starting the personal shopping thing. She had a group of eight here last night, all taking turns in the fitting room. And I definitely don't want to sell. I'm wondering whether I could take over the business myself and let Mum go part-time. But I need a plan to make Joop more profitable.'

'Esme Wilde, that's brilliant!' I abandoned my breakfast and hugged her tight. 'You could definitely run this place by yourself. And I'm so proud of you.'

'Well, money will be tight to start off with so . . . ?' She opened her eyes wide and stared at me.

I cringed. 'I can't really help out, Es. I'm going to need cash for a deposit on somewhere to live.'

'I don't need cash, you plonker,' she cried, thumping my arm. 'I need a lodger. You need somewhere to live . . .'

I smiled at her as I hesitated to give her an immediate reply. Esme would be fun to live with and she had been nagging me to move in with her ever since she first got her own flat, but something held me back. I was reluctant to take the easy option. For once in my life I wanted to force myself out of my comfort zone and try something different.

'Thanks for the offer, Es, but I think it's time to strike out on my own.'

My best friend pulled a sad face. 'Fair enough, but if you need somewhere temporary, you know where I am.'

I kissed her cheek. 'I'll remember that. Actually, I might ask Lord Fortescue if he has anything going.'

'At Wickham Hall?' she wheezed, banging her chest as a morsel of bread went down the wrong way.

'No!' I laughed. 'On the estate. Quite a few of the staff live in tenanted cottages; they're highly sought after, though.'

Jim and his wife lived in Wickham-owned cottages, as did Edith; Lord Fortescue had granted them lifelong tenancies. I wasn't sure I'd need anything quite that permanent, but I was confident that he would be a fair landlord. And it would be good to stay close by.

Esme winked. 'Now that would be handy for when Ben comes back.'

'Two words,' I replied: 'Lady Fortescue. One sniff of impropriety and she'll have me deported.'

She rolled her eyes. 'Honestly.' She sighed. 'When are you two going to wake up and smell the pheromones?'

'Part two of the news coming right up.' I jumped to my feet. 'But first, let's start hanging that new stock.'

There appeared to be far too much clothing for one tiny boutique but Esme assured me that it was less than normal, due to their precarious cash flow. The next two weeks of pre-Christmas and, more importantly, pre-New-Year's-Eve trading would see off most of it, she reckoned. We removed the plastic garment bags and sorted items by colour and collection, with Esme dipping in and out of the task between customers.

'What we really need is for our suppliers to offer us sale or return to avoid all our money being tied up in stock,' she said, after she'd waved off a customer who'd tried on an armful of dresses and bought nothing. 'But that's about as likely as Coco Chanel wearing pink.'

'Hmm,' I said noncommittally, thinking that what she really needed were more customers like Lady Fortescue whose wardrobe capacity knew no bounds.

'Oh! Now this is a dress.' I sighed with longing as I spied a pale gold empire-line tunic with a scoop neck and sleeves that flared out from the elbow to the wrist. 'Esme, I think I'm in love.'

She quirked an eyebrow. 'Fab choice. But it's not a dress; it's supposed to be worn over trousers.'

She inspected the label before foisting it on me. 'Jersey silk – very slinky. Try it on.'

I squinted at the price tag with one eye – ouch – and handed it back to her firmly. 'I'd better not. I might love it, but I don't need it and I haven't budgeted for anything like this so . . .'

Esme looked at me like I was insane. 'So? Live danger-ously for once in your life, Holster, be frivolous. Didn't you just declare a new spontaneous you?'

I pursed my lips. She was right. I grabbed it from her and dived into the fitting room. 'Absolutely.'

I scrambled out of my jeans and top and concentrated on taking the thing of beauty off the hanger without snagging the delicate material.

I popped it over my head and when I straightened up, the cool silk fabric slithered down me and I held my breath. It might have been a tunic for some people (tall ones, mainly) but on me, with my short legs, it was the perfect length. The scoop neck hinted at a bit of cleavage whilst still being classy and the dress had a subtle sheen to it, making it perfect for the Christmas season. I didn't have anywhere to wear it and I almost certainly couldn't afford it but all the same, it was definitely coming home with me.

I took a step closer to the mirror. The colour seemed to make my brown eyes shine and my blonde hair glow.

'I look all . . . glowy.' I giggled, turning this way and that.

'You look beautiful,' said Esme, joining me in the fitting room. 'And it's got a touch of the Elizabeth Bennet about it. Well, the top half has anyway.'

She was right.

'How apt for Wickham Hall.' I bowed to my reflection and performed a graceful curtsey. 'Thank you for a deli-cious luncheon, Mr Darcy,' I enunciated, holding up the sides of the dress.

Esme snorted. 'Mr Fortescue, more like. Any news?'

'Which leads me nicely into part two of my news,' I said, pressing my lips together in a prim smile. 'Or is it part three? I've lost track.'

'I don't care,' she laughed, 'just tell me!'

'I heard from him last night!'

I was still floating on high since getting Ben's message and was only too happy to fill Esme in on its contents. There was a seven-hour time difference between here and Cambodia: he had sent it in the early hours of his Saturday morning when I received it on Friday evening.

Lord Fortescue had been right: there was no internet or even phone service in Mae Chang village where he was based, and it wasn't until he made his fortnightly trip to the nearest city for supplies that he'd been able to go online and so had only just picked up my message.

'Well, we're now friends on Facebook, so that's a good start,' I said, ushering her out of the fitting room so I could close the door and get dressed again without passers-by on Hoxley High Street getting an eyeful.

'And he sent me a message. The school repairs are almost finished and he has been working with the officials to organize careers advice for the students so that their education really helps them to help their own communities.'

'Aww, that's good. And did you apologize for blasting him for secretly contacting your father in Italy?'

My stomach lurched at that but I was saved from answering by the arrival of a customer in the shop. Esme leapt into sales mode and promised to find the lady the perfect outfit for a Christmas dinner dance.

I had replied to Ben last night, of course. Immediately. I'd updated him on all that had happened since he'd left, about the White Christmas theme and even about putting the angel on top of the Christmas tree. And at the end of my message I had told him how sorry I was that I'd reacted the way I did and that if I hadn't completely blown it I hoped that we could still be friends. And after I pressed send I waited for three hours, staring at my phone for a reply. I could only guess that he had needed to leave his internet connection because I hadn't received an answer.

As soon as I was dressed I left Joop with one of their lovely carrier bags over my arm, my new dress tucked into sheets of delicate tissue paper. I had promised Esme that I would try to think up some money-making ideas for her and Joop. I'd loved having a girlie catch-up with her, but for some reason I'd resisted revealing my innermost thoughts about Ben to her. I didn't want to tempt fate, perhaps, I mused. A lady with a Liberty-print scarf over her head opened the door to the tiny old-fashioned hairdressers as I passed by and I caught a whiff of hairspray along with the velvety tones of Michael Bublé singing, 'All I Want for Christmas is You'.

. . . *to come home*, I finished inwardly, *to smile me that smile and wrap me in your arms and never let me go.*

And to tell Lady Fortescue to bog off.

Chapter 35

It was officially Christmas. A magnificently bedecked Wickham Hall had reopened its doors to the guests for the Christmas season five minutes ago and there was a slightly hysterical sense of purpose mixed with the magical buzz of Christmas in the air as we all scurried round putting the final details in place for the first day's activities.

The sixteenth-century building seemed to thrive on all the energy and attention and I felt it breathe a warm welcome as I journeyed through the public rooms, turning on all the fairy lights.

There was a permanent smile on my face this morning, and not just because of the beauty of Wickham Hall. I'd had another message from Ben and . . . he was coming home . . . Hurrah!

Guess what, Miss Clipboard? I'm flying home on Friday. Managed to get last seat on the flight. I've had a great time, but am ready to come home and face the music (aka the parentals), and not to put too fine a point on it the first thing I'll be doing is taking the world's longest shower. Can't wait to see you because I've got loads to tell you. (But after the shower obvs) Ben x

Friday was only four more sleeps . . . I could not wait.

'Welcome to a White Christmas at Wickham Hall,' I overheard Marjorie declare to the first visitors, a middle-aged pair of ladies, who instantly started to unravel chunky scarves and divest themselves of gloves as they stepped through the door.

I beamed at the new arrivals and followed at a safe distance behind them to eavesdrop as they oohed and ahhed at the twelve-foot Christmas tree that stood proudly at the bottom of the wide staircase where Zara had descended in her wedding dress six months ago.

'I was worried it would look a bit plain, being all white,' hissed Marjorie, tugging my sleeve. 'But I'm really impressed.'

I nodded in agreement. The hall looked even more spectacular than I'd envisaged and even Lady Fortescue had capitulated that Andy had been right and had done a splendid job.

'Loving the Christmas jumper, Marjorie.'

She giggled and her bright eyes crinkled at the corners. 'Watch this!'

I widened my eyes as she plunged a hand underneath her layers and started fiddling and huffing. I held my breath, bemused, until Rudolph's nose began to flash and a dubious electronic version of 'Rudolph the Red-Nosed Reindeer' began to play.

'That's brilliant!' I laughed, pleased that she and everyone else, come to that, had joined in with my suggestion of having a Christmas jumper day for staff. I pulled at my own cream and green snowflake-patterned jumper. 'It makes my

Norwegian woollie look very boring.'

'Never mind, dear,' she said, pinching my cheek. 'It's very you.'

'Thank you,' I said. *I think.*

'Tasteful and demure.'

Let's leave on a high, I thought and left Marjorie to welcome the next group of visitors. I carried on towards the Great Hall to check that Andy had everything he needed.

I had only gone a little way along the corridor when Lady Fortescue appeared from a door leading to their private staircase, laden with armfuls of ladies' clothing and followed closely by her husband.

They could barely see over their load and I hurried forward to help them with the door.

'Thank you, Holly. Lady Fortescue is making room in her wardrobe before her trip to Paris tomorrow,' Lord Fortescue said breathlessly, giving me a subtle wink behind his wife's back.

'I'll have to put something down, Hugo, my wrists are in danger of giving way,' Lady Fortescue groaned.

I glanced at the clothing and spotted evening dresses, a tweed something-or-other, several jumpers and countless coats, as well as a bag filled with something over Lady Fortescue's arm.

'Oh goodness, let me help,' I said, relieving her of half of her pile.

'Thank you. Although now I've sorted them all out I'm not sure what to do with them.'

'Well, how about . . .' I hesitated. I could always take them to Mum's charity shop but would she see that as an insult? Besides, I thought, looking at the quality of her cast-offs, they would be wasted in there amongst the musty old rain macs and nylon wedding dresses . . .

Some of these looked good enough to sell in Joop.

And there was Esme's solution: add a barely worn designer clothing rail to Joop! My stomach quivered with excitement. Sale or return, no initial cost of the stock . . .

'You were saying, Holly?' Lady Fortescue tapped her toe impatiently.

'I could dispose of them for you, Your Ladyship,' I volunteered. A second even more brilliant thought occurred to me. 'And the money from the sale can go to a charity of your choice.'

She pondered this, pressing her lips together thoughtfully. 'I did want to do something for charity,' she said slowly. 'And there's plenty more where this came from. What do you think, Hugo?'

'I think my arms are aching and you should hurry up and make a decision.' He chuckled, shooting me another wink.

'All right, done, Holly. We'll put these in your office for now.'

'Perfect,' I said with a glowing smile. 'In fact, if you just put things on the floor, I'll pop out to my car with everything.'

They both lowered their bundles to the floor with relief.

'On second thoughts, I might keep that,' said Lady Fortescue, plucking a fur hat from the top of Lord Fortescue's pile. 'The forecast for this week is snow. I might even get stranded in Paris.'

'You might, I suppose,' conceded Lord Fortescue, looking a mite too cheerful for his own good.

'And Benedict. What about him?' she fretted.

My ears pricked up and I bent down to add my pile to theirs.

'I doubt that the snow will reach South East Asia,' he chortled.

'No, but it might close the airports in Britain.'

'Darling, we've got a few days until he comes back, let's try not to worry.'

'But the BBC said—'

'The BBC is no more in control of the weather than you or I,' declared Lord Fortescue, giving his wife a peck on the cheek. 'So I suggest that you carry on packing for Paris while I pop outside to feed the birds. The ground is frozen solid and they'll be struggling for food. And Holly, if you get a moment, please can you check on Jim in Santa's workshop? There is another spare heater in the gatehouse; I don't want him getting cold.'

'Of course.' I nodded.

He paused to smile at me briefly. 'Thank you.'

I recognized the dismissal and spent the next twenty minutes loading Lady Fortescue's elegant clothes into my car. Back inside, a quick glance at my watch made me quicken my pace to the Great Hall. Andy's first workshop would be starting in the next half an hour and the last time I'd seen him he'd been getting very stressed about the lack of berries on his holly and had begged Nikki to go foraging for some better specimens.

Every other day the long dining table in the Great Hall would be laid for a formal dinner with shimmering candelabra, opulent goblets, elegant silvery cutlery and antique china, but today it had been covered with a protective plastic sheet. Heaps of greenery, moss, wire and ribbon were piled along its length and at the very end sat Andy, snipping at a freshly cut bunch of holly with secateurs.

'Hols!' he grinned, looking up.

The new friendly Andy was still taking some getting used to, but I wasn't complaining. I smiled back when he held a sprig of mistletoe over his head and puckered up.

'I am so looking forward to today,' he said, placing a Christmas kiss on my cheek. 'I've got a full house of fifteen customers and in the next three hours we're going to attempt a garland, a table centrepiece and a wreath. It's going to be fab.'

I couldn't help sharing his enthusiasm as he pointed out all the materials he'd arranged in front of each guest, which included a huge tray of dried clementine slices that Jenny had done for him in the café ovens.

'It looks and smells amazing,' I said, picking up some cinnamon sticks that he'd wrapped into bundles with raffia. 'I wish we'd booked more of these workshops now. I must make a note in my diary for next year. What will you do tomorrow?'

'Gift shop in the morning and then,' his eyes glittered mischievously, 'elf duty.'

We both laughed.

'I can't wait to see you in the green tights,' I said. 'Which reminds me, I must check the rota.'

Whereas Jim was Santa every day, no one had wanted to play permanent elf, so Sheila suggested that we all take turns and I had yet to find out when I was due to do my stint.

'Well, as you've obviously got everything under control, I'll go and see if Santa's workshop is warm enough. I don't want Jim getting frozen to his chair!'

I turned to leave, but Andy caught my arm. 'Wait.'

He produced a small posy of mistletoe tied with a white glittery ribbon and presented it to me. 'For you.' He winked. 'Use it wisely.'

My heart melted and I gave him a hug. 'That is so sweet of you. I'm touched. Truly.'

Who says people can't change? I mused, as I made my way to the gatehouse to fetch the spare heater for Jim. If Andy could change his attitude to me so dramatically, there was hope for others. Maybe even Lady Fortescue . . .

The electric heater wasn't heavy but it was a bit bulky so I tucked the mistletoe posy into the pocket of my jeans as I lugged it along the covered walkway to Santa's workshop. It was only noon, so I didn't get the full effect of the Christmas lights in the gardens but despite the cold air nipping at my cheeks, it was a joy to be out in the winter sunshine.

Santa's workshop was the cutest little wooden chalet ever. It was surrounded by Wickham estate Christmas trees to give the area a foresty feel and inside the space was divided into two rooms: the first being devised as a toy workshop with a workbench covered with wooden toys, piles of gift-wrapped presents and a desk with a long scroll of paper on it. The top of it read 'Good Girls and Boys' and underneath were listed all the children whose parents had booked Santa visits for today. I caught myself scanning the list for Holly Swift and giggled softly to myself under my breath. I opened the door to the second room where Santa would meet the children and was quite startled to find Santa sitting in his rocking chair doing the crossword next to the Christmas tree with a sack of presents at his side.

'Jim!'

I plonked the heater on the floor, produced my posy of mistletoe and gave him a hug and a kiss.

'That's Father Christmas to you, young Holly,' he said

waggling his eyebrows at me. 'Or Santa, I suppose, depending on your preference.'

'But you've got hours until the first children arrive!' I said, dropping onto the wooden stool presumably positioned for the little ones to perch on.

'Well,' he said, patting his red jacket, 'gives me time to settle in, you know, get into character. Besides, if no one knows where I am, they can't give me any jobs to do, can they?' He chuckled.

'That is the most authentic suit I've ever seen,' I marvelled.

Sheila had brought it in from somewhere. It looked hand-made from thick red wool with large black buttons and white fur cuffs.

'I love it already. And very warm. I probably won't need that heater, especially as Jenny has already been across twice with hot soup and a flask of beef tea.'

'Excellent. It's so good to see you!' I beamed. 'How are you? Have you missed us?'

'It's good to be back, and I've missed you all something rotten,' he said, laying his newspaper down on the floor at his feet. 'Although I was quite getting used to Betty waiting on me hand and foot.'

'You deserved a break, Jim,' I said, patting his liver-spotted hand.

'A month, Holly. A month off work. Most I've ever had in one go was ten days and that was when we went to see Betty's sister in the South of France. Did I ever tell you about the time I met Dolly Parton? I didn't—'

I smothered a chuckle. 'You did, Jim,' I said before he recounted the autograph story again. 'Although I didn't know you'd been on your way to France at the time.'

'Oh yes,' he said gravely. 'My sister-in-law lived in

Monaco. She's passed away now, God rest her soul, but she had one of those millionaire apartments near the Golden Square.'

I shook my head. Full of surprises, our Jim; he lived a quiet life in a tenanted cottage while other members of his family lived a life of luxury. 'Betty's sister sounds like she was quite well-to-do.'

'So was Betty when I met her.' He nodded wistfully. 'Elizabeth Charlotte Simpson Jones as she was then. Her father was less than impressed when I asked his permission to marry her. Refused point blank and told Betty that if she married me he'd cut all ties with her.'

'Why?' I huffed. 'I would have thought any man would be proud to welcome you into his family.'

'Albert Simpson Jones was a judge.' He shrugged. 'I was just Jim Badger, handyman at Wickham Hall. He thought I was beneath her.'

'She must have really loved you.' I felt a pang at the thought of the young woman torn between her lover and her family.

'Why? Because she put up with being called Betty Badger? Go on, you can laugh; I don't mind.'

'Sorry,' I giggled, clamping a hand over my mouth. 'No, actually, I think that's a very sweet name. I meant giving up her family and her wealthy lifestyle.'

'What can I say?' he smirked, leaning back and resting his hands behind his head. 'I was worth it.'

We laughed for a moment before his face grew serious.

'I did tackle her about that,' he said, 'because I was worried that one day she might regret it. But you know what she said?'

I shook my head.

'She said that when you fall in love with someone, you

403

fall in love with the person they are and not their job or their bank balance and that people are people and we shouldn't put one above another.' He sniffed. 'So I married her and we've been together for over fifty years.'

'Oh, Jim. That is the sweetest thing I ever heard.' I reached out and squeezed his hand. 'And did her family ever forgive her?'

'Yes. Old Albert was quite a decent chap in the end. So all was well.'

'A happy ending,' I said, standing to leave. 'I'm glad. I'd better be off; our celebrity chef is due any second and I want to check that Jenny doesn't flirt with him too outrageously.'

'Hold on, aren't yóu going to tell Santa what you want for Christmas first?' He settled his red hat on his head and rested his hands on his tummy. 'Go on, I'm ready.'

'Oh gosh,' I chewed my lip. 'Let me think.'

I wanted to be Ben's girlfriend, I wanted Lady Fortescue to be overjoyed for us and I wanted the airmail letter from Italy to bring good news . . .

My shoulders lifted in an almighty sigh. 'I want the impossible, Santa.'

'It's Christmas, Holly, anything can happen.' He laughed, tapping his nose. 'You might get lucky.'

I kissed Jim's cheek and said goodbye, pausing in the workshop to stand on a stool and fix Andy's mistletoe posy to the ceiling with a pin.

Let's hope Jim is right, I thought, *maybe this Christmas I will get lucky . . .*

Chapter 36

I left Jim in his cosy grotto and scurried across the courtyard to the café, wrapping my arms around myself to
ward off the icy wind. But despite the cold, I paused for a
moment at the door.

Decked out in its festive finery, the café looked delight-
ful. Jenny had suggested that all the decorations in here
should be in keeping with the Elizabethan food event
she was running today. So we had held back on the silver
glitter, making use of the abundant greenery from the
grounds instead. Swags of bay, laurel, holly and ivy ran
along the serving counter and around the ceiling beams,
adding traditional festive charm. Tall fat candles encircled
with rosemary and thyme coronets created a gentle glow
and the overall aroma when I opened the door was rich and
pungent.

The usual café tables and chairs had been put into
storage for the day and the space had been set up theatre-
style around a demo table near the kitchen doors. Jenny
had purloined a couple of electric hobs from somewhere
although they didn't have an oven out front, so one of
her helpers would be on hand to ferry food to and from
the kitchens. Rachel, Jenny's sous chef, was at the table

arranging a series of ceramic dishes full of ingredients for Daniel's menu.

And there, sitting at a table to the side of the demo area, almost concealed behind a pile of cookery books, was Daniel Denton himself.

Our celebrity chef had arrived.

I had watched three episodes of his series *Kitchen Secrets* last night back-to-back, so I thought I knew what to expect. His TV persona was of an enthusiastic octopus on speed; he waved his arms endlessly, darted from cooker to fridge to workbench as though his pants were on fire and he could crack an egg with one hand while stirring cheese sauce with another. Even his blond floppy hair seemed to be in constant motion. I felt exhausted just watching him and to top it off the show was set to music with a constant dance beat that he nodded and twitched his shoulders to. He didn't talk much, but he had a habit of winking at the camera just before slamming something in the oven.

But when I crossed the Coach House Café, I was quite taken aback. Daniel Denton was hunched over his coffee, scowling at a coiffured redhead who was brandishing a clipboard. He didn't look at all like his on-screen personality.

Jenny was at my side instantly.

'Come and meet Daniel and Portia,' she said breathlessly, grabbing my arm. 'Isn't he divine? And those pale eyes, so beguiling; I've been a total fan girl ever since he arrived. And yes, I do know he's married, but I can't help myself. Come and say hello and please pinch me if I say anything inappropriate.'

I did as I was told and followed Jenny to where Portia was arranging copies of her husband's books in a fan shape on the table.

'Will you sign one of your books for me now in case

we run out?' Jenny asked once the introductions had been made. She delved into her pockets for her money.

I bit the inside of my cheek to hide my smile; she was so star-struck that she could barely meet his eye and her face had turned a deep shade of pink, which toned beautifully with her aubergine-coloured hair.

'Sure,' Daniel replied flatly, picking up a black pen.

'And we've bought DVDs as well,' said Portia. 'Don't forget to sell those too, Daniel.'

He sighed by way of response.

'So what do you think of Wickham Hall, Daniel?' I asked, undaunted by his lack of interest.

'Yeah, great,' Daniel muttered.

'It is sweet,' Portia conceded, casting a glance around the café. 'Although, you're lucky to get Daniel at a venue like this. We're only here for some practice in front of a live audience. This time next year we'll be aiming much higher.'

Charming.

I heard Jenny exhale through her nose and I was slightly concerned she was going to say something that we all would regret when Daniel's chair gave a screech as he pushed it back and stood up.

'I need some air,' he grunted before stomping out of the café.

Jenny and I exchanged looks but Portia just smiled smoothly and handed Jenny her change.

'My goal, *our* goal,' she corrected herself, 'for next year is to break into the live food show circuit – London, Glasgow, Manchester. They all have a big reach and I think they'll build his brand in a more experiential way than TV. His public need to meet him in the flesh.'

'Absolutely,' I said. Whatever experiential meant.

'Excuse me,' said Portia with a tight smile. 'I'll go and retrieve him.'

Jenny and I watched her leave the café and scan the courtyard for her errant celebrity husband.

'He's a bit . . . well, sullen,' I said cautiously.

'Hmmm,' said Jenny, biting her lip. 'At first I thought he was just remaining aloof, like stars do, you know. He was more responsive when we had a run-through of the schedule and he was very complimentary about the ingredients for today's dishes. He said he'd never seen such a plump goose.'

'She's got him, look,' I said with relief, as Portia and Daniel, hand in hand, arrived back. They looked frozen.

'Phew,' Jenny breathed. 'We're supposed to be starting any minute.'

Tickets to our celebrity chef demonstration had included a tour of the Wickham Hall Christmas decorations first so that all guests, including my mum, would arrive at the café at the same time and right on cue, at twelve o'clock, Marjorie opened the door that led from the hall's main corridor and Daniel's audience flocked in.

'Welcome, welcome,' cried Jenny, extending her arms, 'to Wickham Hall's first ever celebrity cooking demonstration. Please put your hands together for Daniel Denton.'

I waved at Mum who'd managed to be one of the first in, and everyone began to clap as Daniel dragged himself up from his chair, raised a hand briefly and sat back down abruptly.

Jenny's eyes flicked over to me and I shrugged discreetly. I sincerely hoped that he would perk up when he donned his pinny, or this could be Wickham Hall's *last* ever celebrity cooking demonstration too.

'Refreshments are over here, ladies and gentleman!'

Jenny indicated the table at the back of the room, which was laden with tea, coffee, water and a selection of Wickham Hall biscuits.

The crowd immediately surged towards the refreshments and I noticed Portia jabbing a finger at Daniel's book.

'Ooh yes,' giggled Jenny, picking up her signed copy. 'I'd better put this somewhere safe.'

Portia looked as though she was about to erupt and shook the book harder.

I cleared my throat and bellowed in my loudest voice: 'And don't be shy; Daniel will be signing copies of his new book, *Kitchen Secrets*, which will make a perfect Christmas present, or a treat for yourself.'

'Bugger,' Jenny whispered with a grimace. 'I was meant to say that.'

'No harm done.' I patted her arm and made a beeline for my mum.

'Hello, Mum.' I kissed her cheek. 'Having a good time?'

'Best event I've ever been to here, love.' She beamed. Her hair was tumbling out of its bun and she had sparkly Christmas tree earrings in. 'I'm so proud of you.'

I shook my head with a laugh. 'Jenny organized this one; Daniel Denton is her contact.'

'I'm proud of you anyway.' She pointed to her bag. 'I've bought one of his books and had it signed for Steve for Christmas.'

'Oh, nice.' I arched my eyebrows. 'Is Steve a keen cook?'

'Well,' Mum's face coloured and she pressed a hand to her hair, 'to be honest, Holly, I don't really know. But a bit of encouragement never hurt anyone, did it?'

I left her to her cup of tea and wandered off to find Jenny; time was ticking on and we really needed to seat the audience.

It takes time, I supposed, to find out everything about the one you love. That's part of the fun of those early days. Now that I thought about it, I knew all sorts of random things about Ben: he liked mustard on his sausages, often kept a paintbrush behind his ear and, I reminded myself for the umpteenth time, he was coming home in four sleeps . . .

'Psst, Holly!' Jenny hissed at me, bringing me out of my daydream.

'What's up?'

'Give me strength,' muttered Jenny, dragging me into the kitchen. 'Where's his celebrity charisma? Where's his stage presence? I'm tempted to grab him by the lapels of that denim jacket and yell, "Cheer up, it's Christmas!"'

I sucked in a worried breath. 'I know what you mean, Jenny. But at least he's here. I thought for one awful moment that he had left for good when he stormed off.'

'Most of the ladies have been here before to one of my demos. They're expecting something special. And they've paid handsomely for a ticket. I hope this doesn't all go belly up, chick.'

'Give him a chance, Jenny.' I squeezed her arm. 'He was probably up with the lark this morning to get here on time from Manchester. And from what I saw of his on-screen persona, I doubt he could keep that enthusiasm up for long. I imagine he saves the "crazy chef" routine until the last moment to preserve his energy.'

She eyed me doubtfully. 'But all his emails and tweets have been so chatty and bubbly.'

'He's probably just working himself up to it slowly; I'm sure this will be the best Christmas event the Coach House Café has ever seen. If it's any consolation, my mum thinks it's great.' I smiled.

'I hope you're right,' she sighed, smoothing her whites

down neatly, 'because right now I'm feeling less than festive myself.'

'Oh dear. Well, that's probably because you aren't wearing a Christmas jumper.' I raised an eyebrow and flicked at her chef whites. 'Didn't you get the memo?'

She snorted and undid the poppers on her jacket. 'I thought I'd be too hot, but my bra's got jingle bells on. Watch.'

We both giggled as she shimmied and tiny bells tinkled along the top of her bra.

'Perhaps that's the answer to Daniel's depressed face,' I suggested. 'Give him a flash. I defy anyone to keep a straight face looking at that cleavage.'

Jenny shuddered. 'Portia would kill me with one of her stares. I wouldn't dare!'

At that moment, the kitchen doors swung open and Portia appeared, her forehead creased and her lips pressed together sourly. 'Sorry to barge in, but have either of you seen Daniel?'

After five seconds of staring at each other in sheer panic, the three of us split up and went looking for our incredible vanishing chef. Portia decided to brave the men's toilets, Jenny ran along the corridor to the Great Hall and I went outside.

I found him in about thirty seconds.

He was sitting astride Jenny's Harley-Davidson, making revving noises under his breath.

'Daniel!' I exclaimed breathlessly. 'Did you get lost? We've all been looking for you. Portia's beside herself.'

He glanced up at me for a second. 'I can't do it.'

I honestly think my blood ran cold as I imagined having to face a disappointed audience in the café. Not to mention Jenny.

'Look, these people are your fans. Surely you don't want to let them down?'

'I never wanted to come in the first place,' he said morosely. 'I was supposed to be having a day off Christmas shopping with my brother today. Portia kept it as a *surprise*.'

I was confused. 'But you're a celebrity chef; aren't you living the dream?'

'I love to cook,' he said, climbing down off the bike. 'Big difference.'

I frowned, remembering the tweets and emails that Jenny had proudly shown me over the last few months.

Daniel lowered himself onto the step of the kitchen service door and I squeezed next to him, shivering as the cold shot up my spine.

'But you accepted Jenny's invitation on Twitter. Why do that if you never intended to come?'

'Not me; I've never even been on Twitter.' He shook his head, staring down at his feet. 'Portia does all that . . . social media stuff. She says it's important for profile-building.' He shrugged. 'I just want to be in the kitchen, cooking. I never wanted to be a celebrity.'

My heart sank as I looked at my watch. The audience was expecting the demo to start in seven minutes. And I had a celebrity chef who didn't even want to be a *celebrity*, let alone cook.

I scrabbled around for something motivating to say, but before anything profound came to mind, Daniel turned to me and blinked his solemn grey eyes.

'You know my show *Kitchen Secrets*?'

I nodded.

'That started as a joke because I never let anyone else in the kitchen with me. I'm quite a private person; I cook for myself, for relaxation. I crank up the music, throw myself into my cooking and lose myself in my own world. My wife pushed me to audition for TV. Sometimes I think she gets more out of it than I do; it's certainly given her career a boost.'

'But you look completely at home behind the camera, why don't you want to do this demo?' I asked, attempting to keep the frustration out of my voice.

'A camera – yes. Just me and a cameraman in the kitchen.' He gulped and his face seemed to drain of all colour. 'Not several hundred pairs of eyes all staring at me, waiting for me to make a mistake.'

I sighed inwardly; Jenny, our very own chef, could not only cook, but was a great entertainer too. She would jump at the chance to be in his place. What a shame that all these people had come to see him and not her. Unless, of course, they could work as a double act . . .

I jumped to my feet. 'Just wait there, don't move a muscle.'

Ten minutes later Daniel, Jenny and I were assembled in the kitchen, waiting while the audience settled themselves into their seats. Portia was at the book-signing table trying to flog DVDs.

'Jenny will do most of the talking,' I soothed. 'You just do the cheffy bits.'

He nodded nervously.

Jenny winked at me. 'And Daniel, if you start to panic, just hum "Jingle Bells".'

'What? Why?'

His jaw dropped as Jenny ripped open her top and wiggled her chest at him. 'Every time you hum, I'll come to your rescue.'

A smile spread across his face and he shook his head. 'I've seen it all now.'

'Not quite all.' She grinned. 'I've got matching knickers. Now come on, we've got an Elizabethan Christmas dinner to dish up to a hundred hungry fans.'

She linked arms with him and the two of them strode into the café singing 'Jingle Bells' quietly to themselves.

'So now that the roast goose is in the oven, we're going to crack on with the potted pheasant. I'll start the cider reduction, while Daniel prepares the pheasant.'

I hovered at the side of the demo area, completely entranced. I know she's my friend and I know I'm biased, but Jenny Plum really was a star; not only was she able to slice onions at speed whilst making eye contact with the audience, but she was also full of trivia and titbits of the origins of the dishes the two of them were creating. What's more, she was brilliant at drawing Daniel into the conversation . . .

'What are you putting in that pestle and mortar, Daniel?'

'We're going to pack some really bold flavours into this dish.' He held out his hand, looked around for the camera to do its close-up and then swallowed, realizing there wasn't one. Luckily, I was filming it on my iPhone, so I quickly stepped forward and zoomed in. He flashed me a grateful smile. 'I've got some mace, some star anise and some peppercorns to give it some heat.'

'Jenny's a genius,' murmured Portia in my ear. 'I don't know how she's done it, but he's totally calmed down.'

'So you use all of the pheasant?' asked a rotund lady in the front row.

Whoops. Portia had spoken too soon; it seemed Daniel was only calm when he forgot that the audience was there.

'Er.' Daniel blinked at the lady. '"Jingle bells" . . .'

Jenny perked her head up and began to dance on the spot.

Portia's hand flew to her throat. 'What on earth . . . ?'

'We're just using the breast in this recipe,' he replied, with a sly glance at Jenny. 'But the recipe has plenty of wiggle room for personal taste.'

'Potted pheasant would have been a traditional Christmas dish in Elizabethan times. Are there any food-related Christmas traditions in the Denton household?' Jenny asked him.

Daniel smoothed his hair back from his face and thought about it for a moment. 'My grandfather only cooked one dish and that was a raised game pie for Boxing Day. I haven't made one for years, but now that you've reminded me, I might give it a go again this year.' He grinned.

'Interesting,' said Jenny. 'Now the Elizabethans loved pies . . .'

And she was off again, describing the elaborate pies made as centrepieces, one even containing a whole peacock. The audience loved the double act and whenever Jenny asked for volunteers, nearly every hand shot straight up in the air.

The three hours flew by and towards the end, when Daniel was putting the finishing touches to the elaborate fruit cake that was to be shared amongst the audience, the door opened softly and Lady Fortescue slipped into the café.

In fact, I almost missed her; I was so engrossed in watching Jenny modelling miniature marzipan fruits and it took me back to my first day here when she had been making something similar for the Women's Institute.

'Now for this last delicate operation, we need an extra pair of hands.' Jenny smiled at the audience. 'Any volunteers?'

I nearly fell over when Lady Fortescue raced forward, as

415

usual looking effortlessly elegant in soft grey trousers and a silk blouse.

'Lady Fortescue, ladies and gentlemen!' declared Jenny, leading the applause as Her Ladyship donned an apron.

Daniel handed Lady Fortescue a fine brush and then showed her where to add the touches of gold leaf to the icing on the top of the cake, and the three of them brought the demonstration to a close by handing round slices of cake to a delighted audience.

An hour later all the guests had gone and Daniel was stowing the last few unsold DVDs in their car. Lady Fortescue, Jenny and I were lingering over a cup of tea and mulling over the success of the day.

'Just food for thought,' said Portia, 'but would you be interested in taking part in an episode of *Kitchen Secrets*, Jenny? I think you'd be a natural in front of the camera.'

Jenny's face flooded with colour. 'Me? Well . . . if you think—'

'She'd love to,' I interjected. 'And I agree, she is a natural. In fact, how about *Kitchen Secrets at Wickham Hall*? We've got so much history here and I think viewers would love to see behind the scenes.'

'Excellent idea, Holly,' Lady Fortescue exclaimed. 'Um, perhaps there would be a cameo role in it for me?'

My heart soared; it had been so long since any of my suggestions had found favour with Her Ladyship.

Portia took out her notebook and scribbled something down. 'I'll have a word with the director and be in touch.'

Jenny and I braved the cold and the dark to wave off Daniel and Portia in the car park. Jenny shook her head as their tail-lights finally disappeared into the distance. 'I cooked with Daniel Denton. I can't believe that just happened.'

'Believe it, Jenny.' I chuckled. 'I've got the video to prove it.'

'Just think, chick. I could be on TV. I couldn't wish for a better Christmas present.'

I was so happy for her, but even so as I wrapped my arm round her waist and we turned to go back inside a sigh escaped from me.

'Aww, that was heartfelt! Don't worry, your turn will come.'

I laughed softly, shaking my head. 'I've already told Santa today that all I want for Christmas is the impossible.'

'Hey, chick,' she said squeezing my shoulders, 'I just made the miserable Daniel Denton smile and almost got myself a TV contract; I'm living proof that the big man can work miracles.'

'In that case,' I laughed, 'I'd better work on getting myself onto the "good" list.'

Chapter 37

The week sped by and before I knew it it was Friday and I was on elf duty. *Today I win at Christmas*, I thought, pulling on the green and red stripy tights of my elf costume. I caught sight of my painted rosy cheeks in the mirror and grinned; my customary habit of remaining unobtrusive had gone completely out of the window.

I turned slowly to check my reflection in the mirror in the ladies' loos one final time to make sure that my tunic wasn't twisted and my hat was on straight and then hurried back up to the office to hang my own clothes up neatly. It was the Fortescues' Christmas at Home event tonight and although I was working and therefore wouldn't be in a fancy party outfit, I still wanted to make a good impression – especially on Ben, whose aeroplane would be somewhere in the skies right now.

My heart gave a little jolt at the thought of him, as it had been doing all day . . .

After a morning spent emailing exhibitors about next year's Wickham Hall Summer Festival, I'd treated myself to a warming jacket potato for lunch in the café. I was about to embark on my first ever stint as Santa's elf with Jim in the grotto. I was really looking forward to it; if three hours with Jim dressed in that Santa outfit didn't make me feel Christmassy, nothing would.

I peered out of my office window and couldn't help but feel all tingly at the perfect winter sight: the formal gardens were covered in a thin layer of undisturbed snow and the topiary trees looked magical with their sparkly white coats. It looked as though it was going to be a white Christmas at Wickham Hall both inside and out.

I hummed the tune to 'White Christmas' under my breath as I skipped down the stairs, enjoying the sound of the bells on the hem of my tunic jingling as I moved.

The weather forecast had predicted a heavy snowfall for today and we had anticipated a quiet day at the hall with the possibility of cancelled bookings to see Santa. I'd trudged to work in my wellingtons, wrapped up in layers of wool, rather than attempting to drive. On the plus side, that meant that I would be able to treat myself to a glass or two of mulled wine this evening.

Much to my surprise and delight the snow hadn't had the predicted effect on our visitor numbers. The café, back to normal again after Daniel's visit, had been busy with lunch-time customers enjoying bowls of game soup and slices of Jenny's brandy-soaked Christmas cake and there had been a steady stream of visitors to see the White Christmas decorations in the hall all morning.

I had one last thing to do before joining Jim in Santa's workshop. I poked my head into Lord Fortescue's office to see Sheila.

'Hello, have you got a moment?'

'Holly, dear! My, what a picture!' Sheila Beckwith lowered her reading glasses and waved me in.

'Thank you,' I said, jingling my way to the chair. 'I quite like being an elf. Impossible to creep up on anyone in this outfit, though.'

'A tiny bit of bad news, I'm afraid,' said Sheila, pulling a face. 'The storyteller from Henley library has called to make her excuses. She slipped on her front drive trying to clear the snow and has twisted her ankle.'

'Oh, poor thing!'

That was a shame. Now I'd have to find a last-minute replacement. Jim would have been perfect, but he and I would still be handing out presents in Santa's workshop.

Christmas stories around the Christmas tree had been one of our most popular events. Parents simply dropped off their little ones at four and collected them again at five, leaving them with a child-free hour to themselves to browse the gift shop or linger over a hot chocolate and a mince pie in the café.

'But never fear!' Sheila declared. 'I shall stand in myself and love every minute of it. I read to my grandchildren and I'm sure I can manage a larger group.'

'Sheila, that would be a real help. Are you sure you're not too busy?'

'As long as Her Ladyship doesn't start making last-minute changes to the seating plan for tonight's dinner as soon as she gets back from Paris, we'll be fine,' said Sheila with a wry smile.

'Which brings me to the reason I'm here.' I brandished my diary at her. 'Can we just run through the itinerary for tonight, please?'

The sun hadn't put in an appearance all day and the pale grey clouds overhead looked poised to deposit more snow at any moment. I was glad of the heavy fur-edged green elf

420

cloak as I braved the elements to join Jim in the cosy Nordic cabin. Nikki's team had cleared the snow from all the paths and sprinkled salt to prevent any accidents, but even so I stepped gingerly across the courtyard, through the formal gardens and along the covered walkway towards Santa's workshop, musing on the wisdom of Lady Fortescue's plans.

The Fortescues' Christmas at Home reception would begin at six o'clock sharp and end equally sharply at seven thirty, according to Sheila. Then a second wave of guests – personal friends of the Fortescues – would arrive for a formal dinner party at eight o'clock. Why anyone would organize two social occasions in one evening was beyond my comprehension, especially as Lady Fortescue and Zara weren't due back from Paris until later this afternoon.

It was tradition, Sheila had explained simply. 'According to Her Ladyship, there has always been a Christmas reception followed by a dinner as far back as she could trace in Lord Fortescue's ancestors' history. And Lady Fortescue would never break a Wickham Hall tradition.'

'Even if it was inconvenient?' I'd asked, nonplussed as to why she would put herself through the stress. 'Why not?'

Sheila fiddled with the chain on her reading glasses. 'Because from what I understand when she married Lord Fortescue she didn't have any family traditions of her own and so she made sure all of his are strictly adhered to, to pass on to future generations.'

Tradition or not, I thought, the potential for plans to go awry was infinite and added to that I had just felt the icy flutter of snowflakes on my face. I cast my eyes up to the putty-coloured sky; sure enough it looked as if we were in for a heavy snow shower. I just hoped everyone made it home safely.

'Hello, Santa!' I grinned as Jim opened the cabin door to me.

'Just in time, love,' said Jim, nodding to the path I'd just travelled along. 'Our first visitors are about to descend on us.'

'As is the snow. This could be a fun afternoon!'

I made my best happy-elf face as two mums and their toddlers approached, the children shrieking with excitement at the snow and the impending encounter with Santa.

I darted over to the desk and sat down at my list of good children while Jim arranged himself next door in his chair. He and I had magical memories to create for thirty children and their parents in the next three hours before I could even begin to think about Benedict Fortescue.

At four o'clock Jenny sent a tray of tea and biscuits over to us and we closed the door to the cabin for a well-deserved twenty-minute break.

'How have you done this every day, Jim?' I said, sinking on to the stool gratefully. 'I've only been going for two hours and I'm exhausted. And I'm convinced that I'm going to say the wrong thing and shatter some poor child's illusions.'

'You worry too much.' He chuckled, selecting a gingerbread man and dunking it in his tea. 'All you have to do is check their name is on the "good list" and chat to them until Santa is free.'

'Answering children's questions about Santa and the North Pole is a minefield! Every family has their own Christmas traditions and I have to tread carefully so as not to put my foot in it or contradict what their parents have already told them. The children this afternoon have quizzed me on where I live, what I do when it's not Christmas, what

I eat for dinner and how Santa knows what time all the children in the world go to bed . . .'

'And you enjoyed every second of it,' Jim said perceptively. 'I can see it in your eyes.'

It was true. Seeing the wonder and joy on children's faces had been a pleasure to witness. Their excitement and absolute belief that Santa would bring them their hearts' desires on Christmas morning had rubbed off on me.

'This time of year is so exciting for kids, isn't it?' I sighed happily. 'We don't have any little ones in my family – no cousins or nephews and nieces – and I must admit, this afternoon has made me feel broody.'

Jim's eyes twinkled as he flicked crumbs from the front of his red suit. 'Good grief, I'm not sure my role as Santa stretches to that.'

I laughed and waved a hand at his knee. 'I'm serious, Jim, seeing Christmas through the children's eyes has really moved me. I can't explain it other than to say that there's an ache in my heart that I didn't have this morning.'

'No. That'll be the biscuits.' He winked. 'Heartburn. Ginger always does that to me.'

'Will you stop making fun of me!' I laughed and began to turn around as I heard the outer door to the cabin open. 'I'm pouring my heart out here. I've got love to give to— Ben!'

And there he was in the doorway, shivering in a thin jacket, his dark curls flecked with snow.

'Then it looks like I've arrived just in time,' he said and laughed.

I didn't even stop to think about the right thing to do, or the fact that I was dressed as an elf sitting in Santa's grotto. I just took one look at his handsome sun-kissed face, his eyes crinkling with amusement, the line of stubble

423

darkening his jaw and I leapt up and threw my arms round his neck.

Ben dropped his bag to the floor, scooped me up and swung me round in a circle.

'You're back,' I gasped. 'You're here and so tanned . . . and cold and I'm so glad, I've—'

Jim coughed and I felt my face heat up. 'Nice to see you, Benedict.'

'You too,' said Ben, lowering me to the ground. He gave Jim a manly hug. 'Glad to see you looking so well after that bonfire business.'

Jim waved a hand nonchalantly, as though collapsing from smoke inhalation at his age was an everyday occurrence. Ben picked his bag up and took my hand.

'Let's go through to the workshop and see what's in my bag.'

'Don't mind me,' Jim called, 'I've got another three custard creams to get through.'

We walked into the other room and Ben shut the door behind him.

'So,' I said, trying and failing to keep my cheeks from executing their widest smile again, 'when did you get back?'

I perched on the edge of my elf's desk and smoothed the green felt of my tunic against my thighs.

'Ten minutes ago,' he smirked. 'Sheila told me where to find you and I came straight here.'

The closeness of him was making my heart race; it was so good to see him after all this time.

'You're grinning.' I laughed.

'You're dressed as an elf. So it's quite hard to keep a straight face. That and the fact that it's fantastic to see you.'

We stared at each other goofily until I felt a bubble of laughter rise up from my stomach to my throat.

'I've missed you,' we said in unison and then laughed.

'How was Cambodia? Is everyone OK after the flood?' I asked belatedly.

'Yes, the kids were fantastic, as usual, and the people are so resilient. I'll go back out next year. But for now I'm glad to be home.' He reached a hand to my face and stroked my cheek. 'Coming back to Wickham Hall is always a pleasure. But this time . . .' He paused and I held my breath. 'Well, this time it feels different, like this is really where I want to be.'

I exhaled happily. That was exactly how I wanted him to feel about the estate, maybe this time he'd stay. Especially when he heard about the plans I'd been working on. But work wasn't on my mind right now . . .

'Should we hug again, do you think?' I suggested, missing the feeling of his arms around me already.

'In a moment,' he replied, looking serious. 'We need to talk.'

'OK.' I waited, my pulse whooshing in my ears.

'In November I wrote to Antonio Biancardi without your permission and—'

'Ben,' I said, pressing a finger to his lips, 'it's fine, you've apologized and anyway it's me who should say sorry; I over-reacted.'

He removed my finger and caught both of my hands in his. 'Holly, I need to explain my motives.'

'OK,' I whispered, gazing into his earnest brown eyes.

He took a deep breath. 'After you came with me to my exhibition, it felt as though you were distancing yourself from me and I couldn't understand why. We'd had such a good time, or at least I had, and I was confused, especially when you turned down all my attempts at enticing you on a second date.'

I opened my mouth to tell him how I'd felt, that seeing him in his art world had made me realize how hard it would be to give it all up for Wickham Hall, but he silenced me with his eyes.

'I racked my brains to come up with a plan to show you what you mean to me. And in my own misguided, insensitive way I thought that the answer was to put you in touch with your father. I can tell how much family means to you by the way you've tried to persuade me to stay at Wickham Hall, so I thought that tracking down your father would prove to you how much I care.'

A lump had appeared in my throat. I swallowed and managed a smile.

'Thank you, Ben, it was a lovely thought, I mean that,' I said shakily, 'despite storming off and calling you rude names.'

Ben laughed softly. 'I don't know what shocked me most: that I misjudged the situation so badly or that Miss Clipboard said the word "arse".'

We both laughed and I covered my face with my hands. 'Am I blushing?'

'You've got rosy elf cheeks, remember?' He grinned. 'Rather fetching, actually.'

He lowered his head to mine and my breath caught in my throat as he placed a soft kiss on my cheek, but just as I reached to thread my arms around his neck and kiss him back he straightened up again.

I bit back my disappointment as he searched around for the bag he'd brought into Santa's workshop.

'The story of Antonio Biancardi continues,' he said hesitantly. 'If you're happy to hear it.'

I nodded.

He exhaled out of one side of his mouth nervously,

lifting his curls in the process. My mouth lifted in a smile; I'd missed those curls so much.

'I sent the letter to him to the address we had from 1984: his father's business address in Bergamo. I had no idea if he'd even get the letter, but . . . he did. And he wrote back.'

I felt as if my heart was going to thump its way out of my ribcage. So I'd been right: the letter that I'd nearly managed to open in Lord Fortescue's office was from my father.

'It didn't arrive until after I'd left for Cambodia, but Dad realized it might be important and . . .'

My eyes widened at that; perhaps Lord Fortescue had seen more than I thought that morning.

'He forwarded the letter to me. Antonio was asking for information about your mum and you. At the time I didn't know if I was doing the right thing or not, especially after your reaction, but his letter seemed very genuine so I phoned him from Cambodia and we had a long chat,' Ben continued.

My hands were trembling. 'You've actually spoken to him?'

He nodded. 'Then he wrote back again. This time the letter was addressed to you. I asked Sheila to hold onto it until I came back. '

Ben took a letter and a package wrapped in Christmas paper out of his bag and held them out.

The hairs at the nape of my neck prickled. 'I can't believe you actually found my father,' I whispered gruffly.

I took the envelope out of his hands and stared, absorbing every detail. It was exactly like the one I remembered seeing that morning in November: the red and blue airmail stripes, the Italia postage stamp. But this one was from Antonio Biancardi to me, his daughter. I blew out a shaky breath and carefully tore the edge of the airmail envelope to reveal two sheets of paper inside it.

I swallowed as the inside of my mouth dried and my hands shook as I opened the letter. What would he say to the daughter he'd never even known about?

Chapter 38

Dear Holly,
What a beautiful name! I hope that you will forgive me writing
to you directly. When Mr Fortescue contacted me to see if I was
the Signor Biancardi who had been at the festival at Wickham
Hall in the 1980s I almost jumped straight on a plane to
come and find you. Luckily my wife Etta is more sensible and
advised me to proceed slowly.

The news that I have a daughter has brought such joy into
my life and I hope that one day we will meet. I am married, as
I have said, and I have three sons, two of whom work in my
leather business. The other is a chef. But Etta and I have no
daughters and she is just as excited as I am to learn of your
existence.

I have never forgotten your mother, Lucy, and for a long time
after that summer I thought about her often, wondering why she
hadn't come to say goodbye as we'd arranged. Wondering if I
had done something wrong.

But shortly after the end of the festival my father became
seriously ill and sadly died. It was my duty as his only child to
take over the running of the business and I must confess that
with so many responsibilities thrust upon my young shoulders, I
consigned that summer and your mother to the past and began a

new life with Etta, building the leather business and raising a family.

However, the time Lucy and I spent together was a very happy one and I even incorporated a pearl into some of my leather designs to remind me of the bracelet we found in the gardens. Does she still have it, I wonder?

I wish you and your family a very happy Christmas and I look forward to the possibility of meeting you next year if you wish.

Warm wishes

Antonio Biancardi

PS I have sent you one of my bags as a Christmas gift. It's our most popular style. I hope you like it.

I lowered the letter and stared at Ben through eyes blurred with tears, momentarily lost for words.

Ben pulled me towards him in a bear hug and I tucked my head under his chin.

'Happy tears?' he murmured into my hair.

I nodded.

'He sounds genuinely pleased to have a daughter; he even wants to meet me.' I swallowed. 'He sounds lovely.'

My father, I realized, my father sounded like a lovely man. The letter answered so many questions, and asked as many new ones too, but that was OK. We would have plenty of time to get to know each other in the future.

My eyes sparkled with tears as I lifted my gaze to Ben. 'Thank you for doing this for me. I will remember this moment, reading this letter, for the rest of my life.'

'Phew, I've done the right thing, finally?' he said.

'Yes.' I laughed, brushing away my tears. 'This is the best Christmas present I could have wished for.'

'Ah, now *here's* the present he sent you.' He grinned and

handed me an exquisitely wrapped parcel the size of a small shoe box.

I slid off a silver ribbon and tore the ornate wrapping paper open to reveal a box containing the most beautiful clutch bag I'd ever seen. It was the shape of an envelope made of bronze leather so soft that it felt like velvet in my fingers. And the flap of the bag was fastened with an over-sized pearl button.

'Pearl,' I murmured, stroking it with my fingertip. 'My middle name, the bracelet that Mum and Antonio found, your mum's pearls.'

'I guess that means we're indelibly linked?' He grinned.

'I guess.' I smiled at him, my heart beating so wildly against my ribs that I wouldn't have been surprised if he could feel it too. It was all I could do not to bury my head in the soft part between his collarbone and his neck and inhale the irresistible scent of him.

'So if I'm forgiven, I have a favour to ask . . .'

My eyes locked onto his and I nodded. 'Fire away.'

'Would you be my date for my parents' dinner party to-night?'

A dinner party in the Great Hall . . . What would Lady Fortescue say about me turning up?

'Isn't that just for your parents' friends?' I said, chewing my lip.

'And mine,' he added. 'And it'll be much more fun if you're there. Please?'

I pictured the room shimmering with Andy's white and silver Christmas decorations, the soft glow of hundreds of candles and the crystal glasses sparkling in the light. It would be magical and I would be there on Ben's arm . . .

My whole body felt as though it was glowing with happi-ness as I nodded my head slowly; today was just getting better and better. I'd found my father, Ben was home and now this.

'I'd be honoured to be your date,' I breathed.

The last few inches of space between us melted away and I felt his lips brush against mine.

And then my arms were around his neck pulling him closer until I could feel the beat of his heart through his thin jacket. I thought my own heart might burst as the kiss that I'd been dreaming about since the summer was really, nearly happening and—

'Mummy, what's the elf doing with that man?'

Ben and I sprang apart and turned round to see a family of four staring at us agog. I blushed furiously, although thankfully my elf make-up disguised it from our new audience, while Ben rubbed a hand through his hair and laughed.

'Sorry about that, folks.' Ben smiled apologetically at the parents.

It seemed our tea break was over and the next Santa session had begun.

'Who's ready to come and tell Santa what they want for Christmas?' Jim boomed, doing his best to block my and Ben's clinch from prying eyes. The two children began bouncing on the spot, shouting, 'Me, me!'

'My elf is just getting her Christmas wish a bit early, that's all.'

He ushered the children and their parents into his room and turned to me with a twinkly smile. 'Santa officially gives his favourite elf the rest of the afternoon off.'

'Thank you, Santa,' I giggled.

I was going to need it; I'd have to fit in a trip home to change my outfit – my ordinary work clothes would not cut the mustard for Lady Fortescue's dinner party.

'Have you no elf-respect, you naughty girl?' murmured Ben close to my ear as soon as the door was shut.

'Maybe not, but that kiss did wonders for my elf-esteem,' I retorted with a giggle. I stepped back up to Ben's chest but he checked his watch and groaned.

'Much as I'd love to stay, I'd better dash. Got stuff to do before the big Christmas at Home thing. I'll see you there, will I?' He stroked my cheek with his fingertip and my insides fluttered instantly.

'Sure,' I said, pressing a swift kiss to his cheek. 'And thank you. For everything.'

I waved him off and watched him disappear into the deepening snow. I stood there for a moment enjoying the muffled silence and the velvety beauty of the snowy evening landscape and then shook myself into action.

I left the list of children still due to visit for Santa and then, taking Jim at his word, donned my green cloak, picked up my new bag and letter from my father and opened the door of the cosy cabin. As I began to close it behind me, the small posy of mistletoe that Andy had given me caught my eye on the ceiling directly above where Ben and I had been standing and I pressed my lips together in a secret smile.

A kiss under the mistletoe with Ben Fortescue, a Christmas gift from my dad . . . This Christmas was shaping up to be the best of my life.

I set off for the hall, tiptoeing along the snowy paths and trying to tread in Ben's footprints to protect my elf shoes. I got as far as the courtyard and I bumped into Jenny, dressed in her motorbike leathers with her helmet under her arm.

'Jenny,' I squealed, 'isn't this snow beautiful! It makes you want to build a snowman, doesn't it, or have a snowball fight?'

433

I scooped up a handful of snow and threw it up in the air and Jenny yelled as she dodged the falling flakes.

'I think that elf costume has gone to your head.' She laughed. 'Or is there some Christmas magic in the air?'

'Magic, definitely,' I said, grabbing her hands and twirling her round in the snow. 'My life feels like it's falling into place, Jenny. I'm so happy I feel like dancing.'

'Well, chick, you've changed your tune since Monday, when everything seemed impossible,' she gasped, out of breath. 'Does this have anything to do with Benedict, by any chance?'

My eyes sparkled as I nodded.

'He's contacted my father for me, how sweet is that?' I changed my twirling to on-the-spot bouncing. 'And he's asked me to be his date for the dinner party tonight!'

Jenny widened her eyes and whistled. 'Wow! Now, please stop making me bounce, I'm supposed to look cool dressed like this; you're doing my street cred no good at all.'

'You're not going anywhere on your Harley in this weather, are you?' I frowned, coming to a standstill.

'Sure.' She shrugged. 'It's built like a tank. Besides, the roads are clear, it's the pavements that are lethal.'

I grinned at her. 'In that case, can you give me a lift?'

If anyone in the village of Wickham spotted an elf clinging on to a leather-clad chef riding pillion on a Harley-Davidson through the snowy night, they might have thought they'd overdone the mulled wine. But after the succession of surprises I'd had this afternoon, it felt curiously appropriate and the short journey in the freezing-cold air heightened the sense of adventure for me even more.

'Sweet cottage,' said Jenny, as we peeled our helmets off at the doorstep.

My heart stopped for a moment and I blinked at her; something amazing had just dawned on me. I was bringing someone home, a work colleague, and for the first time in . . . at least a decade . . . I didn't have to feel embarrassed about it, or try to explain the piles of clutter in the hallway or make excuses about why it looked like we'd just moved in. Because Mum and I were free of her hoarding, she'd put that part of her life behind her and we were both moving on.

I turned the key in the lock and opened the front door. 'Thanks.' I beamed. 'Welcome to Weaver's Cottage.'

Mum was still out at work and I left Jenny in our tiny living room with a cup of tea and instructions on how to light the fire while I dashed upstairs to beautify myself.

I shivered as I stripped out of my elf tunic and tights and dived into my dressing gown while I mulled over what to wear. Normally at this point I'd phone Esme for her professional input, but she would be busy getting herself ready for this evening and I didn't want to bother her.

A million different thoughts span around in my head, making it difficult to focus: what would Mum make of my letter from Antonio? I'd never imagined that we would get such a lovely response from – let's face it – a complete stranger. My heart melted at the image of him and his wife – what was her name? – Etta, talking about his English daughter and her kindness at being so accepting of my existence.

The clock by the side of my bed beeped to signal the hour and I let out a panicky squeak. One hour until the guests began arriving for the Christmas at Home event and I was still at home, dithering in my underwear.

Right. Hair. Make-up. Dress. Shoes.

I'd start with hair.

I sat down at my dressing table and dragged a brush through my windblown, motorcycle-helmet-flattened hair . . .

'Jenny, are you any good at hair?' I yelled down the stairs.

Ten minutes later Jenny stood up straight and swivelled me towards the mirror.

'Not bad for my first ever up-do.' She smirked.

I turned my head this way and that. 'Wow! Jenny Plum, you're wasted in the kitchen. I'm impressed. I love it!'

She had braided the front of my hair so that it lifted away from my face and loosely rolled up the back. It was casual but at the same time sophisticated – well, for me anyway – and emphasized my neck.

'Who knew strudel-plaiting skills would be so useful,' she said, plonking herself down on my bed. I picked up my make-up bag and started applying foundation.

'Hey, cool painting,' said Jenny, pointing to Ben's canvas on my bedroom wall.

A package had arrived at the end of November containing *Secret Sunrise* and a note from Miles Leith, the gallery owner, advising me to have it insured for an eye-wateringly large sum. I'd gingerly hung it on the wall above my bed so that it would be the first thing I saw when I opened my eyes. Now I started every morning with a smile.

'Present from Ben,' I said, choosing a gold eyeshadow from my meagre selection.

'Well, if tonight goes well, maybe this time next year it'll be hanging in Wickham Hall,' she said slyly.

'This is our second date, Jenny.' I laughed. 'Besides, I've got other plans for it.'

I waggled my eyebrows mysteriously but wouldn't divulge any more; I had a proposal to put to the Fortescues but I wanted to run it past Ben first . . .

'How are we doing for time?' I asked, regretting my decision to try flicky-out eyeliner for the first time; my hands had gone slightly shaky.

Jenny stood and peered out of the bedroom window. 'We should probably leave sooner rather than later. It's still snowing and Sheila will be stressed out if you aren't there at least twenty minutes before the guests arrive.'

I swept a brush over my cheeks and dropped it back into my make-up bag. 'My face is on,' I pronounced with a grin.

'And now for the million-dollar question.' Jenny clapped her hands in anticipation. 'What are you going to wear?'

'Actually, I've got a new dress.' I jumped to my feet and opened the wardrobe. 'I didn't think I'd get a chance to wear it this Christmas, but it'll be perfect for tonight.'

I took out the shimmery pale gold dress that I'd treated myself to in Joop and swished it round in the air.

Jenny widened her eyes. 'You'll be the belle of the ball in that.'

I flung off my dressing gown, slipped the dress over my head and smoothed the fabric over my hips. My stomach flipped; it was even more beautiful than I'd recalled and I felt like a princess.

'Should I wear a necklace? I feel a bit exposed.' I pressed the palm of my hand to the bare skin showing above the scoop neck.

She shook her head. 'Keep it simple. And that little glimpse of collarbone is very sexy.'

'Right. OK. Shoes and bag and I'm done,' I said, conscious of the ticking clock.

I sorted out a pair of nude heels but none of my handbags were elegant enough.

'My new clutch bag!' I cried. 'God, I'm rushing so much I nearly forgot about it.'

I opened the buttery-soft bag, added my phone and lip-stick and flashed Jenny a smile.

'Ta-dah!' I trilled, giving her a twirl. 'What do you think?'

'Oh my God, Cinderella *shall* go to the ball!' said Jenny, fanning her face. 'Everyone will be besotted, especially one particular man.'

I knew of at least one person who wouldn't be besotted – Lady Fortescue. I took a deep breath and stepped closer to the mirror.

Ben could have asked any number of girls to go to to-night's dinner party. But he hadn't, he'd chosen me. And Lady Fortescue might disapprove of me for not having gone to the right schools and not having a father who owned half of Warwickshire, but as long as Ben didn't care about any of those things, then neither would I.

I gazed at my reflection: the dress shimmered under my bedroom light, my new clutch complemented the outfit perfectly and my eyes sparkled with determination. Perhaps Jenny was right, perhaps I could be the belle of the ball. It was time for Holly Swift to come out of the shadows . . .

Chapter 39

The snow was still falling but the flakes were smaller now and although the pavements were treacherous, the roads were passable with care. Jenny steered her motorbike past the gatehouse and up the long drive towards Wickham Hall with me tucked in behind her, holding on for dear life, my dress concealed beneath a long woollen coat.

My stomach fluttered as the hall came into focus. There were lights at every window along the length of the ground floor. The crystal chandeliers over the main staircase sparkled, candles glowed through the windows of the Great Hall and the fairy lights on the Red Sitting Room Christmas tree twinkled magically.

Jenny stopped the bike at the front steps between the two large bay trees glistening with yet more Christmas lights. I climbed down, handed her back her spare helmet, taking care not to ruin my hair do, and she revved away, sending a shower of gravel and snow into the air as she turned the bike towards the staff car park. I pushed open the large oak doors and went inside.

Sheila was in the hallway, struggling to carry a cardboard box filled with Christmas gift bags, and I hurried forward to help her.

'There you are!' she said, sighing with relief as I took some of the weight. 'I thought we were going to have to send out a search party; Jim said you left Santa's workshop hours ago.'

'Jenny gave me a lift home to change. What an experience!' I laughed, brushing the melting snowflakes from my coat.

'Red Sitting Room with these,' Sheila instructed and we began to walk, lugging the box between us.

'Do you think the snow will put many guests off?' I asked as we manoeuvred our way into the Red Sitting Room.

Sheila shook her head. 'We've had a handful of cancellations but not many. Wild horses wouldn't keep most people away from Lady Fortescue's Christmas at Home.' She chuckled. 'And the family have all made it home safely for Christmas, which is the main thing.'

Especially Ben, I thought, that was *my* main thing. 'Oh good. Is Zara here?'

'Yes, although the two of them had a frightful taxi journey from the airport. Zara has gone for a bath and Lady Fortescue is in her room getting dressed for the party.'

The room had already been cleared for the Christmas at Home gathering: armchairs had been moved in front of the French doors for the evening to leave the centre of the room clear, a table had been set up for the refreshments and there was a second table near the door.

For the next few minutes, Sheila and I busied ourselves arranging the Christmas gift bags on the empty table.

'My first Christmas at Wickham Hall.' I sighed contentedly, setting out the last gift bag. 'I don't think I've ever been happier.'

Sheila threaded her arm around my shoulder. 'You know, Holly, you've only been here six months, but you've fitted

440

in so well, it's hard to imagine what we did without you. Such a hard-working girl. We're lucky to have you.'

I blushed at the unexpected compliment. 'Thank you, I feel the same way; I couldn't imagine anywhere I'd rather work. In fact, sometimes I forget it's work, it just feels like this is my life now and I wouldn't want it any other way.'

'Good,' Sheila smiled, 'because I think we make a pretty good team.'

She was right, I mused, glancing round me; this party was a perfect example of teamwork. The room was decorated with greenery from Nikki's gardens to Andy's theme. Sheila had been in charge of the guest list and Jenny and her staff would be providing the food. And each guest would receive a Christmas gift bag as they left at the end of the evening. They had been my idea and as well as a small framed print of the Christmas card designed by Ben, they contained a Wickham Hall calendar and a rosemary and bergamot scented candle from the Wickham Hall range.

By six o'clock, when guests began arriving, Christmas carols were playing in the background and every detail of our Christmas at Home event was perfect, from Jenny's filo pastry mince pies and the punchbowl of mulled wine to the gentle glow of the logs ablaze in the sitting-room fireplace. The tall Christmas tree that Marjorie and I had decorated filled one corner of the room and Lady and Lord Fortescue were ready to receive their guests in the centre.

I took my place slightly behind Lord and Lady Fortescue in the receiving line with the list of guests' names on a clipboard, ready to help them out if they couldn't remember who anyone was.

'That's a lovely outfit you're wearing, Lady Fortescue,' I said, during a lull twenty minutes later. Most of the guests had been ticked off my list and only one or two stragglers remained unaccounted for.

She inclined her head graciously and ran her fingertip along the tiny bugle beads that edged the neckline of her black chiffon tunic. She wore it with matching wide-legged trousers and heels and looked every inch the aristocrat. 'Thank you. It's one of my Parisian purchases. I thought it might double up for Zara's New Year's Eve party at the chateau.'

'Another damn party.' Lord Fortescue tutted disconsolately. 'Left to me, I'd be in bed before midnight with a brandy and a good book.'

'But you won't be, Hugo,' Lady Fortescue said tightly. 'You'll be enjoying the party. Apparently, at midnight in France they all drink champagne, raise a toast to Saint Sylvestre and kiss under the mistletoe.'

'French kissing?' He winked at me. 'I might stay up for that.'

I swallowed a chuckle but my laughter quickly vanished as I noticed Her Ladyship eyeing up the length of my dress.

'You look very nice too, Holly. A little bit short but I suppose at your age you can get away with it.'

'Um. Thank you.' *I think.*

'You look enchanting, Holly,' said Lord Fortescue. 'I think we'll manage the receiving line by ourselves now, so why don't you go and work your magic on our guests?'

I didn't need asking twice.

'Holster!' Esme elbowed her way towards me through the crowd, holding her glass high up over her head. She was wearing an electric-blue tight lace dress, which not only looked exotically glamorous in a room of predominately black outfits but thankfully detracted the attention from me and my short dress for a moment.

'And boom.' She grinned, looking me up and down. 'Red-carpet glamour. Right there. That Joop dress looks amazing on you.' She looked around her and repeated loudly, 'From Joop.'

'OK,' I giggled in a whisper, 'advert over. Glad you approve.'

'But I thought you weren't dressing up? "It's business," you said to me.'

I drew her closer. 'Ben's asked me to be his date to the dinner party straight after this.'

'Eek, that's fantastic,' she squeaked quietly, grabbing my arm. 'And is old lemon face cool with that?'

My head flipped round frantically to check no one had heard Esme's choice of endearment for Her Ladyship. Luckily not.

I shook my head. 'I don't think she knows yet.' I pressed my hand automatically to my stomach, which had just turned over at the thought. 'Fingers crossed she doesn't turf me out.'

'Do you want me to hang around later,' Esme balled her hand into a fist, 'in case things get nasty?'

I couldn't help but laugh as I shook my head; she was such a loyal friend. 'I doubt it will come to that. Besides, there'll be a gong at seven thirty to signal the end of the Christmas at Home event. You'll be given your Christmas gift bag and shepherded out along with the rest of the hoi polloi. I imagine that's when Ben will tell her.'

'Don't worry, Holster. How could she not want you there? You look like a flippin' A-lister in that outfit. Here . . .' She opened up her handbag and doused me with her favourite Chanel perfume. 'As Coco would say: "A woman who

443

doesn't wear perfume has no future." And so now your future is secured. Now enough about you . . .'

I grinned as she told me amidst much eye-widening and arm-squeezing that the barely worn designer clothing section that I'd suggested she add in at Joop was doing really well and she had persuaded her mum to turn down the offer they'd received for the business. Bryony was going to focus on her personal shopping customers for two days a week and Esme would run the shop herself from January.

'I can't thank you enough, Hols. It looks like I'm a businesswoman after all.'

'I never doubted it.' I grinned.

'And – get this – I had an amazing chat with Zara earlier and she's going to rope in all her friends to send their unwanted designer labels to me, too. So that means I'll have younger stuff to sell. Zara's lovely, just like a normal person; no airs and graces at all.'

I laughed, remembering that 'Heirs and Graces' was the name Ben made up for the bogus magazine he said he worked for when we met.

My stomach flipped suddenly; the Fortescues were just people at the end of the day. Just like Esme and me. I was probably worrying about Lady Fortescue objecting to Ben and me dating for nothing.

'Anyway, to me,' Esme raised her glass, 'and my own business.'

Her eyes danced with excitement as we chinked glasses to celebrate Joop's new lease of life.

I was thrilled for my friend; working with the Fortescues directly would bring her into contact with so many influential people, which was just what she needed to boost her sales in the spring.

Just then the fashion editor at the *Stratford Gazette*

caught my eye so I introduced her to Esme and made my excuses. Sheila had instructed me to mingle and attempt to talk to every person in the room to ensure their support of Wickham events for next year so I dutifully began the rounds.

I was making polite conversation with the Fortescues' accountant, who was telling me that she was spending New Year skiing in Switzerland with her husband and two teenagers, when a movement in the doorway caught my eye.

My heart gave a little bounce as Ben walked into the room. He looked handsome in a slim-fitting black suit with a dark grey shirt open at the neck, his hair slightly damp and his face clean-shaven. Totally gorgeous. I gave myself a little shake and tried to concentrate on what the accountant was saying ...

Ben's eyes found mine and his face broke into a wide smile.

Beautiful, he mouthed across the room.

You too. I smiled, feeling a flush of heat in my cheeks, and it was all I could do not to shove through the party and fling my arms around him.

'Now that's what I call an eligible bachelor,' the accountant muttered out of the side of her mouth, straining her neck to follow my gaze.

'Mmm,' I murmured casually. An eligible bachelor who thought I was beautiful and who had chosen me to be his date. I must be the luckiest person in this entire room.

I watched out of the corner of my eye as he greeted people effortlessly: smiling, shaking hands, touching people's arms, kissing cheeks as he worked the room, moving ever closer to my place by the Christmas tree. The accountant continued with her lost passport anecdote but I could scarcely drag my eyes away from Ben and it was

445

becoming more and more difficult to focus on her words. Ben Fortescue, my date. Merry Christmas to me . . .

Suddenly he laughed loudly and as I looked up to see who he was talking to our eyes met. The accountant's voice receded and the other guests faded from my vision until it was just him and me. And I couldn't wait any longer.

'Please excuse me,' I said to the accountant, without breaking eye contact with Ben. 'I think I'm wanted.'

Ben crossed the room heading my way and I edged closer towards him, the pair of us grinning wildly. I had missed so many opportunities to get closer to Ben this year, I realized: in the gardens at the Summer Festival, the times when I'd turned down a second date after the exhibition opening, and then under the stars on Bonfire Night. But he was here now and I had no intention of letting him leave again for a very long time.

Ben smiled me a smile that lit up his face like sunshine and stole my breath for a moment.

'Hi,' I whispered, 'I've missed you.'

'And I've missed you,' he said gruffly. He took both of my hands and stepped closer. 'You look like a Christmas angel in that dress, all golden and radiant.'

'Thank you. You don't look too shabby yourself.'

'Although I must admit to being a bit disappointed you aren't still in the elf outfit. That was sexy. In a green way. But you still look sexy,' he added hastily.

He waggled his eyebrows and gave me the twinkly smile that I adored. The one that hinted that if we could only find a quiet corner he'd show me exactly how sexy. I found myself glancing at the doorway and wondered whether we dared creep off. But before I could speak again he leaned forward so I thrust my cheek towards him, expecting a chaste peck. But instead he tilted my chin and pressed his lips to mine. My heart stopped for a fraction of a second, I closed my eyes and breathed him in, savouring his familiar citrus aftershave.

'Ben!' I murmured. 'What if—'

'Darling, there you are!' Lady Fortescue shoved her head between the two of us, forcing us to step apart.

She beamed at Ben and then at me and then gave a sort of general smile to the people around us.

'Mum,' said Ben, planting a kiss on the side of her head, 'looking as lovely as ever.'

'Benedict, can I borrow you for a moment?' She tucked her arm through his as he nodded his consent.

'You too,' she said to me, flashing me an icy look that brought me out in instant goosebumps.

'Of course, Lady Fortescue.'

My heart thudded as I followed them numbly out of the sitting room and into a small room where the guests' coats had been hung. Lady Fortescue shut the door behind us and folded her arms.

'Benedict, I saw that. In fact, I think everyone in the room probably saw it. Kissing a member of staff . . . What do you think you are playing at?' she said.

'I apologize if I've caused you any embarrassment, Lady—' I began.

'Holly, there's no need to apologize,' said Ben firmly. 'It was hardly obscene.'

Lady Fortescue drew herself up tall. 'Nonetheless, there is such a thing as propriety, Benedict. And as the next Lord Fortescue, I advise you to behave accordingly.'

He flashed me a look of resignation and then, impervious – or perhaps immune – to his mother's outburst, took hold of my hand. 'I've invited Holly to the dinner party, Mum. As my date. That's all right, isn't it? Room for a little one?'

He squeezed my fingers and gave me an encouraging smile; I tried to relax against him, but Lady Fortescue's glare made relaxing very difficult.

'I'd have invited someone suitable for you if I'd known,' she fretted, running a finger along the beads at her neck again. 'That nice girl who came up for the fireworks, for instance – she was very disappointed not to have met you.'

Suitable. Meaning that I wasn't. I felt my hackles rise and had to bite my tongue at that. Not ten minutes ago, I'd been agreeing with Esme that the Fortescues were just people like us. Clearly Her Ladyship didn't feel the same.

Ben pressed a hand briefly to his face. 'Mum, how many times? I don't need or want your help in choosing me a girlfriend.'

'Oh, I think you do,' she said forcefully and then cast me a steely look. 'And you, Holly. I've warned you about your behaviour before, but it seems my warnings have gone unheeded. It's most unprofessional, and I must say it raises doubts about your commitment to Wickham Hall. This is the final straw.'

'I agree,' I declared, unable to keep silent for another second.

'Holly—' Ben interjected.

'I agree; it *is* the final straw.' I stared defiantly at her. I accepted that I wasn't upper class like the girls that she so obviously wanted her son to meet. I understood that, even if I didn't like it. But criticizing my work was quite another matter. 'I think you're being unfair. I work hard and I am very committed. My job at Wickham Hall means the world to me.'

'Well said,' Ben added. 'And, Mum, I kissed her because not only is she brilliant at her job, but she's a very special friend to me. She's coming to the dinner party because I invited her and as a member of this family, I get a say.'

My heart swelled with joy and I smiled up at him, my eyes stinging with tears. 'Thank you,' I whispered, squeezing his hand.

'Very well.' The colour had drained from Lady Fortescue's face as she reached for the door handle. She jutted her chin out and, ignoring Ben, addressed her final comment to me. '*Friend* or not, I really think Lord Fortescue and I are going to have to reconsider your position here. And until Benedict decides whether he will or won't take over at Wickham Hall, he doesn't have *a say* about that.'

She swept out of the room, leaving my heart racing and Benedict momentarily speechless.

I turned to him and took hold of his other hand. 'I'm so sorry, Ben. I shouldn't have said what I did. I've made a mess of everything.'

'Not at all, I'm proud of you for standing up to her.' He looked at me, totally bewildered. 'I don't understand what she's got against you. But one thing is for certain: there's no way I'm going to spend the next five years here doing a handover before they retire. I will come back and run the estate, but on my terms and to my timescale. Right now, the sooner I can get back to London and move into my new studio the better. Wickham Hall can wait for the time being.'

My stomach lurched; if Ben left now, Lady Fortescue would never forgive me and besides, was that really what he wanted, I asked myself, or was he just being stubborn? Today when he first arrived, he'd admitted how good it was to be home. I was sure that deep down, Wickham Hall was where his heart truly lay.

'You're just angry,' I soothed, reaching my arms round his neck. 'Don't make any hasty decisions.'

'Sshh.' He traced a fingertip along my top lip. 'I'm not letting her have the last word. Don't worry. It doesn't change anything between us. And I'll make sure you get your job back.'

He pressed a kiss to my lips, flung the door open and strode after Lady Fortescue.

I sank down onto a chair and exhaled. How could Ben say it didn't change anything? I'd inadvertently already changed *everything*.

'Holster!' A hoarse whisper from the doorway made me lift my head to see Esme sneaking in.

'I eavesdropped. Couldn't help myself, soz.' She grinned cheekily, but her eyes were full of concern.

'Oh, Es,' I groaned. 'I've ruined the party, lost my job and inadvertently sent Ben back to London.'

She perched on the arm of my chair and slung an arm round my shoulders. 'Hmm, that is bad. What we need is a rescue plan.'

'I don't know how to sort things out, Es. What do I do?' I stared at her, blinking away my tears. 'What would Coco advise?'

Esme rolled her eyes. 'Isn't it about time you got your own guru? OK, how about this? Er . . . "The most courageous act is still to think for yourself. Aloud."'

I stared at her, nodding thoughtfully, while I absorbed Coco Chanel's advice. There was something I could say, something I'd only just realized. It might work. It might also backfire spectacularly, but at least I'd know I'd done everything I could to save the day . . .

'Esme, we might need to make a quick getaway after this; there's something I need to say to the Fortescues.'

She grinned at me and punched my arm. 'You go, girl.'

I took a deep breath, tucked my clutch bag under my arm and marched back to the Red Sitting Room.

Chapter 40

I stood in the doorway for a second, planning my next move. Lady Fortescue had stationed herself in the centre of the room and was attempting to pour herself a glass of mulled wine. She looked upset and her hand was shaking so Ben took over and handed her a glass.

Their voices were slightly raised and were attracting attention and Sheila was standing next to the small brass gong and wringing her hands anxiously. Lord Fortescue was further away, talking to the man from the tourism office and, being hard of hearing, was probably unaware of the muted row going on between his wife and son.

Ben folded his arms and stared at the carpet. '. . . humiliated Holly and me. It's never going to work, Mum, not when you still treat me like a child.'

Lady Fortescue sipped at her mulled wine and looked over her shoulder, refusing to look at him. 'Don't you care that you've broken your mother's heart?'

'You've got to take some responsibility for that, Mum. And anyway, it's for the best.'

'How can you say that? I feel less than festive now, thanks to you . . .'

I straightened my spine and threaded my way through

the crowd towards them and tapped him on the shoulder.

'Ben, there's something I want to say.'

He whirled round to face me and his eyes softened. Lady Fortescue, on the other hand, pursed her lips sourly.

At that very moment Sheila sounded the gong, signalling the end of the Christmas at Home party and a silence descended on the room. I glanced around me and could hardly believe what I saw; maybe the body language between the three of us indicated that something was amiss because fifty pairs of eyes were staring at us.

Now what? Everyone was listening. Do I pretend I was going to say something trivial, like 'I'll be off then', and lose the moment, or do I go for it?

My body was humming with the attention of the entire room upon me.

Out of the corner of my eye I saw Esme sneak into the room and stick her two thumbs up above the heads of the guests.

The most courageous act is still to think for yourself. Aloud . . .

I took a fortifying breath and looked him in the eye. 'Ben, I think I have loved you since I caught you in the churchyard with your trousers down.'

I heard a snort of laughter and noticed Zara join Esme in the doorway, eyes wide with hands over their mouths. There were a few other titters too and David the young reporter from the local radio station took his iPhone out of his pocket and held it up.

Ben was staring at me, his eyes soft and full of an emotion that I didn't dare name, but I liked it and it filled me with encouragement to press on. I took his hand.

'I love you for your heart, for your generosity and for the way you light up the room as soon as you enter. I love that you give yourself completely to things you care about.

I love you for your passion for all the things that matter to you like your art and Wickham Hall and, of course, your family.'

Ben reached out and pushed a stray hair off my face. 'And you, Holly, you matter to me too.'

My heart swelled with love as he kissed my forehead and a chorus of gentle 'ahhs' echoed around the room, reminding me that I had an audience.

I can do this, I can say this in front of all these people. I need to do it . . .

'Ben, from you I've learned not to plan everything in my life and to live in the moment.' I swallowed. 'Because that's when the magic happens.'

'Lovely sentiment,' said Lady Fortescue crisply, 'but the party's over now so . . .'

Lord Fortescue appeared at his wife's side and regarded the three of us suspiciously. 'What's going on?'

'Nothing important, Hugo. Holly is just leaving, as are our other guests.' She patted his arm appeasingly.

People began to shuffle towards the door then but I cleared my throat and they all paused.

'Actually, I still have something to say,' I said, squeezing Ben's hand for courage. 'Ben, I'm afraid I'm going to get a bit bossy now: I think you're making a big mistake leaving Wickham Hall.'

'Ben?' Lord Fortescue frowned.

'Hold on, Dad,' Ben's lips twitched. 'Go on, Holly, I love it when you're bossy.'

I smiled back and turned to Lady Fortescue; her eyes were stretched wide in surprise.

'Lady Fortescue, on the first day I met you, you declared that you thought that you and I would get along splendidly. And for the most part we have. Do you know why that is?'

A look of discomfort crossed her face. 'Um?'

'We get along because we want the same things. We both love Wickham Hall; we love every red brick, chimney pot, creaking floorboard, moss-covered balustrade, every Himalayan poppy and every tiny pane of leaded glass. And most of all, we care about what happens to the hall in the future. And,' I paused to slip my arm around Ben's waist, 'we both love this man.'

I gave her a challenging look but she simply stared down at her hands and said nothing.

'And Holly's leaving too?' Lord Fortescue grunted. 'I didn't know that.'

'Mum threatened to sack her,' Ben informed him with a wry smile. 'I'm assuming you don't agree with her unilateral decision?'

'Ben, please. This isn't about me. The thing is that you could find a new events organizer. I am easily replaceable; Lady Fortescue could advertise my job and you'll be inundated with applicants. But Benedict isn't.'

I tilted my face to meet his eyes. 'You are simply not replaceable. You are special. You are the right – the only – person who can continue the amazing work that your parents have done for thirty years. Because you are born for this. You are a leader, Benedict, a good one, and you are more than capable of filling your father's shoes. Wickham Hall just wouldn't be the same without you.'

I finished my speech to a huge burst of applause. Several people actually cheered and Esme and Zara were wiping tears from their eyes.

Sheila took this opportunity to bang her gong again and after several increasingly louder attempts, the noise quietened down a bit.

Ben and I gazed at each other, scarcely aware of Lord

Fortescue delivering a Christmas message to the departing guests. Esme and Zara took over my job of helping Sheila hand out the Christmas gift bags and after a rally of cheerful goodbyes and Merry Christmases to each other the room finally began to empty. I noticed Zara link arms with Esme and drag her off somewhere and then it was just the Fortescues and me.

Lord Fortescue added another log to the fire and began rearranging the armchairs in front of the fire. Lady Fortescue perched on the edge of a chair and Ben and I helped him move the rest.

'So where do we go from here?' Lord Fortescue took a seat next to his wife and looked at his son.

Ben ushered me onto a small sofa and sat beside me.

'Dad, I've tried to fit in over the last few months, but it feels like I've had my wings clipped. Working in the family firm for five years before you retire would suffocate me. I'm used to my independence, the freedom to work when and where I want. Wickham Hall is magnificent and I know how privileged I am, but art will always be my first choice.'

'Benedict darling, no one denies that you're a good artist.' His mother sighed wearily.

'Correction, Lady Fortescue, forgive me,' I said firmly, 'Ben is a very talented artist. Isn't he, Lord Fortescue?'

Lord Fortescue nodded and his eyes looked a bit misty as he looked at his son. 'I'm very proud of your work, son, very proud.'

'Thanks, Dad,' said Ben in disbelief. 'Thanks.'

'But I'd like to make a correction too, Holly,' Lord Fortescue smiled, 'you are also completely irreplaceable.'

'Perhaps we should talk about this,' his wife muttered. He ignored her. 'Benedict, it would mean the world to your mother and me if you'd stay at Wickham Hall, but equally—'

'Equally I need to follow my own path.' Ben nodded at his father.

My heart twanged with affection for them as a look of love passed between them. If I achieved nothing else tonight, I'd always be proud of that.

'There might be a way for you to do that and stay at Wickham Hall,' I blurted.

A shiver of excitement ran along my spine; the plan I'd been working on for the last few weeks was still in its infancy, but this was exactly the opening I'd been looking for.

All three of them stared at me.

'Ben, please listen,' I said. 'I've got a suggestion to make.'

'I'm sorry, Holly,' Lady Fortescue sighed, 'but we have our dinner guests arriving any minute. This will have to wait.'

'Beatrice,' Lord Fortescue caught hold of her arm, 'remember how we were when we were young, brimming with ideas when we first came to Wickham Hall? Remember all our plans? Let's hear her out.'

I gave Lord Fortescue a grateful smile as his wife nodded gently in agreement. Ben edged closer to me and wound his fingers through mine.

'The way I see it is this: you're torn between your career as an artist and running the business of the Wickham Estate. But I think I've found a way that will work for everyone.'

Ben shook his head and gave me a bemused grin. 'I'm listening.'

'Maybe the five-year handover period before your parents retire would work better if you had your own defined role. That way you'd have independence and responsibility for your own area.'

Ben raised his eyebrows doubtfully. 'What did you have in mind?'

I glanced at the Fortescues nervously. 'I've been looking into the art gallery project that you both started years ago.'

Lady Fortescue raised a curious eyebrow and Lord Fortescue leaned forward to rest his arms on his knees.

'At the time the project was shelved, partly because of funding, but partly because there wasn't a high enough footfall of visitors to the hall. But now, the gift shop and the café – not to mention all the events that we run – have changed that beyond compare.'

Lord Fortescue was nodding contemplatively. Phew. That had to be a good sign.

'Imagine, Ben.' I took his hands and gazed into his eyes, willing him to feel as excited about it as I was. 'Imagine starting a collection of modern art at Wickham Hall! You could showcase some of your friends' work, you could even ship over art from your Cambodian students, hold your own exhibitions. It would be a blank canvas. *Your* venture, *your* Wickham Hall.'

'I remember that project. An art gallery . . .' Ben's brow furrowed.

'It would cost money, of course, to convert the old garages, but the space is fantastic. There'd be room for an exhibition gallery, a meeting room for visiting artists to give lectures, plus a large studio for you to work in, Ben.'

Ben's mouth began to twitch. 'You've thought of everything, haven't you?'

'Not quite.' I smiled back at him. 'I haven't had time to research the costs, but I think we could apply for money from the English Heritage fund for a grant to help with part of it.'

'Hugo, what do you think?' Lady Fortescue looked at her

husband and I had to bite back a smile; it was a brilliant idea and she knew it.

Lord Fortescue addressed his son. 'If you choose to develop the art gallery, Ben, we'll find the capital to do so. Holly's right, the reasons that the project failed last time don't apply any more.'

Ben slid an arm around my shoulders and pulled me close. 'It certainly sounds appealing. Although—'

'I know what you're thinking,' I cut in, 'that there'd still be all the running of the estate to do. But if I got my job back, I can take care of the events by myself. And if I'm not mistaken, Lady Fortescue, I don't think you really want to relinquish your role entirely at Wickham Hall, do you?'

She blinked at me and I realized her eyes were moist.

'I'm so sorry.' I was out of my seat and by her side instantly. I knelt down by her chair and touched her arm. 'Have I got it wrong?'

She pulled a handkerchief from her sleeve and dabbed her tears. 'Not at all.'

I frowned. 'Then, why—'

'You really are a very perceptive girl, Holly,' she said shakily. 'I'm not ready to be put out to pasture quite yet. I know Hugo wants to slow down, live a quieter life, but I thought I'd be able to carry on as a figurehead for ever.'

I stared at her. 'Well, that's fantastic! There's no reason why you can't, is there?'

Lady Fortescue recovered herself and took a deep breath. 'I thought I would be usurped if Ben fell in love with someone strong and capable. And I'd so miss hosting events like this . . . Well, perhaps not this particular one.'

We shared a smile at that; a family dispute at the mulled wine in full view of the guests probably wouldn't be forgotten in a hurry.

'Holly, I owe you an apology.' She squeezed my hand. 'With you at Ben's side, I thought I'd be surplus to requirements. I couldn't bear it.'

She turned to Ben. 'And I'm sorry, darling, I've steered you towards some lovely girls but I chose them because they were unambitious, so that selfishly I could retain a role here.'

'Goodness me, Lady Fortescue,' I said, taken aback, 'I'm flattered but I think you're overestimating my abilities. Not only that, you're greatly underestimating how important you are to the running of Wickham Hall. I've absolutely no desire to encroach there, I promise you. In fact, I was going to suggest you hosted a new event next year: a charity fashion show?'

Her eyes lit up and she nodded. 'Love it. Absolutely love it!'

Ben got to his feet and offered me his hand to help me up. 'I think the art gallery idea is brilliant and I think you're brilliant. I need to find out more about the project, but in principle, yes, I'm up for it, if you are, Mum and Dad?'

'Bravo!' cried His Lordship, banging the arm of his chair.

'Champagne I think, Hugo,' said Lady Fortescue, clapping her hands together.

'Wait!' Ben held up his hands. 'I'll stay on one condition: Holly stays too.'

Lord Fortescue cocked an eyebrow at his wife.

'Of course she can have her job back. Holly, I apologize, I overreacted and I didn't mean what I said. Hugo's right, you are irreplaceable,' said Lady Fortescue going pink.

'Thank you, that's very kind of you to say,' I exclaimed. I pressed a hand to my poor thudding heart, but Ben still wasn't satisfied.

'But not just as a member staff. Holly is far more precious to me than that.'

Precious. I was precious to Ben. My heart clenched and I wished more than anything that this awkward conversation was over and I could show him how much he meant to me too.

'Of course, of course,' said Lady Fortescue, 'I understand. Holly, I have been less than gracious, but will you join us for dinner?'

I squeezed Ben's hand. 'I'd absolutely love to.'

'Wonderful.' She clapped her hands and went into hostess-mode. 'I'll put you next to—'

'You'll put her next to me,' Ben insisted.

'And me,' chimed Lord Fortescue.

Zara appeared in the doorway, still with a clam-like Esme Wilde at her side. 'Come on, everyone, all the guests are here. They've been served drinks in the Great Hall.'

A shiver ran up my spine and I fought the urge to pinch myself. I, Holly Swift, was joining the Fortescues for dinner in the Great Hall.

'Excellent,' boomed Lord Fortescue. 'I think we could all do with a drink.'

'OK?' Ben placed a steadying hand at my waist.

I nodded.

'Thank you,' I replied, feeling dazed and overcome and ridiculously close to tears. 'Thank you for saying I'm precious.'

And then a tiny joyful tear did escape and I reached inside my new clutch bag for a tissue.

Instantly Zara seemed to levitate off the ground with a screech. 'Bianca!'

She fell on my open bag and gasped as she saw the label. 'It is! It's a Bianca!'

Esme's and Lady Fortescue's heads popped up like meer-kats.

'Mum, look! It's the Bianca clutch!'

'Good grief, Holly. How did you get hold of one of those?' Lady Fortescue's jaw gaped.

'Mum's been on the waiting list for ages!' Zara exclaimed.

'Bianca bags cost an absolute fortune!' Esme rushed to my side, wide-eyed and looking a little put out. 'Holster! When did you . . . ? How on earth . . . ?'

I gazed at Ben and we shared a look of bemusement.

'It's one of my dad's.' I shrugged nonchalantly. 'He sent it to me for Christmas.'

'Your dad? Antonio Biancardi. Biancardi – *Bianca*,' Esme stuttered, reaching to stroke the leather. 'Oh. My. God.'

Lady Fortescue's face was a picture of disbelief, admiration and envy. 'You're Antonio Biancardi's daughter?'

I swallowed. 'Yes.'

'For the record,' Ben laughed, squeezing his way into the melee and putting his arm around my waist, 'I don't care who her father is. It doesn't make the slightest bit of difference. Does it, Mother?'

'No, no, of course not,' said Lady Fortescue with a high-pitched laugh. She grabbed my arm. 'But do you think he'd like to contribute to our charity fashion show next year?'

'Probably.' I beamed. 'He seems like a very nice man.'

Lady Fortescue shot me a look of confusion but she was prevented from digging for any more information as Lord Fortescue clapped his hands.

'Right, everyone, to the Great Hall, please, we've ignored our guests long enough.' He peered at Esme. 'And will you be joining us for dinner, young lady?'

'Coolio! I mean, yes please, I'd be honoured.' Esme dipped into a bizarre curtsey until Zara pulled her by the hand.

'You can sit by me.'

Lord Fortescue offered his wife his arm and the four of them left.

And then Ben and I were alone in the room. He switched off the chandeliers and the table lamps until the only light came from the glow of the fire and the glimmer of the Christmas tree.

I walked slowly towards the tree, gazing up at the silvery angel remembering Marjorie's tales of Ben as a boy.

'I love Christmas,' I murmured, as Ben slipped his arms around my waist.

'Me too. It's perfectly acceptable to turn off all the lights and smooch in the dark at Christmas.'

Slowly he turned me round to face him and the reflection of the fairy lights danced in his eyes and my heart started to pound.

'You don't have the urge to launch yourself at the tree then, and cover yourself in pine needles?'

'Not at the tree, no.' He grinned. 'Launching myself at you is a different matter entirely.'

He cupped my face in both of his hands tenderly and all I could hear was the crackle of the fire, the steady sound of his breathing and, far away, voices laughing as guests continued to arrive.

'Well, that was all very exciting,' I breathed, suddenly nervous.

Every kiss we'd tried to share so far, every moment, had been interrupted and I was determined that this time nothing would come between us.

'You, Miss Clipboard,' he said, 'are the most amazing, surprising and capable woman I have ever known. And my mother has well and truly met her match.'

He tilted my chin and his breath felt warm on my face.

'I can't believe you went to all that trouble, working on the plans for the art gallery for me. You're incredible and very clever. Plus you have freckles, even in winter; I didn't know that was possible. I love those freckles; I could look at them all day.'

I looked into his eyes and ran my fingers up the fabric of his jacket, linking them behind his neck. 'And I can't believe you found Antonio Biancardi for me. I've got a father. For the first time. And he seems lovely! And the owner of a coveted accessories brand to boot, which seems to have gone down rather well with your mother. I love that you're so impulsive and spontaneous. Plus you have the most beautiful curls; I could run my fingers through them all day.'

'Then we're quits.' He grinned.

'Will you really stay at Wickham Hall?' I murmured.

He nodded. 'Will you?'

I grinned. 'I'll have to, won't I? Someone has got to organize you.'

'Will you be able to cope?'

'With you?' I snorted. 'I think I'll manage.'

But his eyes were unusually serious. 'I mean it, Holly. Being my girlfriend will mean a lot of intrusion in your life. I know how you avoid the limelight. Even opening the art gallery will attract attention. People will want to know about you, talk to you, photograph you even . . .'

I rolled my eyes at him. 'Benedict Fortescue, do you know what I think?'

He shook his head, a smile playing at his lips, as I closed the last few inches of distance between us. 'Tell me.'

'I think you should stop planning for the future and live for the moment.'

'Really?' He traced his thumb across my lips, sending a jolt of electricity down my spine. 'In that case, is this a good moment to tell you that I love you?'

'It's the perfect moment,' I whispered, weaving my fingers through his hair.

'I love you, Holly Swift.'

And then he kissed me to prove it. And I kissed him back. And there was just him and me, a boy and a girl, and it was as if our bodies were made for each other. Suddenly I didn't care about tomorrow or what was in my diary or when I was going to get round to finding somewhere new to live because I had us, now, this second. If this was what living for the moment meant then I liked it. A lot.

'I've just realized . . .' I laughed as we finally came up for air. 'I got my Christmas wish and it was even better than I dreamed of.'

Ben wrapped his arms round my waist and pulled me tightly towards him. 'You must have been a good girl, then.'

'Very good indeed, shall I show you how good?'

And I kissed him again, the man I loved, in my favourite room at Wickham Hall by the twinkling lights of the Christmas tree and the moment was utterly, utterly perfect.

Epilogue

The pale morning light crept through a sliver of space between the curtains and teased me gently awake from a wonderful sleep. This bed was absolute heaven. I smiled and stretched languorously before opening my eyes. I blinked a few times until I could focus; my painting, *Secret Sunrise*, was propped up against the wall on the other side of the room and its colours and energy made my heart sing. I lay still for a moment, gazing up at the golden drapes, listening to the dawn chorus from the trees just outside the window.

I smiled and sank my head further into the pillows; this was the perfect way to start the day. All that was missing was a certain someone . . .

The door opened and Benedict tiptoed in, carrying two mugs of tea and wearing nothing but his boxer shorts and a cheeky smile.

'Good morning, Sleeping Beauty. You look all dreamy and gorgeous.'

A wave of love washed over me as he padded across the carpet. His hair was all messed up and there were still crease marks on his face from the pillows.

'Is this real?' I sighed. 'Is this really happening to me?'

'It is.' He made a space on the Chinese lacquered cabinet beside me and set down a steaming mug. 'Tea. Just how you like it.'

'Hurrah.' I sat up and took my first hot sip.

I loved that he knew how I liked my tea; I loved a thousand other things, too: like the fact that he folded his jeans when he took them off at night and the way he slept with my hand tightly in his . . .

'So,' he murmured, dropping a kiss on my nose. 'How was it?'

'Did you want marks out of ten?' I giggled, setting my mug back down.

He scooted back to his side of the bed and pulled the duvet up. 'No, but as I appear to have made your third wish come true, I just thought I'd ask if the experience lived up to your expectations.'

My third wish: to wake up at Wickham Hall in a four-poster bed. Tick.

I snuggled up to him, resting my cheek against his chest. 'It *more* than did that; I feel like a princess.'

Ben wrapped his arms round me tightly and kissed the top of my head. 'Well, princess or not, you've got twenty minutes to get yourself downstairs and ready for your next adventure.'

'Arrghhh!' I jumped out of bed and ran into Ben's en-suite bathroom.

'By the way,' he called.

I stuck my head back out. 'Yes?'

'You didn't snore.' He winked.

Twenty minutes later, Ben and I were on our way downstairs with our suitcases. Lord Fortescue had very kindly suggested that I move my things into Ben's room while the

Dower House, a lovely detached cottage on the far side of the estate, was being spruced up for us to move into. It was only for a week and we would be away for some of that.

Ben dropped the bags onto the top step and gave me a sheepish look. 'I'll be two minutes, I promise. I just want to check something with the architect before we go.'

'Two minutes,' I warned, chuckling to myself as he ran off in the direction of the old garages. Ben's plans for the new art gallery had been approved speedily, partly because he was able to use the old sets of drawings. The buildings had been cleared and the scaffolding had gone up and Ben spent every spare minute consulting with builders and architects about his beloved project.

'Holly, dear, I'm glad I've caught you.'

I turned to see Lady Fortescue, wrapped in a long robe and still in her slippers, her arms crossed against the crisp spring air.

'Good morning, Beatrice.' I beamed. 'Such an exciting day!'

She nodded warmly. 'And I couldn't be happier for you.'

At that moment, Lord Fortescue's Range Rover pulled up in front of the hall with Ben in the passenger seat. He jumped out, opened the boot and loaded the cases inside.

'Ready?' He raised an eyebrow and reached for my hand.

'Wait,' said Lady Fortescue hurriedly. 'I wanted to give you this, Holly.'

She uncurled her fingers to reveal her pearl bracelet with the diamond clasp.

My eyes widened. 'For me?' I breathed. 'I don't know what to say.'

I held out my wrist while she put it on me and Ben snaked an arm round my waist. 'That's a lovely gesture, Mum,' he said.

'You remind me so much of myself when I first came to Wickham Hall.' Lady Fortescue sighed. 'Wide-eyed at the beauty of the place, full of ideas and energy. I was about your age when Hugo gave me this and now I think I'm ready to hand it over. To you.'

We looked at each other, both of us with tears in our eyes.

I wrapped my arms around her shoulders and hugged her tight. 'Thank you, Beatrice; I love it, just as much as I love Wickham Hall.'

'Bye, Mum,' called Ben, ushering me into the back seat of the car.

He murmured into my ear as he slid in beside me, 'That's it; you'll never escape us Fortescues now.'

I kissed him swiftly and smiled. 'And I never want to.'

'Morning, Hugo,' I said, leaning forward into the front of the car where Lord Fortescue was drumming his fingers on the wheel.

'All set?' he boomed. 'Got everything?'

I checked my bag for the umpteenth time; our passports and flight tickets to Bergamo lay on top of everything else.

Ben smiled that sunshiny smile that lit up my heart. 'Are you ready to meet your father?'

I nodded and squeezed his hand. 'Let's go.'

The Thank Yous

When I was editing this book, *Ivy Lane* came out in paperback. This was the first book I'd published with Transworld; part one launched in February 2015. I held that book in my hands and it struck me just how far I'd come in less than twelve months. That journey was only made possible by the fabulousness that is Harriet Bourton, my editor, and Hannah Ferguson, my agent. I owe you two ladies a huge debt of gratitude and I love you LOADS!

Thanks also to my siblings, Andy, Jenny and Nikki, who unbeknownst to them, have all been immortalised as characters in this book. This is, of course, a test to check that they really do read their big sister's books . . .

Naming my fictitious hall turned out to be quite tricky; everything I thought up turned out to exist in real life! So I appealed to Twitter and Facebook to help me out. I received over fifty suggestions and although I ended up using one of my own ideas, I did use Charlie Plunkett's name – Hoxley – for the village where Esme has her boutique. Thank you, Charlie!

I took to Twitter again when I needed the name of an unusual bird which could be spotted in the middle of Warwickshire. Thank you to Karen Aldous's husband for coming up with the hoopoe.

Now for a very special thank you. A few months ago the cancer charity CLIC Sargent ran a charity eBay auction, which I took part in, offering bidders the chance to have a character named after them in a book. I was delighted to discover that Jill Stratton, who writes the blog Jill Loves To Read, won the auction to be in my book. She asked me to use her mum's name as a character and so, Sheila Beckwith, I hope you enjoy your role in Wickham Hall as Lord Fortescue's secretary! Thank you both for taking part in the Get In Character campaign.

Big thanks to the lovely people at Doddington Hall in Lincolnshire. I needed a beautiful Elizabethan hall on which to base my own version and found this wonderful place only a few miles away. I visited twice in the name of research and enjoyed every minute of it, especially when I came to see the Christmas decorations. Stunning house and gardens and rather delicious cakes!

A massive thank you to my friends who always buy my books, turn up to events, tell their other friends and generally support me when things get tough. And let's face it, some-times things *do* get tough!

Thank you to Isabel and Phoebe for your patience when I show you fifteen versions of my new covers, and ask you to think up names which I haven't used yet, and force you to listen to a very detailed synopsis of my next book when I've got you trapped in the car on long journeys! Love you both loads.

Thank you to my readers (I still have to pinch myself when I write that!) and all the lovely book bloggers who have been my cheerleaders since the start. Not a day goes by without somebody getting in touch to tell me how much they enjoyed one of my books. I LOVE that! Thank you for reading my stories, it is wonderful to know how much they mean to you.

Finally, to Tony, my bestest friend and wonderful husband, without whom life just wouldn't be the same. Love you to the Andromeda Galaxy and back (see, I do listen).

With love
Cathy xxx

You've come to the end of *Wickham Hall*.

But now you can tuck in to another delicious
modern love story from Cathy Bramley:

the Plumberry School of Comfort Food

Verity Bloom hasn't been interested in cooking
anything more complicated than the perfect fish
finger sandwich, ever since she lost her best friend
and baking companion two years ago.

But an opportunity to help a friend is about to land her
right back in the heart of the kitchen! The Plumberry
School of Comfort Food is due to open in a few weeks'
time and has rather gone off the boil. It needs the kind of
great ideas that only Verity could cook up . . .

But as Verity tries to balance stirring up publicity,
keeping their top chef sweet and soothing her aching
heart, will her move to Plumberry prove to be a
sheer delight . . . or a recipe for disaster?

Read on for a sneak peek at the opening chapters!

Chapter 1

My stomach rumbled as I pulled the pan out from under the grill. I'd been slaving over my laptop at the kitchen table since first thing and now it was four o'clock. All I'd had to keep me going were two chocolate Pop Tarts.

Even by my standards, that was a bit meagre.

There was more to making the ultimate fish finger sandwich than met the eye, I mused, prodding the fish to make sure it was cooked. To be proper comfort food, it had to meet very stringent criteria. The bread had to be soft and white. I'd bought a new loaf from the corner shop this morning specially. The fish fingers must be good ones; life is simply too short for anything less. I keep a box of Birds Eye's best in the freezer at all times, alongside my stash of cottage pie, lasagne and tikka masala ready-meals.

I spaced the four golden strips of breadcrumbed cod evenly across the bottom slice, taking care to leave a gap in the centre for easy slicing. Next the ketchup – Heinz, of course. I gave the bottle a firm shake and added a neat stripe to each of the fish fingers.

Rosie, my part-time housemate, steamed into the kitchen wearing a sports bra and shorts and turned the tap on full blast before fetching a glass.

'Just in time to witness my *pièce de résistance*,' I announced, sliding the plate away from the spray of water.

'Please tell me that's not your Sunday lunch?' She waggled her eyebrows sternly. 'Wait till I tell Nonna.'

Her Italian grandmother believed lunch on the Lord's Day should consist of at least four courses, take the entire morning to prepare and the entire afternoon to clear up.

I sliced through the sandwich and sat down at the table.

'Yep. Protein, carbs, vegetables . . . a perfectly balanced meal,' I said. OK, *vegetables* was stretching it a bit, but the bottle did claim to be full of sun-ripened tomatoes . . . 'And more importantly, it only took me twelve minutes. Sorry, Nonna.'

'You should treat your body as if it belongs to someone you love,' she tutted. She twisted the cap off a tub of sea-weed extract and shook two tablets out into her hand.

I watched her knock them straight back with a gulp of water. 'Who do you love – Nemo?'

Rosie choked mid-swallow and spluttered with laughter. 'Touché, Princess Prick and Ping, touché.'

I pretended to give her a dirty look.

She referred to me as that because of my over-reliance on the microwave, although she didn't spend much time in the kitchen either. Nor anywhere else. Rosie was too busy to spend long doing anything. I don't think I've ever seen her relax. Not completely. Even when she watched TV she had her phone in her hand, her iPad balanced on her knee and her laptop on the coffee table in front of her, each device tracking different social media campaigns for her clients. She was totally dedicated to her job and she'd been promoted twice since I'd known her, which was only two and a half years.

She moved in when I needed a lodger to help pay the

mortgage after splitting up with my fiancé. Not that she didn't have a property of her own; she'd had several over the years. In her spare time she bought and renovated run-down houses, selling them on for a profit which she squirrelled away. Her plan was to buy a big house for herself and be mortgage-free by the age of forty. I had no doubt that she'd do it.

'I'm detoxing,' she explained, rattling the bottle of vitamins under my nose. 'Because I love myself.'

'And I,' I said with my mouth full of sandwich, 'love fish fingers.'

I agreed with her actually; food was about love. To cook for someone was to show them how much you cared. My problem was that I'd lost that loving feeling. Or more accurately, that loving *someone*.

'How's the project going?' She sat down and read the document open on my laptop. 'Need any help?'

Spending all day working might not be everyone's ideal Sunday but it had provided the perfect distraction from the sadness of today's date, which I wasn't ready to tackle yet. Besides, tomorrow's meeting was unusually important.

'I think I'm there,' I said proudly, removing the elastic band from my wavy brown hair. I ruffled my fingers through it, wishing for the umpteenth time it was as dark and glossy as hers. 'I've got an amazing idea for improving customer loyalty: the *One, Two, Three Plan*. Instead of in-centivizing purely new customers, this is about giving existing customers reasons to stay with us for a minimum of three years. I've come up with loads of benefits.'

'Sounds great,' Rosie said, stretching her face, a gesture I recognized as stifling a yawn.

'It is, honestly,' I protested. 'Even Liam thought it was good. Better than his will be, he reckons.'

'You've shown Liam?' Her mouth gaped. 'Have I taught you nothing about office tactics?'

I gave her my o-ye-of-little-faith look. 'Of course I have; I wanted his opinion.'

My boyfriend of six months, Liam, was also my colleague in the marketing department of Solomon Insurance in Nottingham. We shared an office, which had worked out just fine so far: not only did we manage to indulge in illicit snogs occasionally at the far end of the office, but we helped each other out with problems and pooled our best ideas for the good of the company. Admittedly most of the ideas came from me, but he was good at other things like persuasion and flattery. And if you'd ever tried getting extra printer paper from our office manager you'd know just how important those skills are.

Rosie lowered her head to the table and groaned. 'Oh, Verity.'

'Look, I know you want me to fight tooth and nail for this job, but that's just not me,' I said with a laugh, laying my hand over hers.

A few weeks ago, Solomon's had been bought out by an American company which had sent in a man with a hatchet to trim the fat from our friendly little firm. His name was Rod Newman. He didn't talk, he yelled. He didn't listen, he yelled. And he had the attention span of a goldfish. So far three people from accounts, five from sales and two from personnel had been deemed as 'fat' and had disappeared the very same day.

Tomorrow it was marketing's turn to display our leanness. Liam and I both had to present a plan to improve profits and we'd been warned that Ruthless Rod would give one of us the heave-ho based on our performance. The other would be promoted.

478

I'd questioned Liam about his plan, but he'd scratched his head and said he was still working on it. He always did fly by the seat of his pants. I didn't dare tell Rosie I'd offered to help him pull his pitch together. If I got the job, fine; if he got it, also fine. These days I just couldn't get worked up about things; *que sera, sera* as Doris Day would say.

She lifted her head and gazed at me fiercely. 'You are the better candidate, Verity Bloom. Make it happen. Make that job yours.'

'Yeah, yeah.'

She sighed and strode into the living room and seconds later I heard her boinging about to her celebrity fitness DVD. I cleared my plate away and closed the laptop.

It was time for the bluebell walk with Gabe and Noah.

Five minutes later, I'd twisted my hair into a messy bun, added a smudge of eyeliner to my green eyes and shoved gifts of a bottle of real ale and a chocolate dinosaur in my bag. I said goodbye to a puffing and sweaty Rosie and was about to slam the front door when I remembered something I'd almost certainly need . . .

'Tissues, tissues, tissues,' I muttered under my breath as I bent down to rummage through my half of the bathroom cupboard, pushing aside bottles of conditioner and body lotion. 'Oh gosh!'

I dropped to my knees and stared at a new, untouched box of tampons on the bottom shelf. I did a quick calculation and my mouth went dry. No doubt about it; I was well overdue my monthly visitor.

My heart thumped and a hand flew to my stomach automatically.

I couldn't believe it hadn't occurred to me before now; it was so unlike me not to be on top of this sort of thing. I gave myself a shake and told myself not to jump to conclusions; sure, the time of the month had been and gone, but more than likely it was just a bit late. Perhaps, deep down, I was more bothered about the threat of redundancy than I realized? That would be it – stress. Very common. A baby, though . . . A thrill shivered through me and my mind whirled with the implications.

I focussed on taking deep breaths as I let myself out of my little townhouse and into the golden sunshine. I jumped into my small car, started the engine and set off in the direction of the Trent Canal.

The thirty-minute journey was the perfect length to examine my potential pregnancy from every angle. My conclusion was this: practically speaking, I probably wasn't having a baby, but if I was, I'd cope. Like always. This wasn't the first time something unexpectedly life-changing had happened to me and I doubted it would be the last. As to how I actually felt about becoming a mother of my own baby . . . I wasn't quite ready to let those thoughts in yet.

As I parked in the lane by the canal I made a deal with myself. I'd buy a pregnancy test on the way home so that I could stop all this speculation. But in the meantime I was putting this new development on hold and concentrating on what really counted, today, this minute, which was being here on this special day with the Green men. (That's Gabe and Noah's surname, by the way, not their skin tone.)

I crossed the grassy bank and started along the towpath. It was bliss to be outside in the warm early evening air and I felt the tension in my shoulders melting away with every step. A row of pretty barges decorated with hand-painted signs and cheerful flower pots stretched along the water's edge, and as I got closer, I spotted the *Neptune*.

'Daddy, she's here, she's here!' I heard Noah squeal.

My three-year-old godson, dwarfed by a bright yellow life-jacket, was bouncing up and down on the deck of their blue and silver boat. Gabe scooped him up into his arms and the two of them waved like mad.

I felt my heart swell with love for them both. Gabe with his tousled curls, baggy jumper and shorts, and Noah, a miniature replica of his father. And all I could think was how incredibly sad it was that Mimi was missing from the picture. Suddenly, the feelings of grief that I'd been holding back all day rushed to the surface and my eyes began to burn.

Today was the anniversary of my best friend Mimi's death.

Two years ago, Gabe had found his wife dead on the bathroom floor. Sudden Death Syndrome at only thirty years old. Gabe lost his childhood sweetheart, baby Noah would never remember his mum and the sunshine had disappeared from my life in a flash. No warning, no explanation and no time for goodbyes . . .

I blinked furiously, plastered on a smile and raised my hand high.

'Hello!' I sped up to meet them.

Gabe lowered Noah to the deck and held out a hand to help me climb on to the boat, and I sent a mental message to my lovely girl.

Oh Mimi, I miss you so much. I'm here with your family and you're gone and that makes me feel terribly guilty. The irony is that you'd love this: all of us getting together for a walk in the woods . . .

'Welcome aboard the *Neptune*, landlubber,' Gabe said with a lop-sided smile. He stooped to wrap his arms round me.

'Thank you, Captain.' I hugged him, feeling the rough wool of his jumper against my cheek. 'How are you doing?' I murmured, looking into his soft grey eyes.

He shrugged and laughed softly. 'Noah gets me through. As ever.'

Noah tugged on my jacket. 'Auntie Vetty, did you know chocolate is in your bag?'

'Noah Green,' I said, holding his hands and standing back to examine him, 'I think you've grown even taller since I last saw you. And yes, I do know that.'

His eyes grew wide when I gave him his chocolate dinosaur.

'You're not too big for a cuddle, are you?'

He launched himself at me and I picked him up, squeezed him as tightly as I dared and buried my face in his baby curls. He was such a precious boy.

'I do love you, little man. You know that, don't you?' I laughed as he wriggled free.

Tears threatened again as I remembered how much Mimi had longed for a baby, and how devastated she'd been when she'd discovered she was infertile. I'd been there every step of the way with her, determined to help her get her wish, whatever the cost. Gabe too, of course. Team Baby Green, we'd called ourselves. We'd stuck together through the disappointments and the tests and the drugs. Our collective joy knew no bounds when Noah was born and Mimi had so loved being a mum to the tiny bundle of boyhood. Only to have her life wrenched away from her a year later. Tragic didn't begin to cover it . . .

And now I had to love her son especially hard to make up for the loss that he didn't yet fully understand.

I met Gabe's gaze and we shared a sad smile. Life could be very cruel sometimes.

'I hadn't even had the chance to say I loved her that day,' Gabe murmured, rubbing a hand across his face.

'But she knew,' I whispered, squeezing his hand. 'We all knew that.'

'Next time I'm in a relationship, I'll tell her I love her every day.'

My ears pricked up; this was new.

'So there'll be a next time then?' I asked.

He shrugged casually enough but I noticed a flush to his face. 'One day, yeah. I hope so.'

'Well . . . good,' I said brightly, looking down at my shoes.

Gabe had never been able to contemplate another woman in his life. It looked like he might be ready to move on and, truthfully, I wasn't sure how I felt about that.

Chapter 2

A few minutes later, I'd kissed Noah's entire collection of soft toys, marvelled at the no-sew curtains Gabe had made for the living area of the houseboat and the three of us had gone back on dry land to begin our expedition to the woods.

Gabe and I each held one of Noah's hands as we ambled along the towpath, both of us content to listen to his cheerful chatter.

The sun's rays sparkled across the surface of the water and the boats strained gently against their moorings. Birds tweeted merrily in the cluster of hawthorn trees which lined the path as they settled themselves in for the evening. Many of the boating people were out on deck, some sipping beers, a few cooking food on barbecues and calling to one another from boat to boat. There was almost a holiday atmosphere along the canal and I felt my happiness gradually returning.

This was heavenly, I thought, which was apt considering the spiritual nature of our excursion.

A month after Mimi had died, Gabe and I had trodden this path with Gloria, Mimi's mum. Noah had been but a babe in Gabe's arms. Our solemn little group had scattered

Mimi's ashes in her favourite place – a clearing in the woodland where the bluebells bloomed – and we'd each spent a few moments alone with our thoughts.

Shortly after that, Gabe had sold up the family home, abandoned his law career and moved himself and his baby son on to the canal and into a narrowboat just a stone's throw from Mimi's woods. He'd retrained as a French polisher and now he restored furniture for a living and, while Noah stayed with his grandparents, Gabe also made extra money taking stressed-out city-types for weekends on the waterways.

Our bluebell walk had become an annual thing and a lovely way for us all to gather and remember happy times.

'Shame Gloria couldn't be here,' I said, during a lull in Noah's running commentary.

'Hmm,' Gabe frowned. 'I've hardly heard from her since her plans to open a cookery school took off.'

Mimi's mum, a former food stylist, had decided at the age of sixty-five to open a cookery school in the Yorkshire village of Plumberry, half an hour outside York where she was originally from. It was from her mum that Mimi had inherited her love of cooking and I guess it had rubbed off on me too. Not that I cooked any more. Not since Mimi died.

'You don't approve?' I looked at him sharply.

He wrinkled his nose. 'I think she's taking on too much at her age.'

'I hope you haven't told Gloria that?' I grinned.

Mimi's mum was one of the most independent women I knew. I couldn't see her taking kindly to that sort of comment.

He lifted a shoulder. 'No. But she's too busy to see us these days, too busy to even make it here this evening because the fitters are late putting the ovens in or something. And the building she's taken on . . . it's an old mill, well, half of one. That's some responsibility.'

I nodded sympathetically but I could see both sides. Gloria had felt so bereft after losing her only daughter that she couldn't bear not to be busy. She'd been involved with food her whole career and when I'd spoken to her at Christmas, she said opening a cookery school would be a new way to use her skills and spread her passion for cooking.

Funny how grief affects us all differently. Mimi and I used to post videos on YouTube of ourselves making stuff in the kitchen. Just a bit of fun, neither of us was professionally trained, but we had a laugh doing it. But as soon as she died, I closed the channel down and deleted the videos. *My* passion for cooking died with Mimi; there was simply no pleasure in it without her.

We turned off the towpath, crossed the wibbly-wobbly bridge where Noah insisted we threw sticks into the water and then waded through long grass to the edge of Mimi's woods.

Spring has definitely sprung, I thought, as we delved under the canopy of the woodland. The trees were covered in a froth of pink-and-white blossom and now and then petals floated down through the shafts of sunlight, giving a magical illusion of snowflakes in springtime. The path was lined with tall stems of frothy white cow parsley and zingy lime ferns and I let my fingers brush gently against their feathery fronds as I walked.

Noah raced around, zigzagging in front of us, pretending to be a racing car and Gabe fell into step beside me, resting his arm casually on my shoulder. The ground was dry thanks to several days of unbroken sunshine and the air was filled with the pungent smell of wild garlic and an earthiness which, in that random way that one thought can lead to another, somehow made me think of fertility, which in turn sent a shiver of something along my spine.

Hope.

It was *hope*, I acknowledged. My internal debate during my drive over here had centred around the practicalities of being pregnant and what Liam was going to think about it and what to do about work. But deep down, I knew that if I was expecting a baby, it would make me happier than I had been for years; probably since I'd heard that Mimi's IVF had worked and that one of the eggs we'd all got our hopes pinned on had been fertilized.

'Toad!' yelled Noah with glee.

'Where?' I stopped in my tracks.

Gabe squatted down for a closer inspection but, courtesy of a poke with a stick from Noah, the creature crawled off into the undergrowth.

'How do you know it's a toad and not a frog?' I asked, impressed.

Three-year-old Noah gave me a look layered with sympathy and triumph.

'Auntie Vetty,' he sighed, dropping his stick and sliding his pudgy little hand into mine. I felt my throat tighten; I hoped he'd never grow out of doing that. 'His back was all lumpy. Frogs are smooth. Everyone knows that.'

'Silly me,' I said with a giggle, and lifted his hand to my lips for a kiss. 'It's a good job I've got you to teach me these things.'

'Look, Verity,' Gabe pointed through the trees to where a ray of golden sun picked out the nodding heads of bluebells in the clearing. 'Thousands of them, I'm sure there are even more than last year.'

He was right and the beautiful sight took my breath away.

'Mummy's favourite flowers were bluebells,' I said to Noah, swallowing the lump in my throat.

He nodded, retrieved a torch from his pocket and wriggled away from me to shine its beam under logs, looking for more toads. 'Cos they are blue like her eyes.'

'That's right, dude,' Gabe ruffled his son's hair. 'And Mummy had the prettiest, bluest eyes in the world.'

Noah stuck the torch back in his pocket and crouched down to examine the underside of a fallen log.

'Turn the torch off, Noah, or the batteries will run out,' I reminded him.

The little boy straightened up immediately and switched it off. 'Like Mummy's.'

'What do you mean?' I asked.

'My mummy's batteries ran out,' he explained, blinking up at me with those green eyes which tugged at my very soul.

Oh my God. That boy.

My heart might explode. I heard Gabe clear his throat and I couldn't bring myself to even look at him.

'Come on,' I said gruffly, giving my godson's hand a squeeze. 'Why don't we pick some flowers to take back to the boat?'

Noah and I busied ourselves collecting bluebells while Gabe lowered himself on to a tree stump and disappeared for a few minutes into the memories of his happy marriage.

I reached for a tissue and dabbed my eyes.

Gabe's doing a great job, Mimi, he is the best dad ever and I know I'm biased, but seriously, Noah is a child genius! I didn't know the difference between frogs and toads and I'm thirty-two.

The novelty of flower-picking wore off as soon as Noah had a plump handful. I looked at Gabe; he had a bunch in his hands too.

'We'd better get those in water,' I said softly, touching his shoulder.

Gabe stood and nodded and the three of us headed back towards the bridge.

'Are you coming to ours for tea?' Noah asked. 'Beef stew will be there. And sweetcorn,' he added, hopefully.

'Yes, please come, Bloomers,' Gabe added.

I gave him a hard stare for using my teenage nickname.

'Sorry, couldn't resist,' he said with a grin. 'Seriously, some conversation *not* about the comparative size of dinosaurs would be hugely appreciated. And I'll share that bottle of ale with you?'

'I'd love to.' I shook my head apologetically. 'But I've got to get home, I'm afraid, boys.'

'Oh,' Noah whined.

Gabe's face fell too and my heart twisted with guilt.

'Wise move,' he said stoically, gesturing for me to go across the bridge in front of him. 'My cooking's not a patch on Mimi's.'

The guilt deepened then; poor Gabe, he was getting better in the kitchen, but before Mimi died he barely knew how to turn the oven on.

'Sorry, but I've got a big day tomorrow, I need an early night.' And I'm not drinking alcohol before doing a pregnancy test, I added to myself. 'But I'll come back soon. Promise.'

'Good, because I need lessons with a needle,' he grinned. 'Noah asked me to sew up a hole in his pyjamas the other day. I sat down on his bed and ended up sewing them on to his duvet by accident.'

As we walked back along the towpath towards the *Neptune*, I wrapped an arm around Gabe's waist.

'I'm so proud of you, Gabe; Noah is a credit to you.'

'Thanks,' Gabe's step faltered and he took a deep breath. 'Verity?'

I turned to face him. 'Yes?'

He swallowed before murmuring, 'He needs his mum.'

My heart heaved in my chest and I was the first to look away.

I could so easily climb into Mimi's life like a pair of jeans that fit perfectly. I loved Gabe dearly and between us we'd do a fantastic, if slightly unconventional, job of bringing up that little boy who meant so much to us both. But deep down, I knew it wasn't the right thing to do; Noah might need a mum, but Gabe and I could never be more than just friends.

I tightened my arm around him. 'I'll be the best god-mother I can be, Gabe, I promise. But I can never replace Mimi.'

I hugged and kissed them both warmly before they climbed back on board their boat and I made my way back to the car wishing there was more I could do to help out that darling, lonely man.

'What's in the bag? Chocolate?' Rosie grabbed the plastic carrier bag from me as soon as I came in the door.

So much for the detox.

'Er . . .' I looked at her shiftily as she pulled my ninety-nine-per-cent-accurate pregnancy test from the bag.

'Holy Cannelloni!' Her dark eyes stared, saucer-like, in the gloom of the hallway.

'Probably a false alarm, but yeah, I might be having a bambino,' I said, going pink. 'And seeing Noah tonight has made me realize that I hope I am.'

Rosie gave me a huge hug. 'If that's what you want, then I hope so too.'

I hugged her back. That's what I loved about Rosie; she was completely non-judgemental. She knew my job was precarious and I had a sneaking suspicion that she wasn't that keen on Liam but, despite that, I knew she'd always be my cheerleader.

'Thanks, Rosie. Liam said he might come over after the party tonight, so we can do the test together.'

'No, no, no. Listen to me.' Rosie stepped backwards and prodded my shoulder in time with her words. 'You. Say. Nothing.'

I began to protest. 'But Liam has a right—'

'Agreed,' she said, folding her arms. 'Tell him after that presentation tomorrow. I know you. If you're pregnant, he'll persuade you to let him get the job, on the basis that you'll be leaving soon anyway. You're too generous for your own good. And if you are expecting a baby, it will be a damn sight more difficult to get another job before it arrives than keep the one you're in.'

'OK, OK,' I agreed.

Anything for a quiet life. But I didn't mean it. I absolutely could not wait to pee on that stick . . .

Get cosy with a cup of tea and Verity's adventures – available for pre-order now!

Cooking Up A Storm – Part One
Food Glorious Food – Part Two
Taking Stock – Part Three
The Magic Ingredient – Part Four

The Plumberry School of Comfort Food is published in March, April, May and June 2016 and as a paperback in summer 2016

You can also enjoy another charming,
modern love story from Cathy Bramley

A takeaway, TV and tea with two sugars is about as
exciting as it gets for thirty-something Sophie Stone.
Sophie's life is safe and predictable, which is just
the way she likes it, thank you very much.

But when a mysterious benefactor leaves her an
inheritance, Sophie has to accept that change is afoot.
There is one big catch: in order to inherit, Sophie must
agree to meet the father she has never seen.

Saying 'yes' means the chance to build her
own dream home, but she'll also have to face
the past and hear some uncomfortable truths . . .

With interference from an evil boss, warring parents,
an unreliable boyfriend and an architect who puts
his foot in it every time he opens his mouth,
will Sophie be able to build a future on her own
terms – and maybe even find love along the way?

Available now

Or you could try the fresh, funny
and sweetly romantic . . .

Ivy Lane

Tilly Parker needs a fresh start, fresh air and a
fresh attitude if she is ever to leave the past behind
and move on with her life. As she seeks out peace
and quiet in a new town, taking on a plot at Ivy Lane
allotments seems like the perfect solution.

But the friendly Ivy Lane community has other ideas
and gradually draw Tilly in to their cosy, comforting
world of planting seedlings, organizing bake sales
and planning seasonal parties.

As the seasons pass, will Tilly learn to stop
hiding amongst the sweetpeas and let people
back into her life – and her heart?

Available now

Or the irresistibly charming

Freya Moorcroft has wild red hair, mischievous green eyes, a warm smile and a heart of gold. She's been happy working at the café round the corner from Ivy Lane allotments and her romance with her new boyfriend is going well, she thinks, but a part of her still misses the beautiful rolling hills of her Cumbrian childhood home: Appleby Farm.

Then a phone call out of the blue and a desperate plea for help change everything . . .

The farm is in financial trouble, and it's taking its toll on the aunt and uncle who raised Freya. Heading home to lend a hand, Freya quickly learns that things are worse than she first thought. As she summons up all her creativity and determination to turn things around, Freya is surprised as her own dreams for the future begin to take shape.

Love makes the world go round, according to Freya. Not money. But will saving Appleby Farm and following her heart come at a price?

Available now

Irresistible recipes inspired by Wickham Hall

Lemon and Rosemary Shortbread Cookies

I'm a big fan of shortbread, especially those fancy tins you get at Christmas, and I wanted to include a recipe that fit with the flavours of Wickham Hall. I'm not entirely sure whether lemons were around, but rosemary was very popular in Elizabethan times, so here we go . . .

You will need . . .

250g plain flour (sieved)

200g butter

100g caster sugar

Zest of 1 lemon

2 tablespoons of washed and finely chopped rosemary leaves

A little extra sugar for sprinkling

Preheat the oven to 190 °C (170 °C fan/gas mark 5) and grease a non-stick baking tray.

Cream together the butter and sugar in a bowl with a wooden spoon or electric hand mixer. Gradually mix in the flour and then add the lemon zest and rosemary. Using your hands, knead the mix together into a smooth ball.

Turn the dough out on to a floured surface and roll out to about 1-2 cm thick. Use a cookie cutter of any shape, pressing firmly through the dough but not twisting, and place on a baking tray. They will take 10-15 minutes depending on the fierceness of your oven.

Remove from the tray and allow to cool on a wire rack. Sprinkle with a little sugar while they cool.

Serve with tea or coffee in your favourite mug.

Helen's Lemon Curd

If you read *Appleby Farm*, you may remember a recipe for Helen Redfern's deliciously chewy pistachio meringues. She features all sorts of recipes on her blog, HelenRedfern.co.uk, and she has very kindly shared this one for lemon curd with me.

You need to get certain equipment ready for this one before you start:

A heatproof bowl that sits over a saucepan of water (without touching the water)

Zester and juicer

Another small bowl

Whisk

Two small jam jars, sterilized

You will need . . .

  4 unwaxed lemons

  200g sugar

  100g butter

  5 egg yolks (leaving lots of eggs whites for meringues!)

Zest and juice the lemons.

Set the heatproof bowl over a saucepan of water. Make sure the bowl does not touch the water. Add into the bowl the zest and juice from the lemons, along with the butter and sugar. Heat gently and stir until the butter has melted and the sugar dissolved.

In a separate bowl, lightly whisk the egg yolks. Slowly pour them into the sugary lemon mixture over the heat and whisk to ensure all yolks are well combined.

Whisk regularly as it cooks for about 10-12 minutes. It'll become thicker when it is done.

Pour into sterilized jam jars and allow to cool. Tighten the lids, then place in the fridge. It'll keep for a couple of weeks.

Asparagus Tartlets

This is the first dish that Holly Swift sees coming out of the Wickham Hall ovens on her first day. In my head, the ones she saw were more quiche-like, but these are far simpler to make. If asparagus isn't in season, or you don't like it, simply replace with something else like red peppers or courgettes.

You will need . . .

  1 sheet of ready-rolled puff pastry

  150g ricotta cheese

  80g fresh parmesan cheese, plus extra for serving

  Zest of 1 lemon

  16 spears of asparagus

  A little olive oil

  Salt and black pepper

Preheat the oven to 200°C (180°C fan/gas mark 6). Line a large baking tray with non-stick baking parchment. Cut the pastry sheet into four rectangles, each about 12x6cm, and place them on the baking parchment. With a sharp knife, gently score a 1cm border on each rectangle.

Wash and trim the asparagus spears, cutting off the woody ends.

Combine the ricotta, parmesan, lemon zest, and salt and pepper to taste and mix thoroughly in a bowl. Spread the mixture on to the pastry, taking care not to put it over the scored border, and top each tart with two asparagus spears. Brush the pastry borders with oil and cook in the oven for 12-15 minutes or until the pastry is puffed and golden.

Add a few parmesan shavings to serve.

Sheila Beckwith's Blueberry Cake

Pssst . . . Sheila Beckwith is not only Lord Fortescue's secretary, she is actually a real person, who won the chance to have a character named after her in one of my books!

She created this cake for her daughter, book blogger Jill Stratton, and Jill reckons it's the bee's knees!

You will need . . .

285g gluten-free self-raising flour
170g dairy-free olive spread
170g caster sugar
3 eggs
Pinch of salt
170g of blueberries

Preheat the oven to 190°C (170°C fan/gas mark 5) and grease and line a 7-inch cake tin with greaseproof paper.

Cream the olive spread and sugar together. Add 1 egg at a time and mix with a wooden spoon until light and fluffy.

Gradually add the sieved flour and a pinch of salt and mix gently. Then fold in the fresh blueberries without crushing them.

Pour into the prepared tin and bake for approximately 30 minutes, until an inserted knife comes out clear.

Tuck in as soon as it's cool enough!

Samantha Tonge's Glittery Scones

At the time of researching recipes for *Wickham Hall*, I was reading *Game of Scones* by Samantha Tonge. Sam's book is a sizzling romantic comedy set in Greece and includes so many mouth-wateringly delicious food references that I couldn't resist asking her to write a recipe for *Wickham*

Hall. Sam not only came up with the goods (thanks a million, Sam) but she photographed them too, and if you look at her website (SamanthaTonge.co.uk) you can find the pictures. Over to you, Sam!

You will need . . .

225g self-raising flour
Pinch of salt
50g butter
1 tablespoon of caster sugar
1 tablespoon of chopped nuts
½ teaspoon of almond essence
150ml milk

For the filling:

2 teaspoons of almond essence
2 teaspoons of caster sugar
200g plain Greek yogurt
1 tin black cherry pie filling
Pink, gold or silver edible food glitter

Preheat the oven to 220°C (200°C fan/gas mark 7). Grease a baking tray.

Sift the flour and salt into a mixing bowl and rub in the butter to form a crumbly mixture. Stir in the caster sugar and the chopped nuts.

Add the almond essence and then slowly stir in the milk (you may not need all of it) until the mixture forms a dough.

Knead the dough on a board well-sprinkled with flour and roll out until about 1cm deep. Cut out rounds of scone using a 7cm/3-inch-wide cutter or cup rim. Place the circles on the greased baking tray and brush the tops with milk leftover from making the dough.

Bake for 12–15 minutes until nicely browned. Allow to cool on a wire rack.

To prepare the filling, mix the almond essence and caster sugar into the Greek yogurt. Slice a scone in half. On one half, spread a thick layer of yogurt. On top of this, spoon on some of the black cherry pie filling. Sprinkle on your glitter. Then complete by adding the other half of the scone on top.

Enjoy! Everyone needs a bit of sparkle in their lives – I hope your glittery scones do the job!

Chorizo and Butter Bean Stew

One of my favourite things is collecting recipes from friends, family and colleagues and so I was delighted when my publicist at Transworld, Sarah Harwood, sent me this one to try. What I love about this one is its versatility, you can dress it up for Sunday lunch or cook some pasta with it for an easy after-work no-fuss dinner. Thank you, Sarah!

This is an easy and quick dish to make, and makes a great summer side dish. I serve it alongside roast chicken and a big green salad, for a lighter, healthier Sunday lunch. It also goes really well with a nice glass of white wine!

You will need . . .

  Olive oil for frying

  1 large diced onion (I like to use a red onion)

  1–2 cloves of garlic, finely chopped

  200g chopped chorizo sausage (chorizo works particularly well in this dish, but any smoked sausage is fine)

  400g jar of passata

  400g tin butter beans, drained

  1 teaspoon of paprika

  ½ teaspoon of cayenne pepper (optional)

Fry the onion and garlic in a splash of olive oil in a medium saucepan over a medium heat.

After 2–3 minutes, add in the sausage and fry for another 2 minutes.

Add the passata, butter beans and spices, then reduce the heat.

Leave to cook for 10–15 minutes, stirring occasionally.

Spicy Couscous and Halloumi

There are lots of people who work behind the scenes helping to make my books the best they can be, and I'm delighted that one of those lovely people, Helen Gregory, has contributed a recipe to *Wickham Hall*. Helen is Digital Publishing Manager, so she's the person responsible for ensuring that every single part of the machine behind the publication of my ebooks is running smoothly. (She's also very healthy!)

You will need . . .

Couscous (60g per person)
Knob of butter
1 teaspoon of harissa paste
Olive oil
Halloumi, sliced
Half a red chilli, chopped
A handful of sultanas
A handful of flaked almonds
3 tablespoons of natural yogurt
A handful of chopped fresh mint

Pour the couscous into a bowl and rub the butter into it. Stir in the harissa.

Pour in boiling water until the water just covers the couscous. Cover with cling film and leave for 10 minutes.

Put your griddle pan on a high heat and add a little olive oil.

Add the halloumi and sprinkle with the chopped chilli. Grill for a few minutes on each side.

Once the couscous is ready, fluff with a fork and mix in the sultanas and almonds.

Serve with the halloumi on top and natural yogurt on the side. Sprinkle with mint.

Bonfire Night Banana Bread

Huge thank you to Transworld Editor, Bella Bosworth, for this delicious recipe. Over to you, Bella!

Bonfire Night always makes me think of mittens and baked potatoes, of stamping your feet to keep them warm, and of tightly clasped mugs of soup. But it also makes me think of that 'ahh' feeling of coming back inside to a cup of tea and a bite of something, while you watch the last of the fireworks from the window. And there's nothing better than a slice of banana bread, still warm from the oven and shot through with dark chocolate. For extra decadence, spread generously with butter.

(For a gluten-free version, substitute the self-raising flour with a mix of gluten-free self-raising flour and ground almonds.)

You will need . . .

- 175g salted butter, softened
- 175g sugar (half light muscovado, half golden caster sugar)
- 2 free-range eggs
- 175g self-raising flour
- 100g walnuts, chopped
- 3–4 very ripe bananas (the browner, the better)
- 175g dark chocolate in chunks

Preheat the oven to 170ºC (150ºC fan/gas mark 3). Line the base and sides of a loaf tin (20cm x 12cm) with baking paper.

Beat the butter and sugar until light and fluffy. Gradually add the eggs, one by one, to the butter-and-sugar mixture, and then mix in the self-raising flour and walnuts. Peel the bananas and mash them with a fork. Gently fold the bananas and the dark chocolate chunks into the mixture, taking care not to overmix.

Scoop the batter into the prepared loaf tin. Bake for between 60-70 minutes, until golden on top and a skewer inserted into the centre comes out clean. This may take a little longer – if so, you can cover the top with foil to prevent it from burning.

Enjoy with a cup of tea!

Gingerbread Loaf

What could be more autumnal than a slice of spicy, sticky gingerbread? This one is very low in fat – except if you serve it warm and smothered with cream or custard, or cold, spread with butter, of course . . .

You will need . . .

225g self-raising flour
1 pinch of salt
1 teaspoon of baking powder
3 teaspoons of ground ginger
55g butter or margarine
55g soft brown sugar (or muscovado if you have it)
8 tablespoons of black treacle
2 eggs, beaten with milk to make 280ml

Preheat the oven to 180°C (160°C fan/gas mark 4).

Grease and line a 2lb loaf tin. (I use silicone pans these days, which are a lot easier.)

Sieve the flour and mix with the salt, baking powder and ground ginger.

Melt the butter in a bowl over a pan of simmering water. Remove from the heat and mix in the sugar and black treacle thoroughly.

Pour the butter-and-sugar mixture into the flour and stir well. Gradually add the egg and milk to make a smooth, thick batter.

Pour into the prepared tin and bake for about 45 minutes, or until a skewer comes out clean when prodded into the middle of the loaf.

Eat warm or cold and top with either cream, custard or butter! The gingerbread loaf will keep for a week in an airtight box and gets stickier the longer it is kept.

Nutty Tiffin

There are all sorts of tiffin recipes out there, but to tie in with Christmas in *Wickham Hall*, I thought I'd go for a seasonal mix of cranberries and walnuts in mine!

You will need . . .

    100g margarine

    25g soft brown sugar

    4 tablespoons of golden syrup

    3 tablespoons of cocoa powder

225g crushed digestive biscuits (leave some bigger bits)
25g dried cranberries
50g raisins
50g walnut pieces
225g milk chocolate

Grease and line a 20cm square tin.

Place the margarine, sugar, golden syrup and cocoa powder in a bowl and place over a pan of simmering water until melted.

Remove from the heat, add the crushed biscuits, fruit and nuts, and stir. Press the mixture into the tin.

Melt the chocolate and pour on to the top of the mixture. Just as it is almost set, mark the top with the prongs of a fork to make wavy patterns.

Mark into squares and place in the fridge to set for an hour before cutting and storing in an airtight tin. If the weather is warm, store in the fridge permanently.

Filo Pastry Mince Pies

I adore a mince pie, me. And these little morsels are perfect: small and crispy and not too heavy, due to being made with filo pastry instead of shortcrust.

You will need . . .

270g pack Jus-Rol filo pastry (defrosted)
75g melted butter

425g jar of mincemeat (splash out on one with added alcohol if you can!)

1 tablespoon of brandy (optional)

100g of white royal icing

A sprinkling of gold or silver edible glitter

Preheat the oven to 200°C (180°C fan/gas mark 6). Grease two 12-hole bun tins.

Separate out a sheet of filo and brush with melted butter and top with another sheet. Cut into 8 squares. Repeat this until you have 24 squares.

Press a square of filo into each bun hole, scrunching the sides to make it fit.

Mix the brandy, if using, with the mincemeat and spoon into each case.

Bake for 12–13 minutes until the pastry is crisp and golden. Allow to cool.

Roll out the icing and use a star-shaped cutter to cut out 24 little stars. Top each mince pie with a star and a sprinkle of glitter. Christmas in one tiny bite!

Kale and Lentil Soup with Pumpkin Seeds

This is another recipe from Transworld's Digital Publishing Manager, Helen Gregory. It is so packed with superfoods that it is sure to ward off any sniffles this winter!

You will need . . .

Olive oil

1 onion, chopped

2 sticks of celery, sliced

2 carrots, chopped

100g green lentils

1 stock cube dissolved in boiling water (follow stock packet instructions for water quantity)

Bag of kale

Pumpkin seeds

Natural yogurt

Heat the oil in a pan. Add the onion, celery and carrots and cook until soft.

Add the lentils and stock. Simmer for 30 minutes, until the lentils are soft.

Add the kale and cook for five minutes.

Leave to simmer.

Toast the pumpkin seeds in a little olive oil and salt in a frying pan until seeds are golden.

Blitz the soup in a blender. Serve with a dollop of natural yogurt and a sprinkling of pumpkin seeds. Now congratulate yourself on preparing something so brimming with goodness!

Cathy Bramley is the author of the bestselling romantic comedies *Ivy Lane*, *Appleby Farm* and *Wickham Hall* (all four-part serialised novels) and *Conditional Love*. She lives in a Nottinghamshire village with her husband, two daughters and a dog.

Her recent career as a full-time writer of light-hearted romantic fiction has come as somewhat of a lovely surprise after spending the last eighteen years running her own marketing agency. However, she has been always an avid reader, hiding her book under the duvet and reading by torchlight. Luckily her husband has now bought her a Kindle with a light, so that's the end of that palaver.

Cathy loves to hear from her readers. You can get in touch via her website www.CathyBramley.co.uk, Facebook page Facebook.com/CathyBramleyAuthor or on Twitter: twitter.com/CathyBramley